Neighborhood Secrets

JAMES AND CARMINE CIOFFI

PAGE PUBLISHING, INC.
New York, NY

First originally published by Page Publishing, Inc. 2015

ISBN 978-1-68139-216-5 (pbk)
ISBN 978-1-68139-217-2 (digital)

Printed in the United States of America

Contents

BOOK II

BOOK I

CHAPTER

1

Raymond

I T WAS HOT, ONE OF THOSE DAYS WHEN YOU JUST CAN'T STAND THE HEAT. Most people seek relief by going to a pool or a beach, but in the city on a day like this the Johnny pump is the only way to get relief.

This story starts here, at the Johnny pump on the corner of 125th Street and Pleasant Avenue. For the uneducated, the Johnny pump is a fire hydrant. For the kids of the neighborhood, it's heaven on earth. There are two essential tools that are necessary for playing under the pump. The first is a wrench to take off the cap and the second is a coffee can with both ends opened to direct the stream of the water. In a jam your hands will do but they really are not quite that effective. On this August day, about six of the neighborhood boys were at the pump. They were young, with ages ranging from nine to eleven, and they were having a typical good time on a hot summer day. The boys were taking turns holding the spray of the water. While one directed the water into high arching cascades, the others would run in and out of the icy waterfall and squeal with delight. This was joy in its purest form. You didn't need a house on Long Island or a house Upstate. This was all you needed. The neighborhood provided for you. The neighborhood was all you knew or cared about.

On that sweltering day, Raymond was the boy who had brought the wrench and the coffee can. He had opened the hydrant and like moths to a lamppost, the other boys had come. There were other neighborhood kids. Raymond knew a few from school, others he had seen at the playground. Raymond was happy. He had planned this day last week when he had heard on the radio that this was going to be the hottest week of the summer. As the water sprayed, Raymond could only smile at how his plan had come together. A perfect day, he thought. Just then a car turned up the block. Raymond smiled and signaled the boys to get out of the street as he moved the coffee can out of the way, letting the water run its normal course into the street. The man in the Caddy waved his thanks and began to accelerate down the block. The other boys waited with sly grins on their faces, trying hard not to give away what was coming. Just as the Caddy neared the water stream, Raymond grabbed the coffee can and directed a torrent of water at the car's open window. The man in the car instinctively hit the break as the water streamed into the window. Then he realized what was happening and wildly accelerated forward. By the time he got out of the car and was running toward the boys, they were already half a block away screaming with laughter and the unbridled joy of summer. Raymond pulled up in the playground breathing hard from running and laughing at the same time. The other boys were slapping him on the back and congratulating him. One boy that he recognized from school was smiling and shaking his head.

Raymond looked at him and said, "What's the matter?"

"Nothing," Johnny replied. "You got balls though. That was a wise guy's car. You're lucky one of his flunkies was driving it or you might've been in big trouble."

Raymond went cold. He was just pulling a prank; he never thought that he could get into any trouble. That was typical Raymond. He didn't think of consequences. He came up with plans and carried them out. This particular situation, however, could be trouble.

There was a pecking order in the neighborhood. The wise guys were on top. They were the most respected, the most visible, and the most recognizable. Everyone in the neighborhood respected the wise guys. They weren't called gangsters and it wasn't like the movies with guys walking around shooting people. The wise guys were neighborhood guys. They had grown up in these streets and they considered them home. They lived in the neighborhood and took care of the people who lived there. This isn't to say they were saints. People got shaken down and people disappeared, but for the most part the wise guys were the guys who wielded the most power in the neighborhood. Most people went to the local captain if they had a problem. The police were feared but for a different reason. Cops were a tight-knit group back then. They took care of their own and that was that. The old-timers in the neighborhood didn't trust the cops. These fears were irrational, but cops were outsiders. Wise guys were part of the fabric of the community and therefore they were trusted more than the police. The kids in the neighborhood would run from the cops from fear of getting their heads split with a billy club. It wouldn't be unusual for a cop to get razzed as he went down the street from a bunch of kids. When it came to wise guys there was none of that nonsense. The local wise guys would cuff a kid on the head or tell them to run a message to the bakers on the corner, and the kid would obey without question. This is why Raymond went cold when Johnny said he had just hosed a wise guys car.

"Oh man, oh man," Raymond repeated over and over and started to pace around the playground.

This was also typical Raymond. He was already thinking of how he could get out of this. Johnny saw Raymond's distress and kept the pressure on.

"Man, if that was Fat Toni's Caddy, you may as well move to the Bronx!"

Raymond was starting to formulate a plan. He would say he did it on a dare. He figured that the wise guys would respect his courage and honesty. Yeah, that would work with those guys. Show that he was tough and wouldn't back down from a challenge. Johnny was still chattering away.

"I hear the Bronx is real nice. You could move in with some Moolies and get a job as a paperboy. Or maybe Long Island. Lots of girls on the beach out there. Although I hear there are sharks in the water. Sharks or Moolies. Pretty tough situation kid," Johnny said with a smile.

Raymond was barely listening. His mind was racing. He actually was worried. His father worked too hard to have him get in trouble with wise guys. Raymond's parents were second generation Italians. His grandparents were from the old country, but his parents had been born in New York. This gave his father an advantage. He went to school and did well, stayed away from the wise guys and had a nice city job with Con Edison. This was a rarity in the neighborhood. Steady work was hard to come by. Raymond's dad worked hard and stressed education and being smart. Raymond's father always said, "If you have street smarts you'll always survive, but if you have book smarts you'll succeed in life." Raymond would listen to his father's speech and think: What if I have street smarts and book smarts? How far will that take me?

It was something that always drove Raymond. He was a tall lanky boy with a dark crop of brown hair. He wasn't the best athlete in the neighborhood but he wasn't picked last either. He relied on his brain in most situations, not his athletic ability. He did well in school and always looked to make life easier for his family by staying out of trouble and getting good grades. He was smart enough to know, even at age eleven, that things weren't easy for his family. He could tell money was tight. He could see how hard his father worked. Hear the tiredness in his voice when he came home. See the sweat stains that spoke of a hard day crawling down manholes. Raymond saw these things every day and vowed that this would not be his life. He would make things better for his family. Their hard work would not go to waste.

All these thoughts flashed through Raymond's mind as he sat there trying to figure out what to do about his current situation. The sun continued to burn down on him and he stopped pacing.

"Hey! Shut up for two seconds," he barked at Johnny. "I'm trying to think."

"You know I hear Jersey is kind of nice, if you can live with the smell," Johnny replied with a smirk on his face.

That was it. Raymond was about to snap. He took one step toward Johnny and began to ball up his fist. Raymond knew he shouldn't start a fight but what the hell. He was already in trouble so he might as well go the whole ten yards.

Just then Raymond heard a voice behind him say, "Alright, Johnny, that's enough. You're about to start a fight and even though you could probably take this kid, I'm in no mood to break up a fight in this kind of heat."

Raymond turned to see who had just diffused the whole situation. Joey was a big kid. He was twice the size of Raymond. Raymond recognized Joey from school, but it was Joey's father that everyone knew. He was one of the toughest guys in the neighborhood. Famous for his temper and equally famous for his ability to drink and fight. Joey's dad was that guy you don't want to piss off in the bar. There had been many a night when, if you looked out the apartment window, you would see Joey's dad out in the street yelling and screaming back at the building. Raymond remembered one night when he had seen Joey's father literally knock out three cops. They had approached him and told him to quiet down and walk it off. Joey's dad had responded by punching the first cop in the face and dropping him instantly. The other cops called for backup and when it was all said and done, it was hard to tell who got the worst end of the encounter. Joey's dad was always around. He was in and out of work, in and out of jail, and all around the neighborhood he was recognized as a person to avoid.

So here was Joey smiling and telling Johnny, "Just cut it out. You know damn well that that car didn't belong to any wise guy. And even if it did, I would have told him you did it and he would have walked right away."

Johnny laughed, "I would have sent him to my dad soaking wet. My pop would have gotten a kick out of that."

Raymond was confused.

"What's going on here?" he asked.

Joey smiled and said, "This is Johnny Abelli. He likes to break balls and was just having some fun with you. My name is Joey and, just for the record, that was a classic move soaking that guy. What's your name?"

"Raymond."

"Well nice to meet you. Looks like the cops are shutting the hydrant. Let's go shoot some hoops," Joey said.

"Let's swing by the club. I got a brand new ball in the back room," Johnny said.

The three boys started to walk out of the playground. Raymond, Johnny, and Joey walked up First Avenue. It would be a scene replayed over and over for the next five years.

2

The Bar

THE BAR WAS THE PLACE THE BOYS WERE HEADED. The real name of the place was irrelevant because the only purpose of the bar was to be a hangout for the wise guys. The bar sat on the corner of 115th Street and Pleasant Avenue. The fact that it was a bar never really occurred to the boys, because no one ever frequented the place besides Franco's crew. Johnny's father was a captain and the one man who everyone went to see in the bar. Franco Abelli came up in the ranks of organized crime the old-fashioned way:; by being loyal, smart, and ballsy. His deeds were legendary. As a kid, he was a notorious fighter and was rumored to have been stabbed on several occasions. The real genius of Franco was his ability to pick and choose the right people to work with and for. It was this ability that led to his quick rise through the ranks from solider to captain. The bar was his domain. The orders were sent out from the back and the up-and-comers were usually hanging around outside waiting to run any errand that would earn them points with the boss. The bar was the central hub of the neighborhood. Grand Central Station of 115th Street and everyone knew it. You didn't go in the bar unless you were asked to, and if you needed to see Franco you sent a message through one of the older kids who were always milling about outside.

The stories that flowed out of the bar were both hysterical and mostly true. As the boys walked toward the hallowed ground, Johnny started talking; he rarely ever shut up.

"The other day you should have been there, Raymond."

Joey began laughing and said, "Tell it, Johnny."

"We were hanging out in front of the bar when Crazy Larry walks in."

Crazy Larry was the neighborhood junkie. He was always begging for money and would do just about anything to get his fix. Larry was the mainstay at the bar. He provided the guys with comic relief. On this day the guys were watching a western and wondered what it would be like to hang someone. They all decided that Larry would do it for fifty bucks. Tony Fat was the ringleader as usual. He pitched the idea to Larry.

"Come on, Larry, we won't let you die or nothing. We'll just let you hang for a few seconds and then cut you down."

Frankie Bags jumped in, "Yeah, yeah. In those movies it takes those fucks days to die. A few seconds won't kill ya."

Larry said, "You guys are sure you're going to cut me down after five seconds?"

Tony Fat started complaining, "For fifty bucks you got to go twenty seconds."

Then Frankie Bags said, "Lets place bets on how long he can stay up. Don't worry, Larry, we'll throw you a piece of the pot."

Johnny was cracking up as he told the story.

"The guys were in a frenzy. They were betting on how long he could hold out and if he would bleed and who would cut him down and how quickly. It was pandemonium and Larry now starts to get nervous because he realizes these guys are really going to hang him. He says, 'It's going to cost you a hundred.' The whole bar broke out in laughter and started yelling at Larry. My dad threw his hands up and said, 'Come here, Larry. Look, kid, I guarantee the other fifty,' and my dad pulls out a fifty and waves it in front of Larry's face. Larry was a junkie and he realized that with Franco involved there was no backing out. Larry was really worried; he knew that when the guys got riled up like this they were dangerous. Now the boys were in a real lather. Charlie the Greek said he had a cowboy hat at home that Larry could wear. They sent a kid straight away to pick up the hat. Everyone was laughing and betting and the party was on."

Johnny paused to catch his breath, and in that moment Raymond realized these were two guys that he would be friends with for life. There was no particular reason why he felt that way, but he just knew. The neighborhood was full of instances like this where friends became brothers overnight. Their bond would be solidified later that day, but in Raymond's mind the bond was already there.

Johnny, after what he considered a dramatic pause, continued the story about Crazy Larry.

"So now the guys got a rope and a cowboy hat. They throw the rope over a beam and make a noose. Larry has the hat on and now it's getting serious. My dad grabs Frankie Bags and Tony Fat and tells them, 'Look. When he gets the noose over his head, Bags, you push him off the chair and Tony will catch him. We don't want to break this fuck's neck.' Tony said, 'Come on. Let's let him swing. He's a fucking junkie.' My dad said, 'Use your brain, you fat fuck. I don't want anyone dying in the bar and besides he's an institution in the neighborhood.' Franco said, 'Who we going to shoot bottle rockets at on the Fourth of July?' Tony laughed, 'You're right. He's worth more alive just for the shit we'll make him do.' So now it's all set and they get Larry up on the chair and the place is going wild. Bags has his foot on the chair and tells Tony, 'On three okay? One … two … three.' Bags kicks the chair just at that moment, Tony goes to grab Larry and misses. The fat fuck slipped! Larry is swinging in the breeze and by the time Bags realized what was going on, he was up there for about three seconds. Now, Bags and Tony both grab Larry's legs and lift him up. They get the noose off his neck. Larry is gasping for breath, his eyes bulging wide with fear as they lower him to the floor. This long raw and bleeding rope burn extending from ear to ear. Fat

Tony is sweating like a pig. And not from fear of almost killing Larry, but because he knew he fucked up. My father gave him a look that told him it was okay and he went to the back room. The bar was in an uproar because they didn't think Larry would go through with it, but once he did they were pissed that their bets were thrown off by Tony and Bags' intervention. Now everyone is cursing, and the term 'Stupid Bastards' is being thrown around by all the people in the bar. Money was changing hands and all the bets were off to the general dismay of all. Larry stood in the middle of all the uproar. He was trying to speak but no one was paying attention to him.

Finally, to get the heat off of him and Tony, Bags yells at everyone to quiet down. The crowd sees Larry shaking his head up and down and looking like this was the last place he wanted to be, but all eyes were on him. The place fell as silent as Sunday mass. Larry looked down at his torn sneakers and then mustered the courage that a dope fiend says when he knows he is close to a score. 'Where … where's … my money?' he stammered. The worst possible thing he could of uttered. The bar exploded with laughter and insults. The consensus was since no one could make any bets, the deal was off. Bobby Eyeball called out, 'You ain't dead. You hung for about three seconds. What the fuck was that? Get the fuck out of here.' With that they threw him out of the bar and into the street. Larry was pissed. He paced outside the bar ranting and raving like a madman. My father sent Nick, his right-hand man, out to talk to him and quiet him down. Nick grabbed Larry and calmed him down, 'Look, Larry, here's the fifty Franco promised you.' As he pressed a crisp fifty into his hands he said, 'Let it go. Get high and get cleaned up. Most of all, stop ranting in front of the bar before Franco gets annoyed.' 'But it's not right,' Larry protested. 'He promised me. Those fucks hung me and promised me at least a hundred dollars and a piece of the pot.' Nicky said, 'That's not my problem or my concern. Get the fuck out of here before I take that fifty back and cut your fucking tongue out to shut you up.' The seriousness and reputation of Nicky stopped Larry in his tracks. He bit his tongue and stormed down the block."

Raymond, in between breaths of laughter, looked at Johnny and said, "Great story. Really unbelievable."

Johnny drew a deep breath and said, "I'm not done. Wait till you hear what happened when Larry came back!"

The bar loomed up the block in front of Raymond as Johnny finished the story.

"So that night Larry comes back. He is obviously high and feeling good. He's got that happy heroine smile and satisfied look about him. Larry was wearing a scarf around his neck to the amusement of everyone in the place. Well, Eyeball screams out, 'Larry? How's it hanging?' and the whole place erupts in laughter! Larry unfazed walked right to Fat Tony and said, 'Where's my money?' Fat Tony starts laughing and tells Larry, 'Get the fuck out of here.' It's at this point that Larry pulls out a .22 and points it at Tony. The crowd seeing this gets real quiet and serious. Tony looked at Larry and says, 'Calm down. Put the gun away before you do something that you can't get out of.' Larry, high and feeling cool, replies, 'Fuck you! You guys promised me money. Now pay up!' My father was in the back room and had no idea what was going on in the bar. He was in the back with Bags and Nicky when he heard the shot. My father ran to the front of the bar. He sees Fat Tony standing there, jaw dropped open with a bullet hole two feet from where he's standing in the floor. Larry had insisted on getting paid and, to show he wasn't fooling around, fired a warning shot at Tony. My father walked over to Larry and said, 'Put the gun down.' Larry, even high, wouldn't disobey my father and put the .22 on the bar. My father said, 'Larry, what's the problem?' 'These fucks won't pay up and we had a deal,' Larry was stammering. My dad said, 'Don't worry. Tony, Bags come here.' Larry looked smug and smiled, figuring my dad would straighten it all out. Tony smiled and turned away from my dad and walked over to Larry. He grabbed him quick as a flash by the neck and the balls, lifting him straight off the floor and over his head. He then took three steps with the dangling Larry over his head and threw him through the front window of the bar. Larry, covered in glass and cuts, jumped up and ran like the devil down the street to the roars of laughter from the bar."

Johnny was wiping a tear from his eye from laughing so hard.

"So what happened to Larry?" Raymond asked.

"He wound up coming around a week or so later and all was forgiven," Johnny said. "I wish I could have seen the whole thing."

"What do you mean?" Raymond asked a bit confused.

"Johnny gets all his information from Bobby the bartender," Joey answered.

"I mean you think his dad would let him hang out in the bar!"

Johnny took offense to this.

"I could go in and out of the bar any time I want!" he bristled.

"Yeah, yeah, you know what I mean."

Joey rolled his eyes at Raymond and Raymond felt another surge of loyalty to these new friends.

The simplest acts are sometimes what cement the bonds of friendship. As they came to the front of the bar, two men acknowledged Johnny with a nod and a smile.

"Your dad's a bit busy in the back. Any problem?" the shorter of the two men asked.

"No, just came to get my new b-ball. We're going to the park to shoot some hoops," Johnny said.

"I'll get it for you," the short guy answered.

And before Johnny could reply, the man disappeared into the bar.

Joey gave Raymond a quick nudge and said a bit sarcastically, "See, the prince speaks and the subjects jump."

This earned a scowl from the taller man outside the bar, but the boys didn't notice it.

Moments later, the short man reappeared with a brand new Spalding basketball and presented it to Johnny.

"Here you go kid. Have fun," he said.

"Thanks, Ronnie," Joey replied, and the boys headed off down the street toward the park.

3

Three Plus Two Equals Five

SPORTS IN THE NEIGHBORHOOD WERE THE GLUE THAT KEPT THE KIDS OUT OF TROUBLE. Every block had a team and every block would venture to various parks to play games. The older kids would play for money and the contests got fierce. Fights broke out and rivalries formed. In the bar sometimes you could still have fights between Franco's men over games that were played ten years ago. The younger kids learned from the older ones and brothers taught brothers how to play. It was a right of passage to move to the older team. To play with the older guys meant you were one of the older guys. The boys' legends weren't pro players but the older guys who came before them. For Joey, Raymond, and Johnny, Zeke Zinecola was the neighborhood legend. He was an all-around athlete who actually went to college on a basketball scholarship and could boast how he once played against Jim Brown in a game and held him to four points. Or Whitey Marsh, who could play baseball like DiMaggio and whose nickname was "Three Sewer" because he consistently hit a stickball three sewer caps away, the equivalent of a football field and a half. In their mind, the park was Yankee Stadium, Madison Square Garden, and the place where legends and friendships were made and broken.

The boys approached the park and, as usual, saw a full house. The park in the summer was packed. The kids buzzed around like flies at a picnic. Every court was full and the ball fields had two or sometimes three games going on at once. The boys went over to the fence that ran along the court furthest from the street. This is where kids their age played. There was a line of boys milling about watching the game and Johnny immediately saw that one of the teams playing consisted of kids from 118th Street.

"See that tall guy? He fouls you every time you go to the hoop," Johnny said.

"That's how they play over there. No respect for the game," Joey said.

Raymond was confident he could play, but basketball was not his best game by far. Joey, on the other hand, was an up-and-coming legend at the park. He played in various leagues and was well-known for his prowess on the court. He was a vicious inside player who took no nonsense. Joey took after his father on the court. He was a hothead and everyone knew it. He was also one of those players you don't piss off, as it only makes his game stronger. Johnny was a decent player but his mouth never stopped running. Everyone knew who he was and that only made him talk more. Many a time, Johnny avoided getting his clock cleaned because of who his father was. In fact, it was usually Joey who told him to shut up when Johnny was getting out of line.

"Who got next?" Johnny asked.

The rules of the court were simple. Win and you keep playing. Lose and get in line. Johnny hated waiting and was known to pay his way to the front of the line. Once on the court, he usually got a good run in, as Joey was always his teammate.

"I got next," said a tall, skinny, black-headed boy.

He was a good-looking kid, but on further notice you could see that his clothes were a bit too worn, his sneakers were ripped on the side, and he had a bit of an unkempt look like he didn't have a use for or access to a mirror. His name was Tommy. Johnny recognized him and knew right away that he could get the court if he wanted it by throwing this kid a few bucks.

Tommy was poor, plain, and simple. His parents had come over on a boat and though they were proud people, the opportunity for them was limited. They saw in Tommy their chance to do better. They were the typical immigrant family who come to the States for a chance not for them but for their son. Tommy's parents were going to see their son as a success. Any money they had and anything they could do was for their son. Tommy would succeed where they failed. It was an awful burden on Tommy. He knew he was poor; he knew his parents were sacrificing everything for him. He felt this pressure and it showed on his handsome face. He went hungry every day, and it was this hunger that made him sit alone sometimes and realize he needed to succeed. Tommy didn't dream. There was no time to do that. Dreaming didn't pay the rent or fill the fridge. He planned his future. He knew what he wanted to do in life. As a kid, he was always fascinated in how things were built. He told his parents to get him broken toys from the trash rather than spend money on anything new. He loved to see the inner workings of things and relished the challenge to fix them. As he grew older, he became captivated by buildings and their construction. His father, when washing windows, would often take him downtown. Tommy would sit quietly for hours watching the construction around him. He would often wake up earlier then his father and wait dressed for him to go downtown to work with him. This only fueled his parents more. They knew they were sacrificing for the right reasons and, though this was never voiced between Tommy and his parents, it was understood by both of them.

Tommy was an excellent student. He knew what vocation he was to follow. He was going to be an architect. He never voiced this to anyone but Peter, his best friend. If anyone in the neighborhood knew his secret, he would be shunned and made fun of. In the neighborhood, if you said you wanted to be a doctor or lawyer or any profession for that matter, the kids would reply what color dress are you going to wear to work? Professionals were beyond most kids in the neighborhood. Most of the kids in the neighborhood were destined to be construction workers, plumbers, or any other number of trades that were out there. Tommy knew that his destiny was to be better than that. It was what drove him. The tired smiles of his parents and the rumble in his stomach were the fuel in which he drew strength. No amount of insults or obstacles was going to get in his way.

Johnny said, "Look, kid, three bucks says I got next." And he gave a quick glance at the ripped sneakers Tommy was wearing. This was the absolute wrong approach to take.

Tommy smiled, "If you weren't playing with Joey, it would be the worst three bucks you ever spent. These 118th Street guys would blow you and your other friend right off the court."

Johnny was not used to being talked to this way and looked at Joey, who only smiled and threw up his hands as if to say "your move."

"Look, Pete and I have next if you want to buy your way on to my squad. See if you can push some of your father's money on those three. They were going to play with us but if you can pay them off, that's fine with me. Deal?" Tommy said holding out his hand.

Johnny stood there with his mouth open, stunned into silence for one of the few times in his life.

Joey, ever aware of the situation, said, "Johnny, go to work on those three over there." Joey grabbed Tommy's hand in the tight grip that showed he was impressed and respected him. Tommy smiled and Raymond could see the bond he had formed with Joey had just happened again between Tommy and Joey. The day was turning out to be quite interesting.

Throughout the whole exchange another boy stood there quietly, not saying a word but taking it all in. His name was Peter. The fact that he was so nondescript was incredible given his size. Peter was built like a brick shithouse, as the saying goes. He was tall and thick around the neck and shoulders. Not quite as tall as Joey but somehow he looked bigger. His soft brown hair was cropped short and his deep-set blue eyes were calm and introspective. He was a dichotomy of sorts. From a distance he looked like a killer, all size and strength, but from up close he had the serenity of an angel. Raymond looked at him and could feel nothing but confusion. He wanted to hear this boy talk to see which of the two he was. He instinctively reached out to Peter and offered his hand.

"Hey. I'm Raymond."

To his surprise and consternation, Peter didn't say a word, he just smiled and nodded shaking hands with Joey next.

Raymond tried again, "Think we can take these guys?" he asked Peter.

Peter smiled and said in a calm and almost soothing voice, "By the grace of God we're going to break their holes."

To this Joey and Johnny, who had returned after securing their place in the next game, broke into laughter. Raymond stood there stunned and realized he could not get a read on this strange hulking soft-spoken boy.

"Let's go, Rock," Tommy said to Peter. "You got forward. Let Joey play center. I'll play the swing and you, Raymond, and Johnny play the guard positions."

The "Rock" was Peter's nickname. Not for his size, which could have easily described him, but for his temperament. Since they first met, Tommy had thought of Peter as an Apostle from the bible. Tommy was not much of a churchgoer, but attended Sunday mass regularly with his parents or his mother if his dad was working. He met Peter one Sunday after mass. Peter was an altar boy and looked very out of place sitting between two boys who were half his size up on the altar during mass. Tommy hung around after the mass to see Father Bob and ask if he knew of any available work in the neighborhood. As he spoke to Father Bob in the rectory, he did not realize that Peter was standing behind him waiting to see Father Bob as well. Tommy knew the shame of having to ask for work and, in essence, charity but having another boy hear it inflamed him with rage as he stormed out of the rectory. Peter grabbed his arm in a grip that could have bent steel.

"Tommy. Right?" Peter said in a voice that was so quiet. Tommy had to lean forward to hear him.

Peter let go of his arm and asked, "You're in my math class. I've failed the last two tests. Do you think you could help me out? I know how smart you are."

"Sure," Tommy said and stormed out of the church.

On the way home he realized what had just happened. Peter was revealing something that embarrassed him to help Tommy save face. It was by far and away the kindest thing he had ever seen another kid do. He vowed he would help Peter and the next day went to him and promised him he would not fail the next test. Peter invited him to his house after school and was asked to stay for dinner. Peter had two sisters and a mother. His father had died in an auto accident but had been a police officer.

Peter was the man of the house and protected his little sisters with the ferocity of a lion. Peter's mother was named Mary and a more fitting name she could not have had. She was the kindest soul Tommy had ever seen. She took him in and it was not unusual for Tommy to eat dinner at Peter's house at least four times a week. Tommy found out later that Peter was actually pretty good at math. The whole thing had been a lie to help Tommy save face. Peter would never admit this but, to Tommy, it had sealed their friendship for life.

Peter was very religious and was involved with the church. At school, he was quiet and a teachers' favorite as he was always willing to help out. His soft-spoken nature often made him the butt of jokes by other students. Peter would never respond and for all his size he truly was a gentle giant. That was not to say that Peter could not handle himself. The incident that stopped all teasing occurred one day when Peter returned home to find his sister, Nicole, crying in her room. An older boy had said some inappropriate things to her and this upset her so much that she did not want to go to school the next day. Peter gently calmed his sister and the next day after school grabbed the boy who accosted his sister. He proceeded to beat the boy and his two older brothers until all three were bloodied. Tommy had stood there and watched. At Peter's request, he didn't jump in. Peter "The Rock" after that day had never had to fight again. His reputation sealed at age of twelve.

The boys played. They held the court for hours. Raymond called out opposing players' weaknesses and Joey and Peter exploited them. Johnny was a relentless pain-in-the-ass, heckling and harassing the opposition to the point of almost starting three fights. When they were done, the boys cooled off in the shade of the park house. There was nothing to say. Their friendship was now cemented. They were a team, a crew, and friends to the end.

CHAPTER

4

Growing Up

"Looking good," Johnny said as Peter came out of the vestibule of the building.

Peter nodded and replied, "Thanks, Johnny. I see you're all dressed up for the first day of school."

"I was talking to your sisters, you big lob," Johnny said as he winked at Peter's sisters who were a step behind him. The girls giggled and stretched up to kiss Peter goodbye.

"See you later, bro. Love you," Chrissie said.

"Why say goodbye," Nicole chirped. "He's going to follow us to the front door anyway."

Peter lived on 117th Street in a four-story walk-up that was typical of the buildings in the neighborhood. Each building had essentially the same architectural design but each had its own personality. Each building on the block had its own cast of characters that created the special fabric of the neighborhood. Some of the characters transcended individual buildings and were legends in the neighborhood, known to everyone. Peter's building had Mrs. Lazaro who resided on the first floor and was always out her window. The guys swore she ran numbers from that window but it could never be proven. She was the classic old neighborhood lady. She knew everything and she watched everyone. She was a staple of the neighborhood. The guys were forever getting chased off of Peter's stoop by Mrs. Lazaro.

"Go-a play in the river!" she would yell in her broken English and the guys would laugh but respectfully walk away. One time the boys were in a heated game of stoopball, the one sport that Johnny actually had the edge on everyone. Mrs. Lazaro attempted to chase the boys off the stoop.

"There is-a no car in the street. Go-a play over there."

Johnny had had enough. He was winning and not about to go anywhere.

"Go-a ba fongul yourself you old witch!" he screamed.

Peter almost fainted. Raymond said sorry quickly and tried chastising Johnny.

"Come on. Let's get out of here," Raymond said.

Joey stood there mouth open, expressionless and staring at Mrs. Lazaro, waiting to see how the old lady would take it. Mrs. Lazaro quietly stood up and pointed a crooked finger from her gnarled and bony hand right at Johnny. She then smiled and slammed the window closed. The boys were shocked. Johnny stood there white as a ghost.

"What the hell was that?" he said.

"I don't know but I tell you it ain't good," Joey replied.

"We better get out of here," Raymond said.

And as he started to turn, the front door of the building opened slowly and, like a ghost coming out of the mist, out came Mrs. Lazaro.

"Mrs. Lazaro, I'm so sorry. He didn't mean it," Peter said.

"You a good boy, Peter," she said and patted him on his arm. "You-a too, Tommy." And she walked away up the block.

"Where the fuck is she going?" Johnny said, and the boys could almost hear fear in his voice.

"Maybe she's going to get a gun and shoot you in your stupid head. How can you yell at an old lady?" Tommy said.

"Let's follow her," Raymond said as they watched her slow and measured gait take her steadily up the block. The boys all turned in pursuit except Johnny.

"What's the matter, Johnny, ain't you coming?" Joey said sarcastically.

Johnny's voice cracked as he said, "No way."

The boys left him rooted to the spot and took off slowly after Mrs. Lazaro.

"She's pretty quick for an old lady," Tommy said amazed as Mrs. Lazaro progressed up the block.

The boys were excited and intrigued. It was rare to see Mrs. Lazaro out of her window and even rarer to see Johnny scared. This was shaping up to be a classic story, Raymond thought as he walked up the block.

"Holy cow!" Peter gasped. Which was as close as he ever came to cursing. The reason for his astonishment was that Mrs. Lazaro had walked right into the bar! Franco's bar! Johnny's father's bar!

"He's dead," Joey said.

"That's balls," Tommy said. "That old lady is no joke."

"Amazing," Peter said.

Ten minutes passed as the boys stood there and continued waiting. Mrs. Lazaro finally reappeared with Franco escorting her out to the street. Fat Tony came out and began chatting with Mrs. Lazaro as they walked together down the street. When he looked up and saw the boys, Tony waved them over.

"You okay, Mrs. Lazaro?" he asked.

She nodded and continued down the block. Tony's expression changed instantly and his tone of voice made the hair stand up on Raymond's neck.

"Go get Johnny. You know where he is. Tell him his father wants to see him. And, boys, he wants to talk to you guys too."

The last words were said with a smile.

Joey said, "No problem, Tony."

And the boys almost ran down the block. When they got back to Peter's building, they were shocked to see Mrs. Lazaro and Johnny sitting on the stoop and quietly chatting. Johnny was nodding and looked truly sorry and respectful.

As the boys approached, Mrs. Lazaro looked up and said, "Good-a night boys." And to everyone's astonishment, she actually kissed Johnny on the cheek before going into the building.

"Kiss of death," Joey said questioningly as Johnny got up and walked over to the boys.

"Oh, this is so bad," Tommy said.

Johnny solemnly walked over to his friends and said, "We need to go see my dad, right?"

"Yeah, let's not keep him waiting," Joey said, and without a word the boys walked back toward the bar like dead men walking to the gallows.

Raymond was scared. He had been in the bar a few times, but as a matter of fact, it struck Raymond that the boys had never been in the bar together. They had all been in the bar but that was with Johnny when he had stopped in to see his dad or to get drinks after they had played ball. This was different; they had been summoned to the bar. They sat at the round booth, tucked into the corner of the bar away from the pool tables but near the back room. The bar was not crowded but the few men in the bar seemed amused to see Johnny and his little crew looking nervous. The boys were quiet. Raymond could swear he heard Peter saying Hail Marys under his breath. Franco was in the back room, and after what seemed like an eternity to Raymond, Franco finally emerged.

Franco was a man who dressed sharp—always. He had on a white shirt and blue slacks and the hint of a gold chain around his neck could be seen as he walked purposefully from the back to the table. He had on a gold watch and two rings. One was a wedding ring and the other was a diamond pinky ring with a J on it. Johnny always said it was the first thing his father had bought after spending six months in jail and it was something to remind him that he never wanted to go back again. It was a good story but everyone in the neighborhood knew the J stood for his one and only child—Johnny. As he approached the table, his face gave away no emotions. He looked over each boy and then his gaze lingered on Raymond for a second. Raymond, for the briefest instant, thought he saw the ghost of a smile slip onto Franco's face but it happened so quickly that Raymond pushed the thought out of his head instantly. Franco gazed longer at Johnny, stone-faced and introspective. The silence was palpable and the boys dared not speak. Franco hesitated for another second that felt like an hour.

Then Franco whispered, "You disappoint me … Raymond."

Raymond felt as if he had been slapped in the face.

He stammered, "Excuse me, sir …"

But Franco had held up his hand to silence him.

"My son tells me you're the one who always has a plan and yet you came in here with nothing. You are ready to accept whatever I was going to say. You have no defense, no excuse, no plan to get your friends out of trouble. It's good to plan things out but sometimes you have to be quick on your feet. Remember that."

Raymond, feeling complimented, replied, "How did you know I had nothing?"

"Could see it in your eye, kid." He laughed. Franco quickly sobered, "Now to the reason we're here," he said coldly. "Let me explain something. When I was a kid, my cousin Frankie lived in your building, Peter. He lived in 4G and we were inseparable as kids. We practically lived on that stoop. Mrs. Lazaro was an old lady to us even back then. Her husband, Tom, was a bricklayer and tough as nails. He would have given your father a few lumps, Joey. He would come home every night all dusty and sweaty, sleeves rolled up showing off these massive arms, and chase Frankie and me off the stoop. We would run when we saw him coming up the block. Mrs. Lazaro would wait for him looking out that window so she could have dinner ready for him when he came in the door. My father, your grandfather, Johnny, would always stop in to see the Lazaros and ask how I was. She looked out that window and watched after us. We didn't know it but she kept an eye on a lot of the kids in the neighborhood at that time. You see, guys, that is how it is. This neighborhood looks out for its own. You little fucks are too young to understand that, but that old lady who you think of as a pain in the ass is really only watching out for you punks and the rest of the block. That old lady cares about the neighborhood and the people in it."

"She looks out that window and remembers how her husband walked down the street and her chasing you away reminds her of him chasing me away. You're lucky she came here to me. Ten years ago, she would have come out and taken a broomstick to all of your asses herself. She asked me to go easy on you and to explain to you that she really cares about you kids. She's too proud to say that and she keeps up the front of being a tough old witch." He looked at Johnny, who had tears welling up in his eyes. "You hurt that old lady deeply today." He addressed them all now, "I brought you guys here to explain to you that the old people in this neighborhood are like gold. They're precious and they are to be cherished and treasured. Remember that or next time I won't be so nice."

With that, he reached out and hugged Johnny. Peter had tears in his eyes. Joey squirmed in his seat. He was not used to having a father show affection to his son.

When Franco released Johnny, he wiped his face with the back of his hand and said, "You know what Mrs. Lazaro said to me, Dad?"

"What?" asked Franco.

"She said she was disappointed in me and that she knew I didn't mean it and then she talked about Grandpa."

"She's a smart old bird," Franco said. "Now for the real reason I called you guys in here tonight."

Franco smiled as he slid in the booth next to Raymond.

Raymond's relief turned to fear again as he pondered what Franco had meant. Franco put his arm around Raymond's shoulder and quietly said, "You boys are growing up. This year will be your junior year in high school and all the little scams you've pulled this summer are going to stop. Remember two things, boys: I run this neighborhood and I keep my eye on my son. You had a nice time this summer. That candy store thing, the bakery, and the money from the basketball tourney you threw."

The boy's shocked faces told all. Franco had been aware of all their activities this summer. They had broken into the basement of Hooley's candy store in June. A brilliant plan of Raymond's, as he had cased the place for months and knew exactly when the new shipments of comic books would arrive. Tommy and Joey had explored the basement of the building and Tommy figured out which door had led to the storeroom of the candy store. After that, it was easy. Peter kept watch while the other four broke in and took all the comics and sold them to some Spanish kids from 120th street. The whole score had netted them cash for a month. To Raymond, it wasn't the money; it was all in the execution. The plan was perfect. Raymond was ecstatic that it had gone off without a hitch. It was his first triumph with all the boys involved. He would learn later that it was not always that easy and that the best laid plans always had flaws. The boys all turned and looked at Johnny who stared fiercely back at them.

Franco quickly said, "My son is not the rat, boys. Remember I keep an eye on him and that invariably led me to all of you."

This comment struck Raymond as extremely important and he filed it away for future reference in his mind.

"What I'm trying to say is this, boys, be careful. Concentrate on school for the next few years. Stay out of trouble and if you're planning anything in the neighborhood or elsewhere, run it by me first. I don't want Johnny getting thrown out of school for taking a kid's milk money. Are we clear on that?"

The boys nodded and realizing they had been dismissed, started to file out.

Franco grabbed Raymond around the shoulders as he left the booth and said, "Remember what I said, kid." And he gave him a sly wink.

As the boys neared the door, Franco dropped one last bombshell on the boys, "Hey, boys," he yelled and threw an envelope to Johnny, who caught it mid-air. "Don't give old man Manginni a hard time. He has a key also."

Johnny opened the envelope and inside there were five new keys. Johnny smiled and looked at his father then showed the boys the keys.

Franco's face turned grim for a second and he said, "I changed the lock but don't ever let me find out you're sampling anything from the wine cellar."

CHAPTER

5

The Wine Cellar

RAYMOND'S EMOTIONS HAD BEEN ON A ROLLER COASTER THAT NIGHT. The fear and the excitement had been bubbling around and playing tag in his brain the entire time they were in the bar. The last turn of events, however, was a triumph beyond his wildest imagination. Franco had given each boy a key to the wine cellar. It was like Franco had given the boys keys to the city.

The wine cellar had been discovered by the boys in May of the previous year. Franco owned a bunch of the buildings on 109th. Tommy, with his fascination of how things were built, loved creeping around the basements of many of the buildings. He was always dragging the guys around the boiler rooms and sub basements. It always amazed the guys how Tommy, even when underground, knew exactly where they were. The walls in the basements were faded and grimy. No one ever really went down there but the superintendents of the buildings. This was where Tommy felt at home. In the basements, he could actually see the layouts of each building in his head. The blueprints he studied in the library came to life. He traced the heating and water pipes up walls and followed them to and from the boiler room, usually with one of the guys in tow. He would point out how certain doors led to the street or the alley. The other guys were lost and, not knowing about Tommy's

34

secret obsession with architecture, attributed his uncanny directional sense to his ancestors being explorers. Every time they would enter a building, one of the guys would crack, "Hey, Magellan, where we going today?" It was during one of these excursions that the boys came across the wine cellar.

On this particular rainy day, the boys were in 155 East 109th Street.

"Follow me, boys," Tommy said as he walked over to a dark corner of the lobby. There was a recessed door that was unlocked and looked little used.

"This way," Tommy motioned and the guys followed him down a narrow stairway to a small narrow hallway at the bottom. Tommy got his bearings and said, "Straight ahead is the alley with the trash cans. That door there," he said pointing to a door on their left.

The door was locked and Tommy called to Joey, "Little help here, Joe."

"Step aside, boys," Joey said.

Quick as a flash, his knife was out. It was a long, skinny, black switchblade that Joey had taken to carrying. With a few cracks and a bit of cursing, Joey stepped back and said, "Okay. Let's see what's behind door number one."

Tommy entered first and flipped the light switch he had noticed as he entered the room. The boiler room was dark, even with the light on. With no windows and no other doors, it looked like a giant dungeon. As you entered the room, the first thing you saw was the tremendous boiler that was used to heat the building and provide hot water. Tommy followed the oil pipe and pointed to a spot about twenty feet over their head.

"That's where the oil pipe is on the street above us," he said to no one in particular.

If you could look past the boiler, there was plenty of space.

"Look, if you walk around the boiler, this room extends as far as the lobby above us," Tommy said as he squeezed through the four-foot-wide space between the wall and the boiler.

The boys followed him in single file.

"This place gives me the creeps," Peter said.

Being the biggest, he was very uncomfortable in tight spaces.

"Are you kidding me?" Johnny said. "The fucking rats think you're Godzilla! What are you scared of?"

Just at that moment, Tommy stopped short and the boys crashed into each other. Tommy's astonishment was missed amongst the many complaints of the boys. The space opened up once you passed the boiler exactly as Tommy had thought. A naked bulb that hung from the ceiling dimly lit the sight before him. A large barrel dominated the room with a press that was used for making homemade wine. There were a couple extra barrels next to the one with the press and rack of old wine bottles, some empty and some full. On the dusty floor, there were the old-fashioned gallon bottles with twist off caps filled with wine. The rest of the room looked unused. In one corner, there was an old couch with ripped arms and thin cushions. There was an old wood table that was stained in many placed where the wine had soaked into the wood. There were two chairs that looked like they belonged to the original table set and a couple of folding chairs stacked in the corner. A workbench sat against the far wall with some tools and an old gym locker, the tall skinny types with a lock on it, at the end of the workbench. That was basically it.

The room was dark and had an unused feel. The walls were peeling and the concrete floor made it cold and damp, even with the heat the enormous boiler threw off. Tommy, while taking all this in, was blocking the rest of the boys, leaving them stuck between the boiler and the wall, and realizing this, stepped into the room and allowed the rest of them to enter in. The boys filed through and were silent as if they had entered a church. They each took inventory of the room as Tommy had done, each keeping their own thoughts to themselves. Finally, Joey walked over to the wine and said, "Merry Christmas, boys," and he picked up a gallon bottle and examined its contents by holding it up to the light from the light bulb. The effect threw the whole room into a pale red haze that was quite eerie.

"Put that down," Peter said. "This place is creepy enough without the red tint. Let's get out of here. I really am not comfortable in here, and anyway, I'm sure whoever this wine belongs to would not be happy to see us in here."

"It's okay, big guy," Raymond said. "I'll hold your hand if you want me to." And that brought a much-needed laugh to everyone, lightening the mood of the room.

As he stepped in, Johnny was not really listening. His wheels were turning and Raymond, sensing this, asked, "Whatcha thinking, Johnny?"

"Well, wouldn't this place make a perfect hang-out for us? I mean we could make this our own club."

Joey was grinning from ear to ear. He saw other possibilities of having a club of their own.

Peter, usually cautious, was also thinking that this was a good idea. "A nice place of solitude that we could study in and do homework," he mumbled to himself.

"Homework? Are you kidding me? I was thinking of some other things entirely," Johnny said.

"Yeah, well, you know, I'm just saying," Peter was trying to defend himself but Johnny cut him off.

"Shut up, I thought I heard something," he said.

They all froze and listened. There was hardly a sound, and at that moment, the boiler kicked in and the noise made all of them jump. They all looked sheepishly around and laughed nervously.

"Cut it out, Joey. You didn't hear anything. You got us all jumping out of our skins for nothing," Tommy said.

They all relaxed and then heard a gravely voice above the sound of the boiler say, "Who is-a trying to steal-a my wine?"

The boys turned and looked at the narrow entrance between the boiler and the exit; filling the entire space and hidden in shadow was a very large man. In his left hand he had a tree branch or some sort of walking stick. His right hand was behind his back and from the position of his body he looked tensed as if ready to crack someone with the stick. The boys all froze and Joey quietly slipped out his knife and shot Johnny a look as if to say, "I'm ready if I need to be." Johnny squinted and in an instant thought he recognized the man. He moved in front of the rest of the boys and made himself visible. The man in the doorway, seeing Johnny, relaxed ever so slightly.

In fact, only Johnny caught the movement and he in turn at once knew who was blocking their exit and whose basement they were in. This was old man Manginni. He was the super of the building and Johnny had known him since he was a kid. The fact that it was Mr. Manginni didn't waylay any of Johnny's fears because, even though he knew Manginni, he was and had always been deathly afraid of this man. As a child, when his father would go to speak with Mr. Manginni in the lobby of the building, Johnny would cling to his father's hand or hide behind his leg.

Mr. Manginni was an old Italian man from the neighborhood. He was a large man with huge hands and a square jaw that looked like it was chiseled out of granite. He always wore a white tee shirt and his left arm had a scar that ran from his elbow to his wrist. His graying hair was thick and his crooked nose was also large. "Roman nose," his father would say, but never in front of Mr. Manginni. The man was scary and a loner. He never was in any of the neighborhood clubs. You never saw him socializing on a street corner or in a bar. He was sort of a mystery. He never was out and about during the day. Usually, if you did see him, it was at night going or coming from his building, which was always kept impeccably clean.

Mr. Manginni recognizing Johnny said in his broken English, "Why you-a here in-a my basement? You-a steal-a my wine, you meet-a my stick," he growled and tapped the walking stick against the boiler gently. The message was clear and Johnny quickly replied, "No, we just want a place to hang out. Sort of our own little club."

Mr. Manginni frowned with understanding, "You boys should-a no be down here," he replied, then he thought for a minute and said, "You stay. But you no touch-a the wine and you use a key. No break any locks."

"I promise on my word that we won't touch a drop," Johnny said.

Joey moaned and Peter laughed at that and all the boys relaxed.

Mr. Manginni grunted and said, "I'll fix-a the lock and leave a key under the extinguisher down-a the hall." And with that he nodded and walked out of the room.

Johnny smiled and turned to the boys and said, "Welcome to the wine cellar, boys!"

The wine cellar name stuck and the boys decided it would not be a social club. Not that it could be. They agreed that the room was to be for themselves alone and no one outside of the crew.

Joey protested, saying, "It would be a perfect place to bring a girl."

"You're a real romantic," Tommy said. "Bring a girl down here for a date?"

They all laughed and even Joey agreed. The wine cellar was theirs and theirs alone. The boys scavenged some extra chairs and an old cot to complete the look of the place. They noticed that the only thing Mr. Manginni did was take the old gym locker out of the room. The boys noticed it missing the next day when they returned and saw the lock fixed.

For Joey, the wine cellar was a special place. He often slept down in the wine cellar because of the problems he had at home. Listening to rats scurrying around was a hell of a lot better then listening to his father rant and rave at his mother when he came home drunk. The boys knew Joey would sleep down the wine cellar and never made a big deal about it. They understood. Raymond was also particularly fond of the wine cellar. It was where he went to plot out his schemes. He loved the solitude and no windows. In a bizarre way, he thought of it like a prison cell and the motivation to make his plans foolproof was so he never ended up in a cell like the wine cellar. The boys spent hours in the wine cellar. Mr. Manginni would occasionally stop by to look in on his wine and the boys, true to their word, never touched a drop.

The night Franco gave the boys keys to the wine cellar it became officially theirs. This was a reason to celebrate but it disturbed Raymond. Everything the boys had done over the last few months, from the wine cellar to the bakery, had come onto Franco's radar. Raymond understood that it was Franco's livelihood to know what went on in his neighborhood but to Raymond this became a challenge. Whatever he planned in the future had to go on unbeknownst to Franco. That was the goal. It was with this in mind that school started in September.

CHAPTER

6

Taken to School

S CHOOL WAS AN UNENDING DRUDGERY FOR JOHNNY AND JOEY. In fact, all the boys preferred summer and the unlimited freedom that it brought, but for Johnny and Joey, school was a nuisance that they found unnecessary. Johnny, in the back of his mind and in his private moments, wanted nothing more than to follow in his father's footsteps. He had been brought up in a world where power was derived from the neighborhood. His father held the most authority in the neighborhood and never had graduated high school. There were lawyers and politicians who sought after his father's audience. To Johnny, this was power.

He didn't want to be a lawyer. He wanted to be his father and to do that school was unnecessary. He needed experience. In his mind, he already had his crew assembled. He was like his father in that he had chosen the right people. His father had confirmed and approved of his choices. Very often at dinner he would comment about his friends.

"That Raymond. You should study more like him. That's a smart kid. Stick with him and you'll be all right. Let me tell you, son, a friend like Joey is priceless. He will take a knife for you and you'll learn that loyalty is the hardest trait to see in people, but that kid's got it. Tommy's hungry. I'd take one hungry guy for ten satisfied guys any day. Peter … heart of gold that kid has. His father was like that."

All these comments had been said in passing, but Johnny listened and took them as his father's approval. Johnny had no illusions about the life his father led and had no doubts that it could end violently, but it was the path he was determined to go down whether his father wanted him down that road or not. School was a place for Johnny to practice being the boss. He was involved in all the school social circles. Doing favors here. Culling favors there. Academics came not second but a distant third. Girls would come second. This was the only joy that school brought to Johnny and he leaned heavily on his friends to make passing grades and get him through.

Joey and Tommy had another view of school. Each boy loved it for a different reason. Joey loved school because it brought a much-needed structure to his chaotic life. Joey was soothed by the normalcy and routine of school. He was average academically and that suited him just fine. He had his petty gambling ring and provided football sheets to students and some teachers alike. School was a safe and calm place for Joey and it relaxed him. He was very comfortable in school, the polar opposite of his home life. For Raymond, school was a place to show his intelligence and to hatch new plots. He loved the idea of getting over on teachers and other students. He was an excellent student and thrived in an academic situation. He also, like Johnny, worked the social end of school moving easily from group to group. School brought about a new set of problems to be solved for Raymond and that is what drove him in life. Always being ahead of the game and the next guy, working the system to his favor and that of his friends.

Tommy loved school. He was always out to prove himself. His grades were excellent and his teachers loved him. He asked questions to the point of annoyance and knew more about topics than anyone in the school. He was a voracious reader and loved math. He would never frequent the library in the summer, but he lived in the school library during the winter. School was a joy; he loved to work hard and improve himself every day. Peter took school like he took all situations, with calm and patience. He was a hard-working student.

Peter, of all the boys, was the most consistent in all aspects of his life. In religion, he found a certain solid rudder to guide his life. As crazy as things could get, Peter always put his faith in God and let everything else fall as it may. The beginning of school meant watching out for his sisters and watching out for his friends, whether that meant keeping Raymond from getting in a fight or keeping Joey from getting thrown out of Latin class. School was fine. "Jesus was a teacher so how bad could school be," he always said.

It wasn't until November that Raymond decided to conduct his first school heist. End of quarter exams would be a hot commodity and by getting them, the boys could make some quick money. The only risk was getting thrown out of school. Raymond began the plot in September by making friends with a janitor who would always smoke a cigarette outside the gym during Raymond's gym class. Through this janitor, Raymond found out who cleaned the faculty and copier room and at what time. The plan was quite simple. Raymond needed the garbage bag from the copier room to get the carbons of the tests after the teachers ran them off. Not very creative or difficult. Once the right guy was identified, it was easy to follow him out to a dumpster and then mark the bag with masking tape so the boys could pick it up after school. Then the boys would take the bag back to the wine cellar and piece and sort the tests.

After making up answer keys, the boys would sell the quarter exam test answers to students. The real stroke of genius was put on by Raymond, who stole the answers but changed enough questions to ensure high-80s grades. Raymond knew if everyone got a 100% it would be too suspicious. An 88 percent from a kid who was failing, and a teacher could say they studied hard for the exam. An 88 percent from a straight-A student would mean he took the exam too lightly. It was brilliant. They wound up with seven tests and, while changing the answers for those seven proved to be a challenge, it was all worth it when they added up the earnings and made $275.

This was the first of many of Raymond's plots. some involved school and some didn't. The boys were always wary when they saw Raymond smiling at lunch. It meant he had hatched a plot and was ready to spring it on the guys.

"What is it today, Dillinger," Joey would say as he saw Raymond. "Fort Knox or a brinks truck?"

And the boys would get a laugh. Raymond would smile and say, "No, seriously, I got a thing." And then the plan would spill out.

It seemed that the litany of plots never ceased. Test, scams, fake raffles, fixed basketball games, providing beer for parties, it seemed endless, and as Raymond's successes became more and more frequent, the boys began to take him more and more seriously. Johnny in particular wanted to step up their operations and start trying some stuff outside school. He pitched his idea in the wine cellar one day after school.

"Let's say we knock over a club. That one on 118th Street, in the middle of the block."

"The Pollack's!" Joey exclaimed. "You've got to be crazy! The Pollack is nuts. I heard he cut a guy's head off over a blackjack game in the club a couple of months back."

"Get out of here. He never did that," Johnny replied. "That guy lost his head for a totally different reason."

Raymond sat quietly and thought about the proposal. In all honesty, he had thought about it himself a few times. A club would put them on the radar that Raymond was desperately trying to stay off of, but he was getting tired of small time scams and wanted to step it up and do something big.

"Too risky a club. Are you serious to take a club? You have to go in armed to get any money and, Johnny, I would like to see you run that buy your dad," Tommy said.

Raymond jumped right in, "I think it could be done but it would have to be done right and, to tell you the truth, Tommy's right. There's no money in it. The risk isn't worth the reward."

"So what do we do next, Capone?" Johnny said to Raymond.

"Haven't thought about it," he said and stretched back on the rickety cot and closed his eyes.

In reality, Raymond was thinking about hitting a club but what he had said earlier was true. There was no money in it. The neighborhood was full of little storefront clubs that passed as social clubs. Every block had a club and everyone on the block hung out in there. The boys as kids would hang around the club on 110th. Now that they were older, they were actually allowed inside and could shoot pool or play cards. On the weekends, they were regulars in the club. Especially in the winter when it got too cold to go outside and play sports. The club was a miniature version of Franco's bar. Where only wise guys and people who were connected, Crazy Larry excluded, were allowed in Franco's bar, all the other characters in the neighborhood were in the club.

While the summer was prime time for the boys, the winter was a time when everything slowed down. There was less freedom for the boys. Hanging out in the summer meant all day and night. The winter meant hanging out in a club. Every club had their own characters. The club they hung out in was in the middle of the block between a bakery and a candy store. The local candy store was the neighborhood version of the convenience store.

The club in the winter was a place to get out of the cold. You would see scarves, gloves, and hats drying out on the radiator. The club on 110th street was a storefront and a back room. The door had a small window and guys would come and peak in to see what was going on in the club. When you entered the club, it had a few folding tables and some chairs that were used for card playing and other gambling activity. Small time stuff. Nickels and dimes to pass time and hang out. The back room had a small bar with an old 12-inch black-and-white TV above it and an old Brunswick pool table. There was a pool rack on the wall with a couple of cues and a number of chairs around the pool table for spectators. The older guys in the club usually controlled the table. Johnny paid his way into games and often got the boys a chance to play. The money was larger on the pool table and that meant more serious competition. Raymond liked to watch the games. He examined that angles and was usually the one making lines for the side bets. This was right up his alley as he got to control the action.

"Three-to-one he makes the shot," he would call out and money would change hands all around the table. The boy's main reason for hanging out in the club was the entertainment. It was a great place to pick up the gossip of the neighborhood but, for the boys, Johnny was usually the best source of information so the club was a place of comic relief. There was always something happening in the club and most of it had to do with the man who ran the club, Joe Landy Moe.

No one knew if that was his real name or if that was his nickname. He opened the place and closed it down as far as anyone knew. He lived upstairs from the club because he was always there. Landy was a tall lanky guy in his late thirties or early forties. His wavy brown hair was thinning a bit and graying at the temples. Jeans and a sweater was his normal attire. He talked loudly and was constantly in motion. It was like he never stood still; twitchy would be a good word to describe him. Landy was involved in every gambling pool imaginable and was a compulsive gambler. He was also a chronic loser. He never won. It was a running joke in the neighborhood. The legend of Landy Moe wasn't built upon his losing, though it was the way he lost. Landy lost in every bizarre way imaginable. There were tons of stories of how he lost. The time a squirrel ran out on the track at Aqueduct and his horse ahead by twelve lengths jumped the inside rail.

The time he lost a college game because the coach pulled the team off the court forfeiting the game because the fans were throwing stuff on the court at the Garden. The stories go on and on and the club was always abuzz with the latest story or a rendition of an old loss that was being animatedly told by someone in the club. One of Joe Landy's greatest losses was actually witnessed by the boys one cold Sunday afternoon. There was an elimination pool tournament going on and Landy was hot. He won two games and made it to the final match against Tony Bracco.

Tony was a good player but he had been drinking all day and was getting a bit looped. The contest was ripe for the taking for Landy and he knew it. He was talking how this was his day and he couldn't lose and "put up your money, boys, I got this." The crowd kept silent and tense. Some guys were pulling for Landy and some were just waiting for the shoe to drop. The game progressed with Landy running most of the table. He made shot after shot and as the excitement built, so did the tension. Finally Landy banked a ball in and the cue ball rolled across the table, leaving the eight ball sitting in the center of the table and the cue at the far end. An easy shot for Landy. He stood up, stretched—just relishing the moment. He had it. It was a lock. With a dramatic flair he whipped his cue around and bent over to take the shot to win. Just as he leaned over the table a fly landed on the cue and just stood there. Landy stood bent over the cue looking at the fly and the fly stood looking at Landy. Everyone in the place held their breath and waited. It seemed like an eternity and it became a contest of wills who would move first, the fly or Landy. Locked in a duel, both stood and waited the other out. The people in the club were just as silent. The air in the room stood still. Time passed as if it had been a spaghetti western. The camera would have shot back and forth from Landy's eyes to the fly's. They waited until finally Landy snapped.

"Fucking fly," he screamed and swung the cue in an arch trying to scare the fly off the cue ball, but instead it hit the cue ball and everyone watched as the cue ball rolled agonizingly toward the side pocket. It froze momentarily and then, as if pushed, dropped in. He scratched! The club erupted in laughter! It took everyone a moment to see how Landy would react. All eyes turned to him. Landy was looking down at the table. You could see his knuckles were white around the cue stick. He was angry and the crowd waited for him to erupt. Finally, Landy looked up and said in a tight voice, "Got him," and he gestured to the fly that lay dead on the table. With that, he walked out of the back room to a stunned silence.

Raymond also took part in one of Landy's greatest and most memorable moments in the club. On Saturday afternoons, the pool table would be used for a game they called Bankers and Brokers. The game relied on getting the deal. If you had the deal you were the banker and played against everyone else. The idea was to hold the deal as long as you could and that way you were able to get the money. With a hot deal you could make a good deal of money. The boys and a multitude of players were playing for fifty cents and a dollar a hand just killing a Saturday afternoon and having fun. Landy, who had been in and out of the back room, settled in to play and immediately got the deal with an ace. Smiling, he grabbed the deck and began to shuffle.

"Place your bets, fellers. Place your bets," he crackled.

The money began to fly. Everyone wanted in. They figured with Landy dealing, they couldn't lose. Tommy put up his last dollar and Joey actually borrowed two dollars from Johnny just to stay in the game. Landy dealt and when it came to his card he pulled a deuce. In this game, a deuce was a loser unless someone else pulled a deuce. Landy scanned the table. Everyone got paid. Next deal, Landy pulls another deuce. Now the place is in frenzy! Everyone is doubling up and kids from the front room are begging to get in the action. Landy deals … three deuces in a row! The place is wild! Landy, now broke from two payouts, had to borrow money from Jimmy the Fox to stay in the game. When everyone's money was down on the table, he began to deal. With each card there followed a line of cursing. Ten of hearts—you bastard. Queen of Spades—your mother is a … and so on around the table he goes. Finally, Landy looks around the table; there are no aces out and most of the cards are non-picture cards. He figures he can't lose this round.

"Time to get all my money back," he says and turns over a two of spades. As soon as the card hit the table no one even had time to react. Landy threw the deck at everyone and ran to the front room. He came back in holding the TV over his head.

"Get out all you motherfuckers!" he screamed and threw the TV against the wall! As it shattered, everyone grabbed their money and ran for the door. Coats flying and people bumping into each other! It was total pandemonium in the club! Through it all, the boys were hysterically laughing as they scrambled out the door. The next day, every one could not wait to get to the club to see what Landy would say. He stayed in the back and when the place was packed, he came out as if it were a press conference to address the crowd.

"Look, I don't care about what happened yesterday. I don't care about losing the money or four deuces in a row," he said in a calm voice. Then his eyes bulged and he went on as the veins stood out on his neck.

"The only thing I have to say is if I ever find the motherfucker who stole the TV tube from the TV, I'll kill him."

And with that, he stormed out of the club. The boys, as well as everyone else in the club, erupted with laughter, except for Raymond, who had taken the tube out of the wreckage of the TV. Peter, seeing Raymond's face, knew instantly that Raymond had taken the tube and elbowed Johnny, who caught on and began laughing even louder. The club was the ultimate place to hang out for the boys but hitting one would be difficult.

7

The Next Job

THE IDEA OF HITTING A CLUB HAD TO BE SHELVED. As much as Raymond liked the idea of planning it out, the risks outweighed the rewards. The fact was, hitting a club, even in another neighborhood, would put them exactly where Raymond didn't want to be, on Franco's radar. The opportunity to pull a big job nagged at Raymond the entire month of November. It wasn't until December that an opportunity presented itself. Raymond happened to be in the middle of a test when he glanced over at Jimmy Chen. Chen was a good math student and an all-around good guy. You would never have known he had been born in Korea. Jimmy considered himself American and all of his troubles in school came from fighting about his ancestry. Jimmy played baseball and basketball, and even though he was on the short side he never backed down from a challenge.

Raymond respected him and his math ability challenged Raymond's own, which led to a friendly competition. The boys would often challenge each other to who would finish tests first and who would get a higher grade. They often would bet on the outcomes and Raymond was not embarrassed to say he lost as many as he won. During the test when he glanced at Jimmy, he saw Jimmy looking into his crotch. Raymond smiled. Jimmy was cheating and

Raymond had busted him. That day at lunch, Raymond approached Jimmy and confronted him.

"Caught you red-handed, Jimmy. I saw you cheating on the math test today," Raymond said with a smile.

"Cheating? Me? Are you kidding? I've been whipping you all year," Jimmy laughed.

"Then why keep looking down between your legs during the test?" Raymond asked.

"The desk was cracked and it was pinching my nuts,"

Jimmy laughed, knowing he was busted!

He sighed and said, "My dad had me working in the laundry till 11:00 p.m. Then he had the machines running all night. I didn't have time to study the formulas for the test. So I wrote them on the desk in homeroom this morning," he admitted as he handed a buck over to Raymond.

Raymond was puzzled, "You mean you slept in the store?"

Jimmy looked a bit embarrassed but that emotion quickly turned to anger. "Yeah, that's my father. He banks every cent. We live in the back of the store with my two sisters and mother. It's like being back in Korea. We have no refrigerator and a hot plate to cook on. My mother is stuck in there all day and every weekend. We came to this country to make a better life and my father treats us like we're still in Korea farming. He rakes in the dough and doesn't spend a dime. I guess I'll have to wait until he drops to see any money. You know, Raymond, I don't mind 'cause in two years I'll get out, get into college, and be free. What kills me is my sisters and mother have to put up with living that way till I can get them out." He said it all so quickly and in a rush, that Raymond really had no way to respond.

"Sorry to unload on you, Raymond. But it gets very frustrating," Jimmy said as he walked away.

Raymond thought about the situation all day, and the more he thought about it the more he thought there was an opportunity to be had. Raymond spent the day hashing out a plan. He presented his idea to the boys in the wine cellar that night.

"Look, forget about hitting a club. Let's hit Chang's Dry Cleaners."

Joey said, "Why Chang's?"

"Look, Chang's is perfect. It's not going to attract too much attention and Jimmy Chen says his dad keeps lot's of cash on hand at the store," Raymond said.

"So what are you thinking? A smash and grab? Go in guns blazing and just take his loot and run," Johnny laughed.

"Johnny, you can't go in and strong arm the guy," Joey explained. "We're too young for that and he probably pays your father to not have that nonsense go on."

"No way! Chen's a proud bastard. I don't think he gives my dad anything, at least not that I know of," Johnny replied. "And I was kidding. Running in a store and sticking it up is not Ray's style, right Ray? So what's the plan?"

Raymond was pacing the floor and paid no attention to Johnny or the other guys.

"There he goes," Tommy said.

"Jimmy told me that he lives in the back of the store. That means there is always someone there," Raymond said.

Peter chimed in, "Look, I know Jimmy has two sisters. What about them? We need to be very careful."

"Let the man think, Pete. I'm sure he's got this all worked out," Joey said.

"Not yet, but I will," Raymond replied and continued to pace the floor.

It took Raymond a week and a lot of spending time with Chen to finally hash out the plan. Over the course of the week, he had found out that Chen was more than happy to discuss his father and his business. Raymond found out that Jimmy absolutely hated his father. The man was an old school Korean and that meant the girls in the family were unimportant. His sisters, even though they were older than Jimmy, were given no respect and their education would end after high school. The only reason they were even allowed to go to school was to learn English.

According to Jimmy, they were both destined to remain in that store and work until his father died. This drove Jimmy crazy. His older sister, Jade, a senior, had extremely high grades and would do well in college. But his father would not even think about it. His other sister, San Lee, was a beautiful girl and was confined to the store. Jimmy figured his father would ship her back to Korea to marry some old farmer. Through all their conversations, Jimmy expressed his hatred of his father and this was the key to Raymond's plan.

Raymond explained it all to them in the wine cellar. They were all sitting around the old wood table as he told the boys what he intended them to do.

"Look, the store has an alarm on the front and back doors. There is a safe that would be hard to crack and even harder to carry out. The cash register is usually kept with a hundred and fifty bucks in small bills in it. The family lives in the back of the store which means someone is almost always there."

Raymond paused here for dramatic effect. The boys were riveted to Raymond and he could see there were many questions that were about to be asked.

Raymond held up his hand and said, "Hold on guys, let me finish."

Johnny smiled and choked back what he was about to say.

"Here's how we're going to do it. We're going in the back door when no one's in the shop and we're going to leave the safe, take the register and the couple of hundred hidden in the bag in the broken machine in the back of the store. There will be no alarms or no weapons. We should be in and out in ten minutes. Clean as a whistle."

The boys stood there with their mouths open and then the questions started.

"How will you know when the store is empty? What are we going to do—watch the place 24/7?" Peter asked.

"No weapons? What if someone is in the store? What then? We need to flash something to scare them," Johnny said.

"How are you going to get around the alarm, clip the electricity? I would need to see the back of the store to see where the wires run," Tommy said.

"Forget all that. How the hell do you know that there is money in a bag in a broken machine?" Joey asked.

With that, the boys all stopped and looked at Raymond who was smiling from ear to ear.

"Yeah, how did you know that?" Peter asked.

"Okay. What gives Raymond?" Johnny asked. "Why the big smile? What are you not telling us?"

"We will be able to bypass the alarm. No one will be home and the money will be exactly where I expect it because Jimmy Chen will have it already for us when we arrive," Raymond said smugly.

"What, you got Chen in on this? How?" Peter asked.

"See here's the deal. Jimmy's mom and dad are going to Korea to a wedding or something. They will be gone a week. Chen will be in charge of the store and on Saturday night he will take his sisters out to dinner and a movie. We will wait till seven o'clock and then use the back door. We can get into the back alley from the building down the block. It should be dark enough so no one will see us. The back door will be left open and the alarm will be turned off. We go in, get the cash, turn the place upside down a little, empty the register, and go. On the way out, we break the back door lock and one of us trips the alarm. By the time the cops get there, we will be here. Everything is nice. I have gloves for all of us so no prints, not that the cops will care—it's a Korean place. Jimmy comes home and is outraged. Plays it off and calls his dad."

There was a stunned silence in the cellar.

Tommy broke his silence, "Sounds great. When do we go?"

Raymond looked at his watch and said, "It's 5:30. We have about an hour and a half. Let's go over the route and the plan again."

"You mean tonight?" Tommy asked.

"Unbelievable," Joey sighed. "Unbelievable."

Three hours later, the boys were back in the wine cellar. The excitement was evident. Joey and Peter were giggling like idiots and Tommy just kept repeating, "Amazing … amazing" over and over. They had counted the money and had it laid out on the table. In all, they had taken about three hundred dollars. An incredible score for the boys, and the plan had gone off without a hitch. Everyone was happy except for Johnny, who was sulking in the corner. Raymond was also upset. He sat on the cot and didn't say anything.

"Oh come on you two. It's no big deal," Peter said. "How about focusing on the positives. That's a lot of loot on the table."

"Really, everything was perfect, Johnny. You can't be upset. And Ray, what do you expect? We are robbing the place. I mean that was the point." Peter was trying to reconcile the two boys.

The heist had gone off according to plan. Everything was just like Raymond had said it would be. The door was open and the alarm was off. The problem came when the guys started trashing the place. The deal was the boys would break a few of the machines and then find the money where Chen had planted it. The trashing of the place was to satisfy the cops. Johnny was in the back and was going through the furniture that the Chens' kept their clothes in. Behind the dresser, he found an envelope taped to the back of the dresser. In it was a wad of cash. There had to be two to three thousand dollars in the envelope.

"Jackpot," Johnny called out!

"Put it back. We came for the money in the bag and nothing else," Raymond yelled.

The argument was short and Raymond won. Johnny reluctantly backed away from the dresser and the guys went about their business. Johnny had been quiet the whole way back, and then as the guys entered the wine cellar he exploded.

"What is this? I thought we were robbing the place? If he left that money there, we should have taken it! Chen knew we were coming. Hide your money if you don't want it stolen. And another thing, just because it was your plan doesn't make you the boss."

Johnny was livid but Raymond didn't back down.

"Look, I don't want to be the boss. I made a plan and if you want things to go without getting caught, then you need to trust me and follow the plan. I agreed to take the bag. That was my deal with Chen. I wouldn't break that deal because what if we do take the extra money and Chen gets pissed and drops a dime on us? This way everything goes according to plan. We hold up our end and he hopefully he holds up his end."

And with that, both boys had sulked off into neutral corners. Raymond was anxious because the next few hours were the real key to his plan. Chen had to hold up his end of the deal and talk to the cops, plus put a good acting job in front of his sisters and all. To the police, the robbery would look like a quick in and out to hit the register. Chen wouldn't report the bag.

So the next few hours would be the key. If the boys could get through the next few hours, they would be in the clear. They all left the wine cellar around 10:00 p.m. and returned home. Raymond spent the entire night tossing and turning. He spent the entire Sunday hanging around his house and keeping busy with homework. He dreaded Monday and his confrontation with Chen. It had been quiet in the neighborhood. Johnny had come by and told Raymond that there was no news in the club and that, as far as he knew, all looked good. The money was given to Peter who hid it in his room under his bed. That day in school, the boys all went about their business as usual. Raymond, however, was worried. Jimmy Chen was absent from school Monday, Tuesday, and Wednesday. It was three very long days for Raymond. He waited patiently on Thursday for Chen to approach him. The meeting took place fourth period in the cafeteria. Raymond and Chen met in the back on an empty table.

"How's things?" Raymond asked.

Chen smiled and shook Raymond's hand. "Thank you," Chen said. "You can't believe what has been going on the last few days!" Chen was very excited and continued, "After the break-in, my father flew back immediately and decided that it was too dangerous to stay in the store. He got us an apartment up the block! My mother has a kitchen to cook in and my sisters have their own rooms. It's unbelievable! Thanks again! The plan was perfect. The cops could care less and since no one was hurt they just backed off and were gone in an hour or two. I mean, everything you said happened. I told the cops I forgot to turn off the alarm and they bought it. Your plan was brilliant! Thanks again, Ray. If I can ever do anything for you, let me know."

And with that, Raymond had pulled off his first serious heist. It would not be his last.

The next week, the elation that the boys felt was quickly dissipated. Johnny came down to the wine cellar. His face was ashen.

"You look like you've seen a ghost," Tommy said.

"It's worse than that. My father wants to see Raymond tonight at the club," Johnny said.

The boys were shocked. Raymond felt his knees go weak. A call to the bar from Franco could only mean one thing. He knew about the laundry heist and he wasn't happy. The guys were all silent.

Peter said, "Don't worry, Ray. We'll all go with you."

Johnny shook his head, "Nah. He wants to just see Raymond. He told me you guys were to stay here."

Raymond tensed up and said, "What time tonight?"

"Seven," Johnny said.

For Raymond, the next three hours were the worst of his life. The guys tried to calm him and tell him it would be okay. Raymond, at around 5:30, asked the guys to take a walk. He needed to think about what he would have to say and how he would explain his actions. He was really trying to figure out two things: One, how did Franco find out and two, what were some questions *he* would ask. These were the questions that occupied his thoughts as he waited and watched his wrist watch. At seven, he reported to the bar nervous and shaking. As he steadied himself, he decided that honesty was going to be the best policy. Fat Tony was waiting for him at the door.

"Franco is in the back. Have a seat and wait for him. He'll be out shortly."

Raymond went and sat down at the same table that they had all met at a few months back. As he waited, he calmed himself and reviewed the details of his story. Franco came out and slid into the seat next to Raymond.

"So how about that laundry job last week," he said smiling. "Anything you want to tell me?"

"We set that up," Raymond said nervously. "It was my plan and we all did the job."

Franco nodded approvingly, "I'm glad you decided to tell the truth. If you had tried to lie to me I would have really been upset. So let's get down to it. I have a few questions for you," he said with a serious face. "First, did you carry any weapons in?"

He waited.

Raymond looked Franco in the eye and said, "No. The way I planned it there was no need for weapons."

Franco looked like he wanted to say something but stopped. He nodded and asked his next question.

"What if someone was in the store? What were you guys going to do?"

Again, Raymond looked Franco in the eye and said, "That wouldn't have happened because I didn't plan it that way."

Franco looked impressed.

"So how did you plan it?" Franco asked.

"We had Jimmy Chen on board. He turned off the alarms and he left the door unlocked. He told us where the cash would be. That way no weapons and no one gets hurt. Everyone is happy."

"What if Jimmy flipped and gave you up," Franco asked.

"He wouldn't. We had a deal and I trusted Jimmy."

"Trust? Hey, you trusted him, that's a big risk in trusting someone outside of your crew."

"It was a calculated risk. I knew I could trust Jimmy and we worked out all the details. I made sure it went according to plan."

Franco smiled and said, "That's why I like you, Raymond. You plan and you're smart. I trust you with Johnny and I believe you will not do anything stupid to put him in danger. You know I want Johnny to go to college and be a professional. I'm not deluded though; I know he wants to follow in my footsteps and, as much as I want to avoid him in this type of life, realistically I think he sees himself as my successor. I want you to watch out for him and keep an eye on him. He needs good people around him and you are someone who I trust to sort of show him the importance of patience, devising, and carrying out a good plan. Maybe he might even get smart and see all his friends go off to college and follow along with you."

"You know," he smiled, "I've been trying to get that Chen to pay me some protection money for years and after your little stunt he came to me looking for an apartment. He gave me a little present to keep an eye on the store. So … your little stunt helped me out. I will tell you, though, Raymond, run stuff by me before you do another thing like that. You may have tried something that would have hurt me and that would not have been good."

Raymond nodded solemnly and secretly wondered if Franco actually knew that the boys were behind the robbery or if he was just making an educated guess about the whole situation. In retrospect, he had probably given it away as soon as he walked into the bar. He was nervous. He probably had guilt written all over his face. A guy sharp as Franco would have easily read his body language, and without knowing it, he was busted before Franco had even asked a question. It was another thing to file away and be wary of the next time.

"Okay, kid. Out,"

Franco's voice brought him back from his inner thoughts.

"Thank you, Mr. Abelli."

Raymond stammered and shuffled out of the booth as he headed for the door. It was here that Franco made an uncharacteristic mistake. As Raymond walked home, he knew that both he and Franco knew it.

As he neared the door, Franco said, "Hey, Raymond. Say hello to Mr. Manginni for me."

Raymond looked back and said, "No problem," and strolled off into the night.

Raymond didn't head directly to the wine cellar after the meeting. He walked around the neighborhood listening to the sounds and taking in the smells of everything around him. The familiarity helped clear his head and organize his thoughts. The meeting had been fine. Much better than he had expected. Franco trusted him and even sanctioned the boy's actions. This was a relief. It meant more action and maybe even bigger stuff. The laundry heist had another effect on the boys. Chen was so happy it made the guys feel great about what they had done. It was a real life Robin Hood type of situation. Good had actually come out of it and that was a new and different experience for the boys who were usually not used to that type of feeling. Raymond was no fool. He knew what they did was criminal but, if done right, he could almost rationalize the crime as being okay. As he continued to walk, he thought about what Franco had said on his way out.

"Say hello to Mr. Manginni."

It was a simple statement but Raymond knew that Manginni must have been reporting back to Franco about their actions. It was an easy fix. No notes or plans left in the wine cellar. He was sure that Manginni wasn't spying on them or trying to listen to their conversations. He was just an old Italian wine maker and super of the building, but it was clear to him that there was a leak in information and he had left notes on what they were planning once or twice on the table. The meeting had once again taught Raymond some valuable lessons. He realized that, as good as this job had been, he still had much to learn. As he walked toward the wine cellar, he felt clam and confident. He had gained valuable knowledge tonight and would put it to good use.

CHAPTER
8

Time to Grow Up

AFTER THE MEETING WITH FRANCO, THE BOYS LAID LOW FOR A FEW MONTHS. Raymond figured they should wait until after Christmas before trying anything big again. They ran a few scams in school, petty ante stuff.

With the holidays over, life for the boys returned to normal, and normal for Raymond was torture. His focus on his grades and school consumed only a fraction of his time. February slipped into March and the boys, other than some small time bookmaking on college basketball, were relatively stymied by a lack on opportunity. Joey had come up with a plan to hit a bakery but it was under the protection of Franco, so a week worth of discussion was wasted as the whole idea was scrapped.

For the most part the boys' routines became mundane. School all week, weekends at the club or in the wine cellar. Joey was playing ball in about three or four different basketball leagues, which provided a distraction for the boys as they went to most of his games. As the weather began to change, the attitude of the boys began to improve. As April approached, the prospect of spring and summer cheered everyone except Raymond, who learned that the Easter break for him would be no break at all. He broke the news to everyone one rainy night in the wine cellar.

Raymond entered the wine cellar shaking off the droplets of water from his jacket and mumbling to himself.

"Still raining out I see," Peter said.

Raymond nodded and walked over and threw himself on the cot with a huge sign.

"What's up? Your goldfish die or something," Johnny said smiling and elbowing Tommy.

"Hey, you okay, Ray?" Peter asked.

"Yeah, I'm okay."

"So why the long face?"

Raymond launched into the story. It all happened Friday during dinner. Raymond's father, having finished his meal, pushed back his chair and looked at Raymond's mom, who nodded. He then looked at Raymond and began his speech.

"Look, Son, I think it's time you started looking at the big picture," he began. "First, let me say, I'm proud of you and your grades. You're a smart kid and for the most part you stay out of trouble. I know you're close to Johnny and Joey and we both know about their fathers."

Raymond's dad held up his hand to stop Raymond's protest.

"Let me finish. Son, you really are a smart kid and your mother, and I are afraid that if you don't start getting some direction in life, you may end up making the wrong choices."

"Dad, you know I stay out of trouble," Raymond interjected.

"Let me finish. I want you to start working. Every Saturday, the entire Easter break and even this summer you're going to work with me at Con Edison. We have couriers who carry plans and do odd jobs around sites. It's like apprentice work and I managed to get you in. Look, Son, you're smart enough to be running that place someday and I think it would benefit you to get a start early. Don't argue. It's a done deal. This Saturday, you and me. 6:00 a.m."

Raymond was stunned to silence and, instead of arguing and putting up any resistance, he reluctantly just mumbled, "Sure, Dad."

"What, what did you say?"

"I said 'good idea, Dad'. I'm going out now to enjoy my last hours of freedom," Raymond said and grabbed his coat and headed out into the rain.

On his way to the wine cellar, he thought about what his father said. The neighborhood was his home but, in reality, what was his future? The reality was that if he continued on the current path he would wind up working with his friends for Franco. As the rain poured down on him, he thought about the people in the neighborhood. The Irish kids became cops or firemen; the Italians would go for organized crime or other blue-collar jobs like his dads. Some opened stores in the neighborhood. Some became mechanics and some went to jail.

Raymond couldn't see himself in any of those situations. In a way, as much as he loved the neighborhood, he felt he wasn't destined to stay here forever. The jobs they had been doing were a distraction. They filled the void in him but they would not be enough, and the realization that he would either join Franco's crew or leave the neighborhood was what really had him down as he entered the wine cellar and saw his friends. These guys were his family and he would have to leave them someday. There were real choices to make and to make soon.

Maybe he should just get a job with Con-Ed and do what his father said and stay in the neighborhood forever, but deep down he knew that that wouldn't make him happy. His friends tried to cheer him up with jokes about minimum wage and cracks that they had more money in the wine cellar than he would make in a year. Raymond laughed and joked along with his friends but as he walked home, through the downpour, the questions of his future still weighed heavily on his mind.

The irritating ringing of his father's alarm clock woke Raymond at 6:00 a.m. The sound was familiar and Raymond usually woke to it each morning. It actually was comforting to him as it signaled he had another hour until he had to wake up for school. Raymond relished that extra hour of sleep; he often had his most vivid dreams during these times. Today though, he sat bolt upright.

"You up, Son?" his father asked as he poked his head into Raymond's room.

"Yeah. Be ready in fifteen minutes," he said and stretched his long and lean body slowly, rubbed the sleep out of his eyes, and began to change.

It was then that he stopped.

"Jeans and sweater okay, Pop?" he asked.

Raymond knew his father wore a uniform to work and wondered if he would get some kind of uniform or have to wear something special.

"Yeah, that's fine," his father said as he passed Raymond's room. "Bathroom's open."

Raymond mechanically moved through his morning routine, and by 6:45 he was walking up Lexington toward the subway station on Lexington and 110th Street. The rain from the night before left the streets clean and fresh smelling, and as he silently walked next to his father, he noticed his dad would almost start a conversation then stop himself. He thinks I'm pissed and don't want to do this, Raymond thought as they paid the fifteen cents to board the downtown local. As they stood on the sparsely crowded platform with the other people on their way to work, Raymond was struck by the normalcy of it all. This was what life was like. Getting up, going to work to scratch out a living, coming home to a wife and a kid, and starting all over again the next day. Raymond's Robin Hood antics were the furthest thing from this and the whole train of thoughts that he experienced the night before replayed in his mind as the train pulled up. Raymond and his father grabbed straps and stood on the rocking train that smelled of coffee and cigarettes. Raymond realized that his father was getting fidgety and Raymond knew he was having second thoughts about the whole plan to get his son a job.

Raymond eased his pain, "So, Dad, do I get to drink coffee and start smoking now since I'm a working stiff and all?" he said with a laugh.

Raymond's father visibly relaxed and joked back, "Sure, Son. As soon as you earn enough money to buy them that is." He grinned and said, "I truly am proud of you son," and lapsed back into his own thoughts obviously feeling much better.

The train ride took thirty minutes. With each stop, there came the crashing of people entering and exiting the train car. Raymond was reminded of the beach with waves crashing upon the shore and then retreating out toward the sea. The train had a similar rhythm to it. It became relaxing and he found himself drifting into sleep. Just as his eyes were closing, his father nudged him, "Our stop, Son. Ready to go to work?"

As they climbed the stairs out of the tunnel, Raymond was blinded by the bright sunlight that shone at the top of the stairs. He chuckled to himself, like going into the light when you die, he thought. The streets were jammed with people all purposefully moving toward their destinations. The Con-Ed plant that Raymond's father worked at was on Forty-Seventh Street and Park Avenue. From that central hub, trucks and men were dispatched. Most had steady assignments or jobs that required men on site for years. His father had been working at the UN building for two years, and the way he saw it, he would probably be there for at least five more the way the work progressed. Raymond was brought into the locker room and, like any proud father would do, was introduced to every one of Raymond's fathers' friends. The names became a blur after the third or fourth handshake and the fifth said, "Your dad talks about you all the time." Raymond cheerfully took it all in stride and sized up the place to keep himself focused.

There were three shifts at the plant: 8:00 to 4:00, 4:00 to 12:00, and 12:00 to 8:00. Each shift had different responsibilities and the locker room was the central hub of all the workers. Raymond was passed off to Mr. Donollo, who would assign him work each day, and he would meet his father back in the locker room at 4:00 p.m. to head home. Raymond's dad gave one last pep talk to his son before dropping him at Mr. Donollo's office.

"Look, you're a smart boy. Be respectful, do your job, and get the lay of the land. I'm sorry we can't have lunch together but I'll see you back in the locker room at four."

He gave his son an unexpected hug and hurried off to work. Raymond knocked on the office door and was greeted by the rough voice of Mr. Donollo.

"If your waiting for the butler, you'll be standing out there all day and we don't pay for standing around, although the rest of the city might have a different opinion of that. Come in. Raymond, right? Your dad's a good man. We love him around here," he said. This took Raymond aback. It was interesting to hear someone compliment his father in this way. He decided he would give his best today and everyday to show these people that his dad was right for getting him the job.

"So here's how it works, kid," Mr. Donollo said as he crossed the room and shook Raymond's hand and gave him an odd look. "We have jobs going all over the city here. At the central hub, we get the blueprints from the architects and we have our engineers diagram the wiring. You still with me?"

"Yeah, sure. But I thought electricians do all the wiring," Raymond replied.

Mr. Donollo smiled, "Your dad said you were sharp. Of course electricians do the wiring. We have to show them where on the master plans. They can tap our lines and, if necessary, send our workers out to install boxes from our mains to allow the electricians to power the buildings. The deal is you will be a courier. You run the plans from here to the job sites."

"So I get a car," Raymond said, smiling.

Mr. Donollo burst into laughter, "You can do what ever you want with the money you earn, but for this job you'll be riding the train. Most of what you'll be delivering is to job sites that are just starting so they're in no real hurry," Mr. Donollo said, stifling his last giggle. "Some jobs are renovations and require a bit more speed. Either way, you ride the train and probably can get three, maybe four, deliveries a day done. If we're slow, you can help out around here. We always need a hand at the loading dock. But spring is a busy time for construction so I expect you'll get a lot of fresh air. Lunch is on your own time. You'll get train fare before each run. Just check with Janice at the end of the hall and keep your lunch receipts. We treat our interns well and usually reimburse them for half their lunch expenses. Just turn them over to Janice at the end of the day. How are you with maps?" Mr. Donollo said as he reached into his desk and pulled out a subway and bus schedule.

"I think I can find my way around," Raymond replied.

"Good! Look, kid, move quick, don't jerk around and you'll have your foot in the door of a great company."

"Thank you for the advice, Mr. Donollo," Raymond said.

"Jimmy. Call me Jimmy, Ray. Okay?"

Mr. Donollo smiled and handed Raymond a tube with a strap around it. To Raymond, it reminded him of those World War I guns so he strapped it on and saluted Mr. Donollo, who again started laughing until his phone rang and he waved Raymond out of the office. Raymond turned, closed the door behind him, and, after getting thirty cents from Janice, stepped out into the sunlight of his first assignment of his new job. It wouldn't be until weeks later that he realized his new job would provide his greatest opportunity.

CHAPTER

9

Work

RAYMOND'S NEW JOB, WHILE ONLY ONE DAY A WEEK, AFFECTED THE BOYS DRASTICALLY. Saturdays for Raymond were spent at work. He would often slip out with the boys on Saturday night for a few hours, but he was often exhausted and was not his usual self. The boys noticed this and, as he continued to work and the Easter break from school approached, Raymond had become more and more into his job. The boys exploited this with some good-natured teasing. On Raymond's birthday, the boys met in the wine cellar.

"Hey, Raymond. You know we would have gotten you a cake but the rats down here would have had a field day," Joey said, smiling.

"Yeah, Ray, we did chip in to get you something, however," Johnny said, and he pulled out a box from under the table.

Peter giggled and Tommy elbowed him to quiet down. Raymond knew it was a prank but played along for everyone's sake.

"Thanks, guys. You really shouldn't have," he said, smiling.

"It was nothing, really," Johnny said and handed Raymond the box.

Raymond eyed all the expectant faces and tore open the poorly wrapped parcel. He pulled out a quite ugly blue and red tie to the roars of laughter from his friends.

Johnny, wiping he eyes and gasping for air, said, "We figured since you're a working stiff now, you probably need to start dressing like one."

Tommy roared with laughter and Raymond said, "Thanks. Where did you get this, Johnny, from your father's closet?"

"You kidding? You think my dad would own an ugly tie like that," Johnny gasped. "No, really, Raymond, since you've been working so hard on going straight we've had plenty of time to go shopping."

The last part of that sounded more sarcastic than humorous and the laughter in the room stopped. After some nervous laughter, the boys began playing cards and the evening went on as usual.

The fact was Johnny had said something that the boys were all feeling. Raymond had not been his usual self. There had been no crazy schemes, no talk of jobs, nothing. And the boys had begun to notice. On the Saturdays that Raymond was working, they had begun to questions whether they could count on Raymond to do any more jobs with them.

"He sure as hell hasn't said anything about anything in a while," Joey said.

"Maybe it's time we started looking for some things ourselves. I mean Johnny, what—it's been three months and we have nothing even on the horizon. I don't know about you, but I plan on having a great summer and the Chen money is getting a bit thin "No Offense"."

"None taken, Joey," Peter replied.

"You guys know that Raymond's with us. He's just seeing how the other side lives. He'll come around. He's appeasing his dad, that's all. He'll come around," Tommy said.

"You believe that, Tommy," Joey snapped. "College costs money."

"What does that have to do with anything? College? What are you talking about Joey?" Peter said.

"Nothing," he grumbled and stared at Tommy. Then, turning to Johnny, he said, "Well what about it? What do you think?"

They all turned to Johnny, who had been unusually silent throughout the entire tiff.

"I have to admit, I haven't seen Raymond this quiet about not doing something since he was nine."

"I kind of agree with Tommy. He's keeping the heat off of himself by working and making his parents happy."

"See, I told you," Tommy said smugly. "However, I agree with Joey. We can't sit around and wait for him to snap out of it and come back with a plan. Let's all keep our eyes open and if we see something that's doable, we run it by Raymond and let him decide if he's in or out."

Peter smiled and clapped Johnny hard on the back with his giant hand.

"Ow! What the hell was that for?"

"For a second I imagined we were in the bar and you were your father," Peter said softly.

"You're absolutely right, and although you're no Raymond," he said with a wide grin, "that's a damn good plan."

Joey and Tommy nodded their approval. Johnny looked at Peter, who grinned and nodded to him.

"Where are the cards?" he said. "Let's not put any pressure on Raymond."

Raymond went home early the Friday night after his little birthday celebration to the jeers of Tommy and Peter, who continued to break his chops about work. As he walked up the block, though, he dwelled on two things. One was how quiet Joey had been, and two was the comment from Johnny about being a working stiff. He realized he was spending less time with his friends and he also knew what Joey's silence was all about. Joey wanted action. They probably all did. They had looked to him to make the plans and without him throwing ideas out, they were getting antsy.

Raymond understood, but he had his reasons. The fact was that he had thrown himself into his work. The first few weeks, he had monotonously gone on with the regular routine of work. He would begin by checking in with Mr. Donollo and then being sent to a workroom with other guys about his age to wait for his first assignment. The other boys were sons of workers also and most of them were nice enough, but he wasn't there to make friends. Most of the chatter in the mornings was basic sports talk about how the Knicks were doing and what-are-you-doing-in-school type of questions. Raymond was friendly enough, but the truth of the matter was that the boys were usually together for only about fifteen minutes a day. Once the assignments were handed out, the boys would make their deliveries and come back to the plant and receive other jobs. Very rarely did they not have work, and if that were the case, they would be sent home so there were really no chances for interactions between the boys. Raymond worked quickly and would get through four or five deliveries a day.

The work was simple. He was like a carrier pigeon. He carried plans or updated work orders for various jobs around the city and dropped them off to whoever was in charge at the job site. He got a badge with his name on it and the Con-Ed logo, which he pinned to his jacket. The work was easy and Raymond quickly became bored. He liked that he got to travel around and after three weeks was quite familiar with the transit system throughout the city. It was during his third week on the job that Raymond realized the opportunity he was looking for had been in his hands the whole time.

He was delivering a set of plans to the West Side, somewhere on Thirty-First Street and Eighth or Ninth Avenue. On the subway ride there, Raymond was falling asleep. He had made three runs already that day and was feeling tired. He wanted to take a nap but feared missing his stop, so in an effort to stay awake, he turned his focus to the package he was carrying. The package was a tube, the hard cardboard type that contained rolled up plans. Raymond unscrewed the top and slid the plans out onto his lap. As he casually looked over the plans, not really concentrating, a realization started to come to him. It crept up on him slowly then began to build as he focused on the plans in front of him.

They were to a diner that was being built, and while he could not fully make out the details of the plans, he understood he was looking at the exits and electrical systems. Raymond was wide-awake now. He was actually on the edge of his seat. He realized with these plans he could devise a way to rob the place. It was perfect. He had the schematics of the building. The more he looked at the plan, the more he realized it would not work. First, the job would not be finished for another six months. The excitement died down as he also realized that the exits were no good. It was one-way in and out with an occupied building next door. This job would not be possible. But the realization that dawned on Raymond as he sat and rolled the plans back up and placed them into the tube was that with the right set of plans he could pull off another job.

It was perfect! He was outside the neighborhood and with inside information it was only a matter of finding the right plans. Raymond smiled as the train pulled into his stop. He hopped off with a renewed sense of purpose. He was excited to get back to the plant and get the next set of plans. He needed to get to the library and study some books on engineering to make sure he could understand all the squiggles and notations on the plans and he needed a backpack and some drawing materials. His mind was racing. He felt all the uncertainty of the last few weeks melt away. He thought about his friends and realized he had to keep this quiet until he was ready and found the right job.

CHAPTER

10

Choices

RAYMOND RAN THROUGH THE GAMETE OF EMOTIONS THE NEXT FEW WEEKS. He was excited about the work for obvious reasons but was frustrated, as day after day he could not find the right plans. In the interim, he prepared. He spent countless hours in the library studying schematics and engineering documents. Often, Tommy was a great source of information and the two spent much of their free time at school in the library huddled over the three or four books that they had at their disposal. Raymond was surprised at the amount of knowledge Tommy possessed. Raymond learned quickly and was deftly able to read the plans he was carrying each Saturday.

Copying the plans was another story all together. Raymond was not the best artist and had a hard time copying the plans. He used a standard notebook at first but quickly found that drawing plans truly was an art. His first attempts were sadly inadequate. He realized that at home he could not understand what he had copied. This was a significant problem. The right set of plans could come to him on any trip and Raymond realized that they would be wasted if he could not make an accurate copy. He brought the problem to Tommy one day at school.

"Writing plans takes years of practice," he told Raymond. "But the real questions is why so interested in this stuff?"

Raymond knew that question was coming and he was prepared.

"They have a junior intern position at Con-Ed and you have to pass a test that requires you to read and write plans. I thought maybe I could take the test and get the job," Raymond lied.

"Really into this work stuff, huh?" Tommy asked questioningly. Then Tommy shrugged and said, "Get a graph paper notebook and use each square as a set number of feet. Then you can organize the distances better and label important exits entrances and such. It won't be perfect, but it will get you into the habit of being more accurate. I don't know if you can use that on the test but it will help."

Raymond saw the benefit immediately and wondered why he hadn't thought of it himself.

As he pondered the possibilities silently, Tommy asked, "Hey, Ray, can anyone take that test? I mean, do you have to work for Con-Ed or can anybody take the test?"

Raymond, concentration broken, mumbled without thinking, "Sorry, you have to work there, Tommy."

And as Raymond began thinking about how this new idea would help him, he barley noticed how Tommy scowled at him and walked away.

Armed with a graph notebook and a renewed sense of purpose, Raymond faced his first assignment that Saturday with a sense of excitement. He opened the plans the minute he got on the train and realized quickly that they were of no use to him, but he fought through the disappointment and began quickly and efficiently copying the plans as best he could. The graph paper was a godsend as he was able to much more accurately reproduce the plan for the running power lines from the street to the new elevator cars to be put into a high-rise on the West Side.

That night at home, he reviewed the four sets of plans he had copied. None offered perspective jobs but each was readable. He had clearly gotten a hundred percent better and was satisfied that, with a bit more practice, he would be ready when or if the right plans came along. He only hoped it would be sooner than later. A strange feeling came over Raymond. It was anticipation of Easter break when he could work for the entire week. Raymond laughed to himself. He never thought he could get excited about work, but with his skills honed he was ready.

"Any sign of Claude Raines," Joey asked as Peter came into the wine cellar.

"No sign," Peter laughed as he took off his coat and sat down. They had taken to calling Raymond Claude Raines, the star of *The Invisible Man* movie.

"Not for nothing, but you haven't been around that much either, Joey," Peter said.

Joey smiled and winked, "You know that Irish girl, Terry? I've been kind of hanging out with her."

The boys all stared wide-eyed at Joey.

"I figured that. I saw you talking with her everyday between fourth and fifth period and I know she isn't helping you with homework," he said elbowing Tommy, who laughed.

"Yeah well her brother plays on the CYO team and she comes to every game and, well, we got to talking and, you know, with my irresistible charm, she couldn't help but fall for me," Joey said.

"Irresistible charm? Please, someone pop his head before it squeezes all the air out of this room," Johnny said.

"No joke. She's really pretty, Joey," Tommy said. "Are you serious about her?"

"Yeah. We're getting married next week," Joey said sarcastically. "We're just kind of seeing each other," he said more seriously. "We went to the movies the other day, and after the picture, we kind of slipped around the side of the theater to make out and I noticed some guy coming out of a side entrance to throw away the garbage."

"Wait! You go to make out and you notice a guy," Johnny said.

Peter and Tommy burst into laughter as Joey snapped, "Yeah, because I thought it would be a perfect place to rob. While you guys are sitting around I have been scouting the place out," he said smugly.

"So the girl is just an excuse to go check out a movie theater to pull a job on," Johnny said.

"Well, let's just say she's a nice bonus," Joey said, laughing.

Peter said, "What theater were you at?"

"The one on Third Avenue. It's perfect, out of the neighborhood and always packed," Joey said.

"Slow down. Let's get the details and hear your plan," Johnny said.

"Look, after every show, one guy cleans the aisles and takes the garbage out the side door. I figure two of us wait outside and take him out when he comes to throw away the garbage. We go in through the side door and two of us are already in the theater. They only have a guy taking tickets and a guy working the projector. If we pull guns out, we can cover them and take the register. Piece of cake," Joey smiled and crossed his arms.

The rest of the boys were stunned. Peter actually had his mouth wide open in shock.

Tommy busted out in laughter, "You're joking, right? Take him out … guns, cover them … what the hell are you talking about," he said, hysterically laughing.

Joey looked at Johnny, who just shook his head.

"Joey, you need to work on that plan a bit," he said and put his arm on Joey's shoulder.

Joey shook him off and said angrily, "Okay. So the plan stinks, but the job is doable."

Peter, coming out of his stunned silence, said, "You know, Joey, it could work. Let's slow down and think about the details."

"I agree," Johnny said.

Joey relaxed a little and said, "Okay. Like I said, they have tops three guys in the place and, to be honest, it really is one adult and two kids who are working. I've been there three times, and on Saturday the last show is 10:00 p.m. and they have a full crowd every show."

"So we're talking about a couple of hundred bucks tops," Johnny said.

"Not a lot," Tommy said.

"Yeah, but if it can be done easily then it could be worth it," Johnny replied. "First, no guns; that makes it a felony crime and we could get in real trouble. Second, we want everyone out of the theater so we have no crowds to deal with."

"Wait," Peter said, "what if we use the crowd? Like, do it near the end of the last show and slip out with the crowd."

Joey smiled, "I like it, Pete. We are there and we do it while the show is going on. That takes out the projectionist."

"Who is probably the only adult in the place," Tommy interjected.

"Okay … okay," Johnny said. "Now we're getting somewhere."

The boys continued to bandy about ideas, and as the night wore on, they became more and more convinced it could be done. They all decided to go to the late show that Saturday and scout it out.

"Joey—bring Terry," Johnny said.

Joey looked quizzically at Johnny and said, "Why?"

"Well, you have been there with her a few times. If you show up there without her, it might look suspicious, and I got an idea that we can use her without her even knowing," he said.

"You sound like Raymond," Tommy said, and at that moment they all thought about Raymond.

"What about Raymond," Peter asked.

"We'll let him know when we're ready; let's not jump the gun. We have to check it out and see if it's really doable first," Johnny said.

They all nodded in agreement, then Joey said, "Hey, I'm going to a dance with Terry Friday night at the Social Club over on 115th Street. It's a basketball thing but you guys should come. Maybe you could pick up a few girls yourself and I could use the backup. You know I'm not so well liked over there."

"What do you mean? Your irresistible charm doesn't work on 115th Street," Tommy said and they all broke into laughter.

11

Spring Break

THE BOYS ENJOYED THEMSELVES OVER THE SPRING BREAK, ATTENDING DANCES, GOING TO THE MOVIES, AND PLANNING THE MOVIE THEATER THING,

Raymond's week went a bit differently. The Easter break meant work all week, and this was a good opportunity to see a bunch of plans. That first Saturday, while the rest of the boys were sleeping in late, Raymond was on his way to work with his dad. He enjoyed spending time with his father and over the weeks gained an appreciation for how hard he worked. As he waited for his first assignment, the mood in the room was quite depressing. Most of the boys were complaining about having to work a whole week. Raymond, on the other hand, couldn't wait.

He grabbed his first assignment and headed out to the street. It took all his willpower to not stop and open the tube right there in the street. He waited until he was on the train and then popped open the tube. With great excitement, he unrolled the plans and, to his great disappointment, he saw they were another set of useless plans. The one thing that did cheer him slightly was his ability to read the plans. His dedication the past few weeks in studying was paying off. He immediately identified most of the symbols on the paper and could easily envision the layout of the floor plan he was looking at.

Raymond reluctantly pulled out his graph notebook and copied the plans in as much detail as possible. He realized his own system was emerging as he scaled down the floor plan based on a 1:4 ratio. This enabled him to fit the entire plan onto one sheet of paper. As he pulled into his stop, he rolled the plans back up and shoved them back into the tube. The next delivery was of a similar nature: another useless plan and another practice drawing. Raymond was utterly dejected when he grabbed his third tube of the day and headed out just before lunchtime. As he got on the train headed toward Midtown, he almost broke his routine. He was going to eat the chicken cutlet sandwich his mom had made for him that morning for lunch but sighed and decided to wait on lunch until the return trip. With the train jostling back and forth, Raymond opened the tube and pulled out the plans.

His first reaction was of disbelief, and as he shook his head, the lights of the train went out. Raymond, for a second, thought what he had just seen could not have been real. The five-second wait for the lights to come back on felt like an eternity to Raymond. When they did, he intentionally did not look down right away. He paused and took a deep breath. He finally looked at the plans. His eyes went wide with excitement. The train was quiet because it was lunchtime. There was a man at one end of the train reading the *Daily News* and an old Spanish lady clutching her handbag to her chest and dozing silently as her head was swaying to the rhythm of the train.

Raymond quickly came out of his reverie. He checked his watch. It was 12:15 p.m. Most of the workers at the job site would be on lunch till 1:00. He had about another twenty minutes on the train and then he could finish copying the plans if he had to out on a bench at the train platform. He quickly pulled out his notebook and began to copy. He was scribbling furiously and had to tell himself to slow down. He paused as the train pulled up to a platform to make a stop and realized his hands were shaking. He laughed and said out loud, "Calm down and focus." No one heard him, and as the train pulled away, he took a deep breath and began copying the plans that would change his life.

CHAPTER

12

The Plans

RAYMOND WORKED QUICKLY AND, FIFTY MINUTES AFTER HE HAD REACHED HIS STOP, HE WAS DONE. He sat back on the bench at the station and sighed. He closed his notebook and rolled the plans back up and, as he went to put them in the tube, a piece of paper in the tube slipped out. Raymond quickly scrambled off the bench and grabbed it. He reopened his notebook and copied down the cryptic information:

> Please note: 7-18-7-20 12-12-15 a/p recalibrate
> after when main grid is complete.

Raymond quickly gathered all the papers and returned them to the tube. He hustled the three blocks to the job site and quickly headed for the trailer, where the site manager would be stationed. As he entered the trailer, there were two workers eating lunch.

"Delivery from the main office," he said.

"I'll sign," the worker closest to Raymond said. "The boss is still out on lunch."

"Thanks," Raymond said and turned the tube over to the worker and quietly left the trailer.

He looked at his watch: 12:50. He timed himself back to the train. It was less then a five-minute walk. On the train he looked at his notebook and smiled. The plans were very accurately copied from the original. Raymond's mind began to work. The security systems could be disabled. He would need an entry and exit strategy. It could be done. The details were swirling in his head as he continued to work for the rest of the day.

On his way home, the realization hit him. This job actually might be too big. Doubt crept into his mind that there were too many factors he couldn't calculate. He slumped onto his bed and thought it through for the twentieth time that day. As he lay there staring at the ceiling, he was losing hope. It was at that moment that Raymond came to a realization. He needed help. It was a hard thing to admit for Raymond. He had always been the one who made the plans. He was the brains of the crew but this was too big. If he wanted to pull this off he would have to get help. The question was would his friends help him on this one and was it even worth it?

He had purposely been avoiding everyone and was consumed with finding the right job. He had dreamed of going to the wine cellar and having a plan to present to the guys. Would the guys even listen? He had been wrong in doing what he was doing. He knew Tommy was angry with him and Johnny had probably already changed the lock on the wine cellar. Raymond realized that what made his crew special was that they all brought something to the table and one person could not do more than five. He was used to being a loner, but that had changed in recent years and he had made a mistake by not letting his friends in. He would have to make it right. He would go to the wine cellar and explain it all to the guys. It would be their decision, all of them, if they wanted to do this job or not. Raymond lay back and looked at the darkening sky outside his window. The rusty fire escape blocked the full moon that was rising. Raymond thought, full moon, it makes sense because they would have to be crazy to rob a bank.

CHAPTER

13

Two Plans?

Tommy and Peter were on their way back from the movie theater that the boys had planned to hit. It was their first trip there to scout it out. Johnny and Joey had gone the day before. It was Joey's idea to go on separate days to make it less obvious, but in reality two boys or four boys would not have made much of a difference. There were bunches of kids at the theater and that made Tommy optimistic that it would make a good score.

"So when are we going to get Ray down the cellar and let him in on the plan," Peter said.

"Raymond knows where we are. I say let him come to the wine cellar himself and if he doesn't show, we go without him."

"That's harsh. Give Raymond a break, Tommy. You know he's still with us. He just needed a taste of the real world for a bit. I wouldn't be surprised if he shows up tonight," Peter said as they turned the corner in front of the bakery on 110th street.

"Who shows up?" Raymond said as he almost walked into Tommy and Peter.

"Holy cow! We were just talking about you," Peter said.

"And how you seem to be absent a lot lately," Tommy added as Peter shot him a nasty look.

"Where are you headed, guys? I was just on my way to find Johnny and Joey," Raymond said.

"Well, lets go together. We were supposed to meet them at the wine cellar," Peter said.

Tommy kept walking and Raymond and Peter began to talk about the movie he had seen. The tension was palpable, and as they entered the wine cellar they were greeted by the laughter of Johnny and Joey, who were cracking up over some story.

"… And then they kick Crazy Larry in the ass and he goes running out of the bar," Johnny was saying through tears in his eyes.

"Stop! You're killing me," Joey was saying as he held his side.

They both turned as the other boys entered the room.

"Oh, the prodigal son has returned," Johnny said, regaining control of himself.

"Who is this guy?" Joey said. "What? You recruit someone from the altar boy squad, Peter," Joey said, pretending not to recognize Raymond.

"Very funny. You look like you've lost weight, Joey. It must be the haircut. And look at you! The one thing I missed most was the Crazy Larry stories. In all honesty, it's the only reason I'm back," Raymond said.

There was some nervous laughter from everyone and Raymond sensed it. He quickly jumped in before anyone could say anything.

"Look, I'm sorry. I was wrong to keep you guys out of what I was doing and I'm an idiot. I should have kept you guys involved but I didn't want to say anything until I had a plan for all of us. I wanted to be the hero but I realized I went about it the wrong way. Look … You guys are my best friends and I was wrong and I'm sorry. From now on, everything we plan, we plan together. I just hope you guys can forgive me and accept the apology."

There was silence in the room. The guys were shocked. They were not expecting this and no one knew what to say. Peter walked over to Raymond and gave him a big hug.

"I told you he was planning something. Of course we accept your apology, you jerk! Welcome back!"

"Thanks, Pete. Now could you let go? You're crushing me," Raymond said.

Johnny smiled and said, "Good to have you back, kid."

Joey just nodded, and Tommy looked at Raymond for a long time and was about to say something then changed his mind and nodded to Raymond and walked over and shook his hand. Raymond knew he would have to talk to Tommy later, but for now all seemed to be okay.

"I told you guys! So what's the plan, Ray? We taking over Con-Ed or what?" Peter asked.

"Slow down, Pete," Johnny said. "We still need to run our plan by Raymond first unless you were planning on doing something tonight," Johnny asked.

"What plan?" Raymond asked.

"What, you think we were just going into retirement since you went straight," Joey said. "We have a job set to go Saturday night. We were going to run it by you before we did it but, you know, you said it yourself you haven't been around much."

"Let's run it through for him," Peter jumped in.

The boys proceeded to explain their plan to hit the movie theater. Ray listened and asked questions that the guys all had answers for. The plan seemed good. It could be done, but Raymond didn't like the idea of having to confront anyone.

He reasoned, "You never know what will happen when you have to deal with another person. Taking the kid out of the ticket booth—what if the kid thinks he's a hero? What if the old man is in the booth?"

There were too many things that could go wrong and Raymond explained it to the boys that way. Joey was confident he could handle the old man or a kid, but he still could see the point. Raymond thought that any number of kids in the neighborhood could identify them and that would not be a good thing. After an hour of going back and forth, the boys were at a stalemate. The job was only viable if they could figure out a way to get the ticket booth clear. That way no one would be able to hurt anyone.

"Hey, you know what? I thought you came here with a plan, Ray," Peter said.

In all the discussion of the guys' plan, they had forgotten about Raymond's plan. Raymond, for his part, had kept quiet about his plan. He knew they would come around to it eventually and, as excited as he was to explain all that he had been doing, he knew that for now he needed to let the guys talk. Raymond was patient and he thought to himself, this must be the new and improved me. First he had accepted the fact that he needed help and now he was showing patience. When the question was finally asked about what he was planning, he took a deep breath and looked slowly around the room at the guys. It could be done, he told himself, and then he launched into the speech he had rehearsed a million times while sitting on trains the last few months.

"Look. Let me start at the beginning," Raymond said.

He then proceeded to tell them about the job and what the responsibilities were. How he opened the first tube on the train that first week and had seen the blueprints.

"Tommy, that's why I needed the help with the schematics. I didn't understand any of the stuff I was looking at."

Tommy smiled for the first time. Raymond took this as a good sign. Maybe the conversation he would have to have with Tommy later would go a bit more smoothly.

"So, you're riding around with blueprints and electrical information to places all around the city?" Joey asked.

"There had to be a bunch of places for you to choose from," Johnny said.

"Yes and no," Raymond answered. "There were lots of plans but they were mostly rewiring jobs to buildings and some stores, but nothing that really struck me as doable. That was until yesterday," Raymond said with a smile on his face.

As he looked around the room he could see that the boys had understood the implications of all that he had been doing. And now they were excited about the possibilities.

"So what happened yesterday?" Peter asked.

"Yesterday, I found a set of plans that will be perfect. I copied them down exactly like I've been telling you guys. Here look."

Raymond pulled out the notebook and dropped it on the table. The boys crowded around and looked at the scribbles and lines drawn on the paper. Tommy picked up the notebook and sat back from the table. Within seconds, he looked up at Raymond with a look of shock on his face. His jaw literally opened. Johnny, seeing this, asked the question the rest of the boys all wanted to ask.

"So, what's the mark?"

Raymond smiled as he looked at the boys and flatly said, "We're going to rob a bank."

"Get the fuck outta here!" was the lone response that broke the silence.

Joey had hesitated like the rest of them letting the shock pass then continued, "A bank? You did say a bank? Are you serious?"

When he realized no one else was laughing he continued, "Tommy, is he serious? I mean, these squiggles are the plans to a bank," Joey said, grabbing the notebook from Tommy's hands.

"There are the floor plans and all the electrical systems for a bank," Tommy said. "With that information, you could conceivably disarm any bank alarm system. It could be done with this information but I have about a million questions for you, Ray."

"It could be done you say? *Could* be done? A bank? A real bank? Holy shit! I knew you were a genius, Ray, but this is unbelievable. We're going to hit a bank. Please tell me this is true. Holy … A bank," Joey said.

He was obviously excited and if Joey could, he would have went right then and there.

"Joey's enthusiasm aside," Raymond said, "what do you think, Johnny?"

Johnny had been quiet and slowly looked at each of the boys. He put his arm on Joey to quiet him down and said, "This isn't no Chen job here. If you're serious and we get caught, we go away. No juvee hall. We go to jail. Have you thought that through, Ray? All things considered, what we've done is kid stuff. This is a whole new level you're talking about."

"I know, Johnny, I have thought about it but this is a one-in-a-lifetime shot. We could do a million Chen jobs and never come close to this. This one job could change everything."

"You're right, it could for good or bad," Johnny said.

The silence in the wine cellar was palpable. The boys each lost in their own thoughts.

Joey said, "Look, Johnny. I'm with Ray on this one. If anyone wants to change his fortunes it's me. If this is my shot, I'll take my chances. Besides, Ray's a genius. He would never let us get caught, right?"

"You got my vote, Ray. I'm in," Johnny nodded and looked at Ray. Their eyes locked and he said, "I trust you, Ray. If anyone can pull this off, it's you. I'm in."

Raymond smiled and said, "This one will take more than me to pull off. I'm not even sure it can be done, but I think it's worth trying. Tommy?"

"It's easier to be mad at you when you're not around, and you're right. You couldn't have even copied these plans without me so I guess I'll have to come along to make sure you don't screw it up," Tommy said smiling. "I'm in."

They all turned to Peter, who sat there shoulders slumped forward. His hulking frame squeezed into a tight ball.

"I'm out," he said quietly, "out of my mind for doing something this crazy," he exploded and came over and attempted to hug all four of them at the same time!

The laughter erupted from them all and then as they settled down, Ray got serious and said, "Let's get to work. It's going to be a long night."

14

The Problem With the Job

THE NEXT SEVERAL HOURS IN THE WINE CELLAR, RAYMOND HAD BEGUN TO GO OVER WHAT HE HAD IN MIND.

"Look, we have a small window to do this in," he said. "According to the plans, the recalibrating of the system takes place on July 21st. The way I figure it, we would want to get in that weekend when the bank is closed; that leaves us three days to work. Really two since the Friday before there will still be workers in the bank."

"Why not wait until the work is over, we have the plans?" Tommy asked.

"Trust me, it has to be that weekend," Raymond replied.

"If we are taking this place at night, then Friday or Saturday would be best because the bank won't open again till Monday," Joey added.

"Either way, the 21st of July is two months away so that's how long we have to get this planned, and here are my problems," Ray said. "How do we get in? What is our entry and exit strategy? The workers access the bank's electrical systems through the manhole outside the bank. We can't climb in and out a manhole on a busy street. So I was thinking of using an old subway tunnel. There's a station a block away from the bank. If we could find the right tunnel, maybe we can get to the same tunnel the workers are in and then leave using the train."

"That will require us to work underground," Tommy said, "and we need to find a way into that service tunnel."

"Right," Raymond said, "I figure we will have to do some tunnel exploring, Tommy."

"If we can't find a way from the train, can we use the street?" Johnny asked.

"I would prefer not, but I guess it could be done," Raymond said.

"So if we find a way in and we get to the main electrical box and turn off any alarms, how do we get into the bank?" Joey asked.

"Good question. Most of the electrical wires run into a back storeroom. There is usually a trapdoor there to provide access for any electrical work. I'm assuming it will be locked so we need a way to break that lock. I was thinking with no alarms active we could do it the old-fashioned way. Just break in."

"According to your notes, Ray, the door locks from the tunnel so a pair of bolt cutters would do it," Tommy said.

"What? Where did you see that?" Raymond asked.

"Here," Tommy said, pointing to a square with a squiggle on it in Raymond's notebook.

"So that's problem one solved. What about problem two?" Johnny asked.

"Well, I don't know about solved, but it is definitely a start. Problem two is one of safety. Ideally, I would like to have a distraction in the area to draw away attention from the bank. That way, if we do trip any unforeseen alarms we may have some backup. I'm also afraid that if we cut the power to the bank we may take out power to surrounding buildings. That would be reported and that would be a problem."

"Is it all business or residential around the bank?" Peter asked.

"Business, I think," Raymond replied.

Joey said, "Do it on Sunday. All businesses are closed."

"That would work, but what kind of distraction could we cause on a Sunday," Raymond said.

"When did you say it was?" Peter asked.

"July 20th," Raymond answered.

"Go home and pray, Ray. The answer will come to you," Peter said.

"Well, we're off to a good start, but we still need to figure out a ton of details," Raymond said.

"I mean, there are a bunch of little things that are needed to go into this. Maybe we should think it through and think about what could go wrong and try to work it that way."

"Pete's right. It's getting late. Let's meet back tomorrow morning," Johnny said.

The boys left. Each excited and lost in their own thoughts. As Raymond walked home, two things were on his mind. What Johnny had said was right. This was a whole new level and he had to be sure he could do this without getting his friends in trouble. As he walked along the gray sidewalks illuminated by the streetlights, he began to lose faith. This had to be perfect. There could be no mistakes. That led to his second thought. What kind of distraction could they cause that would ensure their safety? "Pray for inspiration," Raymond said aloud as he entered his apartment, and there on the kitchen table he saw it on the cover of the *Daily News*.

POPE TO VISIT NEW YORK

And in little print underneath the headline it said:

SUNDAY MASS TO BE HELD ON THE GREAT LAWN IN CENTRAL PARK—JULY 20TH

The whole city would be geared up for the mass and all eyes would be on Central Park. It was perfect. Raymond smiled. Pray for inspiration. He wondered how long Peter would have made him wait before telling him. Raymond didn't sleep much that night. This turn of events had changed everything.

CHAPTER

15

The New Plan

THE SUN SHONE THROUGH THE FIRE ESCAPE AND STRUCK RAYMOND ON THE FACE. He had eventually drifted off to sleep and now he groggily rose from bed. With the morning routine completed, he decided to head to the bakery for a buttered roll and then get over to the wine cellar and start planning. He figured he could tell his parents he was going to 9:00 a.m. mass and then going to play ball in the park, his usual Sunday routine. He was shocked as he opened the door to his building and saw Peter sitting on the stoop bouncing a pinky ball.

"Up early today, Pete," Raymond joked.

"You kidding? I already served six and seven o'clock mass. You know I'm the only altar boy who understands the Latin masses," Peter replied.

"So, you get any divine inspiration overnight?" Peter asked.

"How long were you going to let me hang in the wind?" Raymond said.

"Well, I am here early," Peter replied. "Look, Ray, you know I am religious and the Pope coming here is no joke. I just figured that it had to be more than coincidence that we needed something and God provided it."

"I don't know about that," Raymond started to say but Peter cut him off.

"Look. Whatever you plan, nothing is going to happen to the Holy Father, right?"

"Are you crazy, Pete? I would never have something like that happen to the Pope. I just need a good distraction. I swear, Pete, I will make sure the mass goes off without a hitch."

"I knew you would say that. I just didn't want to say anything in front of the guys. You know Joey would be relentless with the altar boy stuff."

The boys walked silently toward the wine cellar with a stop at Marsh's Bakery for a couple of buttered rolls. The rolls were still warm, and as they ate them, the sun cleared the tops of the apartment buildings and warmed them. To Raymond, a newfound peace had come over him. He had set things right with his friends and if they were really going to attempt this, at least he knew he had the support of all the guys.

In the wine cellar, Peter and Raymond finished their breakfast as Tommy and Joey walked in.

"Where's Johnny?" Raymond asked.

"Went to mass with his parents. He should be here soon," Joey said.

"We'll wait for Johnny," Raymond answered, but inevitably the conversation went straight to the bank.

"There are some major problems with getting in the bank, Ray," Tommy said. "I mean, most banks run on auxiliary power. If the power goes off, that means shutting off alarms as we enter the bank, and we need to really scout out those train tunnels. I mean the subway system has tunnels that were built years ago. We get lost down there, we're screwed."

"What about your distraction?" Joey said. "Does that mean we're not all going, cause I'm going?"

"Going where?" Johnny asked, removing his coat and placing it near the boiler.

"We thought you were out," Joey cracked.

"Naw. I just had to go to mass with my folks," Johnny said.

"That's another problem we have," Raymond said.

"What?" Johnny asked.

"How do we keep this from your father?" Raymond said.

"What do you mean?" Johnny asked.

"I mean, your father has known about everything we've done and that means we have a rat in here."

Johnny instantly got angry. "You think I've been telling my Dad what we've been doing," Johnny said as he walked toward Raymond.

Peter and Tommy jumped up as Johnny got in Raymond's face.

"What are you saying, Ray?" Joey put in.

"Calm down, Johnny," Raymond quickly interrupted. "I know its not you who is the rat. It's Manginni."

"The crazy old super," Joey said. "No way."

"Explain this to me, Ray," Johnny said, backing down a bit.

"When I went to meet with your father, he told me to say hello to Manginni for him. Then he made a quick face. I mean, I almost missed it, but it was something. He knew he made a mistake and I played it like I didn't catch him but I did. Manginni has been watching us and if we want to do this, we need to plan another job to throw off Manginni and your Dad," Raymond said.

"Now we need to plan two jobs. Are we doing them both?" Tommy said.

"No. One must be a decoy and the bank is the main priority," Raymond said.

"We're getting way ahead of ourselves," Johnny said. "We first need to hammer out the details of the bank and we need to do it systematically. Ray, your distraction is the Pope. The mass in Central Park will have every cop in Manhattan there, and it's a Sunday so it's perfect. The only problem is that we will have to do this in broad daylight." Johnny smiled feeling content that he had come up with the solution.

Peter looked at Raymond and Raymond nodded. Peter understood. The nod was saying, let Johnny have this one.

"That could work, but we can't mess with the Pope," Tommy said.

Peter and Raymond exchanged another a knowing glance.

"I mean, it's the Pope," Tommy said.

"It could work and we could do it without messing with the Pope," Raymond said. "Johnny's right. We need to break this down into manageable pieces. First, we have the date, so that's a start. Next, we need to find a way from the subway to the bank underground. I suggest Tommy and I are on that detail."

"No complaints from me," Peter said. "Crawling around with rats in a subway tunnel is not my idea of a good time."

"If you find a way, we will need some basic equipment. Joey and Johnny—that's your job. We will need bolt cutters, rubber gloves, and some basic tools."

"Don't forget the bags to carry the money in," Joey laughed.

They all broke into laughter and continued to discuss the plan for the rest of the morning. The decision was made that Tommy and Raymond would go to the subway tunnels after school and Johnny and Joey would start slowly stockpiling the equipment they would need. Peter was left to think about two things: the distraction and the false job. In reality, they all were on that detail, but Raymond thought it sounded better to have Peter in charge; after all, he had come up the with idea of the Pope first.

CHAPTER

16

Tunnels and Parks

I N THE WEEKS THAT FOLLOWED, THE BOYS WERE EXCEEDINGLY BUSY. They still had to deal with school, and aside from that, "the job," as they referred to it, took up the rest of their time. As for Raymond, he was still working at Con-Ed on the weekends. He still looked at plans but he spent most of his day thinking about the job. June was fast approaching and they were woefully behind schedule. Tommy and Raymond had spent days at the train station by the bank and had come to realize that it was nearly impossible to catch the train platform empty. Without the platform empty, they could never get down to investigate the tunnels. This was becoming increasingly frustrating for Raymond.

On the other hand, Tommy was enjoying himself immensely. He would sit on the platform and look at the tracks and try to figure the general direction of the bank. They had walked the path from the train to the bank a thousand times with the rest of the masses. Every time, Tommy would be silently counting. One day it was steps; another day it was minutes. He timed trains coming in and out of the station, never writing anything down and repeating the process over and over again. For Raymond, this meant spending most of the time in silence while Tommy did his thing. It was in the third week of scouting out the platform when they finally got a break. It was late and the boys were getting ready to go home when all of a sudden, the uptown train pulled in, and as the boys waited, they suddenly found themselves alone on the platform. Raymond quickly looked both ways and headed rapidly toward the end of the platform. A chain was all that separated the boys from the stairs that led down to the tracks. The boys quickly jumped it and headed down the stairs into the gloom of the tunnel.

Tommy instantly warned Ray, "Stay away from the tracks. The middle rail is electrified and it will fry you if you get too close."

"Thanks for the tip."

The boys continued down the track, which became darker and darker. Tommy pulled out a flashlight and led the way as they moved deeper down the track.

Tommy looked at his watch, "We've been walking for two minutes. The next train down this track is coming in ten minutes. If we can't find a side tunnel in the next three minutes, we turn back," Tommy said.

"That's cutting it kind of close," Raymond said.

The air in the tunnel had a musty dirty quality and Raymond started to cough. They were walking through some sort of muck and Raymond could have sworn he had seen things that could not have been rats because they were too large to be rats.

After about ten more steps, Tommy stopped short and said, "Got it, Ray. Right up ahead."

And sure enough, there was a side access tunnel they turned into it and walked in about seven feet when Tommy stopped.

"We wait here for the train to pass outside. It should be about two minutes from now."

They waited in complete darkness and the feeling was oppressive. Raymond started to feel claustrophobic and then he heard Tommy quietly humming.

"You're enjoying this? Aren't you?" Raymond said.

Tommy chuckled, "It's not so bad. What, you scared of the dark?"

He laughed and then began counting down.

"Five."

The entire ground began to shake.

"Four."

To Raymond, it felt as if the walls were about to come down around his head.

"Three."

The whole tunnel lit up and Ray could see there was a two-way branch up ahead.

Raymond never heard the two or one count as the train rushed by. The sound was deafening and lasted until Raymond heard the high-pitched squeal of the train's breaks. The train had pulled into the station and then rumbled off again.

"So, up ahead we should go left," Tommy said. "But we do that next time and we need to bring something to mark our way out. I'm pretty sure I know where we are approximately but we need to be sure we have a way out, otherwise we could get lost and I'm sure we don't want to do that."

"No. We definitely do not want that," Raymond said as he felt something large and furry scramble over his shoe.

"We're going to need boots," he said as they climbed the stairs from tracks to the subway platform and checked to see if the coast was clear.

"Yeah. Real big ones," Tommy said as they walked back onto the platform and sat on the familiar bench waiting for their train to take them back to the neighborhood.

Johnny and Joey had had a much easier time than the two tunnel dwellers. They had set out to find some basic equipment. Much of which could be taken from the bar. They started small. Pocketing a screwdriver here, some wire cutters there. They really had more trouble hiding the stuff they stole than taking the stuff itself.

Raymond told them to just leave it in the wine cellar. That way Manginni would know they were planning something but not know what it was. This would work toward the part of the plan to feed Manginni with disinformation. In the three weeks they had been at it, they compiled an impressive list of stuff. The prize of their cache was a drill that they managed to snatch from a Con-Ed truck while the workman was up a telephone pole. Johnny played lookout while Joey went into the back of the unlocked truck and managed to get the drill and an empty tool belt. They had an assortment of tools, rope, and even managed a pair of bolt cutters. The wine cellar was beginning to look like a hardware store, and by that time Tommy and Raymond had made their first journey into the tunnels. Joey and Johnny were ready for other assignments. Unfortunately for Joey, it would not be the assignment he was looking for.

17

Peter's Plan

PETER HAD TAKEN HIS ASSIGNMENT SERIOUSLY. He decided the best way to approach it was to go to a place where he could quietly think. There was no better place for him to go than church. Peter was a regular at masses during the week and he would often hang around and help Father Bob out. Father Bob was an institution in the neighborhood. He represented everything good about priests. He was a true father figure to many of the kids in the neighborhood. He would make breakfast for Peter and any of the other altar boys after morning mass. He would show up for all the boys' baseball games, basketball games, or any other event in the neighborhood. He did a million random acts of kindness over the years he served in the parish.

When he saw Peter sitting in the church alone he asked, "What's wrong kid? You okay?"

"Yeah, I'm fine, Father. I was jus thinking about a problem I have."

"Anything serious? Your family okay?"

"No, nothing like that, Father. It's a problem I have with my friends. I will work it out. I just needed a quiet place to think."

"Well, son, you know all answers come from God. Just listen and it will come to you."

"Thanks, Father."

Peter sat and thought about the problem. They needed a distraction—a diversion and the Pope will be in Central Park. The silence in the church was peaceful. Peter sat about two pews from the front, and as he stared at the altar, it came to him. They needed to do something in the park on the day of the mass. It could not disrupt the event but it must draw the attention of the police. As he began to work it out, he smiled. He kneeled and said a prayer of thanks and then was off to the wine cellar. As he made his way through the streets, Peter was conflicted. It really wasn't right to steal and he knew it. He had rationalized it out by thinking that his family and friends were above all things. This was different. He promised himself that if they did pull this off, any money he made would be used to help people. It still didn't make it right, but it made him feel better. Peter smiled to himself and entered the building.

The boys were already in the wine cellar, involved in some intense conversation. Apparently Tommy and Raymond had found a way into the tunnels. Peter sat quietly and listened to the story.

"Rats down there?" Peter asked.

"Yeah some big ones, Pete. I don't know if you'll be able to handle it down there," Tommy joked.

"That's okay. I won't be down there," he said.

That got everyone's attention. The room got silent and Peter let them sweat.

"Look, Pete, if you've changed your mind it's cool. We understand," Johnny said.

"Thanks, Johnny, but I'm still in. I won't be in the tunnels because I will be in the park setting up the explosives."

"Explosives? What explosives?" Tommy asked.

"You planning on blowing up the Pope? I thought you were the religious one of the gang," Joey joked.

"Actually we will both be blowing up... well, not actually blowing up but kind of setting off some ..."

"Slow down, Pete," Raymond said. "Let's hear your idea."

"Look, we know the Pope will be saying mass in the park, so all we need to do is set off some fireworks and cherry bombs at different locations in the park at a certain time before the mass. The way I figure it with all the cops in the park and all the security around, a few fireworks going off will set off all those cops. It could cause enough commotion to give you guys time to get in and out before everything settles down and they realize it's just some people celebrating the Pope's visit," Peter continued before anyone could comment. "I talked to Father Bob. The Parks Department has a summer program that takes high school students and I asked him to get Joey and me signed up. The way I see it, we will all be assigned to park duty the day of the mass to clean up and stuff. What better way to get access to garbage cans? We can set up some fireworks to go off in the cans so no one will get hurt. What do you think?"

The boys were dumbfounded. It was perfect. They sat there with there mouths opened for a few seconds, then Joey spoke, "Why do I have to work for the Parks Department?"

"Look, Joey, Raymond has to go. He has the blueprints and will probably be working at Con-Ed this summer anyway. Tommy knows the layout of the tunnels and if anything goes wrong down there they will need him and, no offense, Tommy, but you and explosives don't mix. Johnny could never get a job. I mean we know who his dad is and it would be too suspicious. That leaves you and me," Peter said. "We need two guys on this and I need you to do this. I couldn't handle it myself."

"You really have thought this out well, Pete. I love it. It really could work," Raymond said.

"Yeah, nice plan," Joey said sarcastically. "Fuck you guys," and he stormed out of the wine cellar.

"Wait, Joey," Johnny said and got up to go catch him. "I'll talk to him. We'll be right back. Hey, Pete, by the way, very impressive," Johnny said as he walked out the door.

Peter smiled and turned to Raymond, "Do you really think it's feasible?"

JAMES AND CARMINE CIOFFI

"Yeah, absolutely, we need to make sure you guys are in that park before the day of the mass and we need to coordinate what time we set the stuff off. It's real important that we time it right. You know we might be able to use this to come up with something to throw off Franco. Let me think about that, but really this is fantastic, Pete."

Raymond turned and said, "Tommy, you know the park pretty well. Anything we could use as a target to throw off Franco?"

As the three boys started to talk about some different places and throw out ideas, Johnny caught up with the fuming Joey outside on the stoop.

"Hey come on, man, what's with the drama?"

"Come on, Johnny, you know I live for this more than any of you guys. I wanted to be a part of this and now I'm regulated to picking up bottles in the park. You know it's easy for you with your dad, and Raymond and Tommy and Pete having their own thing going. I wanted this for me."

"What are you babbling about? When everything is said and done you and me will be running this neighborhood someday and you are a part of this. Come on, in all honesty I would rather switch with you. I mean, I got to crawl around in the dark with rats while you get to see the Pope. And if we get caught, you two are free and clear. You know."

"You know that doesn't matter to me, Johnny. I wanted to be in there with you guys."

Johnny got quiet and let the silence sit. They sat on the stoop. He let Joey settle down, and finally Joey said, "Lots of girls in the park in summer right?"

"Yeah, lots. And chicks dig guys in uniforms," Johnny said, nudging Joey in the ribs.

"Yeah, those sexy green jumpsuits. I look good in green," Joey said, smiling.

"You know, I'm glad you'll be the one causing the distraction," Johnny said, knowing that it was resolved and Joey had come to grips with the situation.

"Why?" Joey asked.

"Because the distraction is what keeps us safe and there isn't anyone I trust more to watch my back then you, brother."

"Thanks. You think a couple of sparklers will do it," Joey laughed as he stood up. "Lets go get a couple of dogs. I'm hungry."

"What about the guys?"

"Let 'em sweat it out a while longer," Joey said.

18

The Alternate Plan

ALL OF JOEY'S COMPLAINING ASIDE, THE PLAN PETER HAD COME UP WITH WAS EXTREMELY WELL THOUGHT-OUT. The job was coming together. At least some of it was, as far as Raymond was concerned. The park idea would work as long as they could set up before the mass. They had gotten into the tunnels and Tommy was confident he could maneuver them to the bank. They had all the tools they needed, or so they thought. The one thing that was nagging Raymond was the alternate plan.

Franco didn't run a crew for no reason. While he thought the boys were up to penny ante stuff, he had pretty much known everything they had done since the Chen job. If Franco had any idea, even a hint of what they were doing, they could forget everything. The tools, the jobs, Franco would know something was up and Raymond had to use Manginni to put his mind to rest and clear them for the bank job. As June approached this was one of the priorities on Raymond's mind; the other was the tunnels.

He and Tommy had only gotten down into the tunnel on two other occasions since their first trip. The second time they had gone into the tunnel, they had taken the left branch of the split and come up at a dead end. This had thrown Tommy. He had thought it would be a pretty straight run down the block underground right to the bank. Having to go right at the first tunnel meant at some point they would have to double back, and it was at this point that they had abandoned the second trip. The third trip, the boys had gone down the right tunnel and come to another open track. They had to wait for over an hour to make sure it was not used, and after seeing no trains, they continued along the tunnel until they found three smaller tunnels leading off in different directions. The tunnels had a downward slope to them and Tommy, fearing that they would get lost, decided that it would be worthless to try and explore any of them without a way to mark their progress.

"We need some spray paint or something to mark our path. You know, like Hansel and Gretel bread crumbs," Tommy said.

"Bread crumbs down here would only mean bigger rats," Raymond replied, "but I get what you're saying. This is about as far as I could go without getting lost."

"Ray, we may need to do some research on the surrounding buildings to figure the way around this," Tommy said.

So that was where they were at with the tunnels, which really was nowhere as far as Ray was concerned. Tommy was more optimistic. He had decided to hit the library and go looking for old subway tunnel plans. Ray had insisted he get a fake library card just as a precaution and Tommy was forbidden from asking for any help from any library workers. So while Tommy was investigating, Raymond focused on the problem of coming up with an alternate plan to throw off Franco. After two weeks and numerous ideas, he was left with nothing. He was sitting in the lunchroom one day with all the boys and Smitty.

Jason Smith, "Smitty", as the boys called him, was the one black kid who lived in the neighborhood. While the high school was integrated, with a mix of mostly Italians and African Americans, the neighborhood was not. There were distinct boundary lines between neighborhoods; Smitty was the exception. He lived in the Italian part of the neighborhood and was accepted by all. Johnny insisted Smitty's mother made the best sausage and peppers in the neighborhood.

"Can't wait for the summer," Peter said with a smile to everyone at the table.

"Yeah, just three more weeks," Johnny chimed in.

"What you got going this summer, Smitty?" Tommy asked.

"Me? I'm a working man. Got me a job at the Boat House in Central Park. You know, taking the boats in and out of the water. Renting boats to people. It kind of sucks but at least I'll be outside."

Raymond's ears pricked up. "How'd you get that job?"

"A cousin of mine worked there last year. He said it's real busy, but the pay is decent and the owner is never there. So long as you do your work you don't get hassled."

"Sounds good," Raymond said.

They finished lunch and returned to class. Raymond spent the rest of the day thinking about the Boat House. He had never been there but would have to check it out. It could be exactly what they were looking for.

Two days later after school, Raymond, Tommy, and Joey were on the uptown 4 train. Tommy was heading for the library on 58th Street, and Raymond and Joey were heading for the park to scout out the Boat House. The Boat House had been in Central Park for years. The set up was fairly simple. There was a place to launch the boats by the lake and a small structure to handle cash and store oars and any other equipment. During the summer, it was a popular place for couples to go for a romantic row around the lake, and by the number of boats stacked outside, it probably made a good deal of cash. In reality, it was a pretty good business. Raymond figured you had a one-time cost of buying boats and then repainting them every few years. You hire cheap labor to basically run the stand and then sit back and collect. Joey saw the potential, too.

"Look at this racket. What do you think? Maybe they have three guys working and at one dollar an hour a boat; to rent a boat you figure it about twenty boats going out all day—that's about $400 to $500 a day. Not bad for no real intensive labor."

"Yeah and just about what we would be looking for," Raymond said.

They walked over to the Boat House and grabbed the leaflet that had all the information on it: the hours of operation, the prices per hour, and the map of the lake.

"What do we need these for?" Joey asked as they walked over the stone bridge back toward 5th Avenue.

"A little cheese for our Italian rat," Raymond said, smiling.

The idea was simple. The map, the tools, and then maybe some other hints would be left for Manginni to discover. He would tell Franco and as long as Franco thought he knew what was going on, he would stay out of their way. With school coming to a close, things would really begin to pick up. Raymond would be busy at Con-Ed. Joey and Peter would be starting the job at the Parks Department, and Johnny and Tommy would be doing the tunnel exploring during the day. They also had to keep up a regular routine of being around the neighborhood. That would include basketball in the park, baseball with the Boys Club, and card games at the club.

It had to be business as usual or it would be suspicious. There was a lot to do and most of it was now riding on Tommy. If he couldn't figure a way through the tunnels, then the whole plan might have to be scrapped. Raymond did not think that going through a manhole was a good idea, too many ways to get noticed or caught. He closed his eyes on the train ride back home. The slow rocking of the train put his body to rest. He sighed and thought it was coming together, but not as quickly as he would like. There was still way too much that had to fall into place and time was running out.

CHAPTER

19

Tommy

TOMMY WAS IN HIS ELEMENT. The New York Public Library, with its massive shelves and the smell of paper and leather bindings, always impressed him every time he walked in. He often thought that this was like the great library of Alexandria in ancient times. Entering this vast and immense storehouse of knowledge was always a thrill, but on the last four occasions, his trips to the library were anything but enjoyable. Based on Raymond's edicts, he could not ask for help from anyone and even with his understanding of the library and the filing system, it had taken him a long time to locate what he needed. What he was looking for were old subway plans and the layout of the building where the bank was located.

His problem was not that he could not read the plans, it was that he could not find them. He found numerous books on the architectural structure of New York and had seen many of the building in pictures, but the outside of buildings was not what he was looking for. He needed the x-rays, the guts of the building, and unfortunately those were not very visually inspiring or very interesting to read about, so there was no information about them written in any books. This realization had come pretty quickly to Tommy so he went to his backup plan. He knew the plan had to be filed as public record. They would be in the library, but to ask for blueprints would go against what Raymond had told him. So that was out. The only other option was to hope that the blueprint plans would have been transferred to microfiche to make storage easier. This led him to searching the microfiche indexes and trying to find the right maps.

The benefit to this is that when requesting microfiche, all you had to do is write down the file number on a card. Tommy assumed that the librarians had not memorized every file so even they had no idea what was on the tape. Tommy realized that there was a possibility that someone would come looking for the person who took out maps of the buildings or subways. He rationalized that even if they did, they would get nothing since Tommy had taken Raymond's advice and was working in the library under the name Patrick O'Donnell who lived on 234 West End Avenue. The name and address were both made up and therefore would lead nowhere. His conscious clear, he was still having a hard time finding the right maps. Most of the tunnels under the city had been done over and over during the last twenty-five years.

On more than one occasion, he found conflicting maps of the same area. The idea of using the maps of the train tunnels was getting him nowhere, so he decided after his fourth trip to the library to take a different tact. Today while Joey and Raymond were scouting out the Boat House, he would be looking for plans of the sewer system. Tommy figured if he could find the sewer that the Con-Ed men were using, he might be able to trace it back to the train tunnel. It was a long shot, but at the pace he was on with the subway plans, he could spend months before he found the right ones. Tommy went through his usual routine in the library. He took out three or four books on ancient Greece.

Then he went to a microfiche machine and set the books down. To any one walking by or paying any attention to him, it would not look like he was studying sewers. He then filled out three cards based on the indexes he had looked up earlier. Each film came in little tubes like the ones camera film came in. After loading it onto the machine, you stared at a little screen and rolled the film with a dial.

Tommy began scanning the first film slowly. As good as he was at reading plans, it was still very slow and tedious work. After two hours of nothing, he decided to take a break. He got up, stretched, and went to the restroom to throw cold water on his face. He had seen numerous sewer lines but none had matched the addresses of where he was looking for. Another hour had passed until he finally found it on the ninth roll of microfiche. Tommy sat back, stretched again, and took out his notebook. Now the real work began.

The manhole the men from Con–Ed were working in was thirty feet from the bank, out in the street. The manhole descended fifteen feet then branched off left and right. According to the plan Tommy was looking at, there was a central groove for water run off and a two-foot ledge to walk on. The tunnel that ran to the left sloped downward, but Tommy couldn't tell if the tunnel dropped down to another tunnel or if it was a dead end. On the schematic it just ended. The right tunnel led to a door that doubled back under the sidewalk to an electrical room that also contained the main electrical board that would control the whole block. Based on the schematic, the space was large enough to work in and hopefully there would be access from this room to the bank.

Looking at the rest of the layout, there was no way the main power could be anywhere but in that room. This information, while helpful, would only be useful if they could get into the room without going through the manhole. There was another room off the workroom that looked like it would access a water main or sewer. The schematics weren't specific; they only had the room labeled sewer line A-4.

This was the way in. Somehow, Tommy had to figure out how to access this room from the subway tunnel. Tommy sat back and tried to visualize the tunnel. There would have to be a door that led to the sewer and to his knowledge they were usually marked. All they had to do was find the tunnel and the door and they could access the sewer line and then the power room without having to use the manhole. It might be a slippery climb through the sewer but that would be no problem. Tommy smiled and then just as quickly frowned. There were major problems. First, there would have to be access from the subway tunnel to the sewer room; if they couldn't find that access then they were sunk. Second, they would have to have access to the bank if they got into the electrical room. He needed to get out of the library and walk the route from the street. It could be done, he thought as he walked down the great stairs leading to the street. It could be done!

CHAPTER
20

Summer and Back to the Tunnels

THE END OF THE SCHOOL YEAR WAS A GREAT TIME IN THE NEIGHBORHOOD. The weather was heating up. The city blocks were alive with action out in the streets. The days were longer and the amount of time everyone spent outside seemed to double. The metal folding chairs started to appear outside of all the stores and clubs. You could not walk down the street without seeing someone you knew and stopping to chat. The summer was usually a busy time for the boys and this year things would change a bit. The boys were now getting excited as the job approached, but Raymond decided that barring their jobs they needed to maintain their regular routine in the neighborhood.

"We need to be at the park and we have to play in the Boys Club baseball league."

There had been some discussion about not playing and using Joey, Peter, and Raymond's jobs as an excuse not to play. But Johnny was in full agreement with Raymond.

"Look, we do what we have to, but we need to step up the action in the tunnel. We're a month away and, to be honest with you, if we don't get that tunnel route straight we might as well call it," Johnny said.

"No way we can use the manhole access the workers use if we can't get through the tunnels. I don't care if we have to go in broad daylight, I'm not working all summer to call this off," Joey said.

"Look, I'm sure I can get us through the tunnels, but I agree we need to get down there and see what's going on and soon," Tommy said.

They were all starting to feel the pressure. They left the wine cellar that night with more questions than answers. Peter and Joey had to start work Monday morning. Raymond would be working every day at Con-Ed with the weekends off. Tommy and Johnny would have to do more of the investigating in the tunnels. The clock was ticking and time was running out.

Tommy and Johnny crossed the street from the bank right past the open manhole cover that led to the electrical room. Tommy was explaining the schematics he had found to Johnny as they ran across the busy street.

"The tunnel leads here. The drop down is to account for the basements of the buildings over there," he said as the stood facing the building on the opposite side of the street. "The sewer lines then branch off and run under the basements, or in some cases alongside the structures; the problem is finding the subway tunnel that leads to these sewer tunnels," Tommy explained.

"But I thought the water ran in pipes. We aren't squeezing through those pipes here. Are we?" Johnny asked.

"The water does run in pipes, but sewers aren't like the drains in your house. They are built more like a tunnel because large stuff gets washed down sewers. If they were like the water pipes, they would clog all the time and break, so for the most part they are basically tunnels with nice ledges to and a recessed groove for the water to flow through. At certain points they have grates to block the debris but hopefully we can avoid that," Tommy explained.

They walked toward the corner and then headed toward the train station.

"I have the distance from the bank to the subway station calculated and the general direction we have to travel in, so I can kind of guess where we need to be and if we've traveled too far," Tommy said.

"So what's the problem? This sounds like a piece of cake. You got it all figured out."

"The problem is that the subway tunnels don't run straight toward the sewer tunnels and that means we have to travel the opposite way and double back. We're also underground so it's hard to keep your sense of direction. You'll see," Tommy said.

The boys descended into the subway station. It was around lunchtime and the crowd was pretty thin. The heat on the platform and musty air made Johnny start to sweat.

"Hot down here," he said. "Wait till you get in the tunnels."

"I thought we were in a tunnel," Johnny joked.

Tommy smiled. He knew Johnny had no idea what he was getting into. Tommy checked his watch.

"Here she comes," he said, and almost instantly a low rumble started to sound in the tunnel.

The train then came rumbling into the station and squeaked to a halt.

"Impressive," Johnny said, smiling.

"I have the trains timed, weekdays and weekends," Tommy said.

The few people on the platform boarded the train and the few who got off headed for the stairs. Tommy grabbed Johnny's arm and they quickly headed for the stairs at the end of the platform. Johnny scrambled down the stairs following Tommy. The light at the bottom of the stairway was dim, and as he stumbled along in the increasing darkness, Tommy suddenly disappeared. Johnny had a moment of panic until he saw Tommy suddenly pop out of the wall.

"Stop fooling around. We need to move," Tommy said, and as Johnny approached he pulled him into the side tunnel. Tommy looked at Johnny who was a bit confused.

"You okay?" he asked.

"Yeah, just kind of freaked out a little," Johnny replied.

Tommy laughed. "Just stay close and you'll be fine. Here I brought you a flashlight," he said, handing a lit flashlight to Johnny and taking out another for himself.

Johnny shined the light around. The tunnel was about seven feet high and five feet across. The floor was littered with dirt and scraps of paper. He occasionally heard the scraping of what had to be rats running up and down the tunnel.

"Nice place," he said.

"Oh, it gets worse," Tommy said, holding the flashlight under his face.

"You're really enjoying this," Johnny said, shaking his head.

The boys moved about ten feet down the tunnel and Tommy stopped and pulled something out of his pocket. He went over to the wall and did something.

"What's up?" Johnny asked.

"Reflective tape," he said, shinning the light on the tape.

In the gloom, the tape lit up and Johnny could see writing on it that said "main tunnel 10 feet."

"I figure we need to keep track of what direction we're going in."

"What if anyone comes down here and see that?" Johnny asked.

"First, I don't think anyone is coming down here, and second, I did a little research. Subway workers use this type of tape down here all the time to keep track of themselves. If for any reason a worker comes down here, they won't think it suspicious. I figure that when we leave after the job we just pull the tape as we go. That way there's no evidence."

He didn't want to admit it, but it made him feel much better that they had a system to find their way out of there. He had gone down one tunnel and was already feeling a bit claustrophobic.

The boys headed toward the next split and Tommy said, "This is where we were the last time. I say we go left."

"Sounds good to me," Johnny replied.

As they headed down the left tunnel, Johnny could not help but notice that the tunnel was sloping downward.

"We going deeper?" he asked.

"Yeah," was all Tommy said.

Johnny could swear he could hear him counting. The tunnel made a sharp right turn and then ran on for another fifty feet to a downward slope that had increased drastically.

Tommy stopped and did his tape thing again and Johnny asked, "Why here?"

"Because we just found another train tunnel, and with any luck this is the one we were looking for," he said as Tommy flattened himself against the wall and shined the flashlight ahead. Johnny could see the wide expanse of another train tunnel. He shined his light around and saw old rusted tracks and hanging lights that were obviously in disrepair. The tracks looked abandoned. He started to move forward and Tommy stopped him.

"We wait—to be sure," he said.

"How long?"

"The trains run about every ten to seventeen minutes," he said, turning off his flashlight.

"Why'd you do that," Johnny asked.

"Don't want to run out of batteries," he replied.

Johnny turned off his also and the boys waited in the silence and darkness.

"Don't even want to talk?" Johnny nervously asked.

Tommy didn't reply and after a few seconds Johnny said in a panicky voice, "I hope you're having fun because when we get out of here I'm going to kick your ass."

"Maybe, I'll just leave you here," Tommy said, giggling.

"Real funny," Johnny said.

They continued to talk for the next ten minutes and finally Tommy said, "Okay, let's go see what we can find."

The subway tunnel was definitely abandoned. The boys did get a scare when they heard a rumbling sound only to realize it was a train above them. This confirmed Tommy's thought that they were under the track they originally had come down.

"This is good if we're under the track. Then I can calculate how far we have to go."

The boys crossed the two sets of tracks heading to the far wall, careful not to touch the third rails, just in case. As they reached the far wall and headed down the track, Tommy was shining the light on the wall ahead. They had walked about thirty feet when he saw it. There along the wall was a door. As they neared it, Tommy grew more excited. There was writing on the door. Tommy wiped away the dust on the door to reveal what they had been looking for. Sewer Line A-4.

"Yes," Tommy said quietly. "Johnny, this is it. It's the way into the sewer. We open this door and we can get into the sewer line based on the plans I found in the library. We can use this to get to the power room. It's going to work, Johnny. It's going to work!"

Johnny tugged on the door. It was obviously locked and didn't move.

Johnny looked at Tommy and said, "You know what, Tommy? It just might work!"

CHAPTER

21

Work

JOEY DID NOT FEEL THE EXCITEMENT OF JOHNNY AND TOMMY. While the boys were rooting around in the tunnels, he was sitting in a hot, crowded room full of guys, listening to his duties for the summer. He had been tempted on several occasions to get up and walk out but Peter had always just shot him a dirty look every time Joey even got restless.

"No smoking and no socializing with anyone in the park."

He heard a few grumbles and a couple of "Yeah rights" from the crowd of boys in the room. They were sitting in the main Parks Department building in Central Park. The room was filled with teenagers who wanted to be Parks Department summer workers. The ages ranged from sixteen to nineteen and most of the boys, like Joey, were not here on their own accord. Most of the boys in the room were here because their parents had set the jobs up for them and most of them would have rather been anywhere else.

As it was, Peter seemed to be one of the few listening attentively. He even addressed the old man lecturing them as sir and continued to ask a bunch of questions that, to the old man, were very important. It seemed like after every question Peter asked, the old man would launch into a five-minute response that reiterated to the boys just how much work they would be doing this year. It got to the point that when Peter started to raise his hand a couple of the guys were grumbling.

"Shut up or this old guy will have us here forever," one of them said to Peter.

Joey shot him a look that told the boy to back off and then he leaned toward Peter and whispered, "What, you want to get us killed the first day? I'm almost tempted to start a fight so we an get fired."

Peter smiled and said, "You know, Joey, you really must develop more social skills. I'm just being nice to the old man out of respect."

"Respect for what? He talking to us like he got a fresh crop of slaves off a boat and you want to give him respect."

Peter just smiled his patient smile and spoke to Joey as if he were a child, "You have a lot to learn, my son," he said.

"What the fuck are you talking about?" Joey said and got up and headed toward the door.

The old man said, "Where you off to, sonny?"

"Just going to take a leak," Joey said.

Peter shot him a look and Joey quickly added, "I'll hurry right back, sir."

The sarcasm was so subtle the old man didn't pick it up and Peter shook his head and turned to the old man and said, "If it rains are we reassigned to another duty or do we continue to work in the park?"

"Good question. Now let's discuss the procedure for rainy days," which was followed by another long set of rules and procedures. Joey heard the old man droning and decided to make this the longest leak in history.

Joey heard the shuffling of chairs and figured the lecture was over. He waited for Peter to come out of the room but to his surprise he never appeared. Joey asked one of the other boys what was going on.

"We have to report to the building across the walkway and pick out our prison jumpsuits," he joked.

"Thanks," Joey said as he headed back toward the room fighting through all the boys exiting. When he entered the room, he saw Peter shaking hands with the old man. As Peter saw him, he pointed to Joey and then turned to the old man. They exchanged some words and then Peter, laughing, shook the old man's hand again and walked toward Joey.

"What the hell was that all about?" Joey asked.

"You know, the more I think about this, the more I feel like if we pull this off it will be all because of me," he said in a half serious tone.

"I have no idea what you are talking about."

"Well, let's see. It was my inspiration to use the Pope's visit and it was my idea to get the jobs in the park and use the Boat House as the cover."

"Okay. Slow down."

"Wait, let me finish," he said, throwing a massive arm around Joey's shoulders. "And it was me who just sweet talked the old man into getting us the post near and around the Great Lawn as well as getting the assignment of cleanup for the Pope's visit," he said, pulling Joey's neck into a strangle hold.

"Yeah," he said in a very sarcastic tone, "you guys would have been lost without me."

Joey was ready to give an equally sarcastic comeback but as he looked at Peter's smiling face he said in the most serious of voices, "You know, you're right, Pete."

He left it at that and the smile immediately wiped off Pete's face.

"I was only kidding," he said with a bit of panic in his voice.

Joey saw his distress and said, "I know you were, Peter, but I'm serious. You've done some great work and I know you're too humble to admit it but I want you to know I won't be any trouble. I'll show up for work on time and I'll try not to bitch too much. I think Ray was right for us to work. We all have to play our part and I haven't been playing mine that well."

And with that, he put his arm around Peter's neck and said, "And anyway, Ray and Tommy are too ugly to be working in the park. This will be good for you. I'll teach you how to pick up women, curse, and even smoke."

"I don't know about all that," he said, "but it will be good to be outside instead of a rat infested tunnel."

After about two weeks of work, Peter might have changed his mind. The boys started at 8 a.m. and worked until 2 p.m. They worked five days a week and they had the unfortunate luck of having to work through one of the hottest summers on record. Their day was very structured and routine. Every morning, they met at the main Parks Department building and jumped in the back of an old pickup truck. The boys were armed with garbage bags, brooms, and scoops. They went from can to can in the park and changed the garbage bags from the night before, putting fresh bags in all the garbage cans. The boys would load the bags into the back of the truck and follow it as it moved along the paths in the park. The Parks Department guy who drove the truck was an all right guy. His name was Lou and he would stop every few cans and pull out his paper and read in the truck.

"Pace yourself, boys. Know what I mean?" he said, winking. "It's a long day and we don't want to burn ourselves out."

The message was clear—take your time when Lou stopped, and the boys grabbed their brooms and sort of walked around the paths sweeping and occasionally picking up some trash with the scoops.

"You know," Joey said, cupping the lit cigarette in his hand so no one could see it, "I could get used to that job," he said, pointing at Lou who was basically sleeping with his paper open on his lap.

"You mean you actually like this job," Peter said with a grin.

"No. Actually this sucks. It's 9 a.m. and I feel like I need a shower. I've seen three rats that I haven't told you about and by the time the park fills up I'm bored out of my mind."

Before Peter replied Joey added, "But … as far as work goes, this is far easier than any one of the million jobs I've been through. And if I had to work every day what better job to have than that guy's," he said, pointing to Lou. "I mean, he drives around and sleeps all day. What a racket!"

Walking and changing bags went until about 10:30, then the boys were on their own till noon. They basically had to walk around, sweep up, and pick up any garbage on the paths and across the Great Lawn. They would make a couple of sweeps, and by the third day they had Lou's schedule down. He drove by twice at around 11:00 and right before lunch at 12:00. The boys always made it look like they were extremely busy when he came around and he always said the same thing, "Nice work, guys. Pace yourselves. It's hot out here today," as he rolled the window up to keep the A/C in.

The boys got an hour lunch and then they would go back to patrol, as they liked to call it. At 1:00, Lou would return and they would do the garbage can thing again until 2:00. Then they were then free to go. All in all, Joey was right. The job was easy and it allowed them plenty of time to look around and start planning how they were going to create a diversion.

CHAPTER

22

The Wine Cellar

THE FEELING IN THE WINE CELLAR WAS ONE OF ANXIOUS ANTICIPATION. The boys were all feeling the excitement of the moment. The enormity of what they were doing had not entered their minds yet. They were all talking at once, each throwing out ideas and comments. Raymond settled them all down.

"Okay. Let's see what we have here. We've got two weeks and we still have a bunch of problems we need to figure out by the end of this week."

Raymond was tense. He was working every day and that kept him out of the action. As confident as he was in the ability of his friends, he was used to being the only one in control. The idea that he hadn't seen firsthand the tunnels or the layout in the park made him nervous. He would never show it outwardly to his friends but of all of them he realized the consequences of mistakes more than anyone else. That was why they had these nightly sessions in the wine cellar. To review the plans over and over so he could find the flaws and they all could correct them.

"Let's run through it," Johnny said, rubbing his hands over his face. "Tommy and I have been in the tunnels. We need to get through that one door and check it out to see if it leads to the electrical box."

JAMES AND CARMINE CIOFFI

"The problem is, we don't want to go through too early because the Con-Ed guys are probably still working in there and if they are, we don't want to arouse any suspicion by going in," Tommy said. "We have to get through that door this week for two reasons. One, we need to be sure that it's the right door, and two, we have no idea how to get from the electrical room to the bank. If there is a trap door we need to know how to get through it so, as risky as it might be, we have to go now. We won't have time to figure it all out when we're in there."

Raymond said, "I'm going with you guys and we go tomorrow night."

"I agree. We need more information. Tommy and I have hidden some tools down there. A hand drill, bolt cutters, and a sledge hammer but we really need to see that room to know what we need to bring," Johnny said.

Peter jumped in, "So you guys go tomorrow. That's settled. Our problem is pretty simple. How are we going to set off multiple explosions or smoke bombs in different locations at the exact right time?"

"The problem is the place will be packed and we need to devise a system so we don't get caught doing anything. I mean, we probably will be able to go anywhere in the crowd but Peter is right. We need to be able to set off multiple, let's call them distractions, at the same time and that's got us stumped," Joey said.

They all fell silent. This problem had been discussed over and over with no resolution over the last few days.

"Hey? Why multiple distractions at the same time," Tommy said. "Wouldn't staggered explosions cause more confusion?"

"We need to have them go off at the same time so the cops are confused," Joey insisted.

"Hear me out," Tommy said. "Look. There are only two of you and if you guys set up a couple of smoke bombs and light them, then move to another location, that gives you about a minute or two. Then you set off a couple of cherry bombs, move again and keep moving out from the Great Lawn in opposite directions. If you time it right, the commotion keeps them guessing. I figure two rounds of smoke bombs and two rounds of cherry bombs and you will cause enough confusion to cause a stir without a riot."

"We can't have a riot," Peter said.

"I like the idea of smoke bombs. They are harmless and will cause confusion." Raymond said. "Is there any way you can have them set up ahead of time?"

"The security will be tight. They will be sweeping the area the day before and the day of the Pope's mass. We will probably have to keep the stuff on us. I guess we could plant them while we change the garbage bags that morning," Joey said, looking at Peter.

"Yeah, but how do we set them off?" Peter said.

"I got that figured out. Pete, you're going to have to learn how to smoke," Joey said, laughing.

The boys all looked at Peter's shocked face and burst into laughter.

"I can't smoke. My mom will kill me," he stammered, only making it worse.

The boys roared and Tommy added, "Yeah, let's see, robbing a bank or smoking. I think your mom would go with the smoking."

Joey said, "Relax, Pete. I think I can keep you under a pack a day,"

"Let's hear your plan, Joey," Ray cut in seriously.

"It's simple, Ray. Most of the kids working sneak a cigarette every once in a while so it will be no problem for me to plant whatever it is on our initial sweep. I figure we put it under the cans. Most guys just pull the bags, so if we hide something under the can it should stay put. At the designated time we just change the bag like normal and light the smoke bomb or whatever that's under the can. It's pretty simple; I've run through it a few times already."

"When?" Peter said. "I've never seen you do it."

"Exactly," Joey said, smiling. "I haven't lit anything but I have done the motion a million times and no one sees that I have a lit cigarette. I cup it in the inside of my hand like so," and he revealed an unlit cigarette in his hand.

"You're a real Houdini," Johnny said.

"It's a good trick," Raymond said. "Could you teach Pete?"

"I could try and with the size of his hands he could hide one of Johnny's father's cigars," Joey replied to more laughter from the boys.

"Okay. So that takes care of the two most pressing problems. Tomorrow we hit the tunnels and Pete and Joey start picking the cans to hide the explosives in. Time how long it would take to get from can to can in opposite directions."

Pete was getting lightheaded. He couldn't tell if it was from the heat or the cigarettes he had been smoking all day. The morning had started out typically with the boys riding in the back of the pickup with Lou. Joey had explained to Peter how to smoke and how to inhale and hold the smoke in his lungs. It had all sounded quite easy when Joey explained it and lit up. The experience was totally different. Peter nearly passed out from choking and even Lou woke up long enough to ask if he was all right.

Joey forced him to continue this every half hour and Peter felt he was making no progress and would have liked to quit a number of times had it not been for Joey reminding him that he was sweating through his underwear picking up garbage on a Friday afternoon in July. The heat was oppressive and the boys were drenched with sweat from the moment they met outside of Peter's apartment building. It only got worse as the day crept along, and by lunchtime, both boys had changed shirts three times. Peter was questioning his decision to take on the role of being in the park.

"I don't care if it's a sewer with rats. A nice cool tunnel wouldn't be so bad right now."

Joey, who just nodded, kept sweeping and counting as they walked from one can to the next. Then Joey stopped. He looked at Peter then he looked down at the ground. He continued to look around and for a split second Peter thought he was having a heat stroke.

"Joey, you okay?" he asked.

"You brilliant bastard," Joey said, laughing to himself. "Pete that's it. The sewer. The cherry bombs go down the sewer and that way no one gets hurt."

"What are you talking about?" Peter asked.

"Look, we put a cherry bomb under the garbage can the day of the Pope's visit. This place will be crawling with people. Someone might go to the can and get hurt when it goes off. If we drop the cherry bomb down the sewer, it goes off, rumbles the ground a little, and, if anything, someone gets hit with sewer water. Too bad, but no one gets hurt. Look, there are sewers all along the path. We just need to reposition a can or two near the entrance of the sewer and then we can light the cherry bomb and drop it right down the sewer. Piece of cake."

"That would work, Joey. And you're right. No one would get hurt."

By the end of the day, the boys had the sewers picked out and the location for all the fireworks set. Joey figured it would take about thirty minutes to set off three cherry bombs each and two smoke bombs each. That should cause a good bit of commotion considering how large a crowd they were expecting. Joey figured their part would be done in forty-five minutes. Then they would be sit back and enjoy the mass and pray for their friends.

While Joey and Peter celebrated their plan with a smoke, things were not going so well in the tunnels. Raymond, Tommy, and Johnny had waited over an hour to get down the platform—much to the consternation of Raymond.

"This won't do. We better get here real early the day of the job. We have to be in position at the right time or the whole thing is shot."

"What do you want to do? Sleep in the tunnel overnight?" Tommy asked.

"It wouldn't be a bad idea," he said hopefully.

"Sorry, friend, but I am not sleeping down there. We'll get here early and everything will work out," Johnny said.

The boys arrived on the subway platform at 6:00 p.m., right during rush hour. They had waited till 6:00 knowing that the Con-Ed workers would have been done for the day. The masses of people getting on and off the trains slowly abated and the boys were able to make their way down into the tunnel. The tunnel was pitch black but Tommy knew it like the back of his hand. He could walk it with his eyes closed and actually had a few times. Tonight was the real test however. Tommy maneuvered his friends through the maze that was the tunnel system until they reached the old abandoned tracks.

"We hid most of the stuff down here," he said, pointing toward a dark recess that appeared to be covered by old boards and rail ties.

"Gloves on," Tommy said to no one in particular and reached into his pocket and put on a pair of latex gloves. He tossed a pair to a perplexed looking Raymond.

"We've been practicing working with the gloves on so on the big day we're comfortable with them," Tommy said, smiling at Raymond.

"Yeah, real comfortable. I can hardly unzip my pants to take a leak down here," Johnny said, laughing and snapping his gloves on like a fake doctor in a comedy show.

"Are you ready for your exam, sir?" he joked.

"Get the hammer and the drill. We're going through that door today," said Tommy. "And if I'm correct, we walk up a tunnel right to the utility room under the manhole from the street."

"Let's hope it's that easy," Johnny said, hefting the sledgehammer onto his shoulder.

The boys made their way to the door and Tommy examined it for the hundredth time. It was a steel door with a deadbolt lock. The keyhole and lock were covered with grime and looked as if it had not been in use in years.

Raymond came up alongside Tommy and asked, "What do you think?"

"It's a simple lock standard for these types of doors. Old, which means not cheap. They don't make doors like this anymore. If we had to, we could break the hinges but anyone who comes looking for who did this would know this was the way we came in," Tommy said. "I think we should try and pry it open. I brought a crowbar and if that doesn't work then we try to knock the lock out with the chisel and the hammer."

"Look, either way the cops will be down here and figure out this is the way we came in," Johnny said. "Which means with all the loot, we have to carry out all this equipment."

"Hey, if that's the way it is, then that's the way it is," Tommy said.

"I know, but we could have used that mule Peter down here. He could carry all this stuff with one arm," Johnny grunted as they approached the door.

"Okay. Let's try the crowbar," Tommy said and Johnny propped it in the crack between the wall and the door.

"Tap it in with the hammer," Johnny said.

Tommy tapped the crowbar in and then Johnny and Raymond pulled on the bar. Crack! The sound was like an explosion in the dark and cavernous tunnel. All three boys jumped and the crowbar clanged and hit the floor. The door had swung open and the boys were greeted with a gaping black hole of darkness.

"You think anyone heard that?" Johnny asked.

"No way. We're too far down for anyone to hear a noise like that," Tommy said.

"What about the utility room? If anyone was in there they could have heard that noise," Raymond said.

"I think the noise from the street would mask it but there's only one way to find out," Tommy said, pointing his flashlight at the darkness before them and with those words he disappeared from sight into yet another tunnel.

"Watch your step," Tommy said.

The boys were in a line with Tommy in front. He was excited when he first entered the tunnel. It seemed to slope in the right direction, upward and to the right. According to his inner compass, this was the right direction to bring them to the utility room.

However, thirty seconds into the tunnel, he was starting to have his doubts. The tunnel was sloping upward, which was good, but it was also narrowing. The floor was getting slick as if there had been water in the tunnel and he could faintly hear the sound of rushing water. These were all bad signs. Raymond and Johnny couldn't see anything and had to trust that Tommy was leading them in the right direction.

"I think there's a fork or a room up ahead," he whispered back over his shoulder, but in reality, his heart sank as he realized that it just might be a dead end. All of a sudden he was hit with a wretched smell.

"What the hell is that?" he heard Johnny groan from the back of the line.

"You are in a sewer," Raymond replied.

Tommy ignored the conversation and the smell and continued forward. The tunnel ceiling had shrunk to a point where Tommy was starting to crouch over in order to walk and, in combination with the ever-increasing slope of the floor, made for some treacherous walking. Tommy was afraid he would have to crawl that last twenty feet at this pace and he was terrified that he would slip and take his friends behind him out.

"It getting slippery and tight. Watch your step up here," he shouted, realizing that he had to shout because the sound of the rushing water was now getting louder and closer.

Tommy shined his light ahead into the gloom. He could see something in the air and, after a moment of confusion thinking it was dust, he realized it was mist. There was definitely running water ahead and his heart sank. This was probably a tunnel to a water main or a sewer line, which would account for the smell. He carefully scrambled the last few feet and saw that the tunnel opened up to a small room. The room was ten-by-ten feet and just barely allowed the boys to stand together in it.

At first glance, Tommy was disheartened as he looked down to the source of the running water. There was a metal grate that covered a third of the floor. It was designed to allow a worker to stand on it though none of the boys would. They remained huddled at the entrance of the room. The water was rushing through a massive pipe that was about half filled.

Raymond was shaking his head, "Looks like we're done here."

He sighed and looked to Johnny, who was half in the tunnel and half in the room.

"You kidding me?! Are we done Tommy?" he shouted about the running water.

"We're not done yet," he shouted, gleefully pointing and shinning his light on a door that was on the wall directly across the metal grating. The door was much cleaner than the one they had just come through and was held closed by a chain that ran through the empty lock and was hooked onto a metal spike that was stuck into the wall. Tommy motioned the boys together so he wouldn't have to scream.

"This is a sewer runoff pipe," he said, pointing down toward the water. "The reason the tunnel is slick is that it must overflow during heavy rain. I guarantee that door leads to the utility room. Did you notice it isn't locked?" He continued, "I bet the Con-Ed workers rigged the door in case they need to take a leak or smoke while they're down here they just go right here."

"So, moment of truth time," Johnny yelled. "Tommy, lead the way."

Tommy barely noticed the metal grate or the rushing water below him. He crossed over the grate and unchained the door. Johnny and Raymond were right behind. His heart was hammering in his chest. This was it and he knew it. As he stepped through the door, he could see the side tunnel that led to the manhole cover. There was faint light shinning down, illuminating the tunnel at that spot. The utility room was littered with cigarette boxes and used matches. There was a Wise potato chip bag in a corner and the crust of a slice of pizza.

The air was a bit fresher in this room and across from the boys was the central electrical box. Tommy walked forward and stared at it. There were tags that had systems labeled and switches and wires that were in various states, some were hooked up and some were being swapped out and looked unused. Overall, it was a mess.

There was new equipment on the floor, switches, wires, and various tools laid about. In one corner there was a large wooden crate labeled "main circuit conduit ship to" and an address that was hidden by the wall. This had to be the new box that was going in. The work was almost done and Raymond had been right about everything. They could do this. They would do this. Tommy turned toward Raymond and Johnny, dying to share his excitement with his friends.

"It was a good plan, Ray. I'm sorry," Johnny was saying.

"Yeah but we put so much effort and come so far. This really sucks," Raymond replied, disappointment evident in his voice.

"Who's going to tell Joey he's been working in the park for nothing?" Johnny joked, trying to cheer Raymond up.

"What the hell is wrong with you two? This is it," Tommy said, the confusion and frustration was evident in his voice.

"Tommy, look around," Raymond said gently. "There's no way into the bank. The electricity and wires run through pipes that go into that wall and then probably up to the bank. We would have to drill through the concrete to even have a chance and once we shut the power we wouldn't have enough time. It's over! It can't be done!"

CHAPTER

23

One Last Shot

TOMMY FELL BACK AGAINST THE WALL AS IF HE'D BEEN STRUCK. He gasped and for a moment couldn't breathe. It wasn't possible. His brain could not understand what was happening. He had spent so much energy trying to achieve this goal, so much time, and now they had gotten this far. Could it be possible that they were through?

Raymond placed a hand on his friend's shoulder. "We could never have even gotten this far without you," he said.

"It's alright. This was a long shot at best," Johnny chimed in.

The boys started to head back toward the door to the overflow room as Tommy stood up and surveyed the room again. The boys were right. The wiring ran through a pipe at the back of the box and then up and disappeared into the wall. There was no room or way into the bank. He sighed and shined the light around again and again. Nothing. The bank was above them; ten feet separated them from the greatest score of their lives and there was nothing they could do. He shined the flashlight on the ceiling and sighed. "So close," he thought.

"C'mon, Tommy," Raymond was saying. Johnny had already disappeared from the room.

Tommy started walking toward Raymond, and as his flashlight passed from the ceiling to the wall, he saw a flash as if the light had reflected off of something. He stopped short and scanned the entire ceiling again. As he moved his light lower he noticed the source of flash.

"There's a vent," he said aloud and then louder, "There's a vent!" he shouted, shining a beam of light on a square vent located on about three feet from the ceiling.

"What's with the noise," Johnny said as he came back into the room and saw the two boys looking up at the ceiling.

"I'll be damned," he started. "Are we good Ray?" he asked.

"I don't know, ask Tommy."

Tommy's mind had instantly shaken off the disappointment and was working again. The vent was on the opposite side of where the vault room was supposed to be but he figured it had to double back. There was no doubt that it led to the bank. He would just need to see if it was large enough for them to get through.

"We need to get up there," he said, "and get a better look at the vent before I can answer that."

"How do we get up there? There's no ladder down here. What can we use?"

"What if you get up on my shoulders?" Johnny said from above as he jumped up on the crate.

"It isn't directly in line but if you lean over you could get a look," he said.

Tommy climbed up on the crate and then on Johnny's shoulders. He had to lean over and Johnny grumbled, "Hey, take it easy up there."

Tommy looked over and, using his hands to scramble along the wall, got to look into the vent. It was supported as far as he could tell and wide enough for someone to slip down. As far as he could see, it was possible for a person to slip down into the vent. The vent was held on by four screws that could easily be taken off. They could get in through the vent. Tommy tapped Johnny on the shoulders and climbed down.

"We're back in business," he said, smiling.

Johnny jumped up and down, slapping Tommy on the back. Raymond signed heavily and smiled. The three boys gathered themselves and headed back out of the tunnel. The job was still on.

CHAPTER

24

What If

RAYMOND TOSSED AND TURNED IN HIS BED. They were down to the last few days and, for Raymond, sleep was not an option. As much as he would hate to admit it, he was nervous. No, he was downright terrified! The vent had thrown him off. It was an unknown that he had no control over. He kept telling himself that Tommy would be able to get them through, but in reality there were too many what ifs.

As he tossed and turned, covered in sweat, he would try to go through the what ifs and thereby eliminate them but it wasn't working. He sat up in his soaked sheets and went to the window for some relief. It would have to be the hottest week of the year, he thought as he looked out on the street. He didn't see any movement. The air was thick and the street quiet. He could hear the sound of a fire hydrant running somewhere. He laughed at that. That was how it all had started, at the Johnny pump years ago. He sighed and sat at his desk. In his mind, there were two phases to the plan. His, Tommy, and Johnny's part, which he figured would be the more difficult to pull off. And Joey and Peter's. Joey and Peter seemed confident that they could create a commotion big enough to get a small riot going in the park. Small riot was the way Joey put it to Raymond when Peter wasn't around.

Raymond was hoping that the Pope's presence would bring every cop in the city to the park. In reality, even if it didn't and the guys never got off a firecracker, they probably would have enough time, but who knew what the response would be to knocking out the power to a whole building. That was the first what if. The second was how they were going to get in the tunnel. The subways would be jammed on Sunday with all the comings and goings due to the Pope. Could they get in the tunnel on time? If they got there early enough it shouldn't be a problem—Raymond rationalized. The real problem was the vent. What if it couldn't hold their weight? What if it narrowed and they hit a dead end? What if it was locked on the other side or if it didn't lead to the vault room? These were the real problems he had no answers for.

Tommy and Johnny were sure it was possible but he had his doubts, and in the past, he would never go for a job if he had doubts. He had debated this with himself over and over the past few days and was tempted to pull the plug on the whole thing. He knew Johnny would never go for it and Joey would be real upset. Peter would back him and maybe Tommy. He just didn't know. He sat at his desk with his hands in his head until the sky started to lighten and the street became more active. He heard his father get up and put the pot on for coffee and he dragged himself up and went to take a shower. It would be business as usual today. They were now down to three days and, of all of the boys, Raymond was in a position he had never been in his life. He was unsure of himself.

The day dragged on and as Raymond methodically went about his deliveries, a growing feeling of calm overcame him. They were smart and capable. He trusted his friends more than anyone else in the world. If something came up, they would have to solve it on the fly. The only real worry would be the time. Time was his enemy and there was no way he could deal with the time issue. He relaxed and suddenly felt exhausted. He was glad it was Friday. He would sleep well tonight and get ready for the final preparations on Saturday.

While Raymond was in the shower that Friday morning, Joey was sitting on his stoop waiting for Peter. He was already dripping sweat and not looking forward to another day in the sun. He smiled, though, realizing that they were only two days away from the job. He felt none of the anxiety that Raymond was feeling. The only real feeling he had was jealously. He wished he was the one going into the bank. The feeling went away as quickly as it had come.

He had resigned himself to the fact that he could not be in on that part of the plan weeks ago. He lit a cigarette and sighed, better off, he thought, I would probably end up in jail with my dad. Thoughts of his father made Joey angry and he stood up and paced up and down his block waiting for the familiar build of Peter to turn the corner. He realized he was full of nervous energy and began to breath slowly and deeply. The same thing he did before taking a big free throw in basketball. He needed to stay calm and get through the next few days. Everything would be different after Sunday, he thought and took another deep slow breath.

Tommy woke up early on Friday, showered, and was getting ready to head to the library. He needed to look up some things. Of all the boys, he was the one with the most pressure now. Tommy thrived on pressure. His whole life had been pressure. Most of the guys didn't know what it was like to not know if they were eating dinner that night or if they would be living on the street. He had stopped that from happening just recently with some of the money from the Chen job. He knew what real pressure was and knew how to deal with it. Tommy had spent the last few days dreaming. His what ifs were all the things he could do if they pulled off the job.

He could secure his family. He could secure his future and he could make his and his parents life better. This drove him not to fail and that was why he was up. Not because he couldn't sleep but because he didn't want to sleep. He needed to have everything ready for Sunday. He needed to be prepared because after Sunday he would have a different life.

Peter had been up since 5 a.m. He had volunteered to serve six o'clock mass and then would go and meet up with Joey to go to work. Peter loved being in the church early in the morning. He lit the candles and went through each row checking the missalettes. Peter was also nervous this Friday morning. He was worried about the morality of the situation. Causing a commotion in the park was bad enough, but when the Pope was there, it had to be a sin. He had rationalized the whole bank thing by vowing he would use the money only for good causes and that it would be used to help people who needed it.

This didn't make him feel much better but it was a start. Banks were insured. Regular people wouldn't lose any money and if this worked it might stop his friends from doing further crimes and that would be good. He signed and kneeled down and prayed. Father Bob called out from the back of the church.

"Everything okay, Peter?"

Peter smiled and replied, "Just praying for guidance."

"Well guide yourself back to the kitchen. I made some breakfast for us before the mass begins," he said and headed to the kitchen.

Peter looked up at the outstretched arms of St. Christopher.

"Protect us all," he prayed.

The he rose and went to eat with Father Bob.

For Johnny, there were no doubts. He was confident everything would work out. He went to bed at around midnight and slept like a baby until 10 a.m.

CHAPTER

25

Choices

THE BOYS ALL AGREED TO SLEEP OUT THE NIGHT BEFORE THE JOB.
The weather was so hot they decided to camp out on the roof of Manginni's building. This was nothing new. They had done this as kids for years. On hot summer nights, the boys got beach chairs and would camp out on the rooftop. In the neighborhood, a rooftop was known as tar beach. The hot tar took the place of the real beach and camping out on the rooftop was commonplace. After the sun went down, the roof would cool and as long as they stayed by the doorway, no one underneath them in the apartments would be disturbed by them.

It had been a tradition to bring up sandwiches, chips, drinks, and make it like a picnic. Urban camping—Tommy would call it and the boys would all laugh and make jokes about seeing wildlife like pigeons and roaches. They had beach towels as blankets but with the heat of the last week they were useless, so they rolled them up and used them as pillows. The usually playful atmosphere of their camping trips was replaced, however, tonight by restlessness and unusual bouts of quiet. They were all experiencing that feeling you get before a championship game or big test, an excited nervousness. An almost "can't-wait-to-get-started" feeling.

"We have the bags and the equipment stashed in the wine cellar," Johnny said to Raymond.

139

JAMES AND CARMINE CIOFFI

"Manginni has been through there four times the last week, so as far as he knows nothing has changed," Joey said.

"Yeah, he's going to the park tomorrow, too. I heard my father say half the building asked him to get them passes to the viewing area," Johnny said.

The sky was turning dark and the boys lit up their flashlights and cascaded out in their beach chairs, looking toward the darkening sky.

"Well, boys, by this time tomorrow we'll be counting the loot and celebrating," Joey said as he lit up a cigarette and passed it to Peter, who took it and, with one arm behind his head, took a deep drag and blew out the smoke to the amazement of all.

"What? I could get used to this," he chuckled and closed his eyes and stretched his legs out.

"Anyone have any doubts," Johnny asked. "You know, by this time tomorrow we could be on our way to Rikers or Sing-Sing," he said seriously.

That brought a silence to the rooftop and it lasted for a while until the darkness became complete and the light from the flashlights only lit a small circle in front of the boys. Their voices now seemed to come from the darkness.

"You know, I would have backed out if I had to go in the bank," Peter sighed. "Not because I'm scared but because I can't leave my mother and sisters. I'm the man of the family and it would break my mom if I had to go to jail. I trust you guys and I would do anything for anyone of you, but I couldn't leave my mom alone to protect my sisters. In a strange way, the only reason I'm doing this is to get them secured. I mean, my share will go to making sure they have options in life."

Peter was quiet, and with no response coming from the boys, the silence stretched painfully out.

"Speaking of shares, since it was my plan do I get like an extra twenty or something," Peter joked to break the silence.

The boys all laughed quietly and then Joey spoke.

"You know, I have no one to protect except you guys. My mom had dealt with being alone before and well, you know, with my dad being who and what he is I guess I have nothing to lose. This is the big one. The life changer. The moment in the game when you win or lose. That's how I see it. We win this one and it's all gravy from here on out. Our lives change and I don't need anyone after that. My dad can rot in jail forever for all I care. I won't need him and neither will my mom. She will be safe—you know—financially," Joey added quickly, not wanting to reveal any other dark secret about his father. "And we all become whatever we want. You guys go to college and we set up shop in the neighborhood and everyone comes out clean. Peter can quit his short criminal career. We all can if we want to."

The last part was surprising. Raymond wondered whom it was directed to. Johnny or was Joey talking about himself. The point was that they could stop stealing. After this they could change their lives.

"You know, I was petrified two days ago. I almost called the whole thing off," Raymond whispered to the darkness. "I know you guys would have talked me out of it, but it was close. For the first time since I was three I was scared. Not of going to jail, but of letting you guys down. I mean, if we fail and get out somehow, what do we do? I don't think I can go back to ripping off movie theaters or dry cleaners after this." Raymond paused and let that sink in for a minute. "I mean do you guys realize what we're about to do ... rob a bank. There I said it and it still sounds crazy."

Up until that moment, the bank had been referred to as the job or the thing. It had become like a superstitious thing for the boys they never said the word bank.

"This is big. Our whole lives can change tomorrow, for better or worse. You know it's weird, most people aren't conscious of the moments that change their lives but here we are."

He let that drift and float around the boys for a minute and then, realizing he might be making them nervous, he decided to say something positive but before he could Johnny jumped in.

"It's a job. We planned it. We're prepared; we're ready. It will work or it won't. You guys are making it out to be more than it is. What if we get caught? Well we're screwed, but you know what … we won't. We have this thing figured out and when we succeed we are the same five guys tomorrow night, only with a lot more money. You think Tommy and Raymond wouldn't have gone off to college if we had never attempted this? Peter, you will always take care of your mom and sisters. Money or not. Me and Joey, well, we're destined for my father's crew. So let's not make this anymore than it is. It's a job we're going to pull and let's leave it at that."

Johnny stopped talking, got up, stretched, and walked to the edge of the roof. He sat on the ledge and looked out over the neighborhood.

"You're right about one thing, Johnny. We are prepared and it is a job, but the guys are right. This is bigger than just a job. You guys know how much this means to me and I'm not worried but this will be big for us. This will be the day we look back on and say that was what made it all possible. Whatever we do in life from here on out, tomorrow's outcome will have some influence, good or bad," Tommy said.

Johnny walked back and laid down on his chair.

From the darkness, his voice sounding soft and barely audible he said, "I know, but its easier to take it moment by moment. I'll think about the future tomorrow night."

The silence stretched out again until Joey said, "You know, we really should invite some girls up here."

"Yeah, I agree," said Peter to the shock and laughter of all.

"You really are a bad influence on him, Joey," Raymond said.

"Me? You got him involved in a bank robbery and I'm the bad influence," Joey replied, laughing.

The boys all relaxed and the gentle teasing went on for hours until they eventually fell asleep in their chairs.

Raymond was up before dawn. The sky was getting lighter and the birds had started chirping. The smell of fresh baked rolls was drifting up from the bakery on the corner. Ray could see the racks of bread being cooled out on the street and hear the men loading the trucks with the fresh bread. He slipped on his sneakers and headed down to pick up some warm rolls with butter and coffee. He checked his watch. It was only 4:45 a.m. He went to the bakery and was greeted by Mr. Dinapoli.

"You up-a early today," he said in his broken English.

"I couldn't sleep," Raymond replied. "Can I get half a dozen buttered rolls for the family and some coffee?"

"Sure! That's-a nice, you bring breakfast for your father. He works a hard that one."

As Mr. Dinapoli got the rolls and the coffee together, Raymond stood and thought. His father did work hard and today he would be gambling everything. He could not imagine his father's reaction if today went bad and if it went like planned, Raymond wouldn't be able to help his parents for some time, probably years. He sighed and handed Mr. Dinapoli the money for the coffee.

"No charge today," he smiled at Raymond, refusing the money.

Raymond looked confused and asked why.

"Today is a special day. Everyone gonna remember today. The Holy Father, he-a come to New York. We all blessed today!" He laughed and shooed Raymond out of the store. "Hurry before the coffee, it get's-a cold." Raymond thanked Mr. Dinapoli and headed back to the roof and hoped Mr. Dinapoli was correct.

CHAPTER

26

The Park

"WE THOUGHT YOU SKIPPED TOWN BEFORE THE BIG GAME," JOEY COMMENTED AS RAYMOND CAME WALKING TOWARD THEM.

The roof had already been cleaned up. There were no traces that they had even been there.

"Where's Peter?" Raymond asked as he handed each a cup of coffee.

"He's putting the chairs away," Johnny replied as he gulped down the hot coffee.

Just then, Peter came through the door of the roof, "Those rolls smell good. You saving them for lunch or what?" he asked Raymond, who smiled and handed the bag to Peter.

The boys ate and drank in silence. Then, as they were lost in their own thoughts, Peter laughed out loud.

"What's so funny?" Joey asked.

Peter pointed to Raymond and Tommy, who were finishing up their rolls, "It's like the last supper up here," he grinned. "We should have taken a bottle of Manginni's wine to go with the bread."

"Boy, you sure are corrupted. Now you want to steal from a poor old man too," Joey shot back and they all laughed.

"Down to business, boys. Synchronize you watches," Johnny said to Peter, Joey, Tommy, and Raymond. "It's 5:30, let's get moving."

The plan called for Johnny, Raymond, and Tommy to get the bags from the wine cellar and head for the train station. With any luck, they could be in the auxiliary tunnel before the crowds started arriving at the train stations to head for the park. Joey and Peter had to get to the park early and set up chairs before their morning rounds. Joey had Peter to thank for that. He had volunteered them weeks earlier. Peter and Joey stood in front of Manginni's building waiting for the other boys to come out and bring the bags. They would all take the train together and then split up. Peter lit up a cigarette and Joey laughed.

"Look at you! Like you've been smoking for years," he said proudly.

"You think we got a shot," he asked Joey seriously.

Joey thought for a moment and said, "Would you want anyone else going in there today, Pete? I know I wouldn't. That gives us more than a shot. I think it's going to work." He smiled.

Just then, the boys appeared on the street carrying three large black equipment bags. The bags were stuffed with mostly old newspapers to give them the appearance of being full. There were also a few supplies the boys needed that they hadn't stashed in the tunnels. Two of the bags had baseball bats sticking out of them. The three boys wore red and blue baseball caps with the word Bisons written on them. To any on lookers, it looked like they were heading for a baseball game.

"A little early for ball," Joey laughed and snuffed out his cigarette under his shoe.

Johnny shot Joey a look. It had been his idea to dress like they were going to play ball.

"How we going to get on a train with bags of money?" he had said one night in the wine cellar.

"I never thought about that," Raymond said.

So that plan was to look like they were carrying the equipment with the hats and the bats. They could pass for a bunch of kids lugging all the equipment for a team.

"Well, it's an important game and we want to get there on time," Tommy said. "So let's get going."

The boys would take the 6 train and split up at 86th Street, with Peter and Joey going to the park and the rest of the boys switching to the 4 train down to Wall Street. If all went as planned, they would use the subway for their getaway. It was simple hop back on the train and then straight to the wine cellar. Joey had suggested they steal a car like an ambulance or something and just drive back. But that would involve parking and any other number of things like flat tires or getting in an accident or being pulled over. It was safer to use mass transit. Raymond had insisted. They walked to the train in silence. Raymond, lost in thought, looked at the blocks he had walked a million times as if he had never seen them before. The hydrant where they had first met, the playground where they had spent countless hours, it all somehow looked smaller, different. It would all be different after today. He hoped he would see these places again because there was a distinct possibility that he wouldn't. The boys paid the ten cents to get on the train and waited.

"Another hot one today," Peter said.

"Yeah, it smells great in those tunnels on hot days," Johnny said.

"I'm buying the biggest fucking fan in the world tomorrow," Joey said with a straight face and they all broke into a nervous laughter.

"What you think I'm kidding?!"

They all laughed and relaxed. The plan was set. All that was left was to do it. The nervousness was gone. It was like a big game. The anticipation is what gets you. Once the game starts its all business. That was what they were all feeling as they stepped onto the train.

Joey and Peter arrived at the park at 6:45. You could tell this was no ordinary day right away by the number of people already there. There were a bunch of other summer part-timers standing around, smiling and drinking coffee, but there were a number of big bosses

146

dressed up with white shirts and hats giving orders to the guys who were the everyday bosses.

"Jesus, every mucky muck in the city is here today." One of the guys said to Joey as they approached.

"Yeah, better smoke 'em while we can. They'll be breaking balls all day," he replied.

"Yeah, nothing worse than bosses who know nothing about what goes on but think they do," Joey laughed and, as if on cue, one of the guys in the white shirts came over and said as loud as he could.

"You boys button up those shirts and get over to the Great Lawn and start setting up the chairs."

Joey rolled his eyes and the boys slowly started moving off down the path. Peter grabbed his backpack, which included a sandwich, two packs of cigarette, two books of matches, and a half-a-dozen smoke bombs and eight cherry bombs.

As he walked away one of the bosses said, "What's with the backpack, kid?"

Joey froze and looked back at Peter, who calmly leaned in toward the boss with all of his bulky frame and said, "My lunch and a camera. My mom wanted me to try and get a picture."

"Yeah, I don't blame you, kid. I got my camera in the car. Unbelievable, huh, the Pope here in our park."

"I know, it's historic," Peter replied.

"Hope you get a good shot," he said as he walked away.

When Peter caught up to Joey he said, "I swear, if we pull this off it will be a miracle."

"Very cool under the pressure," Joey laughed and patted Peter on the back. "Let's get going."

The next hour was spent setting up chairs and cleaning up around the Great Lawn. Peter was amazed at how many people were already in the park. You needed passes to get on the Great Lawn and the police had set up barricades around the viewing area, but the area outside and around the chairs was open to anyone and it looked as if people had been camped out all night. By 8:00 a.m., the crowd around the Great Lawn was thick. Joey and Peter went on their first pass, with Lou slower than usual because of all the people. This worked out well, as the boys were busy planting the smoke bombs and cherry bombs under select cans.

"Come on, boys, look sharp today. There are about fifty big wigs walking around so let's actually do some work today."

Lou even got out of the car on three occasions and looked around and picked up a piece of paper or two. The planting of the explosives was easy. The boys had split up the armaments and as they changed the bags they would slip a smoke bomb or cherry bomb under the metal lip of the cans. They should be there later when the time came to set them off. As the day started to creep on toward the mass, the boys began to get a bit more nervous.

"There are a fucking million people here. How are we going to light these and not be seen?" Joey asked.

"I don't know. Let's hope the press of people goes toward the Great Lawn and all the focus is up there," he replied calmly.

He could see that Joey was getting nervous about he whole thing. Although he tried to be cool, Peter was also worried the park had become a zoo. The amount of people flowing into the park was unprecedented. The atmosphere was almost carnival-like. There were people with signs saying "Connecticut Loves The Pope." There were similar signs from a number of different states. Churches from around the tri-state area had run bus trips to the park and set up little camps.

Everywhere you looked there were little tents with people sitting outside eating and drinking. To Peter, it looked like a battlefield with each tent representing a different division. Everywhere you looked there were people. There were church choirs singing and children playing. The whole scene was surreal. To add to all the confusion, the boys were working like dogs. The amount of garbage piling up meant they had to change cans as they filled and leave the bags piled next to the cans until they could be picked up later. They had walked the route several times and had hardly had time to talk.

"This is nuts," Joey said as the sweat poured off his face.

"This is to our advantage; with all the bags around the cans we should have a little cover to do our thing," Peter added.

"Yeah, but the way the cans are filling up there are people near them constantly. We're going to have to be quick and keep moving. If we get spotted, we get spotted, there's no way around it."

"Yeah, I know and have you seen many cops?" Peter replied.

"No, they all seem to be around the Lawn and the barricades trying to keep people out. I thought our job was tough. I actually feel bad for those guys today in uniform and all," Joey laughed.

The boys looked around at the chaos. There were people everywhere and they were still flowing in.

"I don't know how many I can actually set off. With all these people moving around it will be difficult," Peter said.

"I was thinking the same thing. Look, if we get three and three it should do the trick," Joey replied.

Peter checked his watch. 10:45. He looked up at Joey. His face was serious.

"It's almost time."

"How long?" Joey asked not looking at his own watch.

"Half hour. We need to get into position," Peter said.

The Pope was to say mass at 12:00 noon. The boys hoped that all order would be restored by then and it would not interfere with the mass.

"Peter, we get caught it was all my idea. We go with the 'we were just celebrating the event' story. Right?"

"We won't get caught," Peter said in a calm and soft voice.

He then reached out and hugged Joey quickly and said, "Move fast but act natural. I'll see you at the meeting spot."

And with that he turned and walked away. Joey smiled and reached into his pocket, lit a cigarette and fought his way through the crowd toward his first garbage can. There was no turning back now

CHAPTER
27

The Tunnels

S URPRISINGLY THE TRAIN WAS EXTREMELY CROWDED FOR THE EARLY HOUR.

"This is a bad sign," Johnny said. "If it's this crowded already, it will only get worse later on."

"The glass is half filled," Tommy said. "This is good judging by this, the whole city will be in the park."

"Yeah, but how will that effect Joey and Peter?" Raymond asked.

"Good point but not our problem," Tommy added.

"Don't worry, Joey and Peter will do fine. Let's just hope we can get into the tunnel," Johnny added.

Their luck started to turn as the train emptied out after the next two stops.

"Looks like most people are headed to the park. It might be okay," Raymond said.

They sat in silence and waited as stop after stop went by. When they reached the Wall Street stop, their hearts sank. The station was packed. They got off, lugged the bags toward the bench at the end of the platform and waited. To their surprise, the downtown side of the platform was relatively empty. Everyone was on the other side waiting for the uptown trains.

"This is perfect. They will all clear out when the uptown train comes," Tommy said.

If only this was true. When the uptown train arrived, the mass of people surged forward but not everyone could get on the train. When the train pulled out, there was still a crowd on the other side, and as the boys sat there, more and more people flowed down into the station.

"We're never going to get down there," Johnny said.

"Look, we're going to have to make our move when the uptown train pulls in," Raymond said.

"I was thinking the same thing," Tommy agreed.

"It will be close. How much time do we have?" Johnny asked.

"Forty seconds," Raymond and Tommy replied in unison.

They both looked at each other and smiled. They had been timing the last few trains. Johnny shook his head.

"And I suppose you know when the next train is due?"

"Beats me," Raymond said.

"Two minutes and ten seconds," Tommy said, looking at his watch. "Get ready."

The boys stood up and hoisted the bags and looked down the track like they were waiting for the next train. The stairs that led down to the tracks were only fifteen feet away but they would have to move quickly and hope no one would notice. The rumble of the uptown train started to shake the platform.

"Here it comes," Tommy said.

As soon as the train started pulling in, the boys started moving as the breaks squealed to a stop. They were on the stairs and before the second tone of the closing doors went off, they were on the track and heading for the side tunnel.

"Wait here a few minutes," Raymond said. "If anyone saw us, there will be someone down here in a few minutes."

The boys waited in silence and darkness until the next train passed uptown and downtown.

"Let's go," Raymond said.

The boys quickly navigated through the auxiliary tunnels, having done this many times before. They were quickly into the unused tunnel and settled down to wait. The distant rumbling of the passing trains was constant.

"They must be moving the whole city uptown today," Tommy said. "That's good for us, right?"

"Yeah," Raymond replied. "Let's get suited up."

The boys went to one of the duffel bags and pulled out the boots and gloves. They stuffed some newspaper into the tips of the boots and headed into the side tunnel that sloped up to the sewer overfill room.

"The shoe idea was a good one, but going up the tunnel is murder," Johnny said.

"Hey, it was your idea," Tommy called back.

The heat over the last few weeks and lack of rain had made the tunnel a bit less slick. Still, the going was treacherous and as the roaring grew louder, Raymond slipped and would have gone down had Johnny not caught him from behind.

"That was a close one," he shouted over the noise of the rushing water, "thanks."

The boys reached the sewer runoff room and began to unpack.

Tommy said, "Johnny, give me the bolt cutters."

"What for? Did they lock the door to the electrical room?"

The door to the control room was unlocked and looked exactly as it had a few days ago.

"I got an idea. Just hand me the clippers," Tommy said.

Johnny pulled out the bulky bolt cutters and handed them over to Tommy. Tommy walked onto the grate with the water rushing under it. He scanned around and then said over the rushing water, "Here it is."

Raymond and Johnny slid next to Tommy and looked where he was pointing the bolt cutters. The grate had a door that could be pulled up and was locked with a padlock. Tommy, in one quick motion, snapped the top bar of the lock off. The rest of the lock and the cut piece disappeared into the rushing water. Tommy smiled and looked at his friends.

"We dump everything here. When we're done it all gets washed away."

To demonstrate, he went over to a bag and pulled out a handful of the old newspaper. He grunted as he lifted the grate, exposing a two-foot square that led directly to the rushing water. Tommy threw the paper into the water and in an instant it was washed away by the rushing flow of water.

Tommy smiled, "Anything we don't need when we go gets washed away. That way we don't have to carry the tools out or stash them in the tunnel where the cops can find them."

"Very cool," Johnny said as he dragged a bag over and proceeded to throw all the old newspaper into the water. Raymond looked at Tommy and just smiled. Tommy grinned back and then the both of them emptied the other two bags in silence.

The control room was noticeably quieter than the overflow room. The boys settled in and relaxed. The time was 10:25.

"We got almost an hour before the fireworks start," Raymond said, looking at his watch.

"Should we try loosening the screws on the grate so when it's time we can go quick?" Tommy asked.

"Patience, patience. We don't touch a thing until the power is out. No sense stirring up anything before the show in the park starts. Besides, we don't know if there are alarms on that grate or not," Johnny said.

He smiled and sat down on the crate they would use to access the grate.

"You sure look relaxed," Tommy said as he paced the room.

"I told you, it's just a job. It's like playing ball. Get too hyped up and you make mistakes. Relax, Tommy, it'll all be okay."

Raymond laughed but it was a nervous laugh for, even though Johnny appeared to truly be cool, Raymond was another story. He was really nervous. He had kept one last secret from his friends. The one secret that now that they were standing this close, he regretted not telling them. As the three boys stood there in silence, Raymond hoped that they would not have to pay for the one thing he hadn't told them.

CHAPTER

28

Panic in the Park

THE SCENE WAS UNREAL. The papers the next day wrote that they had not seen pandemonium like it since the end of World War II. Joey was on the move. He leaned against a tree some three hundred yards away from the Great Lawn. While he caught his breath and looked at the chaos around him, he recalled the last fifteen minutes. At exactly 11:15 a.m., the first smoke bombs had been lit on opposite sides of the Great Lawn. The smoke didn't attract much attention at first.

Joey had lit the smoke bomb under the first garbage can as discretely as he possibly could. The only real problem he had was actually finding the smoke bomb he had planted earlier that morning. There was so much garbage piled around the can that he had a hard time getting to the smoke bomb. He lit it and immediately started moving. As he walked toward the next drop spot, he listened for the sounds of screaming behind him and, to his surprise, heard none. He risked a glance back as he continued to walk, which was risky due to the hoards of people in the park.

He could see the smoke billowing up across the lawn but he couldn't tell if there was any commotion. He quickly arrived at the sewer where he was going to drop the first cherry bomb. He bent like he was tying his shoe and lit the cherry bomb that he had slipped into his pocket. He dropped it into the sewer and, in one motion, was on the move again. He had taken only two steps when he had heard it. BOOM!

It sounded like a crack of thunder. The difference was that the ground beneath his feet shook. The shock of the explosion froze him in his tracks, and even though he knew it was coming, he was still shocked. By the time Joey regained his senses and started moving again, he could hear the roar. People were screaming and running in all directions. Just as he started moving again, BOOM, the cherry bomb he had dropped in the sewer went off with such force that he was almost knocked to the ground. Amid the screams of panic he realized that the first explosion was the one Peter had set off.

As he regained his balance and looked around, people were rushing everywhere. He tried to keep moving but was being forced off the park path by the masses of people running away from the explosion and the smoke. He kept moving and actually missed the next smoke bomb can but was quick to light another cherry bomb and drop it into the sewer about a hundred yards away form the last one. As he bent down, he heard Peter's second blast. BOOM!

He didn't feel the ground shake as bad as the last one, but by the increase in the noise level he knew it had been as effective as the first. He lit his cherry bomb and started moving again. The screams were growing louder and now Joey could hear sirens. He kept moving, trying to look as if he was running with the crowd. By the look of the people around him, he knew they had caused more than a distraction. This was bordering on a full-scale riot.

He began yelling, "Calm down—it's nothing."

But his voice was drowned out by the screaming. As he moved through the crowd, he heard snippets of what people were saying.

"Someone is trying to kill the Pope."

Joey made his way to the last spot and heard Peter's last bomb go off. Peter had been pretty efficient, he thought. There were more sirens now. Joey could hear ambulances and fire trucks. The park had exploded in a riot of sound. Just as Joey bent to light his last cherry bomb, he heard a voice behind him say, "You alright, kid?" He turned to see a man in a suit with one hand on a walkie-talkie and the other holding his ear.

Joey said, "Yes. Just a little rattled."

"Good. You work for the Parks Department?" The man asked as he looked around.

"Yes. Summer help, sir," Joey said. "What's going on?"

"Just a prank. Some kids lighting off some fireworks. Probably thought it would be funny or something but this place is out of control. Round up whoever you can and head for the Lawn. They are going to need everyone they can to try and restore order over there."

"Okay, sir," Joey said and thanked the man and walked back toward the Great Lawn.

He slipped his hand in his pocket and as an old priest bumped into him he dropped the last cherry bomb on the ground and realized how lucky he had just been. The guy in the suit was undercover and had almost busted him. He leaned against a tree and caught his breath. His heart hammering in his chest. The park was in utter chaos. People were running everywhere. Joey thought to himself— What have we done?

While Joey was contemplating the chaos they had created, Peter was at the Great Lawn calming everyone. He had moved through the crowd calmly assuring everyone everything was okay. He had completed his run of smoke bombs and cherry bombs and had counted the number of explosions he had heard from Joey. When he didn't hear Joey's last bomb go off, he thought the worst but that was out of his hands now and all he could think to do was to try and help restore order to the situation he had created. The mayhem they had created was appalling to Peter and he felt a tremendous guilt for all he had done this day and decided to try and make it right.

In a booming voice he started screaming, "I work for the Parks Department. It was only fireworks. Everything is okay. Please calm down."

He repeated the phrase over and over as he walked back toward the Great Lawn, and to his amazement, people were listening. Peter was like a great ship passing through a sea of chaos and in his wake people calmed down. As effective as Peter was, the park was still a mess. There were fire engines rolling in. The cops were pouring in from everywhere; people were still panicking and it seemed like there would be no stopping any of it. As Peter approached the barrier where the chairs were set up, a cop grabbed his arm.

"Is that true?" he asked Peter.

"From what I heard it is. Why?"

"Why? You fucking kidding me, kid. This place is about to explode. We called every cop and fireman in the city down here to restore order and it doesn't look like we're making a dent. It'll take a miracle to get control of the park."

When Peter thought back on that moment, he would always say it was the closest he had ever been to hearing the voice of God. Almost as if on cue the speakers that had been set up around that Great Lawn boomed and the voice that come out of them was soothing and commanding at the same time.

"People of New York and of God. We come together today to celebrate the greatness of the Lord. Let us all pray."

Maybe it was the shock of the speakers or maybe it was the realization that the Holy Father had begun the mass but everyone stopped in their tracks and turned toward the stage that had been constructed and looked. The Pope went on.

"We are gathered here, O Lord, on this beautiful day in this city of God. All together as children of God."

The realization that it was the Pope speaking swept through the crowd in waves and the silence became a jubilant cheer. The cheering was contagious and, to Peter's amazement, the crowd that was just seconds ago out of control, now turned and cheered for the Pope, who was standing on the stage alone with his arms up greeting the crowd.

"I would ask that the servants of God please turn off the sirens so all can hear the word of God," the Pope said.

One by one, the fire engines and police cars turned off their sirens and a quiet seemed to descend on the park.

The Pope laughed and said, "That is better. Now let us pray."

The crowd erupted in cheers and, to his surprise, he and the policeman were cheering along with everyone else. Peter smiled and said a small prayer of thanks beyond his wildest expectations the Pope had saved the day and restored order.

Joey looked up when he heard the sound. From his vantage point he could see the Pope on the stage and see the waves on people turn and look toward him. The crowd, suddenly aware that the Pope was speaking, forgot all about anything else. The voice of the Pope overwhelmed any panic and everyone as far as Joey could see was settling in and looking toward the stage. When the sirens stopped, the park became eerily silent and then the Pope laughed, actually laughed, and began the mass. The place went crazy in a different way. They were jubilant. Joey laughed and looked around to see if he could spot Peter among the masses of people. Of course he couldn't, but he was so happy that he grabbed the nearest person and slapped him on the back.

"Amazing day, huh, pal."

"You could say that again," the man answered with a smile on his face.

Joey shook his head and, instead of heading for the Great Lawn, leaned against the tree and watched the mass. He and Peter had kept up their end and somehow it had all worked out. His smile quickly turned into a frown as he thought about the guys in the tunnel. They had the real tough job. He laughed in spite of his worries. It would all work out—he hoped.

CHAPTER
29

Showtime

T HE THREE BOYS WERE SWEATING FOR OBVIOUS REASONS; THEY COULDN'T CALM DOWN AND RESORTED TO NERVOUS MOVEMENTS AND PACING.

"What time is it?" Tommy asked for the fiftieth time.

"Two minutes later than the last time," Johnny cracked but he looked at his watch nonetheless. "We got five minutes."

Raymond smiled and stopped pacing. The last hour had crept by and the wait had seemed interminable. They had arrived in the tunnels at 10:25 with nothing left to do but wait. They had already unloaded whatever they would need to disconnect the power and get in the vent. It had been done in thirty seconds, which left them too much time to think and wait. They didn't talk much.

In the last hour, each boy had been keeping his own council. Raymond, for his part, was probably the most nervous. He tried to show a cool exterior but he noticed on a few occasions that his hands were shaking. He had set this all up and he didn't know if he could even pull it off. This was the moment they had been planning for. It had all gone smoothly so far and that was what worried Raymond. As he went over the plan for the millionth time in his head, he was snapped back to reality by the sound of Johnny's voice.

"Guess we got a full-scale riot in the park by now."

"Either that or they are both in jail already," Tommy said half jokingly.

Tommy was feeling the most pressure, even though the toughest part of his job had been getting them to this point, he felt that the tunnels and the vent were his responsibility. He couldn't control the park or the bank once they were inside, but that was it. He had to get them inside. Johnny shot him a terrible look.

"Don't say that. You want to put the *malocchio* on the whole thing!"

"The guys are fine. The park is crazy and," he paused to look at his watch, "it's time we got started."

Johnny was nervous but in a more excited way. He trusted the plan was going to work. The nervousness he felt was like Christmas morning. You knew there were going to be presents under the tree; you just couldn't wait to open them. With that, he smiled at Tommy, who was stunned by the outburst.

"Just trying to get you two to relax. You're making me nuts with the fidgeting and pacing."

Tommy relaxed for about a second and shook his head as if waking from sleep. He couldn't relax. A lot was riding on him and a lot was riding on this day. He could not mess up and he could not fail. It was too important for him.

"Help me get this crate over a bit," Johnny said to Raymond. "We need to pull this thing over directly under the vent so we can get up there easier," he said and motioned Raymond over to where he was standing.

"Tommy, you ready to cut the power? You know what you got to do?"

Tommy grabbed the drill and stepped up to the electrical box. Raymond and Johnny slid the crate over until it was directly under the vent. Johnny hopped on top of it and the top of his head was level with the bottom of the vent.

"Perfect." He jumped down and said, "Okay, boys. Show time!"

Tommy gave the drill a squeeze to make sure it was working and looked at Raymond. Their eyes met and Raymond gave him a slight nod. Tommy nodded back and unscrewed the bolt that held the door of the electrical box closed. He talked while he worked.

"Okay. These are the main switches. Once we throw the circuit breakers, the whole block will go out and the main power to the buildings will be cut off. Then I have about twenty seconds to unscrew the clamp holding the power cable and pull that right out."

"Why only twenty seconds?" Johnny asked.

"The circuit breakers will try to reset. They will snap back after twenty seconds. It's sort of a protection against a power surge or something. If the power goes out, the box tries to reset itself so you don't have to send a man out every time there is a power surge or power drain. Since we are throwing the switches ourselves we need to disconnect the main cable that is running into the box before it resets and I have to be quick. The main power is hot meaning it has electricity running through it. If any of the switches flip back before I disconnect the cable I could get electrocuted."

"Then be quick," Johnny said.

"Do it, Tommy," Ray said.

Tommy took a deep breath and said, "No turning back now."

He flipped switch after switch and the humming from the box gradually went silent. Above them, one by one, all the buildings on the block's power went out. Tommy quickly unscrewed the clamp that held the main power cable and yanked the cable out of the box. Johnny was surprised to see it actually looked like a giant plug. Tommy let the cable fall to his side and released a deep breath.

"Okay, the whole block should be down. Let's get to the vent."

"That's it?" Johnny asked.

"Yep" was Tommy's reply.

"Nice work, Tommy," Raymond said, looking at his watch. "It's 11:33. Let's get moving."

Johnny grabbed the drill from Tommy and quickly unscrewed the bottom screws of the vent.

"Boost me up," he said to Raymond, who kneeled down on the crate and placed his hands on the wall in front of him.

Johnny climbed on his shoulders, and as Raymond stood up, Johnny reached up and unscrewed the remaining screws he said, "Pass the chisel."

Tommy passed it to Raymond, then held it up to Johnny. There was a loud scraping sound as the vent popped loose and fell almost hitting Tommy and rattled onto the ground.

"Sorry," Johnny said as he scrambled off of Raymond's shoulders. "The thing just popped right out."

Tommy jumped onto the crate and now all three boys were standing on the crate.

"Okay, Tommy, you lead. Here's a flashlight. Johnny and I will carry the bags, remember we're heading for the vault room only," Raymond said.

"Vault room? I thought we were breaking into a coffee shop for a Danish," Johnny joked.

Raymond and Tommy did not find it amusing, but Raymond did note that while he and Tommy were covered in sweat, Johnny looked rather cool.

"You're really enjoying this," Raymond said.

Johnny shrugged and put his hands together to boost Tommy up and into the vent. The two boys watched Tommy disappear into the darkness about them. A few moments passed, then they heard his voice.

"It's tight, but I think its sturdy. It should hold all our weight. Come on up."

Johnny said, "After you."

And he boosted Raymond up into the vent. The vent was cramped. Raymond pulled himself in and saw that Tommy was about twelve feet along the tunnel. Raymond was suddenly struck by the fact that he couldn't turn around.

"Tommy," he called, "how are we going to get Johnny in here?"

"Figure it out, Ray. I'm working on another problem."

Raymond was worried. He glanced down at his watch. 11:37. Thinking quickly, he called back.

"Johnny, throw the bags up and in. I can't turn around in here."

Johnny said, "Okay, here comes bag one."

He proceeded to throw each bag up and into the vent. Raymond had slid down a few feet, and when he felt the bag hit his foot, he half-turned and reached behind himself. The position was awkward to hold but he could grab the bags and pull them in front of his body and slide them along that way. Johnny called to Raymond from the control room.

"Ray, stay clear of the front of the vent."

He heard a muffled bang and the walls vibrated around him and then moments later, he heard Johnny grunting and gasping behind him at the entrance of the vent. Somehow, Johnny had made it into the vent as he pulled himself up.

Raymond half-turned and asked, "How the hell did you get up here?"

"I ... used ... the ... hammer to chip the wall and used it as a foothold. Once I got my hands into the vent I pulled myself up," Johnny replied, catching his breath. "Hopefully, I won't have to do that again."

Raymond was suddenly struck by the thought. How would they get up to the vent from the vault room and, for that matter, what was the problem Tommy was having up ahead?

Raymond wiped the sweat away from his forehead and slid down the vent to the back of Tommy's boots. He could see the problem now. The vent split into to different directions.

"C'mon, Tommy. Let's get moving," Raymond said, glancing at his watch again.

It was 11:40.

"Ray, I was never in the bank. I'm not sure which way to go," he said.

"Who gives a shit! Pick a direction! They both have to lead to the bank. Once we get in we go for the vault," Johnny said.

"It's not that simple; we need to be in the vault room. There might be cameras on the doors of the vault room and even in the front of the bank where the tellers work.

"I thought we knocked out the power to the building. Everything should be dead in there," Johnny said.

"We did but I don't want to take any chances," Raymond replied. "We have to make sure we are in the vault room. Whatever you do, Tommy, make it quick. The clock's ticking."

Tommy frowned and said, "Okay. Let's try."

The boys grunted and scraped their way down the right fork in the vent and within twenty feet, Tommy stopped and his heart sank into his stomach. It was a dead end. The vent he was staring at continued onward but at an increasingly smaller rate. He could have gone maybe ten more feet until he would be stuck.

"Go back, Johnny," Raymond said irritably, "and step on it."

He started to crawl back as quickly as he could but the going was slow. Raymond glanced down at his watch. 11:47. It had been about twenty minutes that they were in the vent. Raymond was starting to doubt the whole plan.

He kept muttering, "Too much time, too much time."

Tommy overheard him and said, "Relax, Ray. I don't hear any sirens or alarms. We should be okay."

They had made it back to where they started and the boys started down the left tunnel. The air was thick and it was getting increasingly hotter.

"I'm melting in here," Johnny said.

The going seemed to be taking forever. Raymond glanced down at his watch again and a real feeling of panic overcame him. He was not paying attention and slammed his nose into the back of Tommy's heel.

"Ow," he cried angrily. "What, another dead end?"

Tommy laughed and said, "Tell Johnny to pass me the mallet."

"Why," Raymond asked with the hope evident in his voice.

"Cause we just hit the jackpot," he answered and though no one could see him, he was grinning from ear to ear.

Bang … Bang … Bang!! The vent was knocked loose and clattered onto the floor with a loud crash. Tommy managed to get to his knees and twist himself just enough to get his legs out of the vent. He then eased himself out and hung from the bottom of the vent and dropped himself down the three feet to the marble floor of the vault room.

"Throw the bags down," he shouted up and immediately the bags came flying out of the hole three feet above him.

Raymond emerged out of the gap and awkwardly dropped down to the floor. He landed awkwardly and ended up on his back. Tommy hurried over and picked him up. Johnny came next and this time Tommy stood under the vent to catch Johnny's legs as they hung down. When all three boys were safely on the ground, they turned together and surveyed the room they were in.

"Isn't that beautiful?" Johnny said as he stared at the massive vault door.

The door was made of black wrought iron and was quite impressive. Johnny slowly took the five steps over toward the great black and silver door and ran his hands over the wheel like handles. He couldn't believe what he was seeing. He wanted to jump up and down and scream. They had done it. This whole crazy plan had worked. They were standing in front of a massive safe stuffed with money, he thought. He was stunned.

He ran his gloved hand over metal and wished he could take off the gloves and feel the metal. He wanted to remember every detail of this. He just stood there with both hands on the door, lost in his own thoughts. Meanwhile, Raymond was looking at the vent. It would be tough getting back up into it as there was no furniture in the room. He quickly scanned the room. It was narrow and there was a door that led to the main room of the bank where the offices and tellers were. The vault room was off to the side somewhat behind where the row of tellers would be. There was a small corridor that led to the vault room and once inside there was nothing but the massive vault.

The bank was designed so that customers could just see the vault room. It was a good trick. You could get a peak of the vault while waiting on line. He thought of how many people had stood on that line and dreamed of breaking into the vault. Here he stood with his friends, three kids about to do what millions of people had probably thought of doing. He looked down at his watch. 11:57. He sighed and relaxed, a smile breaking out over his face. It had been tough but they had made it. Raymond was about to walk over to the vault where Johnny was standing. When he glanced at a frozen Tommy.

Tommy said, "Hey, guys, do you see those red flashing lights?"

Raymond looked over to where Tommy was pointing and at first thought it was a cop car parked outside the bank. His moment of elation rushed away and for a second, he thought all was lost. There was a flashing light reflecting off the glass windows to the vault room. Ray instinctively pulled Tommy down into a crouch, then he realized the flashing was coming from behind the teller's desk.

"I think we tripped an alarm somehow," Tommy said, looking around nervously.

"They must have backup generators or some other system hardwired in that doesn't run off the main power."

"We are in trouble, boys. Somebody must pick up this alarm. Ray, how long has it been since we turned off the power?"

"Almost a half hour," he said and glanced down at his watch. 11:59.

"Ray, that is more than enough time for them to send someone out here to check the alarm."

"I know, Tommy," Ray said. "Someone could be showing up any second."

His mind was racing.

"Yeah, that's the least of our problems," Johnny said angrily, walking towards the two boys.

"The fucking vault is locked!"

CHAPTER

30

Alarms

OFFICER SHEA WAS EXPECTING A QUIET DAY THE MORNING OF THE POPE'S VISIT. He had clocked in at 8:00 a.m. and now that it was 10:20, he was settling down to his second mug of coffee and the morning paper. The day had gone smoothly. So far, most of the morning units were already assigned to the park and had left the precinct by 9:00 a.m. The few patrol cars they had out were already doing their rounds and the desk was quiet. They had one kid in the holding tank. A drunken teenager arrested for public urination the night before who was waiting on his parents to arrive and pick him up.

Officer Shea looked at the big clock on the wall and sighed. He sat back in his chair and flipped to the sports section of the paper. He hadn't gotten through a paragraph when all the phones exploded at once. Officer Shea jumped up and looked around. The desk sergeant already had one phone to his ear and was reaching for another when a rookie officer came running up the stairs with a look of panic on his face. Officer Shea put down his coffee and thought, so much for a quiet morning. Ignoring the phones ringing all around him, he snapped at the rookie, "What the hell is going on, Timmy?"

"Sir, the captain called in on the radio. He needs to talk to you immediately."

Officer Shea grumbled and looked down at his radio. He had turned it down earlier and knew he was in for a first-class chewing out. He quickly picked up the radio and barked to the rookie.

"Get on those phones and make sure you get only pertinent information."

He then took a deep breath and turned up his radio.

"Where the hell is the backup?" he heard the captain's voice, which sounded terrified.

"Captain this is Shea. What's up?"

There was a pause and then the radio exploded in officer Shea's hand.

"What? Are you kidding me? The Pope is being attacked. The park is a mob scene and we need every available unit up here to get this situation under control."

Officer Shea could hear the panic in the captain's voice. Something he had only heard on a few occasions and knew this was serious.

"Okay, Cap. Hang tough. I will get every mobile unit there and have them pick up all foot patrols on the way. Do you need SWAT and Mounted also?"

"We're way ahead of you. We already have them on the way with fire and EMS. I just need more men down here ASAP."

"I have five rookies and a desk sergeant here. We're running light today. I could spare the rooks and me and Hanly could handle the house," Officer Shea responded.

"No keep the rooks there. Man the phones. No one goes out unless it's a real emergency. It will be a zoo over there with people calling any minute. Just get me the men who are already out on the street. Tell them to converge on the Great Lawn and await instructions."

"You got it, Cap, be safe down there," Shea said and waved Hanly over. "Get all the units down to the park. Have them pick up all foot posts and head to the Great Lawn. I'll have the rooks man the phones. Nobody goes out without my say so, Cap's orders. Got it?"

"Yeah, no problem, Mike. What's going on down there?"

"I don't know, but it sounds like World War III, and Cap sounds nervous, which means it can't be good. Get the units down there and I'll start with the phones. Keep me posted on their progress."

With that Officer Shea started to pick up the phones. There were reports of shots being fired in the park, two bombs going off, to someone calling to report his tickets stolen for the Papal mass. Whatever was going on down there must have been a mess. So many different reports could only mean one thing ... No one had a clue what the hell was going on.

The hottest summer on record was no picnic for Con-Ed. There had been intermittent blackouts and brownouts all weeklong and crews had been working double-time all whatever it is on our initial just trying to keep service to everyone. The main plant located by the East River was usually pretty empty on Sunday. Today it was even extra empty. The Pope's visit had a lot of people excited and the work crews that would have been in on Sunday had been cut to keep a few crews down at the Great Lawn to make sure everything would go smoothly. As it was, Goldstein only had three crews at his disposal for emergencies. Of the three crews, two had gone out already. They were sent to the Upper East Side, where a transformer had blown and knocked out a building in Harlem. The other was down at the Brooklyn Battery Tunnel, where they were having trouble with two traffic lights that kept intermittently going out and popping back.

Goldstein rubbed his bald head, "This Pope is screwing the whole city today," he said. "I can't get a foot patrol cop to work the light because they are all in the park."

"That tunnel must be a mess with the lights going on and off," his co-worker, David, replied. "Everything else looks pretty quiet. Once the guys finish down there I'm going to tell them to take lunch while they can," David said.

"Yeah. No problem," Goldstein replied as he flipped through the radio dials looking for some oldies music.

10-10 WINS Breaking News … Attack on the Pope

He heard and flipped back to the station.
"David you hearing this," he asked.

> This is Ross Simmons live from the Great Lawn where moments ago shots rang out and a minor explosion has created havoc and bedlam in the park—As this is a scene of mass confusion.

"Wow, that's unbelievable," David said.

Goldstein just shrugged and changed the channel. He could care less.

"Just means more traffic for when we get out of here today," he said.

Just then two alarms went off on the main board.

"Oh great," Goldstein said.

The first was an apartment building on Lexington Avenue. The second was a whole block down in the Wall Street area.

Goldstein quickly looked up both locations and said, "Get Thompson and Kramer on the Lexington alarm."

"But the other alarm is a whole block," David asked questioningly.

"Yeah and non residential. In about three minutes, everyone on Lexington will be calling about the power. There ain't no one down on Wall Street today. Tell Terry's crew they can get down there when they finish the Harlem thing."

"That could take hours with the traffic," David said. "As long as no one is complaining—who cares?"

"Shea … Hey, Shea?"

Officer Shea looked up from the desk. He had one phone in his hand and one phone off the hook on the desk he was writing something down and waved the rookie off.

"So you have an ID on the bomber," he was saying as he wrote. "Go on. What did he look like? Okay, tall, long beard and he was carrying a big black suitcase."

The rookie grinned and Shea rolled his eyes.

"Thanks. We'll check it out. That's the twentieth eyewitness and no two have the same description," he said exasperated.

The rookie waited patiently.

"What you got, Timmy?" he said, wiping the sweat off his forehead.

"Bank alarm down on Wall Street," he said.

Shea thought for a minute and then said, "Call Con-Ed. Check for any power outages. These alarms have been going off all week. If there aren't any outages get back to me. If there are, write down the location and throw it on the pile."

Timmy turned and Shea went back to answering phones.

About ten minutes later he was back, "Looks like you were right. Con-Ed says they have a whole block down that triggered the alarm. They said since it was a non-residential we should send someone down there. They have all their crews out and probably won't get to it for a few hours."

"Yeah, have they turned on the radio today? Why don't we just grab a few circuits and head down town and change a light bulb while they blow up half of Central Park? Throw it on the pile. We'll check it later." He laughed and went back to manning the phones.

31

The Last Secret

"RAY ... RAY ... ARE YOU LISTENING TO ME? That alarm could mean we don't have that much time. I really think we should get out of here. We could go out the front, but with the alarm still on maybe they have a camera or something."

Tommy's voice was beginning to sound frantic at the same time Johnny was walking toward them muttering.

"What the hell is going on? I thought if we turned off the power the safe would unlock. We crawled through that tube and planned for months and the thing is locked. There is no way, Ray, I'm leaving this bank without money. I'm going to the front and taking whatever I can," he screamed.

Tommy heard him and positioned himself between the door and Johnny.

"Johnny, you can't go up front; there may be a camera or you may trip another alarm. We have to get out of here," he said and placed his hands on Johnny to stop him from exiting the vault room.

"Get off of me," Johnny said menacingly.

"Johnny, I know what I'm talking about. We can't get caught in here. We have to get out. Ask Ray," he said pleadingly.

Tommy looked into Johnny's eyes and dropped his hands slowly.

"This can't go down like this," Johnny said with his fists balled. He was on the verge of exploding. He realized Tommy was right and desperately and reluctantly asked, "Tommy, there has to be a way. Come on, you're smart. Figure this one out."

"Johnny, the only thing we can do is get out of here before this place is over run by cops. See that alarm signal," Tommy said, pointing through the glass, "it must tip off someone. We gotta go," he whispered urgently. "I'm sorry, it's the only way."

They both turned to Ray simultaneously and to their surprise, he was smiling from ear to ear.

"Snap out of it, Ray, we have to get out of here," Tommy said.

"No we don't," Raymond said flatly, still smiling and looking at his watch.

"But the alarm," Tommy protested.

"Went off a half hour ago," Ray finished for him. "The nearest police station is about twelve blocks from here. Think about it, even if a cop had walked out of the station when the alarm went off, he could have been here in ten minutes. You hear any sirens? You see any Con-Ed trucks? I agree that alarm goes somewhere but no one is in a hurry to get here or they would have been here already, Tommy. Think about it for a second."

Tommy looked at Raymond, dumbstruck. He took a second and thought about what Ray had just said and realized he was right.

"So how long do we have?" he asked, visibly calming down but still glancing out the glass window expecting to see something.

"I figure we will be out of here in about ten minutes," Ray replied calmly.

That was it for Johnny. He exploded, "Okay, Einstein, so we have ten minutes. Let's get out there and check the draws for some money."

"We can't," Raymond said.

It was as if Johnny had gotten slapped.

"Tommy was right. There may be more alarms and a second alarm will definitely send up a red flag," Raymond said.

"What the fuck?! We are in a bank and we can't get any money? So what, you're happy that we were able to pull it off? That satisfies you? Is that why you have the big grin? You think this is funny or something? You come up with this brilliant idea, we all buy in and put the time and effort and come away with nothing?! This is bullshit!"

Johnny was ranting and shaking from frustration. He went to the vault door and gave it a pull. Then he turned and looked at Ray. Ray just smiled some more, which drove Johnny crazier.

"Yeah, great plan. We got nothing genius, unless you have some magic secret fucking password that will open the vault door."

Raymond looked up from his watch and looked Johnny right in the eye and started counting down from three. "Three, two, one … open sesame."

He smiled as the bank vault silently swung open.

Johnny's jaw snapped shut. He was speechless. The vault now was open a crack. He shook his head in disbelief and looked at Tommy.

Tommy just exhaled and said, "Don't look at me. I have no clue but that was the coolest thing I've ever seen."

"How, Ray? How?" Johnny asked but Raymond was already on the move.

"I'll explain while we work," he said and went over to the grate and grabbed the three bags.

"Pull that door open, Johnny," Raymond said.

As he hit Tommy on the shoulder to get him moving, Johnny reached out toward the door, tentatively almost afraid that if he touched it, it would close again. He grabbed the metal and pulled outward. The door swung open silently and Johnny fittingly was the first to step into the vault. He called over his shoulder. His voice was back to its calm and cool self.

"Hey, Tommy, you may have to change your mind. I admit I have no idea how Ray did that, but I guarantee this is the coolest thing you will ever see!"

Tommy and Raymond stepped into the vault and stood shoulder to shoulder with Johnny.

Tommy whistled quietly and said, "Ray, did you know it would look like this?"

It was Raymond who was stunned to silence this time. He had a hard time registering what he was seeing.

The vault was smaller than he expected. The far wall was covered with safety deposit boxes with numbers running from 1 to 350. It reminded Raymond of the mailboxes in some of the high-rise buildings you see downtown. There was a rolling ladder. Probably used to reach the higher safe deposit boxes pushed up against the row of boxes labeled from 100 to 135. The walls had a thick secure look to them that almost made the room seem claustrophobic. The ceiling was low, maybe eight feet high and the inside of the vault door had the massive locking mechanism. There was a table running the length of the left wall and there were larger boxes lining the right wall with another table and two chairs. Raymond figured that was where they kept the bank's cash and sorted out the money that they would use daily.

The most startling feature of the vault, however, was in the center of the room: There lying in the middle of the floor were three huge pallets of money neatly wrapped in cellophane. As far as Raymond could tell they were all hundreds stacked in neat piles. The pallets were three feet high and about five feet across. Raymond could not even begin to calculate how much money was there but it was a lot more than he had expected.

"Have you ever seen anything like this?" Johnny asked.

"Never," Tommy replied.

Raymond stared at it. He realized he was holding his breath and finally let out a huge gasp of air.

Johnny laughed, "Yeah, some sight, huh. Did you ever imagine there could even be so much money?" Johnny said, nudging Raymond with his shoulder. "Let's get to work!"

Johnny laughed again and took out a pocketknife and proceeded to cut his way into the first pallet.

Raymond snapped out of his trance and said, "Guys, we have to move quickly. We only have eight minutes," he said, looking at his watch, and as he spoke, he took out his own knife and cut the second pallet, motioning Tommy to do the same.

"What's the rush? You worried about the alarm," Tommy asked as he cut open the third pallet.

"Yes, but that's not the real reason I'm worried," Raymond said as he reached across his body and opened the black bag.

"This door is going to close in seven minutes and we need to be clear of the vault."

Tommy paused for a second and looked at Raymond.

"A time lock," he said, shaking his head, "now it makes sense." He smiled at Raymond, who was already stuffing neatly wrapped stacks of cash into the bag.

"What the hell is a time lock?" Johnny asked.

Raymond explained that the first day he had discovered the plans he had seen the little notation on the bottom of the plans that read "12-12-15 a.m. and p.m." and "recalibrate after the main box is replaced." Raymond had figured out that the vault ran on a time lock and that during the final days before the construction was to be finished the code on the bottom referred to the times the vault time codes would be set. Johnny paused and looked up at Raymond.

"And if you were wrong about the code?" he asked.

Raymond shrugged, "Hey, I took an educated guess," he laughed nervously.

"Well, you got some pair," Johnny said evenly as he went back to stuffing his bag.

The boys worked quickly and were soon sweating. Every once in a while, Johnny would lift up the bag to see if he could carry it.

"It's going to be tough getting these things out of here," he said.

"I know," Tommy grunted as he tested the weight of his bag.

"Okay, boys, two minutes," Raymond said unexpectedly.

"What do you mean two minutes?" Johnny said as he continued to stuff his bag with a bit more urgency.

"We got to go in one minute and thirty seconds," Raymond said as he stood up and shook out his arms, which were hurting from the packing of the bag.

He zipped up the bag and looked over at Tommy, who was stretching out his back. His bag was already zipped.

Johnny said, "What are you two doing? You still have room in those bags open them up and fill them until they're full."

"Johnny, we have to go now," Raymond said. "The vault will lock whether we're done or not and if it locks with you in, it stays locked until midnight tonight."

"Come and get me later. We can clean this place out bring the two bags out and come back later and get the rest," he said as he continued to stuff money in his bag.

"Johnny, now," Tommy yelled.

"Okay. Okay. I was only kidding," he said and quickly hefted he bag over his shoulders and walked out of the vault.

The boys waited outside the vault and Raymond stared at his watch.

"Man, just look at that. Isn't it beautiful," Johnny said wistfully.

Two of the three pallets of money were reduced in half. Johnny's was almost three-quarters gone, but there was still a lot of money in the vault. The boys stood and silently watched as Raymond whispered the countdown.

Five ... four ... three ... two ... one ... and the door silently swung back closed and after a series of clicks and gearshifts went silent. The boys stood facing the massive steel door for a few seconds and then, as if realizing what they were doing, Tommy quickly turned and looked back out of the vault room window toward the front of the bank. The alarm was still flashing.

"Hey, guys, we're not out yet. Let's go."

They headed for the vent groaning under the weight of the bags. Johnny grabbed Raymond by the shoulder, looked at him in the eye and just nodded to him. Then a smile broke out across his face and Raymond grinned back. It was Johnny's way of saying good job.

"Let get out of here," Raymond said.

32

Back To The Neighborhood

"HOLY SHIT," TOMMY SAID AS HE STOOD IN FRONT OF THE VENT THAT LED BACK TO THE TRAIN TUNNEL. The moment between Raymond and Johnny was broken as they both looked at their friend. Raymond could see the problem immediately. It took Johnny to verbalize it.

"How are we going to get up there?" he said.

"No idea," Raymond said, looking around the vault room.

Tommy was staring up at the vent, which was about five feet over their heads. Coming out of the vent was easy, getting back up to it was now the problem.

"Whatever you are going to do we have to do it quickly, Tommy. That light is still flashing and eventually someone will come to check it out," Raymond said. "I don't...I mean, is there anything we can use to boost ourselves up there," he asked.

Johnny laughed, "We have three giant bags of money if we stack them up and I climb on top of them I could boost Tommy up. Tommy gets in the vent and we pass the bags to him. He drags the money into the tunnel, then I boost Ray in and then he hangs down and pulls me up."

Tommy looked at Johnny and said nothing.

"What? I'm not a complete idiot. I'm surprised you two geniuses didn't have that planned out already."

He grabbed his bag and placed it under the vent and then stacked Tommy's and finally Ray's. It worked like a charm. Once Tommy was in the vent, Ray and Johnny passed him the bags with a bunch of grunting and sweating. The bags disappeared one by one into the hole. Tommy would drag the bag down to where the vent split and come back for the next one.

After the three bags were in, he called out, "Okay. Let's go."

Johnny boosted Ray up into the vent and Tommy pulled him in. After they slid down and turned around, Ray hung down out of the vent with Tommy holding his legs. Johnny jumped up and was pulled into the vent.

Once they were all in, Johnny said, "One last thing to do."

He turned back and headed for the opening of the vent. He had left a ball of string near the entrance and now pulled the string. The vent cover, which he had placed on the floor near the opening, rose up and Johnny grabbed it and re-secured it in place. To anyone coming into the bank, it would look like no one had ever been there.

The boys silently navigated out of the vent and back to the control room in the sewer.

"The vent cover is in place," Johnny said, panting from the effort of dragging himself and the bags through the vent.

Tommy said, "Let's turn the power back on."

He went to the main power switch and reattached the cable and flipped all the breakers. The box began to hum and Tommy knew the power had been restored.

"Okay. Now gloves, shoes, and any tools into the sewer," Johnny said, leaving the control room and going over to the grate and lifting it up.

Tommy and Raymond followed and they all threw all evidence into the rushing water. The boys picked up the bags and started down the tunnel toward the abandoned train station. In fifteen minutes, they were on the empty train platform. It was 12:50 and they had just robbed a bank.

The uptown train pulled in and the boys got on the train and sat down. The old man on the train looked up from his paper. He saw three sweaty boys in baseball caps carrying equipment bags with bats sticking out of them. To him, it looked as if they had just finished a game and were heading home. He looked back at his paper and paid them no mind.

The boys sat in silence on the ride home. They were physically and mentally drained. The job was over, they were out and the tension of the last few days and hours combined with the swaying train put them in a relaxed state. Raymond looked at his friends and smiled. He was relieved.

The last few days had been torture, and even though he knew they were not totally out of the woods, they could still somehow get caught, he pushed that thought out of his mind for now. He allowed himself to fantasize about how this would change his life. He had no idea how much money they had, but it would be enough for him to choose any college he wanted and that was the real prize. He could tell his parents he had gotten a scholarship or some hardship deal or even say Johnny's father was helping out. His parents would be so happy he was going to college they would buy anything he told them. After school, he could get a job and then maybe help them out. He saw firsthand how hard his parents worked. It would be good to be able to help them out. This was the break he needed. He thought about how many people were as smart as him, but without that one break they never amount to anything. He had decided long ago he would never wait for that break. He would make it for himself and now he had done it.

He looked up at his friends. They were lost in their own thoughts. He wondered about Joey and Peter. He hoped they had gotten out of the park and everything had gone smoothly. He looked down at the black bag at his feet and couldn't help but grin. He pulled down his baseball cap over his eyes and slumped down into his seat. His whole body relaxed. His future tucked safely under his legs.

Tommy looked at Raymond. He looked like he was sleeping. Tommy could understand, he felt as if he had played five baseball games and walked ten miles after that. He was drained. He thought he would be elated but he wasn't. There had been that moment when the boys high-fived when the train had pulled into the station but for the most part they were pretty subdued.

Tommy figured Ray and Johnny must feel as exhausted as he felt. They would celebrate later when they counted the money. He looked down at the bag at his feet for the hundredth time and kicked it a little just to make sure it was full. He shook his head and recapped the events of the last hour.

He liked to replay special moments in his head. It helped him remember them. As he replayed the problem in the vent and the vault door opening, his mind wandered to other thoughts. His parents arguing over how they were going to pay for the rent after his mother had bought him a birthday present when he was seven and couldn't afford it. The times his father would not eat dinner. He would jokingly say how bad his mother's cooking was or say how he had had a big lunch. But Tommy knew there wasn't enough food for the three of them and he was sacrificing his portion. The countless nights his father sat up and paced the floor wondering how he was going to make ends meet. The look on his father's face when he could only give him a nickel to go to school or when he didn't have a present for him on a birthday.

Tommy knew it killed his father every time. It killed his mother too. Tommy remembered those moments. He had used them his whole life. He had used them in the school, in the playground, even in the tunnels. He knew this was his shot. College had been a dream and now it would be a reality. He would make it all right for his parents. They would never be poor again. He would become an architect. He would build his parents a house that everyone would admire. They would never feel like they had nothing again.

He had sworn this his whole life but now, for the first time, the road would be a little easier. He would ask guys to let him give his parents a little money until he was out of school and on his way. He kicked the bag again a little harder this time. His exhaustion had unleashed some pent up emotions. He breathed deeply, calming himself down. He would never be poor he had always sworn, and today was the first day in his life that he wasn't.

Johnny tried his best to stay relaxed. In all honesty, he was exhausted like his friends, but he was dying to open the bags and count the money. Ray and Tommy were deep in thought so he kept quiet during the ride back to the neighborhood. He tried to figure out how much money could be in the bags. The stacks they loaded into the bags were in hundreds. He figured there had to be at least $800,000 in the bags and that was a low estimate. Eight-hundred grand, he thought as his mind reeled. Even his father had never had a score like this. He thought about how they would be legends in the neighborhood.

Then he laughed. No one would ever know. Hell, they probably couldn't even touch the money for years. I mean a couple of hundred here or there, but the bulk of the money would have to be hidden somewhere. They couldn't hide it in the wine cellar. Manginni would find it. This was a problem they had never thought about. Johnny laughed to himself; they had never discussed what they would do if they were successful. They had no plan for that. Wait, how I'm going to break Ray's balls over that one, he thought. He looked at Ray and Tommy. With two guys like that, I could run the neighborhood, he thought. And with the bankroll I will have behind me I could run the whole city, maybe be *capo da capo*. Boss of bosses. He smiled. He liked the sound of that!

"They should have been here by now," Peter said as he got up off the stoop and looked up and down the street for the thousandth time in the last half hour. He was still in his parks department orange jumpsuit. He had pulled the top half down and tied it around his waist. His white t-shirt was drenched in sweat and streaked with dirt.

Joey took a drag from his cigarette and said, "Look, relax. According to my calculations, they shouldn't be back for a half hour or so. Here, have a smoke. It'll relax you," he said, holding out a cigarette to Peter.

Peter lit the cigarette and looked down at Joey, who was lounging on the stoop. He had his legs stretched out and crossed at the ankles, his elbows on the top step.

"Can you believe the day we had?" Joey said, shaking his head. "Even in my wildest imagination I couldn't have pictured it any better."

"We're lucky no one got hurt," Peter said. They had had this conversation about ten times already but Joey couldn't let it go. The boys had met back at the main park house after the mass. With all the police activity and the second cleanup crew arriving, they had no problem getting off work. The bosses were too busy with the regular workers to worry about the summer help. They were dismissed and headed home. On the train ride home, they had told each other their version of the riot and where they were when the Pope restored order.

"Got to admit it," Joey said, "the Pope is one cool customer. I mean, all that chaos and he gets up and settles it right down. That really was impressive."

"I still can't believe no one got hurt," Peter repeated.

"Hey, relax, Pete, it all worked out. No one got hurt and every cop and fireman in the city was in the park. It was beautiful."

"We couldn't have planned it to go any better. Let's hope Raymond, Johnny, and Tommy had it as smooth," Peter said.

Joey sat back and closed his eyes. The sun beat down on him and he exhaled a cloud of smoke. It would all work out. Any minute, Johnny, Tommy, and Raymond would come walking around the corner with bags of money and everything would be all right. His father could rot in prison forever as far as he cared; his mom would be taken care of and he could cruise from here on out. Maybe open a club or a bar after he got out of school, or even a candy store or something to run numbers out the back and have a bookie joint in the apartment above the store. Yeah, that would be the life. He opened his eyes just in time to see Peter's face. He was white as a sheet.

"What's wrong, Pete," Joey said, sitting bolt upright. It was then that he saw it.

A cop car was turning the corner and heading down the block. Peter stood as still as a statue and was squinting, turning to see if his friends were in the back seat. Joey had another vision. He imagined the look on his father's face as he was put in the cell next to him. He snuffed out his cigarette on the cement and stood up. The cop car was twenty feet away and suddenly the lights went on and the siren blared.

Peter almost bolted but Joey grabbed his arm and said, "Look, Pete, they aren't stopping." He sighed as the cop car sped up and raced down the block away from them. Peter almost collapsed. He let out his breath and Joey realized Peter had been holding it the whole time.

"Mother of God," Peter said. "They better get back soon. I don't think I could take much more of this."

"I don't think you have to worry anymore, Pete," Joey said, jumping up and down and pointing to the corner where three boys wearing baseball hats and carrying three black bags were making their way down the block.

"Calm down," Peter said.

Joey was practically bouncing.

"Hey, you were just a ball of nerves and now you want me to calm down. Let's go help them out," Joey said and bolted toward his friends.

Johnny saw them first and said, "Hey, look who made it out of the park."

Raymond and Tommy laughed. As the boys were about to break into a trot to meet their friends, they saw Joey stop short and Peter's eyes go wide.

"How-a you boys do today?"

The voice came from behind them. Raymond, Johnny, and Tommy all turned at once and found themselves fact to face with Mr. Manginni. They were speechless. Manginni smiled. He had an I ♥ the Pope flag in one hand and a glass of wine in the other. It was obviously not his first glass of the day.

"How-a you boys do?" he said again, motioning toward the bags with his glass. "You win-a the game or what," Manginni said.

The boys stared and finally Johnny said, "Yeah, Mr. Manginni, we won big today. Raymond here hit a home run."

"That's-a nice, that's-a nice," Mr. Manginni said and walked up the block in the opposite direction the boys were going.

"How about that," Johnny laughed as Joey and Peter came up to them.

"Everything okay?" Peter asked.

"Yeah," Tommy said. "What about you guys?"

"You mean you haven't heard?" Joey said.

"Heard what? We were underground for hours. Of course we haven't heard," Johnny asked quizzically.

"We can fill them in later," Peter interrupted. "You need a hand with those bags? They look heavy. Are they?" he continued, looking questioningly at Raymond.

"Oh they are … they are," Raymond answered and a smile broke out across his face.

"Enough screwing around. Let's get to the wine cellar and exchange stories," Joey said.

"Fuck the stories! I want to count the money," Johnny laughed and they all joined in and headed down the block.

CHAPTER

33

The Investigation

"SPECIAL DETECTIVE WALSH TO SEE YOU, SHEA," THE ROOKIE POOPED HIS HEAD INTO THE CAPTAIN'S OFFICE.

Shea looked at the Captain pleadingly. He was dreading this meeting.

"Don't worry, Shea, I got your back. There was nothing you did that I wouldn't have. Screw this guy Walsh. Fancy detective from downtown appointed by the Mayor himself. He's just another badge like you and me. Answer his questions straight and don't worry. We are in the clear on this one."

"Thanks, Cap," Shea said and got up off his chair and headed to the interrogation rooms downstairs.

Walsh was waiting for him with notebook in hand, briefcase on the floor. He was a graying man of about middle height, a bit stocky around the middle but still in pretty good shape. He had gray-green eyes that made him look a bit more intimidating than he was. He wore a blue suit and sat comfortably. No coffee. No cigarette. He just kept flipping through his notebook and every once in a while scribbled something down with his silver pen.

Shea had read his file. Walsh had made detective at twenty-nine and worked some high-profile cases. He had friends in high places and some said he had eyes on politics when he had padded his resume enough, but most badges said Walsh was a cop through and through. He lived for the hunt and transferred from homicide to burglary early in his career. He must have had some powerful friends because he always got the high-profile cases. He cracked the Metropolitan Museum of Art heist six years back and then followed that with a big-time jewel thief who had been robbing down in the diamond district. Shea had talked to a guy he knew and asked what type of cop Walsh was. He had gotten a two-word answer: "no joke." Shea opened the door and sat down; he knew he would be there a long time.

He relaxed, lit a smoke, and said, "So, you have some questions for me, Detective Walsh?"

Walsh looked up from his notebook and replied, "Put out the cigarette, and no, I only have one question for you."

He paused and waited while Shea extinguished his smoke. "Why didn't you follow up on the alarm report until eight hours later?"

Walsh stretched his legs and rubbed his temples.

"You okay, Chief," his driver said from the front seat.

"Yeah, Danny. It's just this case is something different. Real hard to crack and if my hunch is right, we have about thirty-six hours to nab these guys or they're gone. If they aren't gone already."

"Where to, Chief?" Danny asked.

"Let's head over to Con-Ed. The only real lead comes from there."

Walsh sat back and reviewed the last twenty hours in his head. The bank opened at 9 a.m. Monday morning and by all accounts, nothing was amiss. The tellers reported in work, went about as usual until noon, when the vault opened and the bank manager noticed the money was gone.

Walsh had checked the bank manager and the tellers they were clean. It wasn't an inside job. He found the scuffs on the wall under the vent made by men's work boots and realized the entrance point. Sure enough, the vent was loose. They came in through the vent in broad daylight. It had to be daylight because that's when the alarms went off. Ballsy, he thought.

The Con-Ed room revealed the old crate under the vent and the missing lock on the grate to the sewer indicated that they had disposed of the evidence through the sewer. Smart, Walsh thought, they would never get any evidence from there. The footprints in the workroom were too numerous to discern any real pattern since there were workers in there all week long leading up to the crime. They could have gone up through the manhole or exited through the subway tunnel. Either way, there were no real prints. Some sneakers in the tunnel but with the graffiti on the walls down there, those were probably kids playing around. He figured the manhole, which had been used by the Con-Ed guys all week long, was loose anyway.

No one reported any strange activity or seeing anyone. Walsh figured this was an expert crew. Had to be. They knew too much. They knew that the bank was a way station for all the other banks in lower Manhattan and that week a delivery of six million had been made that Friday. The money was to be distributed to the other banks all throughout the week. So the crew knew the money would be there. They also took advantage of the Pope's visit. They set off a distraction in the park that caused the whole police force to respond, leaving no one to respond to any alarms. It was well planned and thought out. They must have been working on it for a long time to time it just right. So who could have done it?

Walsh eliminated the idea of a lone guy. Too much money had walked, and the park required careful planning. He had immediately put all his resources into shaking down the five families in the city but not one of them seemed responsible. An outside crew, maybe, or some crew from Europe. But who? Italians would have worked with one of the families and it would have been too complex for the Irish. They were more of the smash-and-dash kind. He couldn't figure it out. The only real lead he had was down at Con-Ed. They were doing electrical work down there and they would have had access to the time lock information. The report from Shea was that the alarm had gone off in the middle of the Pope chaos. They had checked with Con-Ed and there was a power outage so the police ignored the call. Rightfully, he would have done the same given the circumstances.

Con-Ed was busy and, by the time they went to send a crew out to check the outage, the power had come back and they called the police and reported the situation was normal. Shea had actually sent out a car that night to drive by the bank and everything looked okay. So maybe someone at Con-Ed was responsible for the crime. Someone turned off the power and then turned it back on. They knew about the control room and they would have had access to the bank plans. It was his best lead and so he would have to check it. He sighed. This was too clean, though, for a Con-Ed worker to have pulled it off. There were too many parts involved with the Pope thing and the timing of the money. He leaned back and closed his eyes.

"Here we are, Chief," Danny said.

"Wait here. I won't be long," Walsh said and, checking himself in the car mirror, grabbed his notebook and got out.

"So, Mr. Gruber, you're telling me only the foreman would have had access to the plans for the bank renovation?"

"Of course and there is always a copy at the home office," Gruber replied.

Walsh scribbled some notes: plans in the home office and a foreman who probably had the plans lying on a desk in a trailer. No security at all. Anyone who was looking to find the plans could have—he bet.

"How do the plans get from here to the job site?" he asked.

Gruber replied, "We use curriers. Usually high school kids."

"Show me," Walsh replied, snapping his notebook shut.

They walked down the hall and down a flight of stairs. All the workers were interested and stopped when they saw Gruber in the hall. He obviously didn't leave his office much. They turned into a small locker room with a couple of kids hanging around. Some were reading, some were blowing smoke out a window from the cigarettes they were trying to hide, and one kid was sleeping on the floor. Walsh had seen enough.

"This is a waste," he said, walking past Gruber. "These kids couldn't rob a vending machine," he said as he exited the room.

Walsh headed back to Gruber's office. He would hammer the foreman and the workers at the site and see if he could shake something loose, but as every minute passed, he figured the money was going further and further away. These guys probably shipped out hours after the crime. They had a twenty-four hour head start and could be anywhere by now.

He sighed and said, "Gruber, get me some coffee and a list of all the workers down at the site and I want that foreman in here in twenty minutes."

He sat down behind Gruber's desk and rubbed his face. It was going to be a long day.

CHAPTER

34

The Wine Cellar

"WHAT DO YOU HAVE?" Johnny asked, looking at Peter.
"Hold it a minute," Peter said as he was counting hundreds. "I got ten thousand too."

"Ray, each pile is ten thousand," Johnny said.

They were in the wine cellar and they had opened the bags. The money was wrapped in packets. They had loaded thirty-eight packets. Johnny had suggested they break open one and count it. Each packet contained ten stacks of bills. Joey, Peter and Tommy each counted a stack. Joey was giddy. He had been amazed at the story of how Raymond had made them sweat in the vault and shocked when they opened the bag and revealed all the money. Peter had relayed the story of the park to the amazement of Johnny, Tommy, and Raymond. But this was the moment they had been waiting for.

Tommy was talking out loud, "Ten stacks of ten thousand. That's a hundred thousand a pack times thirty-eight is ..."

"Three-point-eight million," Johnny interrupted. "Ray, right? Three million eight hundred thousand," he repeated.

Ray smiled from ear to ear. Peter hugged Joey. Later, Tommy swore he saw Joey crying.

Tommy walked over to Raymond and whispered, "We really did it."

"Yeah, we did," he replied.

Franco pulled his chair out hard and slammed it down as he sat at the dinner table. His wife raised an eyebrow at him and gave him a stern look.

"I'm sorry, dear," he said and sighed.

He threw the *Daily News* down on the table and looked at his plate shaking his head.

"What's wrong, Pop," Johnny said as he shoveled food into his mouth. What's wrong? Are you kidding me? This bank thing has everyone crazy, he thought looking to the paper. Franco couldn't believe what had been going on the last few days. The Monday after the robbery, his whole crew had been picked up and questioned. That fuck, Walsh, had the nerve to send someone down to the bar and ask for Franco himself.

All the families had been shaken down and the funny thing was everyone was innocent. No one in any of the families had been involved. These guys had come in from out of town, had to be. The job was too clean. Franco had ears in most of the police precincts and in the ones he didn't, he knew other bosses who did and they all were singing the same tune. No clues—no nothing.

Walsh was ready to throw in the towel after two days but he decided to appease everyone—he would keep the pressure up for a while. That meant that all business had to stop for the families for a while. The cops were watching everything from car dealerships to jewelry stores. They were looking to see if any big money purchases were going on. Franco told his guys to be careful and not even eat out for a while until the heat died down. Franco had noticed a greater police presence in the neighborhood so even his numbers and gambling rackets had to cool off. It was a nightmare. Franco shook his head again and looked at the headline of the *Daily News*.

TRAILS GROWS COLD IN BANK CASE

Cold, he thought, it had never been hot. The head of the families had also gone hunting and asked their Italian connections. According to the guys in Interpol, there had been no activity, nothing. Franco was amazed. With a crime like this, usually some one knows something, even with all the families' connections and the police. This crew had come in undetected and gone out undetected. The job had been flawless. No loose ends.

"Dad, you okay," Johnny asked again as he finished off his plate and started to get up from the table.

"Sorry, Johnny. Things have been a bit crazy since the Pope left," he said, glancing down at the paper quickly.

"They got away with a lot of loot," Johnny replied, motioning with his head toward the paper on the table as he walked to the door.

"Yeah, that must have been some crew," Franco said admiringly.

"Why do you say that," Johnny asked as he paused at the door.

"No trace, cops got nothing. We don't even know anything. It was an impressive job and to get away with a couple of million. That's some score!"

Johnny smiled and shrugged. "When you put it that way, I would have to agree with you. That must have been some special crew," he said as he walked out the door.

Franco could hear Johnny going down the hall and as he stared at the spot where his son had just been, a chill had crept up his spine. Manginni had said everything was quiet with Johnny and his friends lately. They didn't seem to be planning anything. They were sharp enough to know not to do anything while there was so much heat in the neighborhood. Raymond was a sharp kid. Maybe he had realized education was his way out. They all were smart kids ... real smart.

Johnny froze and for a second he thought ... what if ... Nah, it couldn't be.

Epilogue

THE RAIN POURED DOWN OVER THE CITY. It had come down in sheets all day long. Peter looked out his window at the quickly darkening sky and watched the people below scurry for cabs. They looked like little ants from his apartment on the twenty-eighth floor. He sighed and sat down, taking of his collar and robes. It had been a long day. He had met with the mayor this morning for a photo shoot and they had gone back to St. Patrick's and worked in the office all day. He had skipped lunch and now his secretary would be wondering why he was skipping dinner.

He moved away from the window and sat back in his favorite chair. To anyone entering the room, it would be the last chair they would pick to sit on. It was an old, wooden straight-backed chair. Peter sighed as the chair creaked under his weight. He smiled and thought, one day this old chair is going to collapse under my weight. The out-of-place chair was a memento of Peter's youth. It was his favorite chair from the wine cellar. He had gone back and taken it when he was assigned to New York. He could still remember Johnny saying, "You know, I like to keep the place exactly like it was. But who am I to refuse a request from the Arch Bishop of New York."

Peter ran his hand over the old wood and thought about his friends. After the bank, everything had changed mostly for the better. They had all gone to college. Raymond had gone to California to visit a number of schools and decided on Cal Berkeley, where he became involved in a number of civil rights actions. He took to politics like a duck to water and after graduating decided to work as a public servant for the government. His career quickly brought him fame and in no time at all, he was running with the elite political powers of the state. Raymond had no problem coming up with money to help grease the political wheels and soon he was elected mayor of a small town in California. Raymond was then on the fast track to bigger and better things. He was now the Deputy Governor of California and many in the party were pegging him for the governorship in three years.

Peter laughed out loud at that. Raymond liked to call the shots, but he didn't think he would want so public an office. He might do it as a vehicle to get a cabinet position some day. Imagine that, Peter thought, God willing. Peter smiled, he would see Raymond less if that happened, not that he saw him that much now. Raymond had to keep a low profile. It would not be good for him to be seen with Johnny too often.

Johnny … Peter thought, Johnny had gone to college at St. John's and had gotten himself thrown out sophomore year for allegedly trying to fix college basketball games. The scandal had been the icing on the cake. Johnny had gone to school to appease his father but in reality he was never in class. He set up a bookmaking operation day one, and by year two, he was loan-sharking and dealing in stolen term papers and textbooks. Johnny never needed the money. It was the action he craved.

Most of the cash he made in college went to pay off professors for grades or to throw wild parties and pay off the local cops. Johnny ran St. John's like his father ran the neighborhood. The college basketball thing was a favor for his Dad's boss, the head of the five families. Franco was furious when it happened but he knew Johnny was not destined for college.

In a roundabout way, it actually helped seal Franco's rise to head of the five families. The head of the families handpicked his successor when he retired. Franco's ties to Europe and the respect he had with the other bosses made him the clear-cut choice. With Franco's accession to the top, Johnny inherited his own crew and in no time, not because of who he was but on his ability, he was made a captain. He took up residence in his father's old digs and went about carving out a reputation for himself. One that would one day lead him to taking over for Franco.

Peter stretched and rose from the chair. He called in his secretary.

"Father Matthew, I will be in meditation tonight and am not to be disturbed."

"Your eminence, would you like me to get you some dinner?"

"No, Matthew, I'm going to watch the Knicks game and then turn in early. I do not want to be disturbed. You may retire to your apartment. I can fend for myself," Peter said gently.

"As you wish. Do you think they have a chance?" Matthew asked.

"We can only pray," Peter replied.

When Matthew had left, Peter glanced at the clock and began getting dressed. He put on jeans and a sweater. With a Knicks cap and out of uniform no one would recognize him on the street. He walked through his spacious apartment and turned on the Knicks game and locked his bedroom door. He then headed out through the kitchen to his back door and the service elevator. The elevator could only be accessed by key and Peter turned the key and waited for the elevator to come up.

"You will love this, Pete," he remembered Tommy telling him. "With this elevator, you can come and go as you please and no one will ever know you've left the building. Once you're in the basement, walk all the way to the last door on the right and it will leave you off by the garbage ramp. From there, you can walk out onto the street. Just be careful of the rats by the garbage," Tommy had joked.

The building Peter lived in was owned by Tommy. He had gone to school at Rhode Island School of Technology and gotten his engineer's degree in three years. He then transferred to Princeton and got his MBA.

Tommy had started off small working for a small architectural firm but quickly realized that if he wanted to design building it would be easier to own them first. He started off small, buying old condemned places and redesigning them. With a bit of financial backing from his friends, he soon began developing large areas of land. Over the last fifteen years, Tommy had become one of the biggest real estate moguls on either coast. He owned a multitude of businesses including restaurants, hotels, an advertising agency, and many others. Of all the boys, he was worth the most, although Johnny and Joey might disagree on that.

Peter laughed as he stepped into the elevator. Tommy had donated the top two floors to the new Archbishop of New York of his building on West 56th Street. The move was good publicity and Tommy made no secret that he had grown up with Peter and that they were friends. They met often for lunch when Tommy wasn't traveling. Tommy had actually lived in these apartments himself and had designed the elevator as a way for him to come in or out or for Joey or Johnny to come up and visit. Now that he was so big it didn't matter anymore who he was seen with.

The rain had let up and Peter pulled his coat tight around him to fight off the cold. He hailed a cab and gave the cab driver the address to the trendy SoHo neighborhood. As the streets flew by, he thought about why he was going out tonight. He had arrived home yesterday to find an envelope slipped under his door in the kitchen. The only way someone could access the elevator was with a key and the only people who had those keys were Johnny, Tommy, and Joey. He knew the note was from Joey the minute he saw the handwriting on the envelope.

Peter sat back in the cab and sighed. Joey was his greatest disappointment. Joey had followed Johnny to college and followed him right out. He worked with Johnny for years under Franco and in doing so made many underworld connections. Peter could live with Joey being a boss in the Mob. He could have lived with him doing any of a million things but Joey had branched off from Johnny. Joey's father had become a drug dealer in prison and when he came out he gave up the bottle and focused on the drug trade. With Franco's help, he created a nice business in the five boroughs and did well. When Joey's father died of natural causes, his business was ripe to take for Joey.

Johnny supported him and Joey took his father's business and had tripled it. He was the leading drug distributor on the East Coast and was slowly gaining ground in California. Peter saw the devastation drugs could cause and had pleaded with Joey to get out and do something legitimate but to no avail. The cab pulled up in front of the restaurant and Peter paid the cabbie and got out. The line was halfway around the block and Peter walked to the back of it, then turned the corner and walked toward the kitchen entrance. He saw two limos parked in the alley and laughed. Tommy and Johnny were here already. As he approached the kitchen entrance, he rang the bell and a familiar face greeted him at the door.

"Hello, Pete."

It was Smitty.

"Hey Smitty, what are you doing here," Peter said as he grabbed him in a giant hug.

"Tommy said he was holding a reunion tonight and I couldn't help but drop in to see you guys."

Smitty was in charge of all of Tommy's restaurants in New York and Los Angeles.

"They are waiting for you downstairs. We'll catch up later," Smitty said.

Peter walked through the kitchen and down the stairs. He paused before the door that looked remarkably like the door to the wine cellar of old. The boys all agreed to meet once a year and that meeting had taken place four months ago. They had all agreed that for them to all be together at one time in public would raise too many eyebrows. Peter pulled the note out of his pocket and read it for the twentieth time that day. It was written in Joey's handwriting and all it said was:

Boys meeting tomorrow night. New wine cellar. It's a matter of life and death.

BOOK II

CHAPTER

1

The New Wine Cellar

PETER OPENED THE DOOR AND WAS GREETED BY THE SMELL OF FOOD. Not just any food, the rich smells of pasta with red sauce and sausage and peppers; he closed his eyes and for a second he was back in his mother's kitchen in East Harlem. Italian food always brought him back home it reminded him of his childhood the good and bad.

He continued into the spacious room and smiled, he couldn't help it. Tommy had designed the room to be a replica of the old wine cellar but only with all the modern features they never had as kids. There were beautiful brown leather couches and a fully stocked bar in one corner.

Peter saw the Knicks game on the large screen TV and then, as always, his eyes gravitated to the old out-of-place table in the middle of the room. It was the original from the old wine cellar. It had been refinished and polished to the best condition it could be in, but it stood out like a cheap card table in a five-star restaurant. Only the boys understood the significance of that table and very few others ever came down to this room so it was never questioned by anyone why this old piece of junk was in this otherwise lavish room.

In the instant that Peter had taken to survey the room and get lost in his own thoughts, the other three men in the room had noticed his arrival and were making their way toward him.

Johnny was in the lead, as always; he had grown into a good-looking man just like his father. His dark black hair was cut short and there was no sign of any gray yet. Peter laughed to himself. You would think with all the stress of Johnny's business he would show signs of worry, but Johnny still looked like the cocky wiseass kid Peter remembered from the neighborhood.

His dark suit was tailored perfectly and he wore it like a second skin. Peter noticed the pinky ring that had belonged to Franco, Johnny's father, on his right hand, and the Rolex on his left wrist. He approached Peter arms already spread in a hugging motion and at the last second reached down to kiss Peter's hand. "Your eminence," he said, kissing Peter's ring. Then he looked Peter up and down and said, "What the fuck! You need to stick your hand in the donation box and get some nice suits, you look like a hobo." Johnny smiled and then hugged Peter.

He backed away and said, "You're getting fat, Pete, you better lay off the canoli." By this time, Raymond and Tommy had made their way across the room and were waiting to hug Peter also. Raymond looked very comfortable in jeans and a button-down shirt with no tie; he had grown up, he was beginning to show some gray in his hair and seemed to be a bit older than the other two men in the room but when he smiled, Peter could still see the plotting fierce kid from the neighborhood was still in there.

Tommy was another story. He was the picture of wealth; his suit was tailored even better than Johnny's if that could be possible, his hair was perfect, his jewelry matched the tones of his suit. This was a far cry from the ripped jeans and holes-in-his-shoes kid Peter remembered. He couldn't blame Tommy of all of them, growing up poor was hardest for him. Tommy left that poor kid behind and never wanted to go back. He was the poster child for success in this town and he looked the part.

Tommy smiled coolly at Peter and said to Johnny, "Bet Pete could still take you in agame of one on one."

"Yeah, yeah, only cause he's, what, 6'10' or something," Johnny snorted.

"How you doing Pete?" Ray said.

"Everything is good, and you?"

"Same old, tough to get out here tonight, any idea what's so urgent?" Leave it to Ray to get right to the point thought Peter.

"No idea."

"I thought Johnny might know," Peter replied.

The men turned toward Johnny, who was refilling his drink. "No clue, haven't talked to Joey in a few weeks...last time he was going on about a girl, maybe he's getting married," Johnny joked.

"Matter of life and death , is marriage that bad?" Tommy asked.

"Wouldn't know," Johnny laughed. Peter made his way to the old table and sat down in an oversized leather chair, running his hand over the rough wood. Ray and Tommy sat next to Peter, leaving Johnny at the bar in the corner. "Hey, Pontiff, you want a drink?"

Johnny motioned to the Johnny Walker Black on the bar.

"No thanks, Johnny."Raymond ran his fingers through his hair and tried to discreetly look at his watch.

"What's your hurry, Ray?" Johnny asked.

" I've got to catch the redeye back to L.A. tonight, meeting with Senator Swinton in the morning."

"Fucking big shot, you know what I'm doing tomorrow morning?"

"Sleeping till lunch time," Tommy shot in. They all laughed. At that instant, Joey opened the door and stormed into the room. He bypassed everyone and went straight for the bar and poured himself a drink without saying hello.

Ray shot a look at Johnny, who shrugged and said, "Hey, good to see you too, bro...how ya been...oh, that's great, me too." Tommy started to laugh but Joey shot him and Johnny a deadly look. "Not tonight Johnny,"he said and took a swig of his drink. Johnny sobered up quickly and retorted, "Sure, bro, let's get down to it then you called us here, you storm in like the fucking world is ending or something and then have the balls to warn me to watch my tone. The fucking floor is yours, you seem to be in a bigger hurry than Ray here so spit it out and cut the drama." Johnny slammed his drink on the table and sat down hard across from Ray. Peter was about to say something to calm the situation down but everyone was staring up at Joey, who stood there like he had just gotten slapped.

An expression of sincere sorrow came across Joey's face: "Sorry, guys."It was last thing Peter had expected to hear. Joey's whole demeanor changed; he slumped his shoulders down, grabbed a chair, and sat facing everyone. He took another swig of his drink and leaned forward so he was literally on the edge of his seat. Peter could tell he was struggling with something and wasn't sure how to start so Peter broke the silence.

"Joey, you know we are all here for you just tell us what's wrong." Joey looked up at Peter and caught his eye. Tommy jumped in, "C'mon, Joey, you said it was a matter of life and death, what did you mean?" Joey looked up and rubbed his face wearily and with both hands he steadied him and said, "My death, I'm a dead man."

"Fucking Columbians!" Johnny jumped up. Every one in the room was startled. " I told you not to get to tight with them. Those rat bastards, they will screw you at the drop of a hat."

"No worries. Let me think which crew it is, or is it that fuck Laslo?" Johnny was up on his feet. He walked over to Joey, who started to weakly laugh. "What's so funny?" Johnny asked.

"Johnny, I'm one of the biggest drug distributers on the East Coast; you think a crew of Columbians could get to me?"

"That's like saying the local bookie is going to put you out of business."

"It's nothing like that at all."

"So what is the problem?" Raymond asked.

"I'm dying, I have AIDS."

2

Joey's story

THE ROOM WENT SILENT FOR A MOMENT, LONGER THEN A MOMENT, AS IF EVERYONE WAS TRYING TO PROCESS WHAT THEY JUST HEARD IN THEIR OWN WAYS. Tommy looked confused; he started to say something but then turned to Ray, who was intently staring at Joey as if trying to figure out if this was a joke or not. Johnny was frozen in place, drink still in his hand. Peter looked at Joey again and once again Joey caught his eye.

Pete was compelled with an urge to get up and hug Joey, but he knew this was not what Joey wanted. He knew by the look on Joey's face that he was serious and this was no joke. Pete leaned back in his chair, not even realizing that he had started to get up. He turned to Ray, who now just sat patiently waiting. Tommy was about to say something but Johnny broke the silence. "Get the fuck out of here," he said, taking the swig of his drink. And turning toward Ray, "This fucking guy...almost had me, Ray." The look on Raymond's face stopped Johnny in his tracks.

He turned to look at everyone in the room and then said to Ray, "What, you buying this?" Then his voice lowered and turned to Joey, "How, bro...how?" Johnny sat down and his drink spilled on the table but he didn't even notice it; he looked as if he'd been struck. Tommy saw his friend trying to process the situation and jumped in.

"Look, it doesn't matter how, all that matters now is that we are here for Joey."

Peter stood up and went to embrace Joey. Joey stopped him in his tracks, "Please don't tell me your going to try and hug me," Joey said as a smile briefly crept across his face. Peter said, "You know how I feel, Joey, I was just…" Joey grinned, "I know you big jambrotha, but it's not necessary." Raymond had sat silently the whole time looking at Joey, he stood up and put his hand on Peter's shoulder, guiding him back down into his chair. "Joey, you're not stupid, you and I know there are a million treatments out there and between the five of us I'm sure we can come up with a list of the best doctors in the world, hell, you have enough cash to do that on your own and you wouldn't have had to tell us anything."

Johnny had come out of his stupor and was intently listening to Raymond, a look of understanding started to cross his face; he could see where Raymond was going with this. Joey started to smile but before he could say anything, Raymond continued, "You never mentioned this to us when we met a few months ago, so something must have happened in the last few months that requires all of us, otherwise you wouldn't have had to call this meeting." Raymond walked to within two feet of Joey and looking him in the eye said, "So while you having AIDS is news to us, it's not the whole story is it? You want to tell us the real reason you called us down here?"

Joey and Raymond stood looking into each other's eyes, the other three men looking at them standing there in the center of the room. Johnny broke the silence, he had regained his composure and was back to being his old self again. "This guy, I swear, president some day. Ray, I know you've chosen legitimate crime, I mean politics, as your profession but if you ever need a job you can always come work for me." Johnny slapped Ray on the back still talking, "…sees things three steps ahead of everyone else still," he said with pride.

"So he's right?" Johnny said, looking at Joey. "Right, bro, what's the rest of the story?"

"First things first," Tommy said, "how sick are you? Are you okay? I mean, there's no timeline here or anything like that is there?" he asked, genuinely more concerned with Joey's health than the rest of the story. Joey placed his hand on Tommy's shoulder. "I'm fine, not even symptomatic yet, real early stages, it's my girl who's in trouble, she's in bad shape."

"Girl? I thought you were gay!" Johnny said.

"Seriously, Johnny?" Peter said, shocked that Johnny would say something like that. But as far back as they all went, Johnny and Joey went even farther, it was Johnny's way of showing concern and Joey took it as acceptance of the situation. Joey nodded at Johnny. "It's alright Pete", he said then, turning to Johnny, said, "Seriously, I don't know how long Tiff has, that's why I called you guys, I can't do this alone." Johnny nodded solemnly. "What do you need us to do?" Raymond asked. "Let me give you guys the whole story and then you tell me," Joey replied.

The men all sat down and Joey took a quick sip of his drink then he sighed deeply and launched into his story. "I guess I should start with Tiff. She's my girl; as a few of you know, we started going out about eight months ago and I got to tell you guys, she's the one, I knew it from the start. I know it's hard to believe, but that's the way it is, I love her, have from the moment we met at this club down on Mulberry Street. Well, it's funny she thought I was a Wall Street guy and I guess I let her believe that for a while, in the beginning, but she had her secrets and I had mine."

"What was her secret?" Raymond asked.

"She's an addict, heroine. Kinda ironic isn't it. But anyway, I knew I've been there so I could see the signs. I let it go for a while and then one night I told her everything about me, about what I do and how I became the man I am today."

"You didn't tell her everything did you?" Tommy said with some concern in his voice.

"No, don't worry, I had my father to leave me this legacy. I never mentioned you guys or the 'job.' Once my life was on the table, I told her I knew her secret and I didn't care, I mean, how could I with what I did in the past." He glanced quickly at Johnny who just nodded. "You were there for me too, Pete, back then and how could I judge someone who was like me. We cried and made love and then I got high with her...I know I shouldn't have...but I did, I just wanted her to see it was okay with me. Well, we continued to get high and she must have shared with one of her friends or something and somehow we both contracted AIDS from a dirty needle.Don't start, I know it was stupid and irresponsible but it happened that way and there's no going back."

"Joey, how could you?" Peter couldn't help himself; he had spent countless hours trying to get Joey clean the last time he had used.

Peter caught himself and before he could apologize, Joey looked him directly in the eye. "I'm sorry, Pete, I just couldn't..." His voice trailed off and the room got quiet. Raymond struggled to say something and started to when Johnny jumped in. "Well, that settles the gay thing. Finish the story, I know you didn't call us here to apologize for being an asshole again."

Joey looked at Johnny and regained some of his old cockiness. "I mean really with the gay thing, how fucking old are you? And anyway, I don't see any ring on your finger or anyone else in this room so you could all be gay except Pete."

"Except Pete, what the hell? He would be my number one candidate, he was petrified of women when we were kids," Johnny laughed.

The mood in the room had lightened and Joey grabbed his drink and stood up, taking a deep swig he continued, "So I go to the doctor for a routine checkup a few months back and get the bad news; I had a feeling something could be wrong. Tiff had been in bad shape a few times over the course of a month or two and I figured I should check myself out. Well the doctor starts with there are treatments and the whole fucking pitch about what to do next but I'm way ahead of him. I call around and find the best fucking place to go is San Francisco Medical Center. They're the best in the world."

"Figures Frisco," Johnny said, getting up and pouring himself another drink.

"Don't you ever lay off," Tommy said. "Go on, Joey."

Joey shook his head at Johnny and continued, "So I go out there and get an appointment with a Dr. Flischer. I swear, Pete, I could have gotten an appointment with the Pope easier but after a few strings get pulled, he agrees to see me and I go. I get poked and prodded for an hour and then sit like a shmuck for two hours waiting to see the doctor. He brings me in and starts with the live healthier, eat right, take these combos of drugs and I go back at him that I want the experimental stuff, I want to get into the trials for new drugs stuff that's not on the market. He says that's not possible, I have no insurance and that's when I lose it, I went fucking crazy. I threw two grand in his face and told him I'd buy the lab and...well, I lost it."

"Hard to imagine," Johnny said. "I get it though, those fucks are like leeches, they never give you a straight answer. It was the same with my mother, always some bullshit..." Johnny trailed off and took a long drink. His mother had had a long and painful bout with cancer and with Johnny as her only child, it had been hard for him to watch her slowly waste away and die. Peter had been through that with his own mom and understood Johnny's frustration. "Keep going", Raymond said coolly to Joey.

"Well, the whole fucking place must have heard me go off and I storm out. As I'm about to pull away, one of the lab tech comes running out and stops me. This guy tells me to cool down and that he might have an interesting story for me if I was willing to listen.

"The guy tells me after he left Pfizer he worked for Novacrin for fifteen months. He said they had a doctor there, this guy named Phil Lancaster, real smart guy doing some cutting-edge research according to what the assistant told me. He starts going on about beta-blockers or some shit and virus delivery blockers; it was way above my head but I listened. Anyway, the guy says every few weeks he sees Lancaster meet with these three patients. The first time they come in he says you wouldn't touch them with a ten-foot pole, they looked like walking dead or something. Over the course of the next three months, these guys come in looking better and better.

This guy Lancaster is sleeping in the lab and working around the clock, then one morning he disappears. Supposedly he is transferred to a lab out in New Jersey. Everyone working at the facility in California gets the ax. Novacrin stocks go up five hundred percent, the company comes out with a new treatment for AIDS, and a fat research grant from the government."

"So you need to find this guy Lancaster?" Tommy said.

"I'm not done. My new friend the technician says he checked the blood work of the three guys who were in the trial and met with Lancaster over those three months. All three had AIDS when they came in, and all three were totally clean when they went out. My new friend seems to think Lancaster came up with a cure."

"That's unbelievable, how can you trust this guy and why would he offer the information to you?"

"He didn't offer, I paid him thirty grand for the name of one of the guys who walked out of there and I may be grasping for straws here, but I think if we put our minds to this one we can find a cure for AIDS."

"Are you saying what I think your saying, Joey?" Raymond said.

"Yeah, I think Novacrin has a cure for AIDS and is keeping it under wraps." Peter could feel the blood draining from his face he felt a bit queasy. "Do you know what this means if it's true?" Johnny laughed, "Yeah, millions and millions in cash and research grants worth billions from the government, what a fucking scam."

Peter looked at Johnny shocked. "No, millions of lives can be saved if this is true." Joey stood up and looked Peter in the eye and said, "I found something out, and for once I want to do the right thing. We all changed our destinies with that bank job and I just...I don't know, I guess seeing my girl get sick has changed me. I want to help. I know it sounds corny but I've been selfish my whole life. My dad came out of jail and became a drug dealer. I could have chosen a different path, gone with Johnny, even become a legit businessman. I don't know, I could have done things differently but I didn't. Dealing has done nothing but hurt people. It never hurt me until now. I see things differently now. I guess, Pete, I've finally come around. I want to do some good but I need your help. All of you."Peter got up and hugged Joey. Joey let him and then stepped back as Peter whispered so only Joey could hear him, "You don't know how long I've prayed for this." Joey regained his composure and said to everyone, "Look, I wouldn't ask you guys to do this if I could do it myself, but I need your help on this one. What do you say?"

"I'm in," Peter said.

"You know I will do everything in my power to help you, Joey," Tommy said.

"Of course I'm in, those fucking drug companies. I get the name, they been robbing people for years. If I could bring one of them down why not."

Joey was smiling as he turned to Raymond, who hadn't moved. He sat deep in the leather chair. He was seated in with his hands pressed together, his chin leaning on his thumbs; he looked deep in thought. "Ray, you know if anyone could figure this out its you. What do you say?" Ray sighed and rubbed his temples, he looked weary, " Before I say this, Joey, I want you and everyone in this room to know you guys are my brothers and I will always be there for you."

"I feel a but coming on," Johnny said.

Raymond smiled, "No buts, not for you guys never. I'm in."

"Trying to make us sweat you fuck, ha, like old times, boys, although this time I'm not crawling through any rat infested sewers." Johnny smiled.

3

Lancaster

T HE MEN MET A WEEK LATER IN THE WINE CELLAR. Unfortunately, that was really the only place they could meet. Being who they were, some circles of their lives ran together but some did not. Raymond especially had a hard time getting to New York, especially with his duties as Lieutenant Governor of California. For Tommy, things were easy; Johnny was a known figure and to be seen with Tommy did not affect Tommy's business in any way. No one knew Joey, and Peter out of his robes was almost invisible. The men agreed to meet on a Thursday night. Raymond would catch a red-eye flight back to L.A. that night and be at work Friday morning. The men all arrived around seven p.m. and after a quick meal sat down and began to discuss business.

"So, here's what we have," Raymond said, tossing five folders that were stuffed onto the table. "There are five board members in the company that represent the hierarchy and are the most vested in the company and daily affairs. It goes without saying that if what we believe is true then there would be a limited number of people in on the secret."

"That sounds familiar", Johnny chipped in. "Listen, Joey, I've read through these folders and we have to realize something, this may be a situation that we have totally misread. Lancaster is a brilliant scientist and he may have discovered something that is viable but not a cure. We could be wrong and then this would be just a waste of time and energy."

Joey, who had eaten very little but had made up for it in scotch, didn't want to hear it. "You have time and energy, Ray, my girl doesn't. It's true, I know it is." Raymond could tell he was trying to control his anger, he had seen him like this a million times and he did not want him to blow up. Raymond was about to say something when Tommy jumped in. "I agree with Ray on this. Look, Joey, I looked into some of the guys on this board, nothing serious just searched them on the computer, and there are some pretty respectable men on that board."

"Could we have misjudged the situation? Maybe we should just approach Lancaster and ask for the treatment he gave those three men, I'm sure Ray or I or even Pete could contact him." Raymond cringed inside, wrong tact; he knew it and didn't have to wait long for Joey's reply. "Respectable, so what, cause a guy builds a hospital or puts up fucking schools that makes him respectable, what are you trying to say, Tommy, you trust these fucks more than me?"

"The world looks great from your penthouse; everyone living at that level is a standup guy, is that what you saying? Cause I live down on the streets still and see your so-called standup guys do some fucked up shit. I tell you, these guys have the cure and you want to go and believe them."

"Fuck you, Tommy! Maybe I can do this without you. I'll grab this guy Lancaster and peel his skin off an inch at a time until he talks." Joey stood up; he had lost control and Johnny could see something else in his eyes. He stood and intervened, putting his arm on Joey's and guiding him back to his chair. "Joey, please," Peter said. Joey sat down, realizing that he had lost it. "Look, Pete, you don't see how Tiffany looks, you don't see her in the morning when she can't get out of bed or at night when she's shivering in my bed with ten blankets on. Maybe you shouldn't be here if you are now holier than thou and can't bring yourself to hear these things, but that's how it may have to go down in the end."

"Joey, I will never abandon you or anyone you love but this isn't fifth grade, we cant fight our way to the answer and violence only begets more violence. Would you want to see any one of us hurt because of this, especially when we have no proof of the truth? No one has more faith than me in this room and I want with all my heart to believe in this story, but we can't act rashly listen to Ray, Joey he knows what he's talking about."

Joey didn't seem placated but he relented and kept quiet as Raymond continued, "Look, the way I see it, there are only two ways to corroborate the story: First, we get into Novacrin files and I can't see any way we could do that, we wouldn't even know where to start. The second way is to find the three guys, we have one name; if we can find these guys we can tell if the story is true or not."

He paused. He knew it wasn't what Joey wanted to hear; he waited for an explosion or an argument but was surprised when none came. Johnny took the opportunity and, looking at Joey, said quietly, "I agree with Raymond. We find these guys and confirm the story." Raymond continued quickly, tapping the folders on the table and looking at Joey, who was placated but still seething. "Let's assume you're right, Joey, then we need a plan to get leverage on one of the board members." Johnny jumped in, as Tommy looked through the folders nodding and murmuring every now and then.

"Look, these guys are hard to touch. Called around talked to Little Eddy Botz from Vegas, he put a few guys on it and came up with nothing. I mean, these guys are real big money and they pay to stay under the radar, no girls, no drugs, no gambling problems. At least none that any of my connections could come up with and I are pretty well connected." Johnny leaned back and took a swig of his Johnny Walker Blue. He looked right at Joey and sighed, "Tommy might be right, these guys might be clean." He paused and looked at all the men around the table then spoke quietly, "Look, I also agree with Joey, unless you have some other way, Ray, we may have to muscle these guys to get any information." Johnny avoided Peter's shocked look and quickly looked at Ray.

Raymond stood up and stretched his arms into the air. He rubbed his neck and then spoke. "Again, it's all moot unless we confirm the story but I think we have a few options other then yours and Joey's," he said, looking at Johnny.

Tommy put down the folders that he had been examining the whole time. "I know some of these guys…I mean, not personally but we run in the same circles. I've actually built two hospitals in L.A. for this guy Whitehall about five years back. We're talking real old money there and influence; we had a zoning issue that he took care of in about five seconds."

Raymond smiled and sat back down, sinking into his leather chair. "Look, there's a weak link in any chain, we just have to find the right target and execute the proper plan."

"So who's the target here, Ray?" Johnny asked. Raymond motioned for the folders and gathered the men around the heavy table. He spread the five folders out and put his hand over the first one.

"Roony. This guy is old money, real country club, never worked a day in his life. He was brought into Novacrin by Whitehall, the real businessman of the bunch. As far as I'm concerned, this guy Roony is a clown. He writes checks and cashes them; of all of these guys, he may know the least. Roony's only vice is money so if it's true and they are covering this up, it would cost him billions and a guy… even a stupid guy like this won't give that up so Roony is off the list." Raymond slid the folder to the other end of the table and placed his hand on the next folder.

"Whitehall, brilliant businessman, his father was in shipping, and when he was twenty-five, Mr. Whitehall here took over and turned his father's business into an empire. There isn't a major port on the eastern seaboard that he doesn't have a piece of. He's a philanthropist; he builds hospitals and sits on the board of a dozen charitable organizations. He sat on the board of Pfizer for ten years before he went and helped start Novacrin."

"He learned the business first then went into competition with them, real smart," Tommy said.

"Yeah, real smart. Whitehall is the brains behind this and his public image is so strong I don't think we can do anything with him, he'd see us coming a mile away."

"That's going to make anything you do dangerous," Tommy said.

Peter looked up at him quizzically. "Why?" he asked.

Tommy shook his head, "Peter, these guys' business is knowing stuff and people. I encounter it on a daily basis, who you know is what gets things done and this guy knows everyone." He continued, "It would be like a big heist goes down in Chicago, would you know about it, Johnny?"

"Of course I would. Nothing major happen without me knowing."

"Well think about that on a much larger scale and that's Whitehall," Tommy replied.

"What about this guy Jamison?" Johnny asked as he flipped the Whitehall file to the other side of the table.

"He could be a target, not as smart or powerful as Whitehall but he does all the dirty work for the company," Raymond said.

"Define dirty work," Johnny asked.

"I guess that term is relative to what you do for a living; in this case, I mean he handles all the contracts and decisions in the day-to-day operation of the company"

"Totally different definition from my point of view," Johnny said with a grin.

"Yeah, but don't be fooled, Whitehall is the public face but Jamison is his right and left hand; if you go after Jamison, he'll report back to Whitehall," Tommy said. "I would avoid both of those guys if possible," he added.

Raymond smiled and said, "I agree, I think that leaves us with these two." He tapped the last two folders sitting on the table. Phil Specter, he really has no fit in this group, he grew up in South Philly.

"Isn't that the rough side of Philly?" Peter asked. "No, real good side of Philly, Pete", Joey added as Raymond continued. "Poor kid but real smart, he managed to get into a private school in Pennsylvania and there he met Jamison. They were buddies through college and Specter always seems to pop up around Jamison's business dealings with these cake titles; for example, when Jamison was in New York for a while, Specter was the head of HR for a company Jamison started."

"Tough kid worked his way up, maybe he could relate to us," Tommy asked. Peter nodded but Johnny just shook his head. "You kidding, Tommy, follow the food chain here: Whitehall feeds Jamison, Jamison feeds Specter unless Specter has an ax to grind these guys are his meal ticket, he ain't flipping on them, he's not smart enough to run the business but he's smart enough to know how he keeps getting paid."

"Johnny's right", Raymond said, sliding the Specter folder across the table with the others. "Here's our boy," Raymond said, tapping the folder in his hand. The one guy who was in this for the science and not the money is Lancaster, if we try to find a crack it's through him."Raymond threw the folder down on the table and Tommy picked it up and began to read.

"So what's his story?" Peter asked. He grabbed the folder away from Tommy; in it were various bank statements and a picture of a well-dressed middle-aged man.

"So here is the background on Phil Lancaster: he's fifty-two, divorced, one daughter age twenty-four, co-founded Novacrin in 1992, since its inception the company has skyrocketed to become one of the top three pharmaceutical corporations on the planet. Phil maintains an apartment in Manhattan and a home out in California, where the company is based. He is an avid art collector and, as far as I know, has no current girl or mistress. These guys have big money and pay to keep out of the spotlight. He is frequently in NY, I assume to visit his daughter, who still lives here with her mother."

"Pete, Phil's wife went a little crazy after the divorce and is the religious type. She is a huge donor to your church, that's going to be your angle."

"I will not exploit someone's faith for information," Peter said a bit bristly.

"Look, Pete, just meet with her, you know how it is…people tell priests everything." Johnny smiled. Peter did not take the bait and was still visibly upset.

He shrugged and asked, "How long ago was the divorce?"

Raymond scanned the folder, which he had taken back, and said, "Looks like twelve years. I mean, really, Pete, she may know nothing. It seems like based on this court report that the divorce was ugly." Raymond was trying to soften the blow and make things easier for Peter to accept his role.

Peter, for his part, understood what Ray was doing and smiled. "What's her name?"

"Judy Tannaro, she goes by her maiden name."

Peter sat up. "I know that name, she is a significant contributor. I'll sit with her." It was all he said but Joey slapped him on the back as a sign of thanks.

"Good, but if we are going after Lancaster we need someone to get close to him. Tommy, that's going to have to be you." Tommy smiled, it made sense; he ran in familiar circles as Lancaster, or at least he could. "Tommy, there's an auction at Sotheby's this week. I had a friend check the invite list, our boy's on it," Johnny said.

Tommy laughed, "I was going to that auction anyway, there's a beautiful Gauguin for sale." He stopped himself but it was to late. "Fucking snob," Joey said.

"So what do I do?" Joey asked, eager to hear his part in the whole scheme, he seemed to have equaled out emotionally. Johnny glanced at Raymond before he spoke and then quietly said, "Look, Joey, we want you to lay low right now. This mission requires a subtle touch, not a blunt instrument. Don't give me that look, you'll have your part but for now just lay low, take care of yourself and your girl." Raymond was ready for an explosion. Peter shifted nervously in his seat. Tommy looked up at the ceiling, he was also nervous. Joey glanced quickly around the room and then said, "Okay."

Johnny was stunned he almost dropped his drink, "What? No arguing, no storming out...fuck, I got a whole speech laid out about why this is the right thing." Johnny's voice tailed off and Joey answered, "I trust the plan, Ray, but we better move quick...I don't know how long I can wait."

"Okay then, I'm going to look into finding the three guys who got cured. But I think we should all run the name Joey has up the flagpole and see what we can get. This is our top priority; if we get stonewalled here, we move on to the next option"

"And what would the next option be?" Peter asked.

Johnny said, "I don't think you want to know, Your Eminence."

"I bet I could help you with that," Joey smiled.

"Yes, yes you can," Johnny said. Raymond quickly jumped in seeing Peter getting nervous with the way the conversation was going. "As for me, I'll use my influence in California to see what the company is all about. Novacrin is based in my backyard; I should have no trouble getting some information. We all meet back in a week or sooner if we hear anything."

Raymond sank back into the leather seat. He had a hard time sleeping on airplanes as it was but now with his mind racing he knew there would be no rest for him on this flight. He thought of the implications of what it would mean if Joey's story was true. Raymond wasn't the daydreaming type and in all likelihood the story was false. The medical assistant was probably preying on Joey, who was desperate to believe anything. He sighed, but what if it were true, his decision to go into politics wasn't all selfish, he truly wanted to help people.

He remembered his parents and how hard it was for them to make ends meet. He also remembered the time after the bank job when he had to wait years before he could do anything for his family. Those years had been the toughest for him and for Tommy too. Having all that money and not being able to access it for years was one of the most frustrating things Raymond had ever been through.

He could only imagine the anguish of other families who had to deal with their loved ones dying from AIDS. If Joey's story was true, then finding the answer and the cure would be the most important thing he and his friends could ever do. His attention went from the dark sky to the manila folder on his lap, he opened it for the tenth time in the last hour. Novacrin would be a tough nut to crack. They had influence and power the likes of any big oil or tobacco company. Moreso nowadays with all the focus on cleaning up the planet and getting rid of smoking, the health care industry had become the real gravy train in the last decade.

Raymond flipped through the notes he had made on his legal pad. Novacrin was well under the regular corporate tax rate for California. He was going to try to use this angle to get a look inside their books and see if he can get any leverage on the company to maybe bring them in and get some answers. That's where he was stuck answers to what. Whitehall donated more money to charities in the last three years than they had gotten away with in the bank. He was a public figure in L.A. and sat on the board of a dozen influential companies.

Raymond could tell that Tommy thought this was all bullshit and Peter, while his motives for going along with the plan came with the best intentions, had no clue what this meant in terms of the real world. Peter of all of them had dedicated his life to helping people. He saw the best in everyone; it was a quality that made him the archbishop. Peter had faith; Raymond didn't live in that world, he had to face reality. The reality was, while he believed it could be possible, he also believed they may be powerless to do anything about it. He rubbed his eyes and looked down at his watch, three a.m., it was going to be a long day tomorrow.

Joey was avoiding the question. He looked out the window in Johnny's limo; the dark black tint made everything seem surreal and muted. Johnny had insisted on taking Joey home as the cruised up Lexington Avenue. Johnny had asked, "When you start using again? And I don't mean with your girl, I mean regularly."

Joey had avoided the question long enough. "I got it under control, Johnny", he said without looking at him. Johnny put his hand on Joey's shoulder, forcing him to turn and look Johnny in the eye.

Johnny looked at him and said, "I know, but for how long? I need you to keep it together. I know Tiff is sick but you going off the deep end isn't going to help anyone. Jimmy tells me T.J. has been handling all the business and I know he's your right-hand man from way back but when he takes over you're usually a mess."

"Is there anything you don't know?" Joey joked as he looked back out the window.

"Yeah, I don't know what you're thinking about when you use? You and I both know you're the best at what you do when you're straight. Last time we had to do this it took three months for you to get it back together and right now, if what your saying is true, and I believe it is, then I'm going to need you right. Cause whatever Ray and Pete and Tommy think, in the end, I got a feeling we're going top have to do this our way, you understand me?"

"I can't lose her, Johnny. I can't, and if we don't do this soon I will."

He turned and looked at Johnny, this time intentionally looking him in the eye. "When your mom was sick I saw the pain you were in, you took it and you dealt with it. You're stronger than I am, Johnny. I can't watch her die in front of me. I shoot up to deal with it, simple as that."

Johnny nodded silently, those were tough times for him. "You've always been stronger than me, Joey. Always. Things have been easy for me my whole life. You...you had to fight for everything you've got. Just don't let that shit beat you." Johnny left it at that.

Joey had never, in all the years they had been friends, said anything like that to Johnny. Johnny understood the pain he was going through. He also understood that no matter what he had to do he would use all his power and influence to help his friend.

CHAPTER

4

Meetings

RAYMOND SAT AT HIS OFFICE. He finally felt like he had caught up with his sleep. It had been three days since his meeting at the wine cellar and he had moved to subpoena the records for Novacrin and was waiting to hear back from the judge, who owed him a favor. His office was called Spartan by some a mahogany desk with a nameplate and a calendar. There were a few knickknacks, like a crystal globe and an old-fashioned model of the state building. There was a framed California state flag on the wall and a picture of the president and Raymond shaking hands at some formal dinner and that was about it.

The leather couch in the corner of the room was worn from many late nights at the office, and the bathroom off to the left of the office had a shower and small closet for spare clothes. Raymond sat at his desk and was looking over some plans for the downtown civic center renovation when his intercom buzzed. He picked up the phone, "What is it, Stacy?"

"I have two things, Raul is on the phone from the orange growers union and Senator Hatch just stopped by to see you, he just arrived and said no hurry." Raymond could tell by the tone of Stacy's voice that she was nervous; there had been no scheduled meeting with Senator Hatch today and drop bys usually meant trouble.

Raymond played it cool, "No worries, Stace, tell Raul I'll be by tomorrow for lunch, and give Senator Hatch a drink, the good stuff, and send him right in." Raymond straightened out his hair and stood up and stretched; he started crossing the room just as his door opened. The senator was a squat man with gray hair. He was impeccably dressed and moved with the air of confidence that men of power always seemed to have. He met Raymond halfway and shook his hand vigorously, not spilling a drop of his drink.

Raymond said, "Senator, what a surprise. You should have called, I would have cleared my schedule. Please sit, what can I do for you?"

The senator sat back in the oversized leather chair facing Raymond's desk. "Look, Ray, sorry for the drop in but I need to ask you…well, actually, I need to know something and I didn't call because this is strictly off the record. You understand?"

Raymond did not outwardly show it but his stomach suddenly tightened this could not be good. "No problem, Senator, is everything alright?"

The Senator smiled; he was savvy enough to know exactly how this looked and Raymond's nervousness was the appropriate reaction to a drop in visit by a superior. Knowing this he paused, make him sweat a little, the senator thought to himself. He leaned forward and gave Raymond a glare. "You tell me," he asked.

"Tell you what?" Raymond asked, confused.

"Look, Ray, I know you, you didn't rise this fast by being stupid and I expect you will have my job someday if that's your desire, but I hear you've been poking around Novacrin lately and I need to know why. And please, no bullshit, I'm getting to old to be jerked off."

Raymond sat back in his chair and thought a moment; he paused long enough to let the senator know he was searching for the connection. "Novacrin…oh, the pharmaceutical company. I asked Judge Rutolo if I could get a subpoena to get a look at their finances. They are paying forty percent below the average tax rate for major corporations and I'm looking to raise money for the downtown civic center restoration so I've been checking out all the major corporations to see if I can squeeze them a little more to make ends meet."

The senator took a moment to read Raymond, staring as if he could see something in Raymond's face that said he was lying. After a moment, he relaxed and sank back into his chair. Raymond could tell he was relieved. "Look, son, shake anyone you want but Novacrin is off limits." He took a deep drink and swirled the ice around in his whisky. Raymond decided to push the issue since it was on the table. "May I ask why?" The senator glared at Raymond and said gruffly, "Because I said so, because they donate heavily to our party's campaign and if we want to stay in office, and that we means everyone in the party, then we need that support. Back off them, Ray. In two years they'll fund you whole re-election campaign or your run for governor, I can see to that. Do yourself a favor, leave Novacrin alone."

Raymond backtracked quickly, "I'm sorry, sir, I'll back down, and I didn't even know they were that heavily connected to the party."

"They pay extra for that." The senator stood up to leave. "I see this was an innocent mistake on your part though I'm surprised, I would have thought with your reputation you would have had all the big fish sniffed out already?"

Raymond replied sheepishly, "Guess that one slipped past me."

The senator stopped and reevaluated Raymond with his stare. "I told you, son, don't bullshit me, you thought about shaking that tree a little harder and seeing if a couple of more bananas fell out!"

Raymond realized his mistake and quietly said, "Yes, sir."

"Look, Ray, there are some companies that are above even our hypocrisy. These guys over at Novacrin are untouchable. And mark my word, you get on the wrong end of them and you won't be able to run for a school board. I see you get my meaning. Just back off and do it quickly."

"Yes, sir."

The senator finished his drink. "You're going to make the whole party proud someday, son. I hope I'm still around to see that."

"Thank you, sir." Raymond said, and with that the senator left the office.

Raymond sat back behind his desk and ran his hands through his hair. He pulled open the bottom drawer and pulled out the Novacrin file, under it was the picture that he always kept in the drawer. It was the picture of him, Tommy, Johnny, Peter, and Joey as kids; they were in a park on 116th Street all wearing green and yellow baseball caps that said Bison's. The picture was taken a week before the bank job. Raymond took the picture out and placed it on his desk. He looked at the file then back to the picture. Raymond smiled and opened the file; for better or worse, he was all in.

Tommy had spotted Phil Lancaster about fifteen minutes into the auction; he was a slight man, no, thin and healthy looking would describe him better, he wore glasses and was well-dressed but not wearing a suit. He looked more like one of those .com millionaires or a software geek than a doctor. All in all, he was pretty nondescript. He had brown hair slightly graying at the temples and his skin was tanned. Tommy watched him as he moved through the crowd. Lancaster didn't really socialize with anyone unlike Tommy, who was stopped every few feet by someone he knew or had business dealings with.

Tommy was relieved when the auctioneer called everyone to the opulent auction room. He picked up his paddle and tried to maneuver himself near Lancaster but the closest he could get was three rows behind him and across the aisle. As the auctioneer began, Tommy had to keep reminding himself to watch Lancaster; he had a tendency to get caught up in the action. Tommy loved auctions; he had dreamed of being able to afford anything he wanted and know that it was a reality, he didn't mind spending large amounts of money on anything that caught his eye.

The auction crept on with the usual intermission with more champagne and fresh fruit platters; it wasn't until late in the afternoon that Tommy saw the jewel of the auction, an early Gauguin. To his surprise, Lancaster opened the bidding at 120,000 dollars. Others quickly jumped in and the bidding started to escalate. The fervor in the room rose as he saw Lancaster raise his paddle at 345,000 dollars. It was time to make his move. "Five hundred thousand," he called out to gasps from the crowd. Lancaster immediately raised his paddle without even looking back. Very cool, Tommy thought and again jumped the bid by yelling out, "Six hundred fifty thousand." Tommy had just increased the bidding by seventy-five thousand and he could see the hesitation in Lancaster. Tommy thought, I have him now, but to his surprise, Lancaster called out, "Seven hundred twenty-five thousand." The crowd now was charged and they cheered, the sound seeming to shrink Lancaster down into his chair; he obviously didn't like the attention.

Tommy smiled and countered, "Eight hundred thousand," to which the crowed cheered again. The auctioneer began his usual, "Going once, going twice, last and final call."

"Too rich for me", Lancaster called out, cracking up the entire crowd.

"Sold to number 4121." The gavel slammed down and the crowd clapped as Tommy got up and headed for the cashier.

Tommy waited for the cashier at the post-auction reception and saw him making his way toward the door. He quickly grabbed two glasses of champagne and cut him off before he could reach the coat check. "Hey, I don't know whether to thank you or be angry with you," he said, offering the champagne to Lancaster. Lancaster hesitated then grabbed the glass and said, "What do you mean?"

"Well, were you really interested in the painting or were you just bidding me up? Because of you I probably paid two hundred thousand more than I should have," Tommy said in a friendly manner.

Lancaster looked quizzically at Tommy and replied, "You definitely paid two hundred thousand more but I wanted that painting. Now, tell me, are you a fan of Gauguin or are you an investor?"

"Dangerous question. I'm a fan; if I were a collector I wouldn't have paid that much. I have three of his paintings and need this fourth to balance out my wall," Tommy said sarcastically.

Lancaster hesitated again and then laughed. "Well, I don't feel so bad then."

Tommy held out his hand. "Tommy Russo."

Lancaster took his hand and shook. "I know who you are. I was hoping you didn't show up today. I would have had a better shot at that painting. Dr. Phil Lancaster."

"MD?"

"No, PhD, microbiology."

"Interesting."

"Not really, but I can appreciate the minute strokes of a paintbrush in great art."

"I never thought of it that way. I guess I just go for the aesthetes, being an architect by trade."

"I thought you were only real estate?"

Tommy laughed. "One of my many pursuits. I grew up wanting to be an architect, the rest just kind of fell into place."

"I know what you mean, I just wanted a little lab and investigate microbes but then things changed. Now I'm on the board of a pharmaceutical company and rarely ever get in the lab."

"Hey, would you like to get some dinner? I'm heading over to one of my places on the East Side; it's the least I could do after winning that painting?"

Lancaster looked Tommy over then said, "You're absolutely right. What's the address? I'll meet you there."

On the car ride over, Tommy felt very proud of himself. Then in a moment of panic he thought, so I've made contact, now what, ask him, "Hey, you got a cure for AIDS you're hiding?" It seemed ridiculous. Tommy had doubts about Joey's story for a lot of reasons but would never air them in front of the guys. He decided to enjoy his dinner and see what happens; as far as he was concerned, he had accomplished his end of the plan now it was up to Johnny to find the guys who had gotten cured.

He shook his head. Find three guys from one name given by a money-hungry lab assistant, what were the chances of that? His dinner with Lancaster was not what he had expected. Phil was a regular guy; he was funny, engaging, and easy to talk to. They discussed wine, art, golf, and other things that only men of their type of wealth could discuss. The evening flew by and they had made arrangements for golf the following Wednesday. Tommy had dinner two more times with Phil that week and they both attended a charity function at the Plaza, where they hung out.

The more time Tommy spent with Phil, the more he felt Joey could not be correct. He hated to admit it, but Phil Lancaster was becoming a friend and he just could not see this man holding out on a cure for millions. When the summons came for the meeting at the wine cellar, he was fully prepared to explain to Joey that Lancaster was a good guy and that the lab technician must have scammed him. He was fully expecting the meeting to produce nothing; he could never imagine how wrong he'd be.

"Your Eminence, your three o'clock is here." Peter's assistant poked his head into Peter's office.

Peter was kneeling in prayer. He was in full robes, even kneeling was almost the size of Michael standing. Peter looked up, "Give me three minutes and then send her in please."

"As you wish, Father." Peter stood up and went over to his desk. There were papers everywhere. He sighed, his desk was a mess and whenever he saw someone in his office it was always a source of embarrassment to him. He looked up at the picture of Jesus and whispered for the greater good. The he assumed the priestly posture, hands folded as if in prayer palms flattened together, and waited.

The woman who walked in was stunning. Elegantly dressed from head to opened toe shoes; in fact, Peter was almost taken off guard. He quickly regained his composure and stood to his full impressive height. Judy Tannaro crossed, no glided, across the room and took Peter's hand and kissed his ring. "Your Eminence, it is a pleasure to finally meet you," she said. "I regret this meeting is one that is long overdue, and I apologize for that."

"As one of the church's most generous benefactors, we should have done this a long time ago."

"The fault is mine, Your Eminence, and I know how busy you must be. Two years is not enough time to get up to speed in a parish such as this." She glanced down at the messy desk and Peter felt a wave of shame run through him.

"Then let us agree that we both share the fault and move forward from there." Peter smiled and motioned for Ms. Tannaro to sit in the chair opposite the desk.

"I've never been back here in these offices. It is truly amazing how large it is back here; I would think the church takes up most of the space."

"You should see the Vatican, talk about space. I once got lost there for two days," Peter joked and Ms. Tannaro laughed heartily.

"I must admit farther I am honored you called me but I am curious to know why."

"Well, I was thinking that some benefactors such as yourself are so giving that I thought you should have a say in the way your money is spent. I feel it is important to have people involved, mind you, only if it is something you wish to do. I realize people are busy and trust us to do the right thing with the funds we receive, but I also realize people have causes that are more important, for personal reasons, and would want to be a partner in the good works we do."

Ms. Tannaro looked overjoyed. "Your Eminence, I have been a benefactor for many years and never question how or where my money is spent, but if you are offering me a chance to be involved with how my donations are spent then I would love to be part of the process."

"Very good, we will set up a schedule for you and your husband to meet with us so we can discuss some of the programs we support and any you would like to add to our list." Peter noticed a quick tightening of her jaw as he said the word husband and waited for a reply.

Ms. Tannaro shifted nervously in her seat. "Your Eminence, my marriage was annulled by the church twelve years ago. I realize some checks come to the church with his name but we are no longer in touch. Unfortunately, his wallet is much deeper than his faith".

"I am so sorry...I did not know." Peter stumbled over the apology but Ms. Tannaro quickly rebounded, "Do not worry, Your Eminence, it was a long time ago, and with Christ's guidance I made it through the dark times of my marriage."

Peter smiled, " Christ will do that for us, won't he? Well, I will have Michael give you a list of organizations we support for you to look at and we can meet again next week at the same time, if that works for you."

"Are there any substance abuse programs that you support?" she asked.

"Yes, quite a few," Peter replied.

Ms. Tannaro stood up and again Peter realized how very beautiful she was, he stood up too and once again, she took his hand and kissed his ring.

"Thank you, Your Eminence, I look forward to our meeting next week." Peter watched her exit and slumped into his chair heavily.

He looked at the picture of Jesus again and muttered aloud, "For all those who are suffering, Lord." Peter picked up the phone and called Raymond. "Raymond, yeah, she just left, seems nice enough but I don't know if it will lead anywhere. In all honesty, I hope it leads nowhere. I understand the greater good here but right now it doesn't feel like it. You know, every day since the park I've been trying to make the right decisions; don't get me wrong, I have no regrets about that day but I feel like I did back then, conflicted. I don't know, Ray, tell me I'm doing this for the right reasons." It all came out quickly and Raymond paused before answering.

Peter was different; as much as Raymond hated to admit it, they all were. They weren't kids anymore, this wasn't a fight in the schoolyard, and for Peter especially this went very contrary to his moral compass. Even for himself, he had made his decision he would always put his friends first but at what cost; Peter and Raymond had the most to lose. For Raymond, it could mean his career, Senator Hatch had made that very clear; for Peter, this was testing everything he now stood for.

Raymond could hear it in his voice. He tried to think of something to say that would comfort his friend and allow him to deal with the situation in terms he could understand. "I know how you feel, Pete, I went through the same thing all those years ago. It's even harder now, I mean, we were kids back then…sometimes I don't think we ever understood the consequences, now it's different. But, Pete, we all have done good in our own ways, even Johnny, you know what he does for the community. And for Joey maybe this is his chance to do the right thing. And if we can help him achieve that and find a cure then we all win."

He heard Peter sigh again through the receiver of the phone. Raymond waited for Peter's response. "If the girl wasn't sick would we be having this conversation, Ray"? It was a question he had asked himself many times on the flight back from New York.

It was Raymond's turn to sigh, "Maybe not, Pete…but if he is right."

"I hear you, Ray, and I have to have faith that this is God's will. Maybe all the years I've prayed for Joey to change maybe this is the one thing that will finally save him; last time we changed our destinies, if Joey is right maybe we change the world"

"That's the key, Pete. If he's right, for all we know we may be getting ourselves worked up for nothing."

"Yeah, I guess finding those three men will be like Moses finding the promised land after wandering forty years in the desert," Peter joked.

Raymond laughed, " Yeah, but no offense, Pete, if I needed to count on someone to get this job done my money's on Johnny."

CHAPTER

5

Johnny's meeting

I T WAS RAINING AGAIN AS JOHNNY AND JOEY SAT IN THE LIMO HEADING TOWARD THE NEW WINE CELLAR. Johnny lamented it always seemed to be raining when they met lately. He had a million things on his mind. He smiled; he wondered if his father had felt this way. He missed his father. It's funny, as you get older you appreciate the ones you love more and more, even when they're gone. Johnny looked at the city blocks rolling by and thought about family. He had never married or had kids.

It wasn't that he didn't want to have a family, he was always afraid of the consequences that having one would bring. Johnny couldn't imagine how his father had dealt with that. Times were different back then, he guessed, there was an honor code, woman and children were off limits then, not anymore. He had sacrificed that to be in the position of power he was in today. It made this whole situation even more important. Joey, Raymond, Tommy, and Peter were his family. He watched their rise with same pride his father had shown toward him. Johnny rubbed his temples and took a deep breath.

He had cleared time for this and was leaving most of the day-to-day operations to his captains. More stress, that's all it was. He would deal with just like his father had right up until the day it killed him. Johnny ignored Joey's babble with Jimmy Shoes, who was driving tonight. The screen on the limo was down and Joey was leaning through the cutout, talking Knicks basketball with Jimmy. Johnny was glad he had brought Joey along, it kept him busy and kept him straight. He understood Ray's plan to keep Joey on the sidelines; Joey was prone to make rash decisions and that may work in his business but in the real world, rash actions led to big consequences.

In Joey's line of work, people ended up dead. Johnny thought of his father again; he had taught him to have good people around him and always stay three moves ahead. "There are strengths and weaknesses in every organization, play to your strengths, cover your weaknesses, see the whole field. The guy in the local deli knows more about the neighborhood than the fucking mayor." Franco had been great at having those people, the people who lived in the neighborhood, as his people. It had been a lesson Johnny learned well.

As the neighborhood had evolved, things changed, but the lessons Johnny had learned from his father still applied. Joey and Jimmy were arguing about the Knicks backcourt now and Johnny chimed in, "What the fuck, forty-five games if they're lucky," to which both men went on a tirade about how crazy he was. Johnny smiled. There were about fifty things he had to do tonight after this meeting. He rubbed his eyes; it was going to be a long night.

The limo pulled into the alley behind Tommy's restaurant. Joey bounced out right into the rain and walked calmly to the kitchen door. Johnny waited for Jimmy to come around with the umbrella and walk him to the door. "I'll call you when we need you," Johnny said and then turned to the door. Once inside, the men were greeted by Smitty, who led them to the new wine cellar. Johnny smiled, "How's your mom, Smitty?"

"Great, you know, it's getting like old times seeing you guys every other week." Smitty laughed.

"What are you talking about, Smitty, I'm never here?" he said with a quick wink.

Smitty smiled. "Of course, you're not, Johnny."

Tommy, Raymond, and Peter were already waiting when Johnny and Joey arrived. "So what's the big news?" Peter said as he crossed the room to embrace Johnny and Joey.

"Slow down, you big fuck, can I get my fucking coat off?" Peter scowled at him and Joey laughed.

"Drink, Johnny?"

"Yeah sure." Johnny took off his coat and hung it next to the others on the wall.

Raymond smiled at them and said, "I take it you have some important news, that's why you're making us wait."

Johnny smiled, "You know, you used to be more fun, Ray, the political arena has made you a sourpuss." Joey laughed and handed Johnny a scotch.

Raymond could tell he was bursting to say something so he asked, "You find anything out?"

"Yeah, we pretty much confirmed the whole story," Joey said, smiling. Johnny looked at Raymond and nodded.

Tommy whispered quietly, "That's amazing. It really is true, I can't see Phil..." he stopped himself before continuing. Peter was stunned to silence and sat heavily into one of the leather chairs.

Raymond smiled and said, "Tell me the story."

Johnny looked at Joey, who nodded and began, "So we decide to go looking for the three guys who died after they supposedly got cured. You know we only had the one name so I figured we give Joey's friend a shout and see if he can get the other two for us."

Joey jumped in, "We were ready to pay anything for the names and maybe see if the guy has any other information."

"Funny thing, though, no one could find him," Johnny said.

"What do you mean?" Peter asked, finally saying something.

"Yeah, he supposedly resigned two weeks after our conversation and no one has heard from him since," Joey said.

Raymond considered this for a minute and then said, "you think any foul play was involved?"

Johnny laughed. "We'll get back to that in a minute," he said. He took a swig of his drink and then said, "I took the one name we had to this guy I use for various things."

"Guy, he's a kid, what, twenty-two, twenty-three tops," Joey added.

"Guy, kid, doesn't matter, he's a fucking genius. He could tell you what you paid for lunch yesterday and what you ate, computers and stuff."

"What, is he some kind of hacker?" Tommy asked.

"Exactly! I use him to do various things for me, fake drivers licenses, social security numbers, he can even tap into certain companies and I know when they are moving merchandise. The guy is worth a fortune."

"Yeah, but you pay him in electronics," Joey said.

"Not my idea, he tells me what he wants I get it for him. And don't think that doesn't cost me." Johnny smiled.

"So me, Johnny, and Charlie Irish go see him with the name. We gave him all we had on the guy, has AIDS, went to Novacrin for treatment, and that's about it."

"That's pretty thin," Raymond said.

"Tells us come back in two days. We go back two days later and he pulls out a folder." Johnny took the folder he had placed on the table when he came in and placed it in Raymond's hand.

Tommy and Peter stood up and moved behind Raymond to get a look at the folder as Raymond read it. "This is incredible, all this from a name? How can you be sure it's the right name. I mean, there must be at least a hundred guys with the same name in the country."

Johnny nodded in agreement. "My guy is good, he knows what he's doing and anyway, that's only half the story in there."

Raymond took a minute to read and flip through the documents then he looked up at Johnny confused. "So let me get this straight, based on this, our guy went to Novacrin in February and started treatments, he was defiantly infected with the AIDS virus and went back for subsequent treatments over the next few months. He then stops treatments and is off all medications for three months then he disappears never to be heard from again?"

"That doesn't make much sense," Tommy added.

Johnny grabbed the folder from Ray and said, "Let me fill in the gaps. My kid searched the name and cross referenced it with hospital databases in California and California insurance records. He narrowed it down to our boy there and once he had the right guy, he was able to access all his information: credit cards, medical records, the works. According to medical records, our guy was on a number of AIDS medications; he was going downhill and getting desperate so he contacted Novacrin, see the correspondence there on page three? He got the green light to go in and was treated by none other then our guy Lancaster. Look, the insurance paid for the initial visit to Novacrin and the testing was done by Lancaster himself."

Raymond considered this for a minute and then said, "So our guy checks in and then disappears too."

"That can't be coincidence," Peter murmured.

"Oh, the coincidences are just beginning," Joey added.

Johnny walked over to his coat and pulled out two other envelopes. "What are those?" Tommy asked.

"The names of the two other guys in the trial."

"How the hell did he get the other names?" Raymond asked.

Johnny laughed. "I told you this kid was good."

Joey took over, "According to kid, he accessed a bunch of Novacrin data and when he cross referenced the one name we had, these other two names kept coming up. So the kid runs their info up the flagpole and the stories are similar. Both had advanced AIDS and both were desperate. These three went in on the same days and saw the same guy every time, Lancaster."

Raymond took the other two folders and began reading aloud, "Frank Cerone, Carlos Medina, and our fist lead Jake Gordon, all in the same trial and (pausing to look through each folder) all are missing?"

"What!" Peter said.

"What do you mean missing?" Tommy asked. "Johnny, am I reading this right, Johnny? This guy Carlos' folder says whereabouts unknown, and Frank's folder says deceased. Are you telling me these guys are both dead?"

"They're all dead."

The room fell silent for a moment then Peter asked, "Wait, I thought they were all cured?"

"They were." Joey smiled.

"Would someone please help me out here, I'm totally confused," Peter moaned.

Raymond coolly looked up from the folder he was holding and said, "Relax, Pete, I think there's more to the story."

Johnny smiled and nodded to Raymond. "Sit, Pete, let me clear it up for you." Johnny took another sip of his scotch and leaned forward in his chair. "After we had the names of the three guys and all of their information, we hit the streets. As you know, I'm pretty well connected when it comes to these things," Johnny joked.

"I'm pretty well connected in my circles too," Joey interjected.

Johnny smiled. "Anyway, we started with this Carlos Medina guy, he lived in California, not far from Novacrin really. I called in a few favors from the Big Worm in California, you know, Tony Cantrello, he put his guys out on the street and we traced this Carlos guy down. Supposedly, he was a drug addict, caught the virus from a dirty needle. Once he got cured, he went right back to his old ways, only this time he was given a hot dose and ended up dead."

"What's a hot dose?" Tommy asked.

Joey jumped in, "A hot dose is a bad concoction of drugs meant to kill someone. Sometimes a dealer wants to get rid of a problem, guy he thinks is a snitch guy who owes too much, sometimes you do it just to send a message."

Peter was horrified. "So someone killed him!" Johnny put his hand on Joey's arm to quiet him down, he sounded too cavalier about murder in front of these guys.

"That's the nature of the business, Pete", he whispered.

Raymond jumped in, "Did anyone talk to the dealer? Ask why he hot dosed the guy?"

Joey not quite as enthusiastically said, "The dealer disappeared."

"What do you mean he disappeared?" Tommy asked.

"Dealing on the corner one day gone the next. Most people in the neighborhood thought he got pinched and turned states but no indictments went down and no more heat than usual in the neighborhood, so it's like the guy just vanished," Joey said.

"Is that normal?" Tommy asked.

"Yes, but the next part isn't," Joey said.

"What's the next part?" Peter said.

Johnny sat back. "Same thing happened to Frank Cerone in Jacksonville."

"Whew," Raymond exhaled and sank into his chair.

"This guy was a fucking mess, old man Stratsi said one of his crew knew the guy, a real dead beat, gambler, dope head, no one was surprised when he went missing. According to Stratsi, there were a number of guys who could have done it. I asked Stratsi to look into it and he came up with a dealer who supposedly got paid a nice chunk of change to deliver the dose," Johnny said.

Joey jumped in, "I sent T.J., my right hand-man, down there to see if he could get some information from the dealer, but guess what?"

"He disappeared too?" Raymond asked coolly.

"Bingo," Joey said.

"So these two who got cured get killed and both by a hot drug dose and both dealers who supply the dose disappear?" Raymond rubbed his temples.

"Could it be coincidence, I mean, they were both drug addicts?"

"You fucking kidding me, Tommy, com'on, that's no coincidence. These guys got whacked and the loose ends got tied. It was a dead end, we had nothing but the four murders." Tommy shook his head and took a deep swig of his drink. Peter looked visibly shaken, only Raymond took it all in stride.

"What about the third guy?"

"The third guy, turns out, got it on a fishing trip in Louisiana." Johnny continued, "He was a drug user too but he cleans up his act after getting cured. Takes a fishing trip about eight months after the treatment, goes out about a mile and a half, and the boat disappears, everyone on it supposedly dead from a boating accident."

"Someone really didn't want any loose ends," Peter mumbled.

"How do you know the boat went out a mile and a half, Johnny?" Raymond asked.

Johnny smiled and leaned forward. "This guy, you should have been a detective, I got the guy who did the job."

"What", Tommy gasped.

Johnny smiled. "Me and Joey, we went down to New Orleans to see Fat Sally, he pretty much runs the town, I had him ask around and turns out one of his lower lieutenants heard about the job. It was an outside thing, sort of a side job for him. He sent out one of his men to follow the boat, killed everyone on board, put two holes in the boat, and tied the bodies on and let her sink."

Raymond digested the information and then asked, "Do you know who put out the contract?"

"Well that's the interesting part, it was a guy who called himself Jake. I brought pictures of the board members down to Sally's man. Guess who he pointed out?"

"They actually pointed someone out?" Tommy asked.

Johnny paused his story and turned to Tommy. "It's not like the cops were asking for information here. I mean really, Tommy, you know what I do for a living, there are perks to being me."

"I'm sorry, Johnny, it's just this is all a bit overwhelming."

"Who'd he point out?" Raymond interrupted.

Johnny looked him in the eye and said, "It was Specter."

Raymond leaned back in, thought, and took a few seconds before speaking. "It makes sense. The other board members are money guys; Specter and Lancaster are the only two self-made men and Lancaster is a doctor. Specter has no real skill set, grew up in

Philly, tough neighborhood, went to business school, must have been friends with one of the money guys, probably Whitehall; they crossed paths in collage. He is the muscle, Lancaster the brains, and Whitehall, Jamison, and Roony the money."

"I still can't believe it, I would have never figured Lancaster to be in on something like this," Tommy said aloud and almost immediately regretted it.

"What the fuck you want, pictures? These fucks are holding out, they got the cure. The proof is that there are guys getting whacked all over the place, that's enough proof for me," Johnny said annoyed.

Joey jumped up angrily. "This is no coincidence, these guys got the cure and we're getting it from them!" he shouted at Tommy.

Peter stood up and walked over to Tommy, put a large hand on his shoulder and said, "I hate to admit it, Tommy, but this must be true."

The men sat in silence for a few moments, each contemplating the repercussions of what they just heard. Johnny finally broke the silence. "Anyone else get anything?" he asked with bit sarcasm in his tone.

Raymond smiled, "I had a senator hand me my ass the other day for trying to subpoena Novacrin records. No Shit." Johnny whistled and shook his head. "A senator, eh…these fucks do have some juice. You okay, Ray?"

"No. He said in not so many words that Novacrin supports the entire party and were untouchable. The whole thing makes sense, you test your product on guys who are desperate but expendable, I would bet these guys had no family no ties to anyone."

Johnny nodded in affirmation. "Nah, the two dope fiends no one cared about and the boat guy was divorced years ago, the wife didn't even care he died."

Raymond stood up and stretched. "There are to many pieces coming together for this to be any coincidence, but we need to be careful. In a way, these guys have more influence than us. The fact that they could get a senator to come down on me so quick is proof of that."

Peter looked hopefully at Raymond. "Don't you think the police would have come up with something? Pieced some of this together?"

Johnny looked at Peter and said sympathetically, "Look, Pete, to the cops they see three scumbags with priors, they could care less. But I checked with my contacts on the force and so did Fat Sally, no investigations were done. The boat and crew were reported missing but there was no mention of the passenger. In all honesty, Pete, no one cared about these guys. I know that's hard to believe but that's the way it is sometimes, they were chosen for a reason, they were expendable."

Peter balled his fists. "No life is expendable," he growled. They could tell he was upset. He walked away to the bar and poured himself a glass of wine.

Tommy looked up from his chair and said, "So what is our next move here, Ray? I mean, we need to proceed with caution. Whitehall and Roony are old money, they may have more connections then us."

Joey had had enough as far as he was concerned; they had found their proof and it was time for action. "Fuck influence and connections, I say we kidnap one or two and squeeze them until they talk. Fuck, let's whack two or three of them and then get the others to squeal, I like that even better."

Peter almost dropped his drink and Tommy looked at Ray, shock and nervousness on his face. Raymond saw his friends' reactions and said, "Slow down, we cant just go on a kidnapping and killing spree. We need to think this out and take it slow."

Joey was hot, "You haven't seen my girl, she looks bad and no treatment is working for her. I want them dead before she dies." Tommy stood up and turned to Raymond pleading his case.

"Look, I just need more time I'm getting in pretty close with Phil. I think if you give me a month or two I can get him talking." Ray knew it was the last thing Joey wanted to hear and as much as he respected Tommy, he couldn't believe that he was so naive in this situation.

Before he could gently explain Joey blew his stack again. "Enjoy your martinis and caviar at your next benefit cause I swear it'll be his last public appearance. Are you fucking hearing this Johnny, are we supposed to sit around and wait for a scumbag to start talking? Cause it's been my experience that no one tells the truth until their inches from death."

Ray sat back and looked at the faces of his friends. They were all looking at him to make the call, all except Johnny, he seemed to know what Ray was thinking already. Ray looked at Johnny and then took a deep breath. "Look, I think we need to give Tommy some more time." Tommy smiled and Peter was about to say something but Raymond continued. He looked at Joey, who he could tell was unhappy with the situation, and said, "One month, Tommy, then it's Joey and Johnny's show and we all back off." Joey smiled and nodded he could accept that.

Peter looked at Ray and quietly said, "I didn't sign up for murder, Ray." He purposely looked right into Raymond's eyes as he said this pleading for him to change his mind.

Ray understood and quietly said, "None of us did, Pete, but the greater good may be at stake here, I think I could live with that." Peter looked heartbroken and Ray felt for him but it was the best course of action he could take. He believed that Novacrin had the cure and he also knew that in all likelihood Joey and Johnny would have to muscle Lancaster to get it.

Peter needed to be cut loose from all of this, Tommy too, but now wasn't the time for that. Peter looked at his friends, he hated the smug look on Joey's face, and he registered the nervousness on Tommy's. Tommy had become friends with Lancaster; Peter could tell he did not like this turn of events. Johnny looked sympathetically at Peter and actually came over and hugged him. As Johnny was pulling away from Peter, he whispered in his ear, "Pray for us all, Pete, it'll all work out."

Peter smiled, he wasn't happy but Johnny was right all he could do was pray for them and let God be the judge. Joey broke the silence, "One month, he said, and then I start leaving body parts around." He grabbed his coat and stormed out without saying anything else.

Johnny shook his head and said, "I'll go after him, be safe, and, Tommy, good luck, see you guys in a few weeks." He started for the door and knelt to give Raymond a kiss on the cheek as he left. "It's the right plan brother." he said.

When Johnny had left, Peter turned to Ray. "How could you condone that?" he asked.

Raymond sighed, "I don't, Pete. I just know the odds of cracking this guy are slim, their way may be the only way."

Tommy stood up and said, "Don't worry, Pete, I'll get him to talk."

Raymond smiled. He'd seen that determined look on Tommy many times. "Just be careful and be quick, Tommy. I don't know how long Johnny and I can keep Joey down."

"He's using again," Peter interjected. "I can tell he's not the same when he's using, he never would have said half that stuff in front of me if he wasn't high." Raymod had thought the same but didn't have the heart to voice his opinion. Joey had gone off the deep end before and Johnny and Peter had brought him back; they had spent countless hours with him the last time to get him clean again. Ray wasn't sure what disappointed Peter more, Joey talking about murder or him using again. The three men sat for a few moments in silence, each deep in his own thoughts.

"What the fuck is wrong with you!" Johnny was hot. He waved his driver back in to the car and grabbed Joey and pushed him toward the alley away from the car.

"Relax, what did I say that was so bad?"

Johnny looked at Joey and softened his tone, "Come on, bro, you can't talk about kidnapping and body parts in front of those guys. Joey, we live in a different world than those guys; they have no clue what we do on a daily basis, you can't go around saying shit like that."

"So you saying you don't trust them anymore?"

Johnny was frustrated. "Of course I trust them, they will do anything for you or me, the point is, you shouldn't ask them to do something they can't handle. You were right to come to all of us with this and we will help you in any way we can, but cool out with the chopping up guys talk. Ray's plan is solid, give Tommy a month that fuck could talk a dog off a bone, it's what he does."

"Give him his shot and then if it doesn't work we take ours, we do it our way the way it's done in the streets." Johnny smiled and hugged Joey.

"I swear, I thought Pete was going to piss his pants when you went off," Johnny laughed.

Joey smiled and relaxed. "Yeah, I guess I could have handled that a bit differently."

"No shit," they laughed as they walked back to the limo.

"I'll call Pete tomorrow and apologize," Joey said. Johnny smiled and got into the car.

CHAPTER

6

Novacrin

THE SUN WAS SETTING, THE LIGHTS OF THE GROUNDS WERE STARTING TO BLINK ON ONE BY ONE AS JOHN WHITEHALL WATCHED FROM THE GLASS WINDOW THAT RAN THE LENGTH OF THE NOVACRIN BOARDROOM. He poured himself a scotch and looked wistfully out the window. J.R. Roony, a longtime friend and fellow board member, was rambling on about some political dinner he had just attended and how he had secured yet another connection in the party, which would allow for some more trial and R&D money. It was very boring and Whitehall had tuned him out ten minutes ago.

Whitehall had other pressing concerns on his mind; they were awaiting the arrival of Thomas Specter, another board member, whose report Whitehall was much more interested in. Just as Whitehall was about to tell Roony to shut up, the door of the boardroom opened. Whitehall expected Specter, but instead it was Jamison. Hollis Jamison was the fifth board member; he handled all the public relations and day-to-day operations of Novacrin.

"Sorry I'm late guys." He quickly scanned the room. "Where's Thomas?"

"Late, as usual," Roony smiled.

"Drink?" Whitehall offered Jamison a scotch; he nodded and took the offered glass.

Jamison assumed his place on an oversized leather chair to the right of Roony and asked, "What's this all about? You made it sound important on the phone."

The question was directed at Whitehall but he didn't answer. Instead, he took another drink from his glass and approached the table; he sat at the head, his back facing the window. Whitehall ran his hand across the black marble tabletop; he looked around the room, sparsely decorated but reeking of elegance and wealth. He smiled and said, "I didn't call the meeting, Thomas did."

Roony rolled his eyes and took out a cigar and lit it. "Specter.. ha, appropriately named. What ghost is haunting him now?" Roony joked. Jamison shifted nervously in his chair. Whitehall noticed. Jamison was leery of Specter and for good reason; Thomas Specter was not a man to be trifled with. Whitehall knew Thomas from college and had complete faith in him, but these men had never strayed into the depths Specter had, they didn't have it in them, few did; that's what made Thomas so valuable, he would do the things no one else would. That made him dangerous and that made these men nervous.

"Who's attacking us now…I swear, John, one of these days that man is going to turn on us. I do not know how you can trust that man."

"Trust who?" The voice made Roony jump and spill his drink on the table. Whitehall smiled; Specter had arrived. "Trust who, J.R.?" he asked again, gliding into the room and sitting across from Roony. Whitehall did not offer Thomas a drink knowing he would decline. Specter was in his late forties, tall, thin the short-cropped dark hair on his head cut military style. He wore a dark suit and, depending how you looked at him, you could consider him harmless or dangerous, if that was possible.

Roony stumbled through an apology, "I was going to say we cannot trust you to ever be on time, we've been waiting twenty minutes already."

"Late for the next ball, J.R. Who is it tonight, the House or the Senate?" he replied sarcastically.

"You should be thanking me for having Hatch come down on your latest 'threat' to the safety of our company."

"You're right", Specter said, " but I was right too, I knew it, I told you guys, I was right but did any you listen." He opened his briefcase and threw a stack of pictures on the table. They fanned out and spread across the black marble. Specter gave Whitehall a quick look as if to say we have something here, and Whitehall in turn nodded for Specter to continue.

Roony was already thumbing through the photos. They were various shots of Lancaster and Tommy golfing, eating dinner at different fundraisers. Roony laughed aloud. "This is your threat... Tommy and our boy Phil. What are you jealous, Phil has a new boyfriend, Thomas?" Roony said, nudging Jamison.

Specter spun on Roony faster then he expected and through gritted teeth said, "Listen, you pompous ass, I care about one thing, the safety of this company, because if there are any leaks, all your connections and all your friends will run and hide; you'll go to jail and I'm guessing you won't do to well in there. So keep your mouth shut and listen for a change." Specter had gotten a little too close and Whitehall could see Roony beginning to panic.

"That's enough, Thomas. No one is going to jail and there are certainly no leaks coming from this room, so please tell us your concerns and stop being so fatalistic." Specter looked at Roony and smiled as he backed away.

"As I was saying, I knew that the lieutenant governor coming after us and trying to get a look at the books meant something but I couldn't put my finger on it till I saw these," Specter made a gesture toward the photos.

"You're saying the lieutenant governor and Phil are connected in some way?" Jamison asked.

"No, the governor and this real estate guy, Tommy Russo."

Whitehall looked intrigued. "Explain," Whitehall said as he put down his drink.

"When we got word the lieutenant governor was looking to subpoena us, I got curious, first I had J.R. call in some big guns to shut him down."

"And I explained to you Senator Hatch said it was an innocent mistake," Roony cut in.

Specter sneered at him. "Well, I sent a man down to watch Phil and he seemingly has a new best friend," again he gestured toward the pictures. I dug around on Tommy Russo, seems he grew up in the same neighborhood as the lieutenant governor, heavy contributor to his campaigns. They've even had some dealings together out here in California. They stay in touch and Tommy and this guy Raymond met twice in the last two months at one of Tommy's restaurants in Manhattan."

"Oh please, I've met Tommy Russo a million times at various functions, this is you being paranoid again," Roony said.

Specter didn't respond; he looked at Whitehall and waited. "What are you thinking, Thomas?"

"I'm thinking somewhere there was a leak and these guys know something."

"John, really, are you buying any of this? These men run in the same circles, it is not beyond reason they become friends."

"Shut up!" Specter snapped at Roony but he held Whitehall's gaze.

Whitehall thought for a moment then replied, "What you say is entirely plausible, J.R...but I think we have seen in the past that in matters such as these, Thomas has an uncanny knack for finding out the truth. I think we need to take this seriously."

"Uncanny knack, is that what we're calling it now?" Roony blustered. Specter ignored him.

Whitehall continued, "Do you think we are compromised in any way, Thomas?"

"I don't know," Specter said coolly, "but I'd like to find out."

"And how do you propose we do that?" Jamison asked.

Specter looked at Whitehall, who barely nodded. "First, I'll go talk to Phil and feel him out to see what state of mind he's in. Then, I think we make life a little uncomfortable for our lieutenant governor and his moneyman to show them we mean business"

"I can't see Phil being involved in something like this, can you, John? I mean, we know Phil for years, he's been onboard with us since the beginning."

Whitehall reflected on Jamison's words before answering. "I would like to think this Phil is still with us, but he's been acting distant lately, spending a lot of time in New York at his lab. It is not out of the question but I agree, Hollis, I can't see Phil turning on us."

"I'd like to think everything is on the up and up also," Specter added. Roony stifled a laugh. Specter shot him a cold look.

"But remember, of everyone on the board he is in the best position to sink all of us if he wanted to."

"And if he is talking to these guys, what then?" Jamison asked.

"If I feel Phil has turned on us then I'm inclined to take all of them out," Specter said matter-of-factly.

Jamison shook his head. "Isn't our body count getting a little high and we're talking about Phil here, are you approving this, John?"

Whitehall stretched and got up. He strolled to the window and looked out at the magnificence that was the grounds of Novacrin. He sighed deeply, "If Phil isn't with us he's against us and as I stated before, I trust Thomas implicitly."

"This is ridiculous," Jamison said. "Rooney's right, we're starting to see threats that aren't there."

Whitehall didn't turn around and Jamison looked for support from Roony, who was looking at his watch and offered none. Specter smiled at Jamison, making him squirm in his seat. "It's decided then, I'll leave to see Phil immediately."

Specter stood and made to leave but Whitehall stopped him; he turned from the window and said, "Don't scare him, Thomas. We don't want to give him a reason to turn on us."

Specter's jaw tightened and he nodded. He made to leave again and Whitehall added, "Thank you, Thomas, and please do not do anything without letting me know and I will filter down the news to Roony and Hollis."

Specter said, "Sure, John," and without a word to the other two men in the room, he left as silently as he had entered.

Roony watched the door, waiting as if expecting Specter to return, or maybe he was waiting for him to get a safe distance away before he spoke. "Honestly, John, why do you have so much faith in that man, he's absolutely criminal." Whitehall turned and looked at the grounds; once again the sprinklers were coming on, bathing the lawns in the cool of the evening.

Whitehall spoke without turning around, "Don't fool yourself, Roony, we're all criminals, Thomas just has no reason or desire to hide the fact that he is."

Roony started again, "But he's no more than a street thug--"

Whitehall cut him off. "Don't you have a party to go to or something?" he said.

Roony grunted and stood up. "You're right, John. But mark my words, Specter is the man who will bring us down before Phil or anyone else."

Jamison stood to leave. "See you tomorrow, John", he said. Whitehall nodded and continued to look out the window.

He heard the men leave. He watched the grounds grow dark and finally, after a while, he turned and looked at the pictures still strew on the desk. He felt sorry for Phil ;he would not want a meeting with Specter like the one Phil was in for, his life literally was on the line. He thought about Roony, he was a buffoon, and a clueless one at that; he would trust Specter with his life, he had on more than one occasion, and in turn he brought Specter with him to the level of power they had now. Roony could never understand a man like Specter. Whitehall picked up the pictures on the table and returned them to the folder. The smiling face of Phil Lancaster sticking out of the envelope caught his eye. Whitehall tucked it into the folder and thought, I hope you're still with us.

Tommy was late. He rushed over to the dresser in his bedroom and grabbed his watch. He looked at the time and cursed. He went and grabbed the phone in the kitchen and dialed. "Phil, I'm sorry, I'm running late. I'll be there in twenty minutes, order a round of drinks."

The voice of Phil Lancaster came back through the receiver. "You better hurry, they may not hold our table," he said jokingly.

Tommy laughed. "If they don't, I'll buy the place and fire the whole staff."

"You mean you don't already own this place? You better bring some cash then, it looks expensive," Phil replied, still laughing.

"I'll see you in twenty." Tommy hung up the phone and rushed out the door.

His limo was waiting downstairs and he quickly got in. On the ride over to the restaurant, Tommy reflected on the past few weeks. Phil Lancaster had become a good friend. The idea that he had befriended him for information had melted away weeks ago. He enjoyed spending time with Phil; they had similar interests and similar personalities. The idea that Phil was this evil corporate thief suppressing a cure for millions seemed more and more ludicrous every time they hung out. But Tommy also had a responsibility to his friends, and he figured if he could clear Phil of any wrongdoing, he could get Joey off his and everyone else's back.

He would have to confront Phil at some point; he had told himself this many times over the last few weeks and every time he had backed down from it. He looked out the window and wondered why. Maybe deep down he didn't want to know; he liked this man and considered him a friend, maybe he didn't want to find out his dark secrets. Maybe Tommy would just tell the guys Phil were innocent and Joey was reaching for something that wasn't there. He sighed and leaned back in his seat. Joey wouldn't buy it, he needed a way to prove it without the shadow of a doubt. The limo pulled up in front of the restaurant and Tommy said, "I'll call when I need you, probably three to four hours, Frank."

The driver replied, " No problem, boss, have fun."

Tommy entered the restaurant and was immediately brought to a quiet table in the back where Phil was waiting for him. Tommy sat and looked around. "The décor is nice, I like the statue in the entranceway," he said to Phil.

"It's a cheap knockoff; I don't come here for the décor, I come for the veal, you have to try it," Phil said, sipping his wine.

The dinner progressed with both men eating and drinking and enjoying each other's company. While they waited for dessert, Tommy, feeling a bit drunk, thought of something and smiled. Phil laughed seeing him and asked, "Why so happy?"

Tommy, caught in the memory, shook his head in dismissal then thought for a moment and said, "I was just thinking of a night I spent in Spain a few years back."

"I love Spain, the food, the culture, the wine," Phil replied.

Tommy looked across the table at Phil and seriously said, "You're a good man, Phil, you remind me of my friends from when we were kids, you would have fit right in with us."

Phil looked sad and said, "I never fit in; I was a science geek. I tried but you know how it is, or maybe you don't."

His voice trailed off and he suddenly looked sad. Tommy didn't understand and tried to cheer up his friend. "Hey, you want to know something I've never told anyone?"

Phil looked up suddenly interested. "You serious?"

Tommy smiled. "Yeah, maybe it's the wine...I don't know, I've never told this to anyone but the night I was just thinking about, the night in Spain, well, I was there on business for two weeks and was bored, so one night I go out and meet this beautiful woman. I mean, she was exotic looking, nothing I usually go for but I was in Spain and the wine was flowing. Anyway, we drink and dance and go back to my apartment and make love, and in the morning I wake up and see her sleeping in the bed. I got up and put on some coffee and as I come back to the bedroom, she is getting out of the bed and I realize my beautiful Spanish girl in not a girl at all; I find out it was a man. I mean, if she...he walked in here right now, you would never know it was a man. It's funny because I think back on that night sometimes and I'm sad because that was one of those great nights...a night I would have remembered forever and it was ruined. I sometimes wish she...he would have left and I would never have known. Everything was perfect until that moment; I would have been blissfully ignorant and happy had the illusion lasted a few more minutes and she had just left."

Tommy grabbed his wine and took a deep drink, finishing the glass; he looked over at Phil, who was quietly staring at his wine glass. Tommy couldn't get a read on him and broke the silence by saying, "Your turn."

Phil looked up. "What?"

"Your turn, I told you something you tell me something."

Phil looked confused. "What are we, seven?"

Tommy laughed loudly. "I wish, no really, tell me a secret of yours."

Phil considered Tommy for a moment and was about to protest, instead he took a swig of his wine and looked Tommy in the eye. "You know that woman you were with that night...it could have been me."

It took Tommy a minute to realize Phil was serious then he said, "What? Really? I would have never guessed."

Phil, not knowing what to expect, continued, "Do you think any less of me?"

Tommy smiled. "No. We all have our secrets; who's to judge any of them but ourselves."

Phil relaxed in his chair, he hadn't realized how tense he was before but now he was relieved he smiled. "You really don't care?" he asked again.

"No, I judge people by their character, your secret is safe with me."

Phil nodded still in a bit of shock. "I wish I had more friends like you," he said.

"Did your family know?" Tommy asked. Phil's face turned dark and he flashed back to the one night he had tried to forget for the last twenty years.

Phil silently replayed the night in his mind, his wife sitting in the dark kitchen waiting for him, the smell of alcohol on him, the makeup that had hurriedly been wiped from his face. It was still vivid, the shock of his wife being awake and waiting. He had always suspected she knew something, but he had figured after all the years they had been together she had accepted it and blamed the late nights on work and the long weekends on conferences. He thought there was an unspoken understanding between Judy and him.

Phil thought lately though the nights had gotten longer and the conferences more frequent and the strain on their marriage had become more evident. Judy had been spending a lot more time in church, dragging their daughter with her. She was becoming more distant and in all honesty, Phil had thought this was better. In reality, he hadn't seen this night coming but it had been coming for years. The kitchen light came on and the brightness made Phil cringe as if it burned him. He turned away from it and from Judy, but tonight the avoidance tact wouldn't work. Judy stood up and closed the distance between them and slapped Phil hard across the face.

"You make me sick! Get out!" These threats had come before but they had never come so forcibly and never when Phil was caught so red-handed. Judy had grabbed his bag and spilled the contents on the floor. Women's garments, makeup, and a wig all spilled on the floor, the secret out, the proof there, years of concealment thrown on the floor and exposed in seconds.

"Honey, you know I can't help it, you know I love--"

He had never gotten that last word out she exploded. "Don't... don't say another word, get out, you freak, get away from me and never come back. You are out of our lives, do you hear me, I never want to see you again."

Phil looked toward their bedroom, his clothes were packed in the luggage they had gotten as a wedding gift. He realized Judy had been planning this a long time. He glanced toward his daughter's room but Judy was ready, she must have gone over this a thousand times while she had been waiting for him to come home. "You will never see her again, you hear me? You have any contact with us or her and I swear I will tell the world what a sick fuck you are, you hear me?" Her voice continued to rise. "How will that go over, how will your career go then?" She was screaming now, all the rage of the past years coming out.

She continued to scream insults but Phil hadn't heard them, it had all become a blur. He stood and took it, he owed it to her at least for ruining her life. When he finally looked up, the last image he saw before he left the house was the sight of his daughter, small and frail, leaning against the door of her room crying.

"Hey, you okay?"

Phil snapped back to reality. He was sitting at dinner with Tommy, he had just told him his greatest secret and unlike the last time, this time it was okay. The pain of that one night years ago lifted just a bit. It was the first time in a long time that he felt truly comfortable with who he was. He smiled. "Thanks," he said to Tommy.

"For what?"

"For understanding."

CHAPTER

7

Specter

T HE BAR WAS CROWDED, AS IT ALWAYS WAS ON A SATURDAY NIGHT.
Johnny sat in the back room. Saturday was the main night for
conducting business. At five-minute intervals, men would come and
go out of the back room meeting with Johnny. There were few times
in the night when he was not busy. The captains of his crew ran
the day-to-day operations but there were always petty squabbles and
plans that needed to be run through him for his okay. Johnny looked
up at the clock; it was well past two a.m. and he motioned to Fat
Sally Jr. to get him a drink and give him ten minutes. He only needed
to nod for Sally to understand the message and in seconds, a drink
was brought to him and he stood up and stretched; it had been a long
night. He walked out to the front room, where most of his crew was
hanging out, drinking, playing cards, watching sports.

Johnny smiled, he remembered being a kid and hiding behind
the bar when his father came out of the back room. The bar looked
the same, the TV's were new but the bar itself had remained the
same. The neighborhood outside had changed, everyone had died
or moved out; it was mostly Spanish now but Johnny had kept his
home base in the old neighborhood out of respect for the old days.
He missed his father. He never had kids, he wasn't able to, and if
he couldn't have children, a wife wasn't necessary. It made life a lot

less complicated for Johnny. He had never had any fear as a child, never thought that something could happen to him or his mother, he had never felt threatened by anything. It was only later when he had grown up had his father confided in him that that was always his greatest fear, reprisal against his family. In the old days, that was forbidden and even now, it was still frowned upon but times had changed, the streets were a lot more ruthless these days.

The lack of family made Johnny a harder target. It made him more dangerous; he had no one to go after, no one to threaten. Johnny sighed. He rubbed his temples, it had been a long night. He walked into the back room and sunk back into his booth and closed his eyes, he was just starting to drift off when Charlie Irish came in. "Hey, boss, you really need to hear this, they're talking about your friend Tommy out here." Johnny grabbed the remote and turned on the TV in the back room, he turned on channel 11 and raised the volume.

"And to restate rumors that have been running rampant that real estate mogul Tommy Russo is possibly being indicted in a real estate scandal with the lieutenant governor of California Raymond Sabucco. Early reports say the governor has used his influence to grease the wheels on numerous projects out in LA. The latest being a four hundred million dollar renovation of the downtown civic center. Local business owners are upset that contracts were given to out-of-state companies.

"There is also evidence that Tommy Russo was major contributor to the reelection campaign of Raymond Sabucco last November. We spoke to the district attorney and he says there are no indictments pending and as far as his office is concerned, there has been no wrongdoing by any party involved. Still this comes on the heels of reports that Tommy has linked to a man who claims to have been taken advantage of and forced into having had sexual relations with him while on a trip to Puerto Rico last June. This picture that surfaced in the Post today shows Mr. Tommy Russo with his arm around the alleged victim."

Johnny shut the TV. Charlie Irish, who had been standing there the whole time, whistled softly. "What do you think, boss?"

Johnny busted out in laughter. "What a crock of shit. Tommy's not gay and he's straighter than a fucking boy scout when it comes to business."

"Yeah, well, he pissed up someone's pole cause somebody is really out to screw him. I mean, to drop all these rumors at one time."

Johnny smiled. "Yeah, give me a minute, Charlie," he said and picked up the receiver of the phone. He called Peter. "Hey, Pete, you hear this shit?"

Peter sighed. "Yeah, Tommy's freaked out. You know he hates publicity, especially negative publicity."

"Yeah, I figured he would be. Have you spoken to Ray?"

"I called him four hours ago but he hasn't returned my phone call. What are you thinking?"

"Ill tell you tomorrow. Get Tommy and meet us at the wine cellar, I'll round up Joey."

"Do you think this is bad, Johnny?"

"I think we were right all along and these Novacrin boys just flexed their muscle a little."

Thomas Specter saw Phil enter the zoo. He watched him walk around and stare wistfully at the animals. He sat on the steps of the seal tank and waited. The seals swam in circles and surfaced for air in the same repetitive pattern. Specter made Phil wait; it would make him uncomfortable and that was the way he wanted him. He hated the zoo; he thought of all these animals as having their balls cut off, zoos were like prisons for animals. He smiled; he had come a long way from the streets of Philly. He had fought for everything he had and there was no way this little piss ant was going to blow it. No one would.

Whitehall understood the ramifications of what they had done. Hell, he had masterminded the whole thing. Lancaster was a smart guy but he would never have had the balls to set up the operation

Whitehall had. Lancaster had made the breakthrough but he would have given it away. Whitehall saw the money and power that the discovery could bring and it was an easy sell to Lancaster, you'll still help people, keep them alive, still do research, make the cure viable for mass production, your own lab, money, power, annoniminity. You can live any way you want and no one would ever know. The threat of his secret coming out, that sealed the deal.

Every man has a breaking point, everyone. For some, it was tougher to find than others, but Lancaster was a scientist and in the end, ego and respect in his field were important to him. He didn't want his name in the papers, for better or for worse. In the end, he sold his soul just like anyone else would. Specter smiled, in the end everyone had a price, you just needed to know how much.

He approached Lancaster silently and sat lightly next to him a bit to close. Lancaster jumped, genuinely surprised. "Thomas, you nearly scared me half to death."

Specter smiled, but to Lancaster it seemed like a sneer. "Why so jumpy?" Specter asked.

"Cut the scare tactics, Thomas, I'm not afraid of you." Specter didn't say a word; he hated that Lancaster called him by his first name; it was a sign of disrespect to Specter. He had no problem when Whitehall did it because he respected Whitehall but Lancaster was a different story. "So did John send you out here to check up on me?" Lancaster asked.

"No, I came on my own, we've missed you the last few months."

Lancaster looked at Specter then turned his head back toward the seals. "You know I've been busy with my work and the lab in New York is a better place to do the R&D. I've explained this since we had my lab built," Lancaster pleaded. "Look, you don't need me to run the day-to-day stuff. I'm the brains behind the company."

"You made the discovery but we made the company, you'd be teaching in community college without us," Specter replied.

"Us, you putting yourself in John or J.R.'s class now. Let's remember you're the muscle that's all."

Specter stood up. "That's right, I am," he said coolly. "Let's walk." The two men walked toward the polar bear enclosure. The giant bear was pacing back and forth behind the glass.

"Why the zoo?" Lancaster asked.

"What?"

"Why pick the zoo to meet?"

Specter replied, "Survival of the fittest. These animals are all caged; they aren't free. Do you ever think they would like to get out of those cages and do what comes naturally?" Specter looked at Lancaster catching his eye and holding it.

"Yeah, I know how they feel."

"Look, Phil, we're all caged, we're trapped in what we do and have done. Think about it, these animals, they're pampered, fed, they lead comfortable lives."

"Yeah, but are they really living?" Lancaster said wistfully.

"Look, if they were released into the wild, they would get eaten up in a second. You understand my meaning?" He grabbed Lancaster's arm for emphasis.

Lancaster shook his arm off and replied, "So that's it. Go back and tell Whitehall I'm still with him. Don't know why you would think I wasn't."

Specter smiled. "That's all we wanted to hear Phil, be careful of your new 'friend' Tommy, he may be trying to set you up," Specter said as he began to walk away.

"What? Why would Tommy do that, he has more money than any of us?"

"I don't know his motives, I just know something ain't right."

"Hollis was right about you, Thomas, you're never satisfied unless you have an enemy, and if you don't have one you make one up."

Specter froze and turned. He sneered at Lancaster and closed the distance to get right up into his face. "You're right, and if I were you, I'd try real hard to stay off my list." With that, Specter turned and walked away. If he had looked back, he would have seen Lancaster begin to tear up and start shaking.

Specter was sitting in the airport VIP club at Kennedy Airport waiting for his flight. The sky was darkening. He couldn't wait to leave New York; he had always hated New York. Maybe it was an inferiority complex growing up in Philly, who knows; maybe he just liked LA better. New York was dark and dirty; LA was the opposite, all sunshine and palm trees. Specter would never admit it, but there were too many guys like him in New York. Out in LA, they were soft and a guy like him was feared. He picked up the phone and called Whitehall.

"John, yeah, I just met with Lancaster. I think he's clean but I'm gonna keep an eye on him just in case. Look, I want to send a message to that fuck lieutenant governor and to Tommy Russo too. I'm getting on a plane to New Orleans tonight and getting things set up." Specter waited for the protest from Whitehall knowing it was coming.

"Look, Thomas, do what you think is right. You know I will endorse any course of action you take. But don't you think all the allegations are enough? These men aren't stupid, they'll get the hint to back off."

"Maybe, but I'll sleep better this way so I think its necessary. It'll keep Lancaster honest too. Like I said, I think he's okay but I don't trust him and in all honesty, he's outlived his usefulness."

"I'll make that call when and if the time comes, Thomas," Whitehall snapped.

Specter quickly said, "I hear you, John, no problem but I have the green light to continue with my trip to New Orleans?"

"Do what you feel you must, but please don't bullshit me old friend; you wont sleep better, hell, you hardly sleep at all."

Specter laughed. "You know me to well, I'll keep you posted."

In his office, Whitehall stood and stretched and rubbed his temples; bodies were piling up and so far, no one cared, but Thomas was starting to drift into a realm where people will care and that will change things. Still, maybe a strong message was what was needed to keep the foxes out of the chicken coop. He sat heavily into his chair; he trusted Thomas, trusted him with his life, and that was what made his decision.

Specter hung up the phone and sighed; he was expecting more of a fight from Whitehall. That's what makes him special, Specter thought. He put on the airs of a rich and wealthy man, but deep down he was a ruthless motherfucker. His kind of guy. Specter laughed as he heard the boarding call for his flight to New Orleans. He stood up grabbed his bag and headed for the gate.

CHAPTER

8

Tommy

TOMMY HAD BEEN AT THE RESTAURANT SINCE THREE P.M., it was the only way to stay ahead of the news trucks that were outside his building on Central Park West. He had holed up in the wine cellar and was conducting business all day. Most of the clients he had and people he knew didn't believe a word of the rumors but public perception counted for a lot. He had been putting out fires all day and whenever he thought he had things under control, more people would call.

After hours of this, he called it quits and forwarded all his calls to his secretary. He sat back and waited for his boys to arrive. Johnny came first, arriving in an unmarked car and entering through the kitchen. Peter had picked up Joey with his cab and they entered the front door and immediately went to the back. "These guys play rough, huh, Tommy, love the picture of you and Ricky Ricardo."

"Please, Johnny, not today. The guy thought I was Trump and asked to take a picture," Tommy said.

"Where's Ray?" Peter asked.

"Can't come, too much heat. I spoke to him a few hours ago. We're on the same page but things are tough for him right now, scandal never plays well with those fucks out there; they're all one way motherfuckers. Things go wrong they run for cover," Johnny said. "He's on his own out there, no one will back him until he clears this up," Joey added; his speech was a little slurred as if he had been drinking but Tommy suspected it wasn't alcohol.

"It doesn't help that neither of you are married. The whole gay thing is going to keep coming up," Johnny said with a smile.

Peter interrupted, "Stop, Johnny, but not for nothing, Tommy, you and Ray need to keep your distance for a while. Johnny, do you think there is anything else coming down?"

"Nah, these guys were sending a message, fuck with us and we fuck with you. Tommy, I assume you're squeaky clean, and I know Ray is too slick to have done anything stupid, so it'll all blow over. We did learn one thing from this though."

Tommy put down his drink and asked, "What?"

"They only know about you and Ray, I mean, an archbishop, no offense, Pete, but we could run twenty ten year olds on camera and ruin you in three minutes, and any association with me and Joey, well, that's career suicide for Ray and it won't help you too much either," Johnny said, nodding toward Tommy.

"So where are we at?" Peter asked. Joey went to speak but Johnny gave him a look that stopped him in his tracks.

"Look, I know Phil, I can get him to talk, maybe I can use this to really gain his confidence."

"Maybe," Johnny said.

Joey rolled his eyes and shot his drink down and proceeded to pour another. "I've gotten pretty close with the ex-wife, we've been meeting weekly to discuss her charitable contributions, but whenever I mention her ex-husband she shuts down and changes the subject, so I really have nothing."

"Keep at it, Pete," Johnny said. "Look, I think we know two things, they are afraid of something and they're willing to play dirty. I have to talk things over with Ray. I'll go out to see him tomorrow, he made it clear that we can't risk talking over the phone, but I think we hit back and I think Specter is the target," Johnny said.

"I agree," Tommy quickly added.

Joey had had enough; he exploded, "Of course you do. God forbid we go after your buddy Lancaster. Look, he has the cure, he's the one we should grab."

"I can get him to talk; he's a good guy, he'll talk," Tommy said.

"Good guy holding a cure from millions? Come on, Tommy, are you kidding me?"

"Johnny, come on. This is nuts, you know it." Joey looked to Johnny pleadingly, the frustration building.

Johnny whispered softly, "Joey, I think Ray is going to agree with you. I agree with you, but let me talk to him then we cut these guys loose and it's our show."

Joey looked at the faces of each of his friends and through gritted teeth he said, "One more week."

And with that, he grabbed his coat and walked out. "He's using too much, he can't think straight," Peter said. "He told me Tiffany is in real bad shape; she can hardly get out of bed and Joey is frustrated."

"I know, Pete, but he may be right. I know you don't want to hear that but I won't lie to you, it may have to come down to me and him. I promise I'll keep Tommy and Ray out of it," Johnny said.

"We've already invested in this, Johnny. You can't turn around and pretend we don't know anything," Tommy said.

"Look, Johnny, I appreciate your concern but I don't agree with what you are proposing, I can't agree to that. Let Tommy crack Lancaster; he can do it, have faith in him." Peter added.

"Look, guys," Johnny was about to explain how business on this level had to be done but then thought better of it; there was no use in his explanation, they wouldn't understand. "Okay, I'll try to keep Joey at bay for as long as I can but you guys know Joey, he gets a bug in his ass he wont stop until he gets it out. And he's using, which means he won't listen to me. I don't think he'll listen to you either, Pete., Johnny continued.

"He said a week, can you crack Lancaster by then?" Peter asked.

"I guess I'll have to," Tommy replied.

"Look, I'll call you, Pete, after my meeting with Ray and we can see what he thinks. I'm sure he'll have a plan, he's probably pissed that he got outfoxed by the Novacrin board and will have something up his sleeve." Johnny stood and walked over to Peter, he gave him a hug and kissed him on his right cheek in farewell. He did the same to Tommy and headed for the door.

He turned back and said, "Pray for us, Father, we're going to need all the help we can get." Then he turned to look at Tommy and added, "Get it done quickly, I can't guarantee Lancaster's protection for more than one week."

Tommy poured himself a drink; he knew he was getting drunk and he didn't care. He was still in the wine cellar; the guys had left hours ago. Smitty had come by a few times to see if he was okay. "Lock it up, Smitty, I'll stay here tonight." Tommy had stayed in the wine cellar on many occasions, usually nights he couldn't sleep. Those nights had become fewer and fewer as the years had gone by. Tommy had relinquished a lot of the daily running of his business to others as the years went by.

It was only natural he oversaw all of his empire but he had hired smart and had the best people working for him. A lesson he had learned from Johnny. His stomach grumbled and he realized he hadn't eaten. He laughed, he was always forgetting to eat. He had never had much as a kid and that was one habit that died hard. Pete would joke he was the skinniest restaurant owner he had ever seen. He walked over to the table, the table that had once been in the original wine cellar. He thought of that table as the anchor that held him to his old life, that and his friends. And that was the problem, Tommy was caught between his friends and this life he had built.

He couldn't help think Joey was wrong. This whole thing was a reaction to his girl's being sick. He was grasping for straws and no matter how much the others thought that Lancaster had the cure, he couldn't see it. He had gotten to know Phil Lancaster over the last few months; he was a good man, a scientist, and a guy who had gotten into research to save people. He donated money to multiple organizations and didn't live above his means. He didn't need the money, there was no motivation to hold back a cure. Tommy thought about just coming out and asking him, he almost had at the last charity dinner they had attended together.

They were both drunk and he was on the verge of saying, "Hey, Phil, can I get that AIDS cure you got? My friend needs it." He had almost said it but then he realized if he had, that would reveal him as a guy out for something, as a mole trying to befriend him just to use him; and even though that's how his relationship with Phil had started, it was different now, he had more in common with Phil then he did with the guys. He knew the guys were like his family and he would never refuse his friends. He rubbed his hands over the old table; they had been through a lot, Tommy, Peter Joey, Johnny, and Ray. He would never forget that they were his brothers. Tommy sighed. As much as he hated to pressure Phil, he would have to, if anything for his own safety.

Johnny could talk about Specter all he wanted to but Tommy knew it would be Lancaster that Joey would go for. And that would not go well for Lancaster, not with the state Joey was in. He sighed. He wanted Phil to tell him he had a cure because he trusted him, but it looked like he would have to figure out a way to get him to crack one way or another. Tommy looked at the watch, it was three a.m. He picked up the phone and called his home, there were five messages. Very few people had his home number; he checked them. Two were from his personal assistant, the other three were from Phil seeing if he was alright, asking him to call him if he needed anything, the third saying to call him tomorrow to meet for lunch. Tommy hung up the phone and sank back into the big leather chair. His stomach growled again and he felt empty, but not for lack of food.

CHAPTER
9

Johnny

"THE PLAN'S READY, BOSS, WE SHOULD BE UP IN ABOUT TWENTY MINUTES," JOHNNY SMILED AND SANK BACK INTO HIS SEAT. He could get some sleep on the flight to L.A. He was using a private jet, a favor from one of his "friends;" Johnny had access to this plane whenever he needed it, he rarely used it but for a trip like this the fewer people who knew where he was the better.

"Hey, boss, you got a call. You want me to tell 'em you're sleeping?" Charlie Irish popped his head back into the cabin; he liked to ride in the cockpit.

"Depends, who is it?"

"Fat Sally from New Orleans."

Johnny froze and sat bolt upright. "Put it through." Johnny picked up the receiver in the cabin and waved Charlie back to the cockpit and motioned him to close the door. "Hey, Sally, what's up?" Johnny listened and said nothing for the next few minutes, and then he said, "I'll be there in four hours. No one moves a fucking inch until I get there, you hear me, Sally, no fucking heroes, it would not make me happy. And, Sally, you did real good, I owe you one." Johnny hung up and rubbed his chin. He said aloud, "The fucking balls on that prick." He called out to Charlie.

Charlie Irish poked his head out of the cockpit, "Yeah, boss."

"Tell the pilot we're flying to New Orleans now."

"Yeah, but, boss, we need to file a new flight plan and contact the tower, it may take a while."

Johnny looked sternly at Charlie. "Like I give a fuck about that shit. This plane better be in New Orleans in four hours, you hear me."

Charlie went to say something and then changed his mind. "No problem, boss."

Johnny sank back and whispered, "That motherfucker." He looked at his watch and picked up the phone and called Joey.

Raymond looked like a mess; he looked at himself in the mirror in the bathroom that was off his office. He needed a shave, and a shower would do him wonders also. The reflection in the mirror was one of a tired and haggard looking man. He walked back to his office, the clock read 2:45 a,m. He had been here for almost two days. Since the story had broke, he had been going non-stop. He had probably slept a total of four hours in the last two days. The press was relentless and his fellow party members were worse. He was fielding calls for hours explaining all his business deals, defending Tommy and himself. He knew it was coming; the one thing he had learned early on was that the rats never go down with the ship, they jump as soon as they see water on the deck. That was what was happening, all his political connections were backing away and leaving him to fend for himself. He knew he was clean, he had always made sure that all his dealings were above board, above board as far as political circles ran. Had he pushed buttons to get deals done? Sure, everyone did. There were no illegal actions pending against him, the D.A. had called and assured him of that. Senator Hatch had called and given him an I-told-you-so speech and then went on TV and basically threw him under the bus, offering no support from the party.

So Raymond was on the defensive; he had pulled every contract he had been associated with over the last three years and then he went back to every other civic project that had been done in the last seven years, he trusted the D.A. but he wanted all his ducks in a row just in case. He sat at his desk looking at the piles of paper; he sank back and rubbed his eyes. Those bastards at Novacrin played dirty. Joey would say this was further proof that they were hiding a cure; to Ray, it only proved how powerful they were that they could call down this much heat this quickly, it was a message back off.

Ray smiled. Any young politician would be falling over themselves to backtrack and try to squash this; they would get the message loud and clear and be begging to get back in their good graces. That wasn't Raymond, he wasn't backing down and he could care less about his career, no one was going to push him and his friends around. Ray just had to figure out a way to push back and to do it without getting Tommy in any more trouble. He stood up; he couldn't wait to talk to Johnny. As much as he hated to go that route, a message needed to be sent, a message he, Peter, and Tommy couldn't send. He pushed his chair back and stood up, he needed a shower and a shave and then a few hours of sleep before the phone calls started again in the morning. Ray went to the bathroom and started the shower. He stripped off his clothes and got into the shower, letting the hot water work the exhaustion out of him he closed his eyes.

To anyone watching, the truck that pulled around the back of the state building would have garnered no attention. A white van with an office cleaners logo on it and two men getting out in blue jumpsuits with shop-vacs and brooms at three a.m. was not suspicious. The news trucks with the sleeping cameramen inside that were camped out in front paid no notice to the men as they gathered their materials and headed for the door at the back of the building.

The men moved quietly without speaking. Once inside, they quickly headed for the second floor, leaving most of the tools in a first floor bathroom. The slightly shorter man still carried a broom. As the men approached the offices on the second floor, the taller man gave the shorter man a hand signal. He nodded and headed to the top of the stairs and started sweeping. He swept slowly, almost silently, and never turned on any lights. The sweeping man swept the same spot over and over, never leaving the top of the stairs. The second man walked silently over to the office at the end of the hall, he listened at the door and heard water running inside.

He smiled to himself and thought, all to easy. He quietly tested the door, the knob turned silently and he slipped in like a ghost. The one small desk lamp was on and the man glancing toward the bathroom quickly sat in the desk chair and turned out the light. The shower was still running in the bathroom as the man reached in his jumpsuit and pulled out his gun. He looked around; the office was a mess. It could use a good cleaning, he thought, as he silently waited for the lieutenant governor to emerge from the bathroom.

Ray emerged from the shower feeling relaxed. He toweled off and slipped his trousers back on. He opened the cabinet under the sink and pulled out an old t-shirt that said Bison's on it. He slipped it over his head and yawned. A few hours of sleep would do him wonders. He checked himself in the mirror and rubbed his eyes, they were bloodshot and the dark circles beneath them verified he need some rest. He turned and walked from the bathroom to his office, which he hadn't noticed was now dark.

BANG.

"You're dead." Ray nearly jumped back into the bathroom; he hit the wall hard and, rubbing the back of his head, said, "Johnny, what the fuck, you nearly gave me a heart attack. What the hell are you doing and why do you have a gun on me?"

Johnny smiled. "Sorry, bro, just carrying out the contract," Johnny said as he got up and went over to hug Ray. "Although, your skinny ass is worth five hundred thousand g's right now so maybe I should cap you myself and collect."

"What are you talking about? What contract?" Ray asked. "And why the dramatics? You could have called, we could have met elsewhere, you didn't have to come sneaking around scaring me half to death."

Johnny sat back in Ray's chair. "I'm sorry. Sit, we have a lot to talk about."

Ray sat across from his own desk, the weariness and sleep pushed away, replaced by the rush of adrenaline from the scare he just had and surprise to see his friend here. "So what's this all about," he said irritably.

"You used to be more fun, Ray," Johnny said. "This job is making you to serious."

"Well if you hadn't noticed, I've been a bit busy lately."

Johnny smiled and put his feet up on Ray's desk. "Look, I'm serious about the contract. Specter went down to New Orleans and put a five hundred thousand dollar tag on your head."

"What? Why? Because of one subpoena? That seems like overkill," Ray said.

"Yeah, imagine if you had insulted his mother too," Johnny cracked.

"Stop fucking around. This is serious. Are these guys really that crazy that they would kill a public official?"

"My guess is they aren't, just Specter he gets off on this I bet. I know guys like him, they like killing people without getting their hands dirty," Johnny mused.

"How did you find out about the contract?" Ray asked.

"Look, when that story broke about you, I put it out that anything concerning you or Tommy was to be put through me. I was coming out to see you and I got a call from Fat Sal in New Orleans. The same lieutenant who had done the boat job got a call to do another job, this one a lieutenant governor. Sally called me straight away and I flew down there to see him. It was Specter, he wants you gone. I told Sally I would handle it and he told his guy to tell Specter he would do the job but it would take a while to work out the details. That buys us some time but I think we have to act on this one quick. This guy may try for Tommy also and while I'm pretty well connected, I don't know everyone so we need to be careful."

"Well at least Specter hasn't made the connection between you and me; if he had, he never would have went to Fat Sally to do the job. I guess Pete's in the clear too, we haven't heard any scandals about him either,"Ray said.

"I told the guys the same thing. I figure Specter wouldn't think to look at where I went to school or he figures we run in such different circles there's no way we would be friends. The same goes for Joey."

"Well if he goes by his own experience, the rest of the board members are the furthest thing from wise guys, so it makes sense. As for Pete, no one probably even knows his real name," Ray said.

"So what's the next move, Ray? I got to tell you we have dissension in the ranks. Joey is hot, he's using his girl's dying in front of him and he wants to kill everyone and anything in his path. I know Tommy's not gay but he's real tight with Lancaster; whether he wanted to or not, he became friends with the guy so he still thinks he's going to get him to talk." Johnny paused.

"I know, maybe it was a bad idea to send Tommy after Lancaster. They're too much alike, they couldn't help but become friends," Ray said.

"C'mon, Ray, don't second guess yourself. It was the right play, none of us would have gotten within twenty feet of that guy and you know it."

Ray shook his head in the affirmative and said, "What does Pete think?"

Johnny laughed. "You know Pete, he's worried about everyone but getting nowhere with the wife."

Ray sighed and the weariness came back to him all at once; he slumped into his chair. "Did you tell anyone else about the contract?" Ray asked.

"Nah, only the three of us know…" Johnny paused, he knew what was coming next.

"Three?" Ray asked.

"Yeah, you, me, and Joey. They killed the other two guys by injecting them with bad drugs. Joey runs all the dealers in the city, I told him to keep his ears open."

Ray rolled his eyes and rubbed his temples, he knew the answer to the next question but asked anyway, "How'd he take it?"

Johnny answered, "Look, Ray, I may have fucked that one up. Joey is not right now, he's shooting up and getting sicker; he went fucking bananas, he wanted to fly out here and blow Novacrin sky high."

"It's not about the cure anymore, is it, Johnny? He's out for blood now."

"I know, but if we can get the cure, we can get him right again. Look, I got him clean the first time years ago and I can do it again, but we need to resolve this first," Johnny said.

"Is Tommy safe?"

"You know I can't guarantee that, Ray. I have the word out, but even I'm not that powerful."

Ray sat up and put his elbows on his knees. "We need to get back to New York."

"You're not going, Ray. If this goes wrong, you need to be shielded," Johnny replied.

"Screw all this, Johnny…"

Ray was about to continue but Johnny cut him off. "No buts, you got a pretty good set up here, Ray, this is what your meant to do. I know you're willing to sacrifice all this, but to what end? You going to come work for me, plan dry cleaning robberies again? I know your heart's in the right place but it's going to get ugly, you need to do damage control and get yourself back in everyone's good graces out here. I just came here to warn you and ask your advice. I want to know what you think our next move should be."

Raymond thought to protest but reconsidered it; he paused for a minute, his brain working, and then said, "You know, this doesn't matter to me as much as you guys, but you're right…I feel…okay. Look, we need to keep any eye on Tommy and he needs to crack Phil.

If he can't, then we may have to look at another of the board members and apply some muscle. You may have to take care of Specter."

Johnny smiled and stood up. "Don't worry, that fuck crossed the line when he put a hit on you. I'll wait but Joey won't. He gave Tommy until the end of the week, I just hope he can wait that long."

Ray stood and nodded. "Go back, watch Tommy and make sure Joey doesn't do anything. Keep me posted."

Johnny hugged Raymond and zipped up his blue janitors overalls, he patted the gun in his pocket. "Five hundred grand, you're getting pretty big in this town," he said, joking. Then Johnny got serious. "Watch you back, brother."

It was Raymond's turn to laugh. "Why, that's your job." They hugged one last time and Johnny slipped out of the room.

10

Phil

PHIL TURNED OFF THE COMPUTER AND SIGHED. The visit from Specter had shaken him but the friendship and understanding that Tommy had shown him sealed his decision. For better or worse, he was resigned to the fact that he would stick to the decision he had made over the last few days. The relief had been amazing. He felt giddy as he picked up the phone and dialed Tommy. "Hello," Tommy answered.

"Well, you could have told me you were gay," he said, laughing.

"Very funny, I thought it was you who leaked the story since you're the only one I told about Spain."

Phil was shocked and panicked a bit. "Hey, Tommy, you know I would…"

Tommy laughed. "Of course I know, I'm only kidding."

Phil felt relieved. "How are you doing really?"

"Well, I've been talking to clients for two days and I'll be having a press conference tomorrow to clear things up, or at least tell my side of the story."

"Come to dinner with me tonight, I have a present for you that will make your press conference the press conference of the century."

Tommy laughed. "What are you going to give me, some of your clothes to dress up in?"

Phil would have been mortified in the past but coming from Tommy he laughed. "No, but that would be good. Just come to dinner, I promise it will be worth your while."

Tommy said, "Okay, but make it an out-of-the-way place, the press is all over me."

"I know a great place in the Bronx, Louie's Seafood on Tremont, see you at eight." Phil hung up the phone and smiled.

Tommy wanted to get excited but he held it in; Phil sounded giddy and he knew he had gained his trust with the story about Spain. Could this be the break he was waiting for? He decided that tonight he would ask. Tonight he would find out one way or another if there was a cure. The phone rang again and he jumped up to grab it, expecting Phil again. Instead, it was Peter. "Hey, Tommy, how are you doing?" Pete asked. "Are you ready for your press conference?"

Tommy sighed. "Not really looking forward to it but I'm ready?"

Peter continued, "What are you doing tonight? Would you like to come over for dinner?"

"Sorry, Pete, I'm staying in tonight." Tommy hated lying to Pete but he thought tonight was the night he was going to crack Phil and find the truth and he wanted to be able to surprise them all.

"Okay, get some rest, I will pray for you."

"Thanks, Pete."

Tommy hung up the phone and went to take a shower. Tonight was going to be big, he could feel it; this was the night he found out the truth.

Tommy thought about driving himself to the Bronx. He rarely did that, but on occasion when he wanted to see Johnny, or even Pete, sometimes he would drive himself. He would have his limo pick him up and then drop him off in an underground garage where he kept his car when the limo left; anyone following him would assume he left. He thought that tonight was a perfect night to use that trick. What, with the way the press had been hounding him. He made the switch to a town car and told his regular driver to drive around until midnight, by then he would be home safe and sound. The whole drive to the Bronx Tommy was nervous. It reminded him of the time in the tunnels years ago. That anticipation, the nervousness. He had done multibillion dollar deals with no sweat, but this was different, he wanted to prove his friend innocent. This wasn't about money, he thought, it isn't even about saving people to him anymore, it was about friendship and loyalty.

Hopefully tonight he could reconcile the loyalty he felt for his old friends with the friendship he felt for Phil. He ran through a million scenarios; There was no cure, there was a cure but Novacrin had kept Phil out of the loop, there was a cure and Phil was being blackmailed to keep it a secret. The one scenario he didn't run was the one where Phil was a criminal, and that was the one scenario he feared. The car pulled up to the restaurant and parked, he sat in the car for a moment thinking. He sighed and got out. This was it, one way or another, he said to himself and entered the restaurant.

The restaurant was crowded and small. The smell of Italian dishes wafting through the air. Tommy scanned the crowd and found Phil talking to a waiter. He went over and Phil jumped up to greet him. They shook hands and sat. Phil looked different, as if a weight had been lifted or a veil removed from his face; he was alive energetic, not reserved at all. He looked comfortable. "Nice place," he said. He looked over the menu.

"Try the veal, best in the city," Phil said.

"You realize the place is called Louie's Seafood," Tommy joked.

The small talk went on for a while but after they ordered, Tommy thought it was time to press the issue. Tommy sat back and looked Phil in the eye and said, "So what's this big news you want to tell me that will save my press conference and my reputation?"

Phil was about to take another sip of wine but the glass never made it to his lips; instead, he placed the glass carefully down and looked up at Tommy, the levity was gone, he was dead serious now. To Tommy, he looked like he was struggling with something, but only for an instant.

JAMES AND CARMINE CIOFFI

Then he said, "Look, what I'm about to tell you is strictly off the record, it could probably get me killed, but what if I told you I came up with cure for AIDS?" Tommy was stunned, there it was. Lancaster had just blurted it out, just like that. Phil took Tommy's silence as him being stunned and continued. "Look, I know it's shocking but it's true. I've isolated a protein that will allow white blood cells to bind and kill the virus."

Tommy smiled. "This would be the most amazing discovery ever. What do you mean it could get you killed?"

Phil's voice dropped and he looked at the tablecloth. "What if I told you I did that five years ago?"

"That would mean you've been suppressing the information while hundreds of thousands of people have died. That would make you a criminal."

Phil looked as if he'd been slapped. "I know, I never wanted it like this...the company was skyrocketing, our pharmaceuticals were working, the cure would effectively put us out of business. My partners, they wouldn't listen and I went along with it to. I don't know, maybe it's time for the secret to come out. Maybe it's time for you to put it out there, blow the whole lid off it. I've reconciled with the fact that what I did was wrong, I was afraid of them saying... you know about me and my other secret. So I played along with the board at Novacrin, I made millions but I was never happy, I'm still not. It all needs to come out and if I burn for it, so be it. Tommy, you're my only true friend, I want you to be the one who blows it all up."

Tommy replied sympathetically, "Couldn't you talk to your partners, reason with them? You're all wealthy beyond belief, put it out now."

Phil sighed and played with a fork. "They wouldn't, they are greedy as I was, and they will kill me before they let the billions go. That's why I want you to put it out."

"Me?"

"Yeah, come back to my apartment, I'll give you all the data on a disk I have. You present it at your press conference and blow everyone out of the water."

Tommy smiled. "On one condition." Phil looked up. "You stand up there and present it with me. We tell the whole story, we say you've found the cure after years of research and the past five years go away, the board will be embarrassed to deny it, hell, it'll keep them out of jail, and once it's out there, they'll have no choice but to go along."

"But what about all those people I could have saved?"

"Some secrets stay secrets. The past is gone, you have to live with that."

Phil was shocked. Tommy was giving him a way out. He smiled. "It could work. I only worry about Specter, he's on the board, he's a nasty piece of work."

Tommy smiled. "Don't worry, I'll introduce you to some of my friends, you'll have nothing to worry about."

Phil lifted his glass and drained it. "One more drink and we'll head to my apartment and get the disk."

"We need to go over how we are going to present this," Tommy said.

The two men got up and headed out to their cars. Phil saw Tommy stagger a little. "Tommy, give me your keys, we'll take my car. You're in no shape to drive. You're drunk."

Tommy laughed and handed the keys to Phil. "But you're in no shape to drive either."

"Sure, but I have my driver here to do that." Both men headed to the car and got in.

Tommy smiled as the car started. The last thought he had was, we did it, we won.

CHAPTER

11

Joey

JOEY CALLED PETER. "Hey, Pete, you talk to Tommy? How's he doing?"

"He told me he was staying in to prepare for the press conference."

"That's good," Joey replied.

"How is Tiffany?" Peter asked, though he knew it was a touchy subject and usually set Joey off, but he was surprisingly calm.

"Not good, Pete. Hey, Peter, I'm sorry for the way I've been lately, it's just frustrating seeing my girl dying and these fucks walking around. Look, I have some business tonight with T.J. so if anything happens to me, see that Tiffany gets taking care of."

Peter said, "Of course, Joey. Is your business dangerous?"

"Nothing out of the ordinary, Pete, but I'm just paranoid now. I want someone to take care of her if something happens to me."

Peter was sympathetic. "Please be careful, Joey, and know I will look after Tiffany like she was one of my own sisters."

Joey smiled. "Thanks, Pete." With that he hung up the phone. It had been all he could do to hold back the anger he felt and talk calmly with Peter.

He went over to the bedroom. Tiffany was in the bed, covers piled high; she had lost a lot of weight, she hardly ate anymore. "You okay, baby?" Joey asked. She managed a weak smile and began coughing. Joey turned away and went into the bathroom; he couldn't stand to see her dying like that right in front of his eyes. He took out his kit from the vanity and pulled out a new needle and went through the motions of preparing his dose. After he shot up, he went out and shot Tiffany up too. She hugged him and he held her, feeling her bones through her thin t-shirt. Even high it enraged him. "Lie quiet," he said into her ear. "I've got business to take care of, I'll be back soon."

She whispered, "I love you." And he pulled away and smiled at her.

He left the bedroom and went into the kitchen and dialed his partner T.J. "You ready?" he asked.

"Yeah, yeah. I been following this fuck all day; he just went into a restaurant in the Bronx, we need to move. I was just about to call you."

Joey quickly got the information and said, "I'll see you in twenty minutes." Joey went downstairs and waved his driver over. "Let's go, we're going to the Bronx up in Pelham Bay."

On the drive over to the Bronx, Joey got madder and madder; he couldn't believe the balls on these Novacrin bastards, putting a hit on Ray, disgracing Tommy. He had had enough. As they neared the restaurant, Joey said, "Pull over here. Now go back to the apartment and wait downstairs until I come back. If Tiff needs anything she'll call you."

Frankie looked confused. "You want me to leave you here, boss?"

"Yeah, don't worry, I'm meeting someone," Joey said as he got out of the car.

"You sure you don't need any back?" Frankie asked again.

"I got it. I'll see you later." Frankie pulled away and Joey stood on the corner and lit a cigarette. He looked around and saw a car flashing its lights across the street; he smiled and crossed over to the car.

T.J. was waiting. "Hey, partner, we haven't done this in a long time," He said, smiling as Joey got in the car.

"Yeah, it's been too long coming on this one," Joey grumbled.

T.J. knew Joey long enough to know that he was a little high and more than a little angry and made for a bad combination. "How's Tiffany?" It was the wrong question and T.J. knew it but fuck it, he was going to polite.

"Not good. Thanks for asking."

"How are you? You been hitting it a little hard lately. No disrespect, but we're not heading for a repeat of last time are we?" Joey shot him a look that would cut glass. "Look, man, we go way back and I'm worried about you, that's all. Don't get pissed, I know something big is going down or it wouldn't be me and you out here but I need to know your holding it down."

Joey softened a bit, T.J. had been with him from the start, he was his partner, he was concerned. Joey reached across the car and hugged his friend. "I'm good, man, I'm good." They sat in silence and T.J. started the car and drove slowly past the restaurant.

"This should be easy. He parked two cars down from the restaurant so we may need a distraction."

"Really like the old days." Joey smiled.

T.J. continued, "He went in alone about forty minutes ago so I think we need to get moving." Joey nodded in agreement. "So you remember the drill, what you want, the plant or the distract?" T.J. said.

"I'll plant it," Joey said. T.J. pulled out a small device and handed it to Joey. Joey slipped it in his pocket and T.J. parked further down the block.

T.J. got out of the driver's side and the two looked at each other. "Follow my lead, bro." T.J. started up the street; he stopped in front of the restaurant and lit a cigarette. He began talking real loud, screaming at a parked car. "You got to be kidding me, man, this shit ain't right. Can you believe the bullshit?" With that, he stumbled over to Phil's town car. He banged on the hood. "You got to be kidding."

The screaming got the attention of Phil's driver, who jumped out of the car. "What the fuck's your problem, man?" the driver said, looking at the hood of the car.

"What you looking at, boy?" T.J. screamed at the driver.

He took a few steps toward him and the driver backed away then said, "Look, you drunk idiot, I'm not looking at you, just take it down the street before the owner calls the cops."

"Cops, fuck you, man. Figures, see a Puerto Rican and you want to call the cops."

T.J. stepped even closer to the driver. This time he held his ground. "Come on, man, I don't make enough for this shit, just take it down the block."

T.J. stopped a few feet from the driver and smiled. "You're right, my brother, these fucks never pay us enough. You got a light? My cigarette went out."

The driver was relieved. "I think they got some matchbooks inside, just stay quiet alright. Be right back." He turned and went inside.

The whole time T.J. was putting on his act, no one would have noticed the tall slim man who strolled down the street and briefly paused to tie his shoe. Joey had watched T.J. and made his move. As he bent down to tie his shoe, he stuck the small object in the wheel well of the car. Then he was up in a flash and gone. "Thanks, man." T.J. grabbed his matchbook from the driver and was off down the street; he made the first right he could down a side street and heard the horn of his car beep.

Joey drove up and rolled down the window. "Need a lift?" he said.

T.J. laughed. "Get your high ass out of my car," he said, "before you crash." Joey pulled over and jumped into the passenger seat. "That was fucking smooth, I never even saw you till you turned the corner," T.J. said.

Joey smiled. "Pull it over there," he said, "across the street and down the block from the restaurant. Now we wait," Joey said and he pulled out his drug kit. "You don't mind, do you, T.J.?"

T.J. frowned but nodded. "Guess I'm keeping watch," he said and positioned his seat so he could get a view of the restaurant. Joey shot up and was drifting off to sleep. He was half conscious when T.J. woke him. "Oh shit, he just got in the car, bro, but I think someone else is with him."

Joey was still groggy and mumbled, "Fuck him, this is for you, Tiff." He pulled out the small remote control and pressed the button. The explosion was loud, it ripped down the block, shattering windows and setting off car alarms. The fireball raced toward the heavens, lighting up the street like midday. Joey fell back in his seat as T.J. calmly pulled away from the curb and drove in the other direction. "For you, Tiffany," Joey said and passed out.

Joey woke up about an hour later. T.J. handed him a beer. Joey's head hurt and his mouth was dry. "Here, bro, you earned it. That was one hell of an explosion."

Joey smiled, it all had come back to him. "How long have I been out?"

"About an hour." Joey looked out the window, he was close to his home. "Figured you would want to be getting home," T.J. said.

"Any news?"

"It's been on 1010 WINS, no details, just an explosion in the Bronx."

Joey laughed. "Thanks, bro." He downed the beer as T.J. pulled in front of his apartment. Joey got out of the car and immediately Frankie came running out of the building.

The happiness Joey felt melted, he thought the worst. "Boss, it's Tiffany. She's hysterical, I can't get her to stop crying." Joey was relieved, he thought Tiffany had died.

He raced into the apartment to find Tiffany on the floor of the bedroom sobbing uncontrollably. "What's the matter?" Joey said and bent to comfort her. Tiffany pointed toward the TV. Joey froze and looked up at the TV screen, the scene was from the Bronx and there were fire trucks and police all over the place. Joey turned up the volume of the TV.

REPORTER:

"We're live here in the Bronx where a car explosion has taken the lives of two prominent businessmen, one whom has been in the news recently. Tommy Russo is reportedly one of the victims; the other is Phil Lancaster, the head research scientist at Novacrin, a pharmaceutical giant based out in L.A. Mr. Lancaster's driver was also reportedly in the vehicle."

ANCHOR:

"Jen, do you have any details on the explosion?"

REPORTER:

No. Right now the police are not ruling out foul play, but based on the recent allegations against Mr. Tommy Russo, the police are not ruling out a suicide."

Joey felt as if he had been punched in the gut. He stood there in shock for a second until Tiffany grabbed him and said, "My father...he was in that car." Joey was too stunned to answer. Tiffany continued, "My father was Phil Lancaster, he was in the car..." and then she began crying again.

Joey looked down at her and stood up. "No," he whispered. Then he screamed, "NOOO!" and grabbed a lamp from the night table and fired at a wall. He ran from the apartment, pushing past Frankie as he was running in to see what was wrong. Joey bolted out of the building into the night, realizing he had just killed his girlfriend's father and one of his best friends.

CHAPTER

12

Novacrin

WHITEHALL SAT AT THE BOARDROOM TABLE. The mood around the office was sullen, everyone feeling the effects of the death of a board member and colleague. Whitehall thought that was the proper face, to put on the tragedy and so that was the position the company took. Roony had set up a fund for the now deceased scientist, some scholarship at Caltech, and they were in the process of renaming a wing of a hospital in Lancaster's honor. For once, Whitehall was happy to have Rooney aboard, he was in his element in all this grief; he did all the speaking for the board, had already been interviewed seven times, and was the most quoted in the papers as the "personal friend and confidante" of the late Philip Lancaster. Whitehall could never have done that. Be that phony.

In truth, Rooney despised Lancaster. He thought he was useless and replaceable. Whitehall sighed; truth was Lancaster was the only reason for their fortunes in this company and replacing him would be difficult. Whitehall figured they could live off of his research for another ten years then it would be time to go, but he wouldn't share that knowledge with anyone except maybe Specter. As if on cue, Thomas Specter entered the boardroom. The three men sitting there in silence looked up.

"Bravo, Thomas, now that was some show," Roony said effusively.

"I must say that was a bit extreme, Thomas," Whitehall added seriously. His tone was meant to say he was unhappy with the way that removing Lancaster had been handled.

Specter slammed his briefcase down on the table and sat with a grunt. "I didn't do it," he mumbled.

"What did you say?" Jamison asked.

Specter was annoyed, "I DIDN'T DO IT," he said clearly and loudly.

"Ha," Roony laughed. "That's why you're in such a foul mood. So who cares? Our problems are behind us. Yes? Maybe it was a jealous boyfriend, maybe that Tommy fellow really did want to off himself, I say even better we aren't involved."

Specter shot a glance at Roony then turned to Whitehall. "If I didn't do it ,who did, and more importantly why?"

"Is it that important?" Whitehall added.

"Only if it was a message sent by that lieutenant governor," Specter replied.

"Thomas, why would he kill his own friend?"

"That's what doesn't add up," Specter said, rubbing his chin.

"Maybe it was just an accident," Jamison said.

"You ever see a car blow up like that on its own? That was a hit, and one meant to be noticed," Specter replied.

"What do you suggest we do?" Whitehall asked.

"I bet whatever it is it involves more bodies," Roony said smugly.

Specter was ready to pounce on him, instead he controlled himself and said, "Only one. I'm leaving the contract on the lieutenant governor but that will be done quietly and, J.R., I'll need you to have the party members pretty quiet after it's done."

Roony smiled and in a serious tone said, "No problem, Thomas."

Whitehall stood up. "So I guess that's it."

The other gentleman left but Specter hung back and waited until he was alone with Whitehall. "This just isn't right and you know it."

"I know, Thomas, but this is one of those rare occasions where we are not in control. Is there any way Phil could hurt us from beyond the grave?"

Specter smiled. "I had a friend search the house, lots of basic stuff but he did come up with this from the safe in Lancaster's bedroom." Specter pulled out a computer disk and slid it across the table. "My friend says it's the original so we can assume there are no copies, guess he kept it for insurance."

Whitehall took the disk and opened it. He turned it in his hand and then slipped it back into its case and slid it back to Specter. "He was a smart man, keep that safe." Specter put the disk in his coat pocket and left Whitehall staring out the boardroom window.

CHAPTER

13

Peter

"FATHER, YOU HAVE A CALL ON LINE THREE," THE INTERCOM BUZZED.

Peter pressed the button. "John, unless it's the Pope I do not want to be disturbed for the next forty minutes," Peter responded angrily. Johnny sat slumped in a chair across from Peter's desk. He was weary and had been crying. Peter looked at his friend and wondered when the last time Johnny had actually cried, it didn't look right. There were no words to describe how he felt and looking at his friend in so much pain didn't help the situation.

Johnny looked up and through red and weary eyes said, "This is my fault, Pete. I told Joey they put a hit out on Ray and he must have went fucking crazy."

Peter placed his hand on Johnny's shoulder. "He called me last night. He asked if I'd talked to Tommy, I told him he was staying in. I had talked to Tommy, he said he was staying in and getting ready for his press conference, I didn't know...Maybe I should have insisted on him coming over, maybe I should have called Tommy again...I had no idea Joey was planning something..."Pete's voice trailed off and he was silent. The tears beginning to well up in his eyes.

Johnny looked up at Peter. He said sympathetically, "It's not your fault, you didn't know what he was planning, Pete. I should

293

have sent some men to watch him…I should have brought him with me to LA. I could have…" Johnny kicked the desk angrily. "I knew what he was capable of, I knew he was on the edge and using, if anyone could have prevented this it was me," Johnny growled.

Peter regained his composure. "It's no one's fault. There was nothing we could have done…we need to find Joey."

Johnny shook his head. "I have the word out. I spoke to T.J. this morning, he hasn't seen Joey since…since he dropped him off. The girlfriend said he just walked out."

"I wish we would have known Tiffany was Lancaster's daughter, maybe I could have used that on Mrs. Tannaro, or Tommy could have used it to crack Phil. You would think he would want to save his own child."

"Who knows, they hadn't been in touch in years." Johnny sighed and slumped back into his chair.

"So that's it? We lose?" Peter questioned.

Johnny laughed. "Yeah, I guess we do. With Lancaster dead, we have no way of getting any proof the cure exists. We have to find Joey and then I have a score to settle with that fuck…sorry, Pete, you don't need to hear that last part. But you're right, we lose this one."

Peter shook his head, "How's Ray?"

"How do you think? He's politically dead. He's linked in a real estate scam with a man who is accused of being gay and just killed himself. He looks guilty as hell."

"But he is clean, in all this how can that matter?"

"Come on, Pete, it doesn't matter. No one will touch him with a ten foot pole; he's lucky they don't ask for his resignation by week's end."

Peter whispered, "How could this have gone so wrong?

Johnny didn't say anything; he sat quietly, the sound of his phone breaking the interminable silence. "Hello…MOTHERFUCKER!" he screamed into the receiver and slammed the phone down against the desk, smashing it into a worthless pile of twisted metal and plastic.

Peter looked afraid and shakily asked, "What's wrong?"

Johnny looked up at Peter, his eyes filled with tears again, "It's Joey," he said. "He's dead."

CHAPTER

14

The Wine Cellar

THE ROOM WAS MUCH SMALLER THEN THEY REMEMBERED IT. The three men stood in the cramped space silently, each lost in his own thoughts. The old workbench was still there and the old wine bottles. dusty and cobwebbed, lay in various spots along the floor. The bottles still gave the room the smell of over-fermented grapes. The boiler pipes would occasionally rattle as the boiler kicked on, and the heat it gave off gave the room a warm uncomfortable closeness that the men had never noticed as kids.

Johnny broke the silence, "They found him here three days ago, he'd been dead two days at least. I should have sent someone down here…I never figured he would come back here."

"It makes sense," Ray said. "Hell, I still have my key. If I were going to end it all this sure would be a fitting place to do it." He continued, "I never thought he would kill himself…not Joey."

Johnny began to tear up. "He was drugged up. Tony left everything in place till I got here. There were at least five bags of heroine on the floor; he probably tried to overdose then, knowing that impatient fuck, he figured it was taking to long so he put a gun to his chest and blew his heart out." Peter was sobbing quietly as Johnny continued, "We cleaned everything up; as far as the world knows, he died of a heart attack."

Peter said, "This has been some day."

"Yeah, no shit," Johnny replied. They had buried two of their friends today: a very quiet ceremony this morning out at St. Raymond's cemetery in the Bronx for Joey that was sparsely attended, and a big public funeral up in Westchester for Tommy's remains.

The latter was a media circus and attended by many of Tommy's work associates and colleagues. Peter thought it was nice to see people put aside the ugly rumors that had been circulating in the papers and show their respect. Johnny had said it was a joke and that most were there because cameras were there; either way, it had been a nice ceremony. Peter was surprised that Ray had come in for the funerals.

"Who cares, at this point I'm pretty much finished. I don't think they will let me finish out my term," he said. The three men had made their way back to the old neighborhood, where it had all began so many years ago. They all agreed to meet at the old wine cellar since during the day they did not have a chance to talk.

Johnny looked around. "It's smaller than I remembered it," he said.

Ray laughed. "Hey, is the hit still out on me?" he asked.

"As far as I know it still is. You would think that bloodthirsty bastard would pull back now but I guess not. Don't worry though, I'll let Fat Sally know that you're off limits," Johnny said.

"So what do we do now, Ray?" Peter asked. "This was to do some good and we've done nothing but lose two of our brothers."

Johnny sighed. "It can't end like this, Ray."

"I'm sorry, but I don't have a plan, Johnny. We're beat for the first time, we got beat," Ray replied. "I have a press conference later this week. I'll try to clear Tommy's name and then I'll probably be asked to step down."

Johnny sat wearily on the cot, he was experiencing a feeling he rarely felt, all three men were. "I just can't believe it," he said as he rubbed his hand across the blankets of the cot. They were warm and clean, one of his men had washed them but the bloodstains were still evident. The three men stood in silence and defeat.

15

Peter

PETER SAT IN HIS OFFICE STARING AT THE PICTURE OF THE FIVE MEN AS BOYS THAT HE HAD HUNG ON THE WALL EARLIER THAT WEEK. In the picture, the boys were in the park on 105th. Peter smiled and thought they were unrecognizable now, they had all grown up. In the picture, the boys had been playing basketball: Johnny was holding the ball, Joey had a cigarette in his mouth, Ray was looking away, probably sizing up the next team they were going to play, Tommy and Peter stood next to each other, an odd couple, Peter towering over Tommy who looked frail and thin.

The last two days had been a blur. As a priest, he had dealt with death often, and he always put the priestly spin on death that it was a new beginning a new life in Christ. But this was different, he couldn't bring himself to see the bright side in all this. He wanted to be depressed. He went about his duties robotically, often crying and staring at the picture. He was snapped back from that activity when the intercom rang on his desk. The voice of his secretary came through on the box, "Your Eminence, a Mrs. Tannaro to see you." Peter was not in the mood but he thought she must have been feeling pain at the loss of her husband. Peter thought of her needs above his own and told his secretary to send her in. Mrs. Tannaro did not look upset; in fact, she looked as she always did, elegant and beautiful.

While Peter had forgone the earthly desires, he was still human and often wondered how Lancaster could have left a woman of such beauty. He smiled as he always did when she entered the office.

"Your Eminence, I'm so sorry to bother you but I had to see you immediately," she said. Peter showed her to her seat and sat across from her at his desk.

"How are you? I'm so sorry for the loss of your husband," he said.

"Your Eminence, I cut all ties with that man years ago. I feel for your losses; it was my understanding that you lost two friends this week?"

Peter made a mental note to reprimand his secretary for divulging too much information. He nodded and said, "It is true I lost two friends this week; it has been a trying time. How can I help you?"

Ms. Tannaro reached into her purse and pulled out an envelope and a small brown package; she hesitated for a second and then passed them over to Peter. "This came to me two days after Phil died. I almost threw it away but I opened it and read the letter, here it is." Peter took the letter out of the envelope and read:

Judy, I know you would not want to hear from me and I guess sorry is an empty word at this point. I am about to do something that could change the world. Unfortunately, it could get me killed. If that is to happen, you must do a favor for me. The contents of this disk contain information that could mean salvation to millions. I am not a religious person as you know but I trust you to get this into the hands of someone who can spread this truth. Phil

Peter was stunned. He sat in silence and Mrs. Tannaro took his silence as a signal for her to continue. "I wanted to throw it away. I have not heard from Phil in years and when that came after his death, I figured the right thing to do would be to give it to someone and let them decide what to do. I'm sorry to put this burden on you, father, and if you like, send it anonymously to the police or destroy it yourself," she said. "I don't know what's on the disk; all I know is that

I'm giving it to you, father, what you do with it is your decision, I only ask that I am never brought up, and that this conversation never took place. That man has caused me to much pain in my life." With those words she got up and left. Peter was shocked; he sat there and reread the letter and looked at the package in his hand.

CHAPTER

16

The Disk

PETER, JOHNNY, AND RAYMOND WERE HUDDLED OVER THE LAPTOP
IN PETER'S OFFICE. He had called Johnny and Raymond as soon
as Ms. Tannaro had left. They had come immediately and now, after
opening and loading the disk, it was the moment of truth.

The disk opened and Ray saw seventy-six folders. He clicked on
the one that said clinical trials; pictures popped up of, some very sick
men. Ray recognized one of the men that Joey had found out about
months ago. "So is this it, do we have them?" Johnny said.

"I don't know, there are a lot of files on this disk but it looks good."
Ray clicked on a file that said research. There, lists of contributions
popped and government contracts and R&D monies that were paid
out to Novacrin. Ray hit another file and a page of information
popped onto the screen, the language was very technical and Ray did
not understand a lot of it by just skimming the information.

"I got to be honest, I don't know if the cure is on here but I got
to assume it is. The data is beyond my understanding, but they've
gotten hundreds of millions of millions over the last few years for R&D and
that was only one file. I think Phil sank the company and I have to
assume the cure is on here."

"It's a miracle," Peter said.

"Yeah, Pete, it is!" Ray laughed.

"So what do we do now, Ray?" Johnny asked.

"Oh, I have a plan!" Ray smiled.

The press conference was packed. The reporters from every major news station crowded the steps of the Capitol building expecting to hear the resignation from the lieutenant governor. Raymond stepped out into the sunshine and faced the mob. He raised his hands for silence and began, "Ladies and gentleman, I am here today to make an important announcement. I would like to confirm the rumors that have been swirling around me and my dealings with Tommy Russo. It is true we did have dealings on the downtown restoration project." Raymond paused for effect. "I also would like to say that Tommy Russo was a dear childhood friend of mine and we were involved in another scheme together." The crowd erupted into a frenzy of questions. The sound drowned out Ray, who stopped talking. Senator Hatch and the governor emerged from the building to stand near Ray, who waited and then put his hands up for silence again.

The crowd settled down and waited for the announcement. Ray smiled and continued, "Three months ago, an unnamed source sent me a tip about wrong doings at the pharmaceutical company Novacrin. I decided to investigate the charges and asked Tommy to help in the investigation by befriending one of the CEOs of the company, Phil Lancaster. It is no coincidence that they were both murdered recently in New York. Before the murder, I received a computer disk that has since been turned over to the proper authorities; the disk contains information on an antiviral formula that has been tested and proven to cure the AIDS virus. It also has information that Novacrin has been suppressing this cure and making hundreds of millions of dollars. Not to the mention the millions of lives that could have been saved. The slanderous allegations against myself and Mr. Tommy Russo were done in an effort to discourage us from finding the truth. The board members of Novacrin were indicted today on multiple charges, including fraud and murder; I would like to thank the governor and The Honorable Senator Hatch for all their help with the investigation. I will answer any questions now."

"Hey, Johnny, the news is coming on." Johnny emerged from the basement of the club, his sleeves rolled up and his hair a bit disheveled. He grabbed a drink from the bar and asked Joe Landy to turn up the TV.

REPORTER 1:

The shocking news today at the press conference of Lieutenant Governor of Californiahas sent shock waves throughout the country. Hospitals are being overrun with requests for the cure, as people infected with the HIV virus are overjoyed at the chance to be cured. The murder of Tommy Russo and Phil Lancaster are being blamed on the four other board members, three of whom have been indicted and were led away in handcuffs. The fourth board member, Thomas Specter, is still at large and a worldwide manhunt is under way. We were at the J.R. Roony arraignment. Roony, one of the accused Novacrin board members, had this to say as they led him away this morning from his mansion in Beverly Hills: "It was all Specter, he set us up. I had no idea this was going on. I'm innocent. It was Specter and Lancaster, they were the ones," Roony was saying as he was led away in handcuffs.

"Turn it down, Joe. I can't stand that fuck's voice." Johnny smiled as they cut to a picture of Ray shaking hands with the senator.

Just then his cell phone rang; it was Ray. "Hey, Johnny!"

"That was some plan. You're going to ride this one to the White House." Johnny laughed.

"I want Tommy to be the hero here."

"Yeah, the more you say that the more the public loves you," Johnny teased.

"Johnny, how's the other part of the plan going?" Ray asked seriously.

"He just cracked. He's a tough fuck but it'll be over soon. I want to hear him beg one more time for his life before I end it," Johnny said coolly.

"Two of them are singing like birds. Once Specter disappeared they thought he went state's evidence on them to save his skin. Except Whitehall, he's been quiet," Ray said.

"Fuck him too, they'll all burn," Johnny said.

"You know, Pete is the real hero." Ray laughed.

"The disk contained everything; the cure should be in production by the end of the month and Tiffany will be getting doses by the end of the week," Ray replied.

"Poor kid, her father and Joey," Johnny said.

The joy left Ray's voice and he whispered, "We lost too much on this one, brother, we lost too much."

The silence stretched as Johnny thought about that statement. "See you in a few months, Ray," Johnny said and hung up. He took a swig of his drink and headed back down the basement steps. There at the bottom of the steps was a figure tied to a chair surrounded by three men with guns.

End

About the Author

CARMINE CIOFFI WAS BORN AND RAISED IN THE NEW YORK CITY NEIGHBORHOOD OF EAST HARLEM IN THE 1950's. Coming of age in a close-knit community like East Harlem—where friends and neighbors constituted an extended family—inspired the story told in "Neighborhood Secrets." Carmine moved to the Bronx with his wife Christine and his three children.

James Cioffi, the son of Carmine, was born and raised in the Bronx. He attended Cortland State University and received his master's degree from Fordham University. James has been an elementary school teacher for the last 15 years. He currently resides in Westchester NY with his wife and two children. Like his father Carmine, this is his first Novel.

Carmine and James would like to thank Frankie Pellegrino, and Dennis Calbi for all their help and support. They truly are "neighborhood" guys.

CPSIA information can be obtained
at www.ICGtesting.com
Printed in the USA
BVHW071609270722
643146BV00002B/251

9 781681 392165